PITFALL

BRACE RUBEN

Printed in the United States of America

Print ISBN: 978-1-953910-26-4
E-Book ISBN: 978-1-953910-27-1

**Canoe Tree
Press**

4697 Main Street
Manchester Center, VT 05255

Canoe Tree Press is a division of DartFrog Books.

This story is dedicated to my wife who is my Islander, my best friend and oh yes, my favorite content editor. Thanks for your unwavering support. I want to make you proud of me. Love you.

CHAPTER ONE

"Let me give you a hand."

That's the service line I offer to morticians if they need help moving a body from the gurney to the prep table where the work begins and ends. Dead weight is purely that and can't be resolved without serious leverage from the un-dead. If the body is in full rigor, that is, stiff as a board, one person grabs the heels and slides the butt over to the table while the other accomplice grabs the nearest arm and tugs until it's secure on the other surface. Believe me, that's not easy. Then, it's a matter of centering and placing the head block underneath the skull. Otherwise, both dissection and embalming are disadvantageous. On the contrary, if rigor has yet to set in, a battle of wills ensues unless the legs and arms are fastened in place by waxed string. Without string, legs, arms, and even the torso do whatever gravity allows.

The irony of the string is the original term: butcher's string. Most funeral homes I've visited refer to it as such. Of course, the over-weight deceased render a special set of skills and that's where a strap lift comes in handy. Mom and pop funeral homes seldom have one installed meaning that whatever help you can get is appreciated. Translation: autopsies are to answer for the dead and teach the living. Aside from the lifting, this one has me busting a gut.

This day began so promising. Then there was this meteoric thunderstorm, and the highway was strewn with fallen debris. I zig-zagged between tree limbs the size of telephone poles. To make matters worse, my ruby-red economy rental had the clearance of a twin bedframe on these pocked-paved highways, and every defect was enunciated in Super Bowl decimal level.

"Son of a bitch!"

If I was not so sleep-deprived, this might sound like the plot of a fish-out-of-water comedy. A *Three Stooges* versus Boris Karloff. An *I Love Lucy* meets Vincent Price. Unfortunately, they don't make those kinds of whacky shows anymore. Weeds and sticks poked out of my car bumper like an off-road dune buggy, clattering on the pavement like pieces of cardboard I used to secure in my bicycle spokes to make the sound of a motor.

That was then, this is now. I'm fogging up behind my goggles and chuckling so much that my surgeon's mask keeps slipping beneath my dripping nose and becomes a trough of snot and tears. At times like this, it might be best to keep the morgue door locked from the inside. Otherwise, I might be straight-jacketed and carted away to the loony bin. Not to pass judgement, but this behavior is the total opposite of medical ethics. Despite everything, I can't get this damn absurdity to disappear in my head.

I'm clenching slippery organs, hovering over a maggot-filled corpse, side-stepping puddles of dark fluids, and inhaling stagnant plumes of decomposition billowing into my face shield. This should be a gag fest. But once again, it's my bizarre comfort zone and is also the cause of my meandering attention span. Dr. Wrists-in-Way-Too-Deep is off the edge today. I think back to my Aunt Hilde. It's because of her that I'm losing it. She needs to take some blame.

There's this bizarre arena stirring conflicted memories of growing up. For instance, the stench. It's no great mystery that we can recall so many different smells, like a steeping bowl of homemade vegetable soup with carrots the size of a kid's forelimb, followed by a platter of Teutonic-style, God-awful smelling bratwurst - - the kind that dear Tante Hilde placed between my younger brother and me by design at the dinner table during our visits to their farm on holidays. Within a brief period of two or three minutes, the meal transposed from winter-food-delicious to December-indigestible. The anti-Ivory Tower in all its glory and yet, my mother continued to gush in full-maudlin mode.

"These are the best that I have ever tasted. You must give me the recipe."

That was a direct contrast to brother and me ralphing into our napkins. That serving dish of steaming, oily, kraut-smelling sausages stole breathable air from the dining room. Like now. I prefer to think it was her mitochondrial DNA, only carried by females, is the rationale butchering and anatomy followed me from the farm to the university, to years of practicing medicine. It's punishment and, for that simple argument, I continue to learn a life lesson from her. Dab my face, wipe my chin, spit the partially chewed swine into the napkin, place it on my lap underneath the table, and slip the toxic tendrils to the stealth, mangy farm hound lying by my feet. With that sleight of hand, I became a magician. Thank you so much, Tante.

With that caveat, and because of those life ordeals, I abhor liver which I used to love fried with onions. At the cutting board, I usually leave that waste-filtering organ for one of the last to examine. Alongside my surgical boot-covered feet on this blood-stained tile floor is a red plastic viscera bag stuffed into a five-gallon bucket to be knotted, then dumped back into the body cavity. In Aunt Hilde's house, the extended supper table hid from view a well-known secret: the original viscera bucket, the farm dog. Tootsie lurks underneath, looking for that friendly drop of a gagging globule. Her bristly coat always brushed my pants legs and smeared a disgusting odor of still damp brown dirt and other suspicious barn smells. Life was hard, my aunt always reminded the two of us, so eat up. But for my brother and me, choking down those spiced tubes were far worse. It's aligned with scrutinizing through this main course of organs in front of me - - except I exchanged a tarnished knife and fork for an insect-laden scalpel and a pair of dull scissors.

That look on my brother's face was sidesplitting, too. Crossing his watering eyes like sieves as he brought the steaming, stuffed sausages to his mouth. A tentative twitch as he hoisted the forkful to his lips. It was way too much fun and right now, I need to buckle down and stay in the present.

I came to the realization early that medical school was far easier compared to the overwhelming high school German class.

Cramming complicated Deutsch terms into a meaningful conversation was, in this farm boy's opinion, as awkward as the first school dance. Now that was an alien nation. Those who survived needed to climb onboard the linguist train quickly or be slid off the table like these whittled organ pieces in my hands.

There were hundreds of words to memorize, not to mention the *virtless* dialogue. The language of Nazis flowed freely at home between my parents. Every Christmas, my Aunt Hilde, who still longed for the Fatherland, communicated in a version of this dialect called lower German. Her "Old Country" sounded like "Alt Kvuntchree" and with enough eggnog, she'd peer over her rimless eyeglasses from the cabbage pot, much like I am doing right now, except my pot is not bubbling. Between dishing out cooked potatoes and bread, she was spilling World War II secrets from which only the original family tree had branches of knowledge.

I slice open the heart on the cutting board using a serrated broad blade with the blunt tip, chamber by chamber. Tracking inflow to outflow. Looking for bad coronaries or valves or scars. Something to answer the cardiac cause of this person's demise besides the obvious cauterized hole in his left temple. If I didn't know better, this male looks an awful lot like my best friend in high school, Brandon, only decades older and minus the parts and bloody pieces.

Fifty years ago, I had finally become the touted high school upper classman. With this new liberation from tenth grade, there was hope that I passed the sophomore torment. No more gauntlet-style bashing by the seniors between classes. No more duty, lugging *their* books to *their* class first. We were in for that nearly every day. When I saw a senior boy look my way, I'd race in the other direction to beat the bell. Teachers loved to see the dweebes sweat and I honestly believe they were in covert operations with the older boys. Detention notices were like receiving speeding tickets. I survived those hell days. Now, I can saunter into the classroom with attitude and slouch into my desk chair just because. The smugness is written all over my face: head cocked to the side, eyes narrowed, checking out the chalk board, reading the crowd. Take note ladies. I have arrived.

My friend, Brandon, is impatient, fidgeting, and squirming in his seat across the aisle from me. He has goofy quirks to match those piercing hazel eyes. Looking for that perfect comfort zone. Milking that vacant stare. Making a gesture to his face as if there is a huge bugger dangling from my lip.

I am overly sensitive that my nose has the manifestation of an over-ripe strawberry. Freckles and sixteen on the girls are cute, but on me, it's girlish. I woke up this morning with a huge zit. While waiting for the school bus at our driveway, I attempt to hide the beast by dabbing on my older sister's pasty Covergirl makeup that I keep as a stash in my coat pocket. This smoke-signals some of my turncoat friends to reign torment from hell. It's the curse of the pale-skin bloodline. It's that sea-sonal raging pigments battle and the eventual loss leaving an unflat-tering blotchy, scaly scar. Like a bad habit I constantly scratch off the thin layer on the tip of my nose until a blanching, permanent pinpoint depression exists. In any case, it doesn't bleed or crust up anymore. Come to think of it, neither does this poor soul lying in front of me.

Today, in this one-person classroom, I claim temporary owner-ship to a once-alive, suddenly departed cadaver. There is an unman-ageable, limp water hose on the edge of the prep table that continues to slip off the table. The radio on the counter blares twangy country songs, but I'm fixated on postmortem clean-up duties and catch-ing up afterwards which consists of diligently checking my texts, answering emails, filing delinquent case reports, and conferring with the attending physician.

Forty years ago, summer was freedom, a no-pencil-or-text type of unencumbered freedom. Back in high school days, I'd methodically mark on my bedroom calendar the number of days without a single copy of Jack London or William Shakespeare until it closed in on fourteen weeks. I rarely cut my hair. Shoulder-length trim is a better descriptive and it's easier to comb. My mane is much shorter now and easier to maintain plus, it doesn't smell like decomposition. Yet, I still know medical associates clinging to the past with crazy-thin, graying ponytails pulled so tight that it renders their faces taut. That constant fear of losing the urban professional look and morphing into a Dr. Marcus Welby-type push them into poor decision-making. Lengthy and frizzed is thankfully out of style, but there are still some interns looking like walking hair mops.

In school, the senior high girls' predominant hairdo was bleached and straight as a ruler compared to the guy's shaggy look, which was a foppish Herman of Herman's Hermits. Imagine a buzzing classroom half full of adolescent high school boys all twitching their head side to side, or slowly fingering oily bangs across their acne-pocked faces. Compound this with a dry smoker's cough masked by heavy duty spearmint candy and the habitual tap-tap on their shirt pockets. The evolution of Midwestern Boys-to-Men begins. I never understood whether we were that insecure over our so-called veiled smokes or accepting what lay before us. I still smile when I think of how longevity was never a topic standing next to our jalopies.

The class settles down with a "Guten tag," or a "Guten morgen." Brandon leans over to me to ask the ultimate question.

"So, how was Bible Camp?" He smirks and cocks his eyebrows a couple times.

He's always been gangly, and with the typical Scandinavian pointed chin and thin lips, I can't help but think of one of the mario-nette puppets in a carney side show.

With the introduction of the British Invasion to small town Minnesota, the arguments became one-sided. Dad shook his head in disgust at my friends. For me, going to church was a living hell. Seasonal stories and biblical parables were repetitive to the point where I yearned for reprieve. We were pounded with endless guilt, combined with the fear of God's wrath for even swearing which, by the way, is how my father began each morning outside of my bed-room door. I never understood the idea that religious people are never good enough, and hellfire is around the corner if your thoughts slip or you nix at the offering plate. By the way, a great majority of my generation were conceived in back seats.

Weigh the right lung. Six hundred forty-five grams. From the looks of it, I'm thinking congestive heart failure. Spongy texture, wet and dark red. Not the expected pink color. Be sure to take a couple slices through each of the three lobes. No masses or tumors, only frothy, bloody fluid. Retain pieces of lobes and bag the rest.

"It was only ok," lowering my voice, looking around. "Some of the city kids were spoiled rotten."

By city, I mean those grunts shipped out from Minneapolis to be ground into religious hamburger for a week or two or longer. The metropolitan congregations delivered their youth by the busloads for us to babysit. If they were especially in need of Christianity, or their parents preferred an extended break from them, the stay might be longer. Our job as counselors was not so much to mess with their vulnerable opinions, but rather keep them occupied and somehow entertained. There were softball challenges between cabins, swimming competitions in the murky lake water, and bored-to-death silly grade school song contests. The camp was co-ed, but fortunately the cabins weren't. Testosterone fluttered overhead like manic Dragonflies, but only landing with the casual tease.

"How were the chicks?" He reaches over and pokes me in the ribs, his head slowly nods, he cocks his eyebrows.

Now, on to the left lung. Five hundred ninety-seven grams. Repeat slices looking for any abnormalities. None, grossly. Exactly like the right lung. Take two fish filet-sized samples from each lobe, drop into formalin container, and discard the rest into red bag. Next organ.

If he wants to compare notes between his part-time carpentry gopher job with a dirge of potheads and my riding herd on a bunch of whiney, boney boys, there is no contest.

"Nothing to speak of because we were all in the same boat. Us counselors were so turned off by their childish immaturity. By Wednesdays, Pastor Williams had each cabin reproduce a replica map of Israel with sand and colored river stone outside the Chapel front step. Between the vandalism and thunderstorms, I can now appreciate the Arab conflict we learned about. Anyways, girls always win out in the artsy stuff easily."

I prop up my head with my fist and begin flipping pages in the textbook. Brandon is searching for specifics and leans in toward my desk.

"Didn't you have any free time to hang out or anything?"

"We had a couple hours each night," I answer. "Most of that was spent drinking pop or sitting on the dock. The local brown nosers went home if they wanted. But the three-mile choppy boat ride across the lake to Wasoon City smothered their misery like reading a spooky novel. We even tried to scare them to death sometimes by making stupid sounds in the woods. Of course, we denied it. All in all, they needed to have a good reason to leave the island."

Grab and separate liver from body cavity with my scalpel. Slippery. Firm. Heavier than usual. Hoist up to scale. One thousand nine hundred thirty-five grams. At least four hundred grams above average for his size. Surface is knobby and cobblestone. The dense texture is not the typical dark butcherblock brown-tan. Off yellow, like an old egg yolk with a green tinge, as if the gallbladder were obstructed and bile was unable to drain. If this is not cirrhosis, then I've wasted forty years of practicing pathology. Take some extra slices to be sure there's no tumor. None. Cubed pieces in formalin. The rest in the bucket.

I wasn't raised near lakes nor cared too much about boating. It was all tractors and chores. In a sense, those few weeks as a counselor was my vacation. It was a baptism, a chance to truly dangle my feet in warm, algae-filled lake water and practice my poorly defined social skills.

"I read you loud and clear, Kevin. Loud and clear. It all sounds extremely exciting." He rolls his eyes. "Actually, mine wasn't much better. I spent a considerable amount of time either drunk or wasted. My grandma died in July, so we went up to Ada for the funeral. I saw tons of dorky hillbilly cousins. We had nothing in common. Johnny Cash and Jack Daniels. That's how we spent our time."

For any unknown catalyst or excuse, we try to magnify our sheltered existence with drummed up legends. Someone, somewhere, led better lives than us. The funeral component I deemed fact. The whacking out bit was largely legend.

Look at stomach in situ. Surface is smooth and glistening. There are no palpable masses. Open longitudinally. I don't see hemorrhage or other gastric contents like a partially digested meal. Again, there are no masses. Place two equal strips into formalin, the rest into bucket. Next: kidneys.

"There was someone..." I began, but our German Princess teacher at the front of the class, who took great pleasure in dressing up for the part, knuckle-taps briskly on her desktop. Adorned in a traditional culture attire of an Old-World hoop skirt and matching bonnet, she begins the roll call.

"Later," Brandon whispers and leans back in his chair, tapping his pencil erasure.

"Later" for me was the very subject I needed to brush up on. It began with "I'll meet you later" and ended with "It's getting late" or "We should go."

Erin Garner was my age and like me, looking forward to leaving this island penal colony and becoming a high school senior. She attended a small high school located sixty miles north in the unincorporated portion of the state where vast forests of Norway pine and the occasional honed-out farm site existed. On a brief visit to the Lake of the Woods as a kid, we passed through multitudes of run down out buildings and outdated machinery. Compared to where we lived, this was third world. So much poverty. So much of nothing.

But when I first put my eyes on her, she was sitting between two other girl counselors. It was first day orientation and I could tell she was bored. Her chagrin matched mine as we stood when introduced, and regurgitated a mini-biography of our lackluster, but Christian-worthy lives. Then came cabin assignments followed by polite applause. At that exact moment, when she finished her story and sat down, I was both out of her league and crazy smitten.

Her wavy brown hair was pinned tight to the back of her head. A ropey ponytail chased down the small of her boney back like a fleeting fox. She wore this distracting green plaid headscarf perched on top of her head like a baker's cover. A drab olive-green sweatshirt hung loosely on her narrow shoulders in a valiant attempt to hide her full hips. With her combination of brown-rimmed glasses, a cautious hello, and a thin-lipped polite smile, it became apparent that Erin was like me. Unhappy and stranded.

Over the first week we drew random dual duty for lifeguarding, crafts class, and the melting-messy ice cream social. There was a total of eight youth counselors: four boys and four girls. During relays against the cabins, our three-legged race was unbeatable. She ran like the devil. We'd lock arms for the forty-yard dash, the rope knotted around our joined ankles leaving semi-permanent abrasions. Not by surprise, this became a psychological advantage with other games. We were always flashing it like a war wound, but I didn't care. Wherever she might be at any moment was where I wanted to be.

Erin taught me patience and envy at the same time. At the end of outdoor activities, her skin became the color of copper in the sun while mine had the elegant tint of boiled hot dogs. She was a natural leader and perpetually positive, always looking at the cup half-full instead of half-empty. I never heard any of her cabin girls complain. They always seemed motivated, hustling along to the planned activities. On the contrary, the held-back sloth trio in my charge began with the idiot: Lavender, a Bible Stumper named after his father, Pastor Laverne; Eric, the momma's boy; and Hoover, the mutant eating machine who always led the cabin to the brunch table. Their famous line "You can't tell me what to do" was the laughing canker sore in my cull. I was helpless with a praying patsy, a fat-ass pouting pussy, and a trucker's mouth as my roomies.

When the eight of us counselors got together, it was like therapy to me. We'd vent and sit around the camp firepit passing a joint that was covertly sneaked onto the island by a fellow Counselor, Nate the Great Dane, named because of his unusually large ears. In my light-headed stupor, I found myself next to Erin, watching the embers reflect off her eyes like a glassy prism.

And then it took a new turn.

Get back to work. Concentrate. Right kidney: 186 grams. Left kidney: 177 grams. Both look normal. Bisect each. Circulatory and collection portions are well-demarcated from each other. Both have smooth surfaces and no masses. Slices look normal. Select routine pieces and the rest is bucket duty. Rinse the excess off the cutting board and continue.

Erin and I became more than co-workers inhabiting a satellite community filled with middle schoolers. We were circling a larger globe and the attraction was overpowering. My heart was weighted to hers. As luck would have it, we strategically stood in line together or matched up boy-girl-boy-girl combinations of our cabins in contests. She wasn't the best at fielding a softball, but that girl could scoot around the bases before anyone came close to putting a tag on even if she goaded them to try.

At outdoor devotions led by the resident pastor, I'd skedaddle alongside and touch her hand in the flickering campfire beyond any watchful eyes. I had a crazy crush. It was my personal rapture. Even Jesus would have endorsed my actions. Love thy neighbor girl counselor with all thy heart. My feelings for her developed an acuity, like having a great mystery revealed. When she took off her glasses her eyes had a soft tawny hue that teared easily on our last days together. As for me, the campfire smoke from her grubby corduroy jacket and hair lingered like unforgettable perfume. Every kiss, every snuggle, every hug, everything about her usually kept me awake all night back in my bunk after we would say goodnight.

At season's end, we'd clean our cabins with Lysol and soap to rid the rooms of the stench of sweat and dirty clothes. On that last Sunday afternoon, my parents unexpectedly arrived early. I peered out my doorway to the sound of crunching gravel as my father parked and got out of the car. He was looking at cabin numbers down the lane. With no going back, he'd found mine. He spoke to my mother who was still seated in the car. Erin was in my room lying on the bunk, watching me pack, her arms were folded in front like a mummy. It was time to say good-bye and I was not prepared for what was next. I stuffed the remaining week's musty belongings into my duffel. Her sadness tore at my chest as the mood in the room plunged like a deep winter freeze. Tears ran down her cheeks. Who knows what another week together might have accomplished? Anyhow, it was safer this way. Behind the door in my cabin, we hugged and kissed one lasting time. She trembled in my arms. This room felt suddenly old and silent.

"Do you have my address?" she said between sobs.

"Right here in my wallet," I told her, patting my hind pocket.

"Call me sometime, anytime."

She kissed me and stepped out the back entrance and out of my life as my parents came through the front door.

Carve out the remaining pelvic organs as a unit. Prostate is enlarged but not overly-firm. BPH. Common in men over sixty but still might have some atypical changes microscopically. Better take some samples of the rubbery parts to be safe. The filled bladder has some smelly old dark urine. Take a sample for toxicology. Done. Rinse. Mucosal surface is flat from the distended pressure. He forgot to pee. Probably had other things on his mind.

"Well, Son, how about a tour?" My father emerges at the doorway. Proud. Chest out. Flaunting a gratifying smile. Hooking his thumbs into his belt loops. My devoted mother always covered her mouth when excited about something religious with me. It was her wish that one of her sons take the first step into the seminary and begin a ministerial career.

An hour later we're motoring down the winding rock-strewn road off the island and heading home. The past week's exhaustion pushed me into a deep, necessary slumber and I woke up stiff from leaning my head motionless against the car door frame for the past couple hours. In the ensuing two-hundred-mile drive I went from scented pine and infatuation, to flat farmlands and the fermenting stench of manure-infested barnyards. But I underwent a harvesting of sorts - - a maturity not taught, but learned and shared.

Erin and I never again connected except for two letters within the first week apart. Her sudden disappearance was not statewide news. According to the story, she was driving to the nearby filling station around nine o'clock one night. School was to begin the next day. Witnesses reported a late model car had pulled in behind her. There was some communication between the driver and her. The passenger door opened, and she hopped in. The car drove off, leaving her car at the pump and a few groceries still in the front seat.

Erin was never seen again. With each passing day, I agonized over the lessening news coverage on the radio and television. People were more in tune to runaways than abductions. How does a person vanish? Days went from weeks, to years, to lifetimes. My fitful dreams of her faded, but never dissolved.

Forty-one years is a long time to grasp at paper straws. No more what if's, just what was. Missing person dramas are merely that... dramatic. In my mind, the loon drake still glides gracefully in solitude over the moonlit pond where we once professed momentous choices. What we became was only a cabin door away.

Before finishing, check other smaller organs for abnormalities. The pancreas, adrenal glands, thyroid glands, lymph nodes appear to be normal. Nothing unusual. Follow- up with an overview of the major vessels. This lost soul has a brittle, calcified aorta, and large distended veins in the legs. Each is filled with gelatinous, dark red clot. His neck muscles are mushy-soft and pliable. No hemorrhage, tears, ruptures, or true emboli. A summary of my findings: heart disease, pulmonary congestion, hepatic cirrhosis, bad coronary vessels, poor dentition, age-related thickened toenails, under-nourished, and dehydrated. One more thing. A self-inflicted gunshot wound of the left temple. Death by suicide. We'll all get to this point eventually unless something like cancer or an accident calls first.

I missed that calling for Erin and it persists, unending, inside-out, like an autopsy of my soul.

CHAPTER TWO

I see their faces. In my sleep. In my head. Hundreds of autopsies and absolutely none of them look like they are napping. Unlike the movies, these mouths are gaping, their rigorous jaw muscles forming an ominous oral cave, spewing up watery brown gastric contents and staining the cheeks and lips. Their last breath was more than likely a bubbly gurgle and not one of those trivial poetic gasps - - the kind most every televised police drama pushes.

A dull, fixed stare is not pretty. Droopy eyelids that don't close. There is no shocking "What the hell happened?" look. Sometimes the corneas are as cloudy as a drab winter day. Sometimes they are amber, an indicator of a feckless liver metabolism working all sorts of internal havoc, as in alcoholics. The face might be puffy or as scarlet as a cardinal eating suet from a birdfeeder, the tongue protruding from between the cracked lips. This is likely a suicidal hanging or death by suffocation. In the contentious battle to live a lost cause, such as cancer, the eyes convey the endless suffering. Diseases can do that. Secrets can do that.

If I begin with the face, the lifeless face, I can pretty much envision how living was at the end. The face quite often tells me the times gone by. Being at peace is bull. I'm able to harbor-up a few ideas or possibilities and go from there. Sometimes, even without a medical history, I can hit the proverbial nail on the probable head. For example, beneath the skeletal framework, cancer might have spread and latched like spilled curdled milk over the entire belly. Rotting flesh and purulent green ooze are tools of the trade. Noxious odors can linger on everything for hours. Even showering doesn't take it away.

It recalls how I arrived at the San Antonio airport today with my tool kit and a carry-on. The overhead terminal speaker blares departure times. After the sprint from the rental car return to the terminal, my back drips with sweat, plus I'm as irritated as a caged badger. Curbside check-in is faster than counter service and, in my haste, I bang my shin into the cart ahead of me. A weeping dark red blotch, the size of a silver dollar, begins to form on my pants leg. As I am about to go through TSA my phone buzzes.

"This is Dr. Michaels."

It is another referral and, no doubt, the beginning of a lengthy phone conversation. I step aside. Passengers with bags in one arm and personal belongings in the other give me the once-over. Another salesman refusing to give up on a distant client. Little did they know. The family of a photographer/adventurer is calling. My services might be in need somewhere in northern Minnesota.

"We spoke to him scarcely two days ago," the calm, but detached female voice informs me over the phone. She is calling from rural southern Minnesota, a start-up community outside Rochester. I hear large machines, like bulldozers, in the background.

Back in California, my home is my office, outside the retirement community of Auburn. The western Sierras border my front office-bedroom view while a rock-strewn zinfandel vineyard frames the back ten acres. The new buzz word is organic, but these irrigated vines are moss green, and the berries are gaining ripeness with each sunny August day. In a couple of months, harvest will be complete, and the dry leaves will begin to fall and blow into my unraked front yard. My tool shed and I have never been the best of buddies. Aside from a few garden tools, it's as bare as Mother Hubbard's pantry. I catch shit from the Homeowner's Association on a weekly basis, but I'm rarely home long enough to even care. They can't say anything about my workplace, though. A modest IKEA desk set and two vinyl-covered chairs. More than likely there will be an ordinance for that too, by the number of revisions stashed in my mailbox weekly.

"Dr. Michaels, he was extremely excited about this. He said this might be the one."

If I earned a nickel every time somebody told me this, I'd retire a wealthy physician.

"The one?" I walk over and look out at the assortment of aircraft. Two male baggage handlers heave luggage onto the conveyer belt. Clearly, this is a call for help, but right now is not the time to discuss business. My stomach roils, looking for a way to get out of this conversation.

"Yes. That ship he discovered last year sunk off the southern coast of Africa and was supposedly from the late nineteenth century. It was one of only a few known scientific vessels to sail around the Cape. My brother, Uncle Ole, as he's lovingly called, had been tracking it through journals and ports of call."

She speaks as if I understand its importance to mankind. Pessimistically, I picture a grizzled explorer, standing astern an eighty-footer holding steady to a telescope on a piece of ocean, dipping up and down beyond the primitive Ivory Coast, a Moby Dick of the twenty-first century. I jot down "Ole Paul Madagascar" in my notes. His proper name was a humbling Orvil "Ole" Olson from Wasoon, Minnesota. As she describes him, I learn that Orvil Olson was a philandering Christmas tree farmer, but how does this tie in with the Indian Ocean? Sadly, the only things that sail in those northern woods are homespun deer hunting trips and desiccating bear dung.

"Uncle Orvil had spent four years researching the scientific fleet of maritime adventurers, especially the African expeditions. To him, it was more than a story. It was a journey."

Through the receiver I hear her rustling through paper sounds. She gently blows her nose.

"He resigned from the Naval Academy a full captain and taught naval history at Wasoon Community College for the next twenty years, an elective for the historians as you might presuppose. There is not much need for an old sailor back in the north woods, but Uncle Orvil turned to books. Before you knew it, he was somewhat of an authority on ocean research vessels. He complained that he was schooled in the art, but never practiced the skills. Uncle used to joke that he was too young to attain history. That was sort of his humor: indirect, old fashioned."

As she continues talking about him, I begin to sense the pain of his passing is still fresh. This woman wishes to convert her relative's unfinished life's chapters into obituary book form. I encounter this quite often on the receiving part. First there is surprise, followed by bitterness and anger. Someone needs to be held accountable for this death. Someone will pay, whether it is the doctors, hospital, nurses, or the like. When resolution takes root and the naturalness of death is not a germinating seed of contempt anymore, my client's grief can become a cause. It is only then can attempts at answers be sought.

As for myself, I'm batting about .500 and riding an agonizing slump. Work and family don't often balance. I still yearn to help those who are suffering loss and yet I am not good at sharing my own. It's the old sports analogy. I hate to lose when I am competing, but there's a comfortable familiarity to playing the game. Only a few get to win on a regular basis which is how the matter stands. As for me, my step to the plate took a dump a few years back. People I trusted betrayed me with unsubstantiated lies. It literally beat me up to a point that I considered quitting medicine. Living on the breadline with the homeless would have been more satisfactory.

"Dr. Michaels. Would you say based on your experience that this patient's mistreatment of his hypertension led to his death?"

"As I have already indicated, an autopsy cannot address standards of care. It can only detail postmortem findings."

"Detail. Detail is such an interesting usage of terms, isn't it, Dr. Michaels? After all, wasn't there an appendectomy scar that you failed to mention in your external examination?"

"There was. I did not recognize the subtle skin changes initially. The body had been decomposing. Internally, the organs were autolyzed and friable. That means the tissues were badly decomposing."

"Isn't that a rather important detail to miss?"

"I did not miss it. If you read my report, I mentioned that an appendix was not identified. This is a part of the routine internal

examination. Only pending medical record review can I be certain of an appendectomy."

"But you went along with the autopsy anyway, didn't you, Dr. Michaels?"

"Objection."

"Sustained."

"Yes. There was a timetable issue. Next of kin wanted to complete the funeral and burial arrangements."

"I see, and you felt compelled to hurry through the autopsy to satisfy their wants as soon as possible."

"Objection."

"Sustained."

"Absolutely not, I conduct my examinations in a routine fashion. I am well-organized and quite efficient. The family is Jewish. Their religious beliefs prefer burials within twenty-four hours, and I try to accommodate that whenever possible. What is the issue here? Is it the fact I did not take three or four hours to complete the case?"

"I'll ask the questions, Doctor. Your Honor, move to strike the last statement."

"Move to strike so granted. The jury will not recognize the previous testimony."

"Thank you, Your Honor. Getting back to the hypertension: what qualifies you to determine clinical hypertension in a dead person?"

"I am a Board-Certified Forensic Pathologist, not a clinician. What are you?"

"Move to strike, Your Honor. Request to treat the witness as hostile."

"Dr. Michaels, please restrain from personal attacks. Answer the questions only."

"I will answer any intelligent question, Your Honor. I will not be badgered into saying why a once living person ended up on a morgue table without giving my professional opinions."

"Dr. Michaels, do you remember a tiny detail regarding an unidentified body that you performed an autopsy on named Jane Doe?"

"I do a fair amount of Jane Doe's a year, Counselor."

"Yes, I understand. But this Jane Doe was someone's once living daughter. You okayed some of the organs to be used by the medical school for dissection. In fact, the heart was sliced into hundreds of pieces for conduction studies. Could you describe for the court what exactly are conduction studies?"

"Conduction studies, in this case, were histological tissue sections of the cardiac nervous system to get a better understanding of how certain neural bundles are able to generate pumping stimulus in a damaged organ."

"Did this patient have hypertension?"

"This patient could very well have, based on the anatomical findings."

"Your impressions were on a dead person, were they not?"

"Objection."

"Sustained."

"They were."

"Did you happen to know that person was Jewish?"

"I did not know at the time."

"Is that an overlooked detail? How about an authorization to perform a postmortem examination? Was that ever issued by the family?"

"The body was identified by fingerprints two days later."

"Dr. Michaels, do you always perform autopsies on unidentified persons?"

"Objection."

"Sustained."

"Not always."

"But you just stated she was identified by fingerprinting, did you not?"

"I said the identification was eventually made."

"Why didn't you wait for the identification in advance of harvesting the organs?"

"There was no toe tag. My assistant told me this Jane Doe was next and we proceeded."

"Is that proper enough protocol for you, Dr. Michaels? Someone tells you what might be correct, and you begin?"

"No. There was an error in communication. I..."

"Dr. Michaels, how many autopsies did you perform on Wednesday, the tenth of October two years ago?"

"I am not sure. I believe you have that answer."

"Why, yes I do. It was thirteen. Thirteen death cases in a shift of nine and one-half hours. Isn't that a little excessive, Michaels? That is less than an hour per case. Thirteen families needing answers from you. Your expert opinion. Let me ask you: How did your wife die?"

"Objection!"

"I'll allow it."

"My wife died from cardio-respiratory failure brought on by pregnancy hypertension and disseminated intravascular coagulopathy. In other words, she had intrauterine bleeding and couldn't produce enough platelets to clot. She kept bleeding internally until her heart gave out."

"On what day did she die, Dr. Michaels?"

"Sunday, October seventh, two years ago."

"That was only three days prior to those thirteen autopsies, was it not?"

"It was, but I accomplished all those cases to the best of my ability."

"Did any of those patients have appendectomy scars, Dr. Michaels?"

"I do not recall."

"Was one of your last cases of the day a badly decomposing young woman?"

"I do not recall."

"You do not recall. Is that because you might have been distracted with your wife's death?"

"Objection."

"Sustained."

"No."

"What is the average number of autopsies performed by the coroner's office per day?"

"Between three to ten."

"Between three to ten? How did thirteen happen? Was there an outbreak or something?"

"Objection. Badgering, Your Honor."

"Sustained."

"Each day or week is different from the other. Twice the number on any given day is not that unusual. We were short on staff pathologists. I felt compelled to help."

"Do you think you were at the top of your game on Wednesday, the tenth of October, Michaels? Afterall, you performed over twice the average number of cases."

"My name is Dr. Michaels. Don't go there. You don't know jack. So, what if I missed an appendectomy scar? So, what? Is that as important as losing your wife and child on the same day without apparent cause or any way to stop it? Think about what you're implying. Think about who YOU are."

"Dr. Michaels. I will not instruct you concerning these outbursts again."

"I am not sorry, Your Honor. This trial is a farce."

"Can we go on please, Judge? I have a few more questions for Dr. Michaels. If I may, Dr. Michaels, how old was your wife when she died?"

"She was forty-four."

"Isn't that rather old to be pregnant? Aren't there higher risks to both mother and fetus in older females?"

"Studies indicate a higher percentile of pregnancy complications. Bear in mind that each case is dependent upon the state of the patient's health."

"How was the state of your wife's health, Dr. Michaels?"

"Not good."

"I have no further questions, Your Honor. The defense rests."

My gut feels hard as if a large rock has formed in the lining. There is a lump in my throat, and I can taste bile, berating myself over the decision, obsessing. How am I ever going to reverse my role and be honest? This internalizing, this blaming the deceased. I want out.

I ask the caller for her name.

"It's Gail, Gail Nevers. I, err, we, live in Sather, a little farm hub south of Rochester about sixteen miles. It's agricultural, like Wasoon and situated in a river valley. Come winter, people bring toboggans and make a day of it." She chuckles. "Actually, it's quite peaceful and unimposing. But you can't compare the Rocky Mountains to Southern Minnesota river valleys for skiing or sledding."

"Sounds nice," I add, although terms like "terrific" or "peaceful" came to mind. I want to summarize in three or four sentences, but those are speedbumps that potential clients don't want to hear.

"It's been daunting with his passing," getting back to her brother. "No one seems to care except for me. All I want are some answers, like was he sick or was there cancer?"

Hopelessness trails off in her voice like trying to stop a landslide.

"I can't believe how many pathologists have refused my autopsy request. Either they were too expensive, too busy, or too late to do the necessary toxicology testing. At least you have listened to my story despite this frustration. I'm sorry to have bothered you. To be on the safe side for everyone concerned, let's cancel this whole mess."

"Ms. Nevers, calling it off doesn't address the concerns. It shelves them. Nothing is gained by forgetting your uncle's dreams. At least through the autopsy, we can eliminate or factor the anatomical findings into completion. I can gather information from the tissues that can give you an explanation. Often, it is natural, such as a heart attack or pneumonia. But if he was aboard a ship in international waters, food contamination or malaria is a possibility. Don't you want to know? That's why you called in the first place."

The pause on the other end is my signal to let *time-out* step to the plate. She needs to huddle with her thoughts rather than giving me a firm decision. A death within driving distance is much easier to fathom.

"You know, I've ordered the body to be shipped stateside. It will arrive in Minneapolis by this coming Tuesday at the latest."

"That only allows us four days to decide, then." I conclude cautiously, trying not to groan over the receiver. My thoughts steer toward the condition of the body, actual date of death, refrigerated or embalmed, or frozen. These are natural thought processes for anyone going the private autopsy route. Because of the uncertainties, and the fact that other pathologists have gone sour on this case, am I going to be able to help her?

"I need to discuss this with the twins, the actual next of kin. I'm merely their bothersome Aunty. They manage Ole's small resort in northern Minnesota lake country."

A lake getaway. Another enviable summertime pleasure beyond my narrowed scope and unconsciously, I push my chin forward and pinch the skin on my throat.

She continues.

"In actuality, Aaron and Davie are young men, but still act like boys in my mind. Olson's to the death. As far as that goes, they wouldn't be mistaken for their father. They pick their battles, put together lousy business decisions, and are close to running their resort into the mud like that catfish farm venture they nearly had me invest in between paychecks. Neither of them ever had much time for Orvil when he was alive and less for him now. If I can convince them of an examination, what are we talking about for turnaround time and expenses?"

"About four weeks and forty-eight hundred dollars plus travel expenses, providing I don't require special studies like toxicology or histology stains to detect specific microorganisms. If I am unable to give you a definitive cause of death, I will deduct the added travel expenses although I doubt that will happen. But up front, some deaths are not explainable, and families shouldn't be penalized for that."

"Well, I'll get back to you," she said hurriedly, as if not wanting to add any more details in the negotiation at this point. People in unsettling situations such as death need extra time to commit to anything else. These are lasting decisions if there ever was such an animal for the next of kin. I've known disgruntled clients who sue for damages years later. Present company included.

"That's perfectly fine. Please take your time. Call me if you have further questions. You have my cell number."

"Dr. Michaels, I don't want to take more of your time, but I hope this is not prying. How did you get started in this business?"

I give her the patented need to help with closure and answers to questions. I went on about how my father died at fifty-five of heart disease brought on by forty years of smoking. I discussed how legal rhetoric comes to litigation. In the end, the death call gave me a sudden kinship of my own. It's someone's loss. I'm there for her if she wants. I'm most likely the only one.

"Because I think people like you need me, Ms. Nevers, and I'd like to help."

We hang up with cordial good-byes. A passenger jet lifts off into the northern horizon.

God, I'm so homesick. If I were home, I'd be watching a flock of Canadian geese silently glide past instead of people lined-up to check through airport security. My view is a valley of towering eucalyptus and magnificent heritage oaks while the migratory birds take up residence in the nearby lake. Touchdown for them is Lake Idaho, a reservoir encased by million-dollar homes, a country club, and a strip mall. Financially, I'm holding my own on the outskirts with a modest two-bedroom cottage on three acres of mostly boulders and rattlesnakes. It's a mishmash of a sparingly furnished and seldom inhabited dwelling since I am either on a plane or the road a major percentage of my time. I can appreciate the view and the greenery, but never have time to explore it. I don't even know my neighbor's last name.

The privately gated community of retirees down the hill from my house dress as if every day begins with golf, followed by Sunday brunch with unlimited cocktails. Their marbled kitchens, their quaint lifestyle, contoured and efficient. I don't even have matching silverware. Regrettably, there are spired mountains of marble and granite to the eastern slope that I do value and promise to visit soon.

Both my parents are buried here as is my beloved wife, Cassie. No one said childbirth was easier as you got older. In her forties, it was stupid and dangerous. She was in good shape: biking and hiking up to the eighth month. But thrombi were forming and torpedoing throughout her left leg, dropping off mini-time bombs into her kidneys, lungs, and brain. No one prepared me for this, and I was supposed to have all the answers. But this time I was on the questioning end. Answers eluded my cross-examination, but they perched on her tombstone next to the roses I planted two short years ago.

On purpose, I'd reach into the bushes to watch the thorns scratch me, draw blood, get infected. Only glistening white scars remain, like drying old spackle on my forearms. That was the part that healed. What I could not save was myself.

I haven't been wholly truthful with that dear woman from southern Minnesota. The patented answer about helping the living through death, that's the sales pitch. I might be the most cordial professional on the phone, but there is a compulsion because of it. I still see Erin Garner, or at least I think it's her. Sometimes she brushes me in a crowded auditorium. Other times, I will be alone and, out the corner of my eye, a shadowy female form materializes, standing quietly. A variant of sorts, but I know it's Erin. It's as if she is teasing me to catch her, find her. She never smiles, but watches me, observes my habits, knows my thoughts. She has become my guardian angel of some sort, although I gave up on that religious stuff decades ago. She is still missing. It still haunts me. There stands that shy, assured fireplug that helped me navigate some rough patches in my complicated existence. Erin is not always in human form, but her presence is a breath, a someone-is-standing-behind-me sensation.

It has taken me years to understand this paranoia. Instead of fear, I became comfortable with her nearness all over again. She was there when I walked crowded college corridors or watched from behind as I wrote laborious journal articles on the timeframes of putrefaction, uncertain if she had passed those stages decades ago. I'd look over to see her sitting in the passenger seat as I drove endless snow fallen miles to mountain funeral homes. We'd dine together in silence and stood in line at shoddy truck stops. She would watch me shower away the one-night stands that I had with women other than my wife. I was certain that I was tilting headfirst into the loony garbage bin, but I dared not discuss this with anyone.

Erin is my measuring stick, my voice of reason, keeping tabs on my mental health first and foremost. I know there's a mission behind this. Somewhere out there, Erin is still waiting for me. She wants to escort me to that temporary residence - - not unearthed, but undiscovered. That's how I define this sanity. She is directing my decisions in a host of ways. Autopsies have become an obsession, a lost suitor in the big dance. Every time I open another body, subconsciously, I am looking for her, seeking the lost answers.

Years have passed, and I have become more complacent. No matter when or how, my life went on while hers was suddenly stunted. On matters concerning psychiatrists, they diagnosed it as a guilt complex. Sometimes, it's weeks before I see her and then one day, I stand on a street corner waiting to cross and Erin stares out from a shop window. Her reflection is in my face. She wears jeans and a sweatshirt. On her head is a green scarf. Some of her curly brown hair pokes out on the sides. It's a sad look and her mouth is downturned. Her appearance triggers another innocent memory of etched distant recollections, like the soapstone necklace I gave her on our last day at Bible Camp. That favorite headscarf always adorns the head of her ghost replacement, tied securely in a telltale double knot. It is Erin's sign, all right. Finish me off entirely, why don't you. A forty-three-year-old piece of a colored headscarf has me by the psyche gonads.

Necromancy. The quirky thing I remember from med school anatomy and all of us residents joked about it. Summoning up the dead. Invoking the future.

Hello, Erin.

Funny how you are summoned-up by that phone call once again. I haven't been to Minnesota in decades. Will this time be the last?

CHAPTER THREE

For a fact, I'm an earth-bound junkie. Regarding the anatomy of the land, I'm hooked. The perception of glittering mineral-types on hikes in ancient mountains, glaciers transformed into farms, how the land is chosen to inhabit, or where to dig a burial site have always drawn my attention. What grows where, natural borders versus linear boundaries. It's like land anatomy without a bone or organ. I was initiated early on when No Trespassing signs weren't meant for neighbors, when barbed wire fences separated cattle from the highways, when abandon ranch houses had to hold their own against the changing seasons.

Flying high above the Rocky Mountains granite vertebral columns from seven thousand feet morphs the Great Plains into chessboard farms. Dome-shaped water towers stand sentinel watch over communities like lonely pawns. I canvass the Mississippi River Valley through my window seat behind the jet's wing. The sun reflects off each of the hundred or so lakes and ponds, like earthy hazel eyes that blink with the tree-lined shores.

My three-hour flight from desert to mountains to flat agricultural vistas provide a vivid reminder how much I miss coming here more often than once every two or three years. The vegetation in the summer is lush and continuously rinsed clean by humid storms. There is that desperate flurry of annoying insect activity, feeding and laying eggs, as if the first frost is nearly around the corner.

In comparison, people of this region are not like that. Midwesterners never hurry anywhere, especially on Sundays. On approach, it comes as no surprise the pace is downgrading to a crawl as the plane glides low and hard over the cars and semis on Interstate 494. The jet's screeching tires, the stewardess' monotone "Welcome to Minneapolis. For your safety, please remain seated..."

introduction, and anxious people standing up and grabbing their carry-ons from the overhead bins is universal.

I stand in line at the rental counter, checking my cell, rubbing my oily complexion. In a matter of minutes, my car assignment pulls up and I follow basic procedure: sign a release form, stuff my luggage in the trunk, crank the ignition, press the air conditioning button, dial up some tunes, and plug in my phone.

Besides the state license plates bragging about the "Land of 10,000 Lakes" even the raptors are on the increase. I can't remember ever seeing red-tailed hawks this late in the summer. Blackbirds and sparrows fly low reconnaissance swooping through the airport overpasses like only Minnesota birds can. Cars on the freeway change lanes without first signaling. A semi swerves to avoid a collision with an old model van. Sports cars weave in and out of traffic. Muscle cars with tinted windows blow by. Monster trucks leave me choking for air. Is this Minnesota or California?

Upon request by Gail Nevers, I'm to meet with the brothers sooner than later. It's explained to me that the peak tourist season prevents them from leaving the business for long periods. She suggests to me that they are the hands-on type, although I have been wrong before. We schedule a meeting at the funeral home prior to their father's remains arriving. This earmarks only a couple days to get reacquainted to country roads and rolling pasture vistas. Such a dilemma. I mull over my options: a little fly-fishing, a good book by a local author, or just chillin'.

Wasoon can be considered a rural town in the Midwest with a population holding at eleven hundred hardy folks. It has a 1950's water tower, a 1960's grain elevator, a two-story 1970's red brick bank building, a 1980's filling station with a two-stall garage, a 1990's sports bar advertising the best cheese fries in the county, and of course, an old-fashioned funeral home. According to the website, the original building from the thirties had been replaced. The accompanying photo shows a driveway lined by statuesque pines and a double-wide modular with an A-frame chapel painted white. There is a classic rectangular sign at the turnoff with the name: Wasoon Family Funeral Chapel. On the bottom, in small print, cremation services are also advertised.

The trip is not as idyllic as I had hoped. Every twenty miles or so there is end-of-summer road construction marred by scruffy, tar-streaked flagmen wearing burnt orange vests. My patience is thread thin and I need to remind myself to calm down. Replaying the sticky day being spent behind the wheel and the seemingly endless, dusty, forty-mile detour has me exasperated. By highway's end, this scene has repeated at least a half-dozen times and I am looking for the silver lining to no avail. What's more, I was rewarded with a speeding ticket from a preying, over-zealous city cop sitting in wait behind the city limits billboard.

His "Have a nice day" never sounded so cynical.

I pull my road weary rental onto the driveway next to a listing birch sapling that is held vertical by an Excalibur-style wooden stake. How severe are the winters up here? The hazy sunlight is filtered with construction dust from pavement graders and dump trucks. Dry summer conditions don't help matters and the heat bakes the ground into a glaze-like sheen. The popping and pulverizing of stones under my tires ignite a throaty German shepherd guard dog that repeats angry warnings next-door. I'm famished and my concentration is foggy as I rock back and forth in the car seat trying to stay alert. A lukewarm bottle of Diet Mountain Dew and a partially melted Snickers bar rest on the passenger seat. It's not a good idea to skip meals on the road, but first things first. Sensibleness has demonstrated to me that navigating new locations has never been one of my favorite pastimes and that's the logic behind pushing the pedal to the metal this time.

I unpeel like wet adhesive off the backrest and step out into the heat. Sweat dribbles down the crack in my butt. Four hours of genuine sleep in the past thirty-six of which eleven were either in or driving to an airport, or delays, or browsing through newsstand magazine racks, or catching up on reports with my laptop. A late model dull gray pick-up truck with a raised bed rumbles in next to me. Its wheels are pricey off-road type with two-inch treads meeting me at eye-level. The driver and the passenger are enjoined in a shouting spiel. I look back to the main building pretending not to hear, get out, and head for the entrance.

Each step on the plywood ramp squeaks louder than the previous one and the wobbly guard rail is in dire need of a good paint job. The double door to the funeral home is sun-damaged and its pattern is French style and not that Renaissance impression from the website photo. What other surprises will this building hold? Is this the right address? Deciding that a knock is unwarranted, I step inside. The waiting room is dark and quiet. An air conditioner drones out the resonant road construction with an icy blast. I linger next to the vent to dry my back, hoping that negotiations are carried out right here. It could be no one will notice the perspiration stain of my arm pits. To the left is a forest green door that automatically opens with a soft chime to reveal the chapel portion lined with about ten or so pews on each side and a center aisle covered by dark carpet. A metallic casket pedestal is situated at the far end and is centered by a tempered bronze-colored coffin. From my perspective, bouquets of flowers, mostly carnations, line the opened lid displaying the elevated head of someone's elderly male relative under the soft spotlight. I get a whiff of recently sprayed floral air freshener and Windex.

This view transports me back to a funeral I attended last summer in the South Dakota Badlands. A respected friend, Waylon Two Bucks, died at the unlawful early age of fifty-three. We had known each other in college. I went on to medical school whereas he moved back to the reservation after Vietnam and became a law enforcement officer. Over the years, Waylon worked on several jobs. He loved playing cards with the elders. As a member of the local Legion Post #66 he became an Honor Guard at cemetery interments. Waylon once confided in me of his failed marriage and the incessant bouts of alcoholism within his immediate family. These were tremendous challenges to overcome and I felt sorry for his dark history. College for him was a blessing.

One day, the violence that was bred into the reservation youth gangs pinned him down in a ransacked house on the outskirts of the village where he had gone to serve papers on a suspected spousal abuse felon. Two shotgun blasts later, he lay lifeless against the screen door. At his funeral, I remembered seeing Waylon's prominent Indian features for the last time. Except for the forehead wrinkles and crow's feet, he looked exactly how I remembered, with perfectly braided salt and pepper hair capturing his stoic face. Unafraid. Aloof. Proud of his heritage.

We paired up in microbiology laboratory where his exceptional knowledge to detail carried both of our grades. I was forever obliged to him for surviving that semester and he never let me forget how he single-handedly got us through blood glucose studies in diabetic rats.

"Hey, Michaels," he teased. "Do any fecal smears, lately?"

That was an inside joke about my peculiar interest in how to identify parasitic eggs in mammal feces. He used to call me Dr. Fecal Smear, a name that literally stuck through undergraduate biology classes. I was often invited to Lakota brew fests where he introduced me as "The Token." It yielded interesting conversation at keg parties until my indigenous male counterpart defined its meaning to some of the most beautiful female coeds I had ever seen. I was usually alcohol-infused, slurring with that shit-faced grin. Not a winning combination. A few minutes of blabbering and they would walk away in disgust. A hard lesson, so I kept my majoring in biology a secret.

The funeral for Waylon was filled with a gauntlet of raw sentiment. He was the oldest male member of his family and fluent in the Dakota language. Representatives from the Bureau of Indian Affairs attended. The women wailed in haunting death melodies during which the men pounded continually on leather-skin drums. At the front sat his two daughters who bore an uncanny resemblance to him. I hadn't seen them since they were toddlers. They must be in their late thirties by now. His ex-wife, Helene wasn't in attendance. That was not a surprise. Some things never change. He fought to keep the traditional ways sacred, but she never bought in. Values are passed onto these children, but the paradox is this: elders are expected to die of old age and teenagers are expected not to live in jail until they're elders. Waylon Two Bucks went on his spiritual journey, the Wanagi Tacanku, on a blustery Friday afternoon, a week before Thanksgiving.

I skip out of my daydream as the office door opens and a middle-aged man emerges wearing a short-sleeve white button-down shirt and slate blue khakis. His hair is thinned, wavy and cut close to the shiny scalp. Flecks of gray adorn both his robin-red moustache and sideburns.

"Can I help you?" His eyes meet me at chin level and his greeting builds with a slow smile as he pushes up the glasses on his hawk-like nose.

"Dr. Michaels," I reply, reaching out for a handshake. "I'm here to meet with Aaron and David Olson. The potential autopsy on their father, Orvil Olson."

"Sounds good. They are supposed to be here anytime soon. I'm Roland Purdy, the Director of Wasoon Funeral Chapel. Won't you please come in?"

He moves aside to allow me to pass first. The office is supplied with a modest desk, phone, notepad, and a daily calendar. Curiously, there are no children or family pictures and no calling cards.

"We are remodeling," he explains. "This is a temporary facility until construction is completed in the spring."

He nervously rubs his cheek. "That was *two* Springs ago."

In my travels, small community funeral homes can't survive only on funerals. Usually, there's a business like a furniture store or transport service accompanying it. I suspect this building is open when the need dictates. The entrance door rings, and the two young men hesitate before stepping inside. One of them constantly checks his watch. Except for mostly identical facial features, it's obvious that they try to not dress the same. The one nearest to me is comfortable with a button-down plaid work shirt and blue jeans. The other wears camouflage cargo shorts and sandals. Number One's hair is combed long and straight and to the side hiding some acne scars. Number Two's mane is darker and not quite as oily as his shirt. Both brothers have matching hazel eyes the color of pristine lakes and their scrutiny penetrates my skull. Brother Number One locks onto something behind Roland and me and chuckles to himself. I follow his gaze out the window. The menacing German Shepard lifts its leg on a rear tire of my rental car and marks the territory with a long stream.

Neither of them exhibits a honed set of social skills as they sidestep me and stand next to a vacant chair. It doesn't feel like hostile category but just to be safe I keep my fingers crossed behind my back. The exit door behind Roland's desk is calling me. Dressed-up Olson brother extends his hand first.

"I'm David Olson and it's nice to meet you. But I'm afraid you have come a long way for nothing."

Widening his stance, he gives me a 'let's get this over with' dismissive nod. This is not the time to pull rank. I'm in enemy territory.

"Your Aunt Gail wanted me to discuss an autopsy," I tell him. "She is concerned about the cause of death. I can settle that issue for all the family."

"Dead is dead. Nothing is going to change it."

He shuffles and gawks at the displayed coffin in the next room.

"I'm not here to change it," I respond. "I'm available to answer the questions of how it happened. People contact me all the time. I'm here to help if you want."

This is not the way I prefer to defend autopsies, but the resistance forces are gathering like berms in an ancient battle. Over the phone this conversation ends long ago but standing face to face and travelling two thousand miles runs counter to common sense.

"Well, I just don't know," David begins to shuffle back and forth. "I respect Aunt Gail and all that. She's been pretty good to Aaron and me and she even got us this here resort business started. When Dad wasn't around, she was our rock, checking on us, asking how we were doing and such. Mom died ten years ago of a stroke. Dad got bored with living up here and wanted to study shipwrecks. Hell, I'm all for that on his own time. But both of us needed a little support."

He casually shrugs it off and glares at his brother who is busy checking the messages on his cell phone.

"Shoot. I missed a call from Paige. Davie, we got to get going pretty soon."

David smirks, "Dr. Michaels, if you're going to do an autopsy on anyone, how about starting with my dopey brother. Paige is this new girlfriend; except she doesn't know yet." He offers up his hands in matching quotation marks. "She keeps on calling and it's really annoying."

He pokes his brother in the shoulder. "Hey, Dingbat, how about a little respect?"

Aaron intervenes. "Guess you met David. I'm Aaron, the hand-some one."

His grip is like holding a dead fish and I end up shaking for both of us.

"Are you here to do an autopsy or something? Dad's body was to arrive yesterday and now it looks like Wednesday or Thursday at the earliest. It has to do with international customs. Roland expects to pick him up once the call comes in from the airport."

"He is not embalmed," Roland cuts in. "However, he has been placed on dry ice. If my records are correct, that was the Tuesday before last, the twenty-second."

"When did Mr. Olson die?" I inquire, envisioning the unstoppable decay, thawing a couple hours, skin turning black and greasy from sulfurous bacteria and tropical temperatures, tissues shedding, soggy-Kleenex style, the trapped putrefaction gases expanding the zipped body bag much like blowing helium into a balloon.

"He was discovered in his berth aboard the *Pinkett*, the research boat," interjects Aaron, his interest in adding to the conversation perks.

"A research vessel in the Midwest is a fishing boat," jokes Roland. "One doesn't come across legions of ships or sailing vessels. Boating is not sailing."

"His berth," I probe, "not his bunk or quarters?"

Generally, the family interprets the information prior to a post-mortem to their favor. Phrases or terms will have bias for the deceased such as "He was fine yesterday," or "She was hospitalized, but a nurse gave her a pill and she threw up after that." It's a natural response and sometimes the term usage is misinterpreted. Protection of the loved one and blame ride shotgun on opposite sides of the same bloodline fence.

"I think they came across him on the floor in front of his berth. His face was blue, and he wasn't breathing. They tried to resuscitate him, but..."

Aaron's voice trails off and he shrugs.

Roland Purdy adjusts his stance and comes from behind his desk to stand with the rest of us, leaning in toward the brothers. He scoots the empty visitor chair that separates us back to the wall.

"Hey, Aaron, this might be a good cause to have an autopsy. Suppose David or you carry some genetic code, making you suscepti-ble to heart attacks or something. If it were me, I'd want to find out?"

Roland's "owt" resonates like a Canadian discussing a hockey game in a blizzard. In my opinion, transplants to the Minnesota tun-dra all sound alike.

"Yeah, I suppose so. But isn't it like gutting a deer? You open them up with a knife, pull everything out, and dice away?"

If he is trying to be clever or shocking, it's not working.

Now is the perfect time to explain my work.

"The entire autopsy is both visual and structural findings. I detail the body with an external examination and then go through the entire organ system individually, looking for departures from the norm. If I discover something out of the usual, I note it, collect representative samples, perform laboratory tests, and compile the results."

Most families don't want to know the specifics. They want assur-ance that the body is properly respected. Aaron pockets his cell phone and begins to rub his scalp.

"What do you think, Dave? Roland does make a good point. Perhaps

Dad avoided us intentionally because he knew something was wrong. I always thought he was purely short of breath from being a lifetime ciggy-smoking stack, but it can very well be something else."

David speaks up.

"When you put it that way, I guess you are right. I'm not so opposed to the autopsy like I was in the beginning. Aunt Gail wants it, that's for sure. That's why she called. I say we go ahead with it and see what comes out the other end. Let's give ourselves some sort of peace of mind."

He straightens and faces me.

"Dr. Michaels, we accept the terms. Go ahead with the autopsy. My brother and I will sign the consent form. When the body arrives, we'll finalize our burial decisions. Is that all right with you, Roland?"

"Sounds good, Dave," the funeral director says, clapping his hands together.

Roland walks back to his desk and pulls open the top drawer.

"Here is the autopsy form Dr. Michaels faxed me last weekend. Let's get this underway, boys." He hands them each a pen. "Sign here," pointing to the bottom of the page.

The brothers curl their pens crablike. Aaron looks over David's shoulder who uses his index finger to read word by word prior to signing. An exasperated Aaron clicks his pen, reaches across and scribbles on the crowded line. Roland applies the Wasoon Family Funeral Chapel notarized stamp below their signatures and boasts a sigh of relief.

"At last. I thought there was going to be a struggle with you two. You surprised me."

"Well, we can't do a fricking thing about Africa, but we'll get the last word on Daddy." David nods to his brother.

"Hey, Aaron, don't we still have that cottage next to the pool vacant for the week?"

"Yep," he agrees. "That stupid guy from Sauk Center cancelled out at the last minute. What's on your mind?"

"I say we offer the doctor an opportunity to visit God's Country for a couple days on us. It's best that we keep the custodial staff busy and he might bring us a couple California clients someday. You are invited to join us, Dr. Michaels. It's entirely up to you."

"I'm in without a doubt."

My grim reluctance to delve into a rotting body gives way to a rewarding aftermath of homemade apple pie and a chilled local brew. We agree with a handshake and David gives me a friendly pat on the back. Meanwhile, Aaron is pulling out his cell phone and scrolling.

CHAPTER FOUR

My dad's idea of a vacation was to stay home and watch his crops grow until harvest was in the bins. Winter was a six-month holiday. By the time April rolled around he set his internal stopwatch for field preparation, fertilization, and planting, all needed by mid-May. There was no other getaway -- period. Travel out of the county to compare corn or soybean fields? No problem. Whereas an unnecessary sojourn out of the state? Big problem. Like my dad, farmers are out of their comfort zone as tourists unless there is someone to visit, a wedding, or a funeral. On the other end of the road had to be another relative, hopefully a farmer. An acquaintance or someone with common interests was helpful, especially with an overnight place to stay. If an itinerary is not written down on a piece of paper with both the arrival and especially return times, forget it, because they are not into sightseeing.

My parents always arrived without any forethought to see anything of interest. As far as I was concerned, travelling with them became a chore. Their sole purpose was to wolf down truck stop burgers, then get back in the car for the sanctuary of home. Their restless spirit fed a sense of urgency, but they preferred status quo. I have firsthand know-how on this with my father. He would bicker all the way down the driveway until the farm was out of sight, or five miles, which ever came first. That is why I can appreciate the Olson brothers' anxiety when they had to travel beyond their self-assured boundaries of the resort. This is *their* farm, their comfort zone. The funeral home is not. Their spinning truck tires fling out gravel chunks at both my rental and the scavenging sparrows.

As they prepare to leave, I am given meager directions in case we become separated. But to the contrary, that definition is lost at the first mile. I see the auspices of a speed trap and the same city cop stalking behind the billboard sign and decide to slow. Speeding tickets are easy income for these little towns, not at all like the metro area. A missed exit in a Little Rock, Arkansas, suburb emptied my wallet by three hundred dollars. I was late for an appointment in Fayetteville and that didn't go well with the funeral director either. I assume by now, the brothers are miles ahead, so the scenic route is the best alternative. Over the course of a few short miles, I am left to fend for myself in unknown territory.

It's been years, but some of the landmarks are still visible. There's the slate gray water tower with a large W on the south side, the John Deere implement store with the now sagging roof, and the family-owned lumberyard. If I remain on this highway out of town, the Bible Camp-Deluxe Resort of my youth is roughly ten miles ahead.

I drive north into once endless timberland that is now a potpourri of broad pastures and road ditches covered in foxtails and colorful bushy weeds wafting in the wind. Well-fed dairy cattle forage where groves of birch and poplar trees once stood. Driving along the shaded portion of the road, I am in awe as the tree trunks take on the gentle sunlight and offer back a majestic olive-green foliage as if traveling amongst an African savannah. Ole need not trek halfway around the globe to savor this. Despite the twin's hearsay, I admire his perseverance to give up most everything to chase a silly dream. For the near future, that whim isn't in my playing card deck.

Overhead, migratory Canadian geese wedge across the clear northern Minnesota skies. Oftentimes, I persuaded Erin to sit beside the lake to watch the exodus, but she was growing wise to my ways. Our free time from counselor duties led to those secret nesting ponds where we discovered special ways to unwind. Today's drive is an excellent reminder of how beautiful lake country can be as summer ends, and how head-over-heels I was with her.

It also goes without saying that those statuesque trees guarding the highway can open onto colorful meadows of bluebells and goldenrod that leaves me in awe. Around the bend an endless lake enters the panorama, and the opposite shore is a spattering of whitecaps. I lift my foot off the accelerator to gently brake as if there were imaginary warning lights ahead. The horizon is pristine. Lake foam laps the surface beside me, and postcard perfect cottages and cabins line the shore. If only I were a better swimmer, the urge to pull off the road and leap in, sans clothes, would be a baptism of sorts. God only knows how far removed I am from my last religious intervention.

Roadside signs on my right announce the entrance to Ole's Resort. I ought to have known the casual way *Ole's* fell off the tongue that the brothers were not wasting time on advertisement. There is a wide array of sixties-style signs, Old Spice-like, on the approach to the resort, propped upon freshly painted wooden stakes every couple hundred yards. Welcome to Ole's. Only a quarter mile away. Did you pack your toothbrush? The smiles and miles just keep on a comin'. By the time I arrive at the entrance, I am spent. Those catchy phrases compounded with the road time have left me burned out and desperate to get out of the car.

My well-used rental car is feeling the effects of on-and-off deceleration as I churn into the security gate, whereupon it putters, then falls into dead silence. The grounds have a familiar ring, like the old Bible Camp, but uncertainty on my behalf takes precedence.

Out of the security booth in the shape of a painted loon, beckons a uniformed man holding a clipboard, signaling me to stop. I roll down my window. The lanky officer with a weak chin and chapped lips stiffly leans forward and rests his elbows on my door. His canvas uniform shirt has damp stains around the collar. A breeze lifts the brim of his cap and he reaches up to hold it down. From my position downwind from him, he either forgot or needs a shower.

"Who might you be?"

Not the sort of welcome I was expecting. He's about thirty or thirty-five. Yesterday's stubble under his chin is a perfect match for his hollow brown eyes and yellowing front teeth. Judging from the stack of magazines on the floor beside his stool, I know for a fact this is not a career move. Four and a half job duties: greet vacationers, stay cordial, point them toward registration, have them sign in, and get back to fishing reports. I could never pull off that type of greeting, no matter how important, for ten hours each day.

"Dr. Michaels. Here by invitation of the Olson brothers."

I was unsure how detailed to be for his acknowledgement.

"Uh-huh. I tink I know dem," he guffawed. "Dey said you were coming right behind dem, but dat was over twenty minutes ago. Did you get lost, den?"

"Actually, they lost me," I explain. "It's safe to say that they know the roads better than me."

"Dat's true. Dey have a heavy foot to boot. Up here da roads have a way of getting to know you. Dey see if dey like vat is on dem."

He has a high pitch giggle and an interesting way how he gives the road a personality. It brings back thoughts of my father and his tractors.

"I don't know if they mentioned my stay at the cottage rental. Do I register here?"

"I tink da best ting to do is da guest sign-up at da office over der," pointing to an old Victorian three-story house shaded by rising northern pine.

"Dey should be able to help you. As for me, I vasn't tolt anyting except dat you vere coming. If you vant to speak to either Aaron or David, it vill have to vait. As soon as dey arrived, dey split. A spur of the moment ting. Plumbing problems. Said dey will be back around suppertime."

He pauses to study me, cocking his head to the right.

"I hear you're from California. How do you deal with all dose earthquakes?" He brandishes a weak smile as he scratches his cheek. "I wasn't sure about dat land of kooks and gays."

"We do all right," I said. "Come out for a visit sometime and see for yourself."

"Oh, I've bin dare a couple times. Saw Disneyland and Hearst Castle. Liked it and hope I git to go back once my leg stops aching. I'm a big history buff and git off on Civil War stories. Nothing dat exciting ever happens up here. It's da shits dat dose Twins can't hold a lead."

Twins? Lead? Am I missing something through any of this conversation?

"I'm talkin' baseball: the Twinkies, ya know? Carson gave up a dinger in dah ninth last night and dat added up to a short-lived twelve-pack of Miller Lite."

I was more than ready to bounce with him back into the present.

"Aaron is a fairly goot ball-player. He even got called up from Double-A for a try-out last spring. He is as close to a local hero Wasoon ever had."

He exhales deeply and looks past the hood of my car.

"Vell, dat's life."

Losing is something rabid these baseball fans live with on an annual basis although I believe the glass half empty logic is inbred here. I think under that uniform exterior he is a family man or wants to be someday. He's the type of person to count on to come upon a sensible solution or two. I envision him retiring from this booth in twenty years, peeling his arthritic hands off the same clipboard, a little grayer around the temples, and more sarcastic.

"Well, thanks for your help." I notice his badge hidden under the chest pocket flap.

"Perry Brown. You can call me Perry. Say, did you by chance bring your ball glove? We play softball most every night all summer. A bunch of us workers got a couple leagues going. Rich folk don't have a clue how to hold a bat, but when it comes to cocktails, dey vill gladly step up to da plate." He rights himself. "Err, you're not one of dose fellers, are you?"

"I wasn't aware of it. But if possible, can I borrow any right-handed fielder's glove?"

"Lefty?" he backs off the door frame and slaps his thigh. There is a tentative smile, like the answer to a great mystery has been revealed.

"More or less every day," I joke. This is the second invitation to join that I'd received from the time I arrived this morning. My kind of hospitality.

"Vell, settle up and veel check in vid you later." He tips his officer's cap brim with his thumb and forefinger like a real cowboy and I am officially released to continue my journey.

I turn on the sputtering engine and shift the car into gear, the exhaust is cloudy and blue. I introduce myself. "My name is Kevin Michaels, not Dr. Michaels, not Doc, just Kevin. I bat left and can play a mean first base. I'll be waiting for your call."

"I'd have dat checked out soon if I were you," Perry remarks, head-pointing to the front of my car. "Sounds like a fuel filter problem."

"Roger that," I salute, military-like, and drive away. In the rearview mirror I watch as Perry reaches inside the Loon's bill, pulls out a phone receiver and begins to converse. Directly ahead of me I recognize the main office and registration as the Vacancy light is turned off.

CHAPTER FIVE

In the spirit of concocting a tale of how the brothers left me in the dust, I expected to pour out my apologies to the resort reception-ist, but she isn't buying it. Her spunkiness overrides my attitude like a new mom chiding her two-year old. My arrival was expected, and my room is vacant and cleaned. All she had to do was punch in a few computer commands and issue me a key with brochure. Afterwards, I proceed to my rental and unfold the map to review the layout of the cabins. The resort is surrounded by a well-manicured golf course with a grand fairway view on the other side of the horse-shoe drive. There are descriptive photos of various activities like pickleball and swimming, aerial views of the lake, and the resort restaurant with outdoor seating. Within a short walk from the main building there's a deli cart advertising spicy hot dogs, organic-fed brats, and moose burgers. The caterer, wearing a white apron and chef's hat, is out front setting up the napkin holder and condiments counter. Dressy restaurant aside, I suspect few locals frequent this upscale place and even fewer can afford the stiff membership fees.

I motor toward my cabin. Paved roads lead to gravel and one-ways. The bike lane is wider than most, like cruising through a national park, minus the annoying shuttle service and need for a Visa card. My assigned cabin is near the activities center where golfers and bocce ball players abound, not to mention the nineteenth hole drinkers. In some sense, this is the old chapel site, now remodeled into livable quarters for tourists. It occurs to me I know why this cottage was vacant at the last minute. No privacy. People are milling about everywhere except at my front entrance. Alongside the picnic tables, currently invaded by swirling yellow jackets, couples of elderly men are taking turns at the horseshoe pit, the clanging and whoop-ing are matched with guffaws. There is a fifty-five-gallon garbage drum a moderate distance away, filled to the brim with soiled paper plates and beer cans. Under a canopy of pines near the edge of the tree line, a group of women in Bermuda shorts, matching tops and tennis shoes perform some sort of stretching exercises to the sound of country music. In retrospect, this island-inspiring Biblical past of mine never held any buzzing and metallic booms.

A storm front had passed through last night leaving the air fresh, but still breezy. Lower humidity meant fewer complaints and a happier clientele. Their pocketbooks open a little wider for that extra round of golf or cocktail. I overhear an occasional friendly yip of a small-sized dog. Pet-friendly business is everywhere these days. There is a poop bag dispensary alongside the trash can. Overall, the grounds are well kept and inviting to a weary driver. A golfer has the best of both worlds. Immaculate putting green for practice and grand views of fairways formed out of the pines. A couple of duffers wearing neon-colored Bermuda shorts and white polos look out of place, at least in my opinion, for such a reserved culture.

Everything is green and manicured including the freshly painted door jams to the cabins. There is a forever-forested theme with petite front lawns and paved, S-shaped sidewalks leading to each doorstep. I pay attention to other color-coded lots: reds, blues, and whites. Sales offices, maintenance, conference centers. At any rate, I was GREEN, and happier than an Emerald Isle leprechaun.

Anything recognizable from a previous Bible Camp had been landscaped out. Back in the day, the most secure building was the easy-to-spot Chapel with its lightening rod spire aiming to the heavens and that gold-plated cross. Us grunts tried to be true believers. I recall that once during a hymn practice, an afternoon thunderstorm produced a couple sanctuary-dimming electrical jolts. We joked that it was because of our failed harmony. Presently, I suspect at least the old woodwork is part of the new registration building where I was handed my key, but I'm unsure where the old portal once stood.

The main building is now a two-story ranch, Victorian-style conversion, paneled with cedar to give the outdoorsy-rustic look, whereas the cottages are modular-style with matching fronts. The grounds beyond the tennis courts are undergoing foundation preparation for what looks to be additional housing. A handful of men wearing hardhats huddle around the back of a pick-up truck, the tailgate down, architectural plans flapping aimlessly in the wind underneath their outstretched hands.

All in all, I approve. Our living quarters back then were quite Spartan. With respect to the present, there are a dozen or so dead pine trees undergoing removal and the backhoe is leveling off a hilly area behind the offices. Workers with shovels are perched on the lip of a deep trench even though the backhoe creeps forward at a forty-five-degree angle. With a little elbow grease, I can recognize the value of how this island might one day be something even the Old Guard speak of with pride.

A very sunburned, twenty-something mother is dragging her knobby-legged whiney son across the heated asphalt. Someone is having a bad day, but I'm nearly certain, with ninety-nine percent accuracy, that the respective jovial spouse is on the links having the day of his life no matter how humid it is. I have attended enough conventions and seminars to know how it eventually works out. Despite the scenery and climate, trophy wives retain their crowns, wearing miniscule floral swimsuits to accent their ample bosom. Meanwhile, their big-headed husbands play golf with their own type of foursome. This young lady was either from the Twin Cities or out of state. No one from the surrounding five county areas is ever caught in public showing that much skin and midriff. Her bountiful breasts jiggle beneath the see-through top as she speaks childlike to her boy.

"We don't talk like that to Mommy. Do you need a time-out?" She adjusts her halter-top and pans around, hoping someone notices her non-mommy physique.

As they pass in front of me, the crying continues as if he's being tortured. She clutches a bag with towels close to her chest. The kid's inflatable toys are secured under her free arm like a rubber octopus' appendage. I'd wager that never a day goes by without some regret how far she's had to go with this "I do." Marrying money got her this far, although "show me the money" is, without a doubt, in the prenup agreement.

My cabin key is also brassy-green, like the door. I remember being issued a spare during my counselor days here. Because of its size, you always felt it jingle in your pocket next to quarters and nickels for the soda machines. It's one of the few connections to the past that remain. I unlock and step inside. The room is air-conditioned with a queen-sized bed and a quilted patchwork spread. Additional Camp Ole's literature is strategically placed on the adjacent nightstand. There is the customary, oak-laminated, clock radio that flips to two forty-five. An antique dresser with two refurbished drawers, part of the old chapel furniture from the rectory, is positioned along the wall adjacent to the bathroom door. Next to the cabin window is a small table with two straight back chairs where I toss my weighted travel bag of dissection goodies: saws, scalpels, towels, scrubs, and plastic containers. A scan of the modest bathroom doorway reveals a standard toilet, sink, and shower stall with matching green towels on the rack. Not that I was intending to steal them, but green is the constant theme at least in this cottage. I give it a Good Housekeeping Seal of Approval.

Suddenly the groundskeeper zooms past on a riding mower the size of a small storage shed. Damp mounds of grass shavings accumulate in the bulging rear pouch and the sharp pinging sounds of the blades encountering loose stones and fallen branches provide a constant reminder to those nearby to keep a safe distance away. Traveling through both the Pacific and Mountain time zones is beginning to catch up with me like an old-fashioned steam train chugging along uphill. I study the inviting bed and rotate my neck a couple of times. Nap or explore? Shoes or slippers? When Cassie accompanied me, there was always the exploring option first, so we'd get a map, buy a cola and sandwich, and be gone for a couple of hours. But now, it's easier to slide into seclusion.

The occasional invitations offered to me from others were seldom accepted. I have become a perpetual loner, but not very professional about it. I'll oblige a cocktail or two and participate in a little catch with my older sister's boys during Thanksgiving break and such. But it's easier to use work as an excuse. My traveling lifestyle has become hectic and sometimes strained. In contrast, I visit parts of the country that Cassie and I often talked about via a tent and a big dog. The rigors of the job don't allow me to embellish life. Performing autopsies on women that were Cassie's age still bring painful memories. There's no way to get over the liability of her death that hovers at half-mast.

I strip down, tossing anything that resembles travel or work clothes into a heap then take a hot, cleansing, five-minute shower. That pool beckons me, and I rummage through my bag for some comfortable shorts, tee shirt, and sandals. Ole's Resort is going to be second nature prior to sunset.

I enter the complex and close the chain link gate behind me. A dozen or so unclaimed guest towels are neatly stacked on a folding table. Some of the strays had blown off and are strewn against the fence line collecting splash overflow from boisterous young boys playing Marco Polo in the water. There are more older adults than I expect at this hour. In my travels, the swimmers are usually young parents with obnoxious children. No one looks up as I sneak in and grab the nearest chair.

"Howdy. Care for a margarita?"

She comes out of the shaded cabana wearing khaki shorts and a blue resort polo shirt with the Ole's logo on the breast pocket. A broad visor keeps the sun off her face, but I notice a spattering of freckles on her cinnamon-colored nose. Her lips are glossy with sunscreen. There is an inquisitive, wide-eyed look that captures my attention. Privacy aside, I point to the side gate leading to my cabin.

"I'm passing through, getting a grasp of my temporary surroundings. So far, I'd give this a nine on a scale of ten, but the water is a little choppy." I clear my throat at my terrible come-on line.

"I think last night's thundershower combined with those spoiled brats has something to do with that. It's usually quiet out here and calm like bath water."

Her eyes are the color of burnt pecans and her dark hair is cut short above the ears. Her summer pigmentation is natural rather than painted or applied with a brush. I'm not a reliable source telling ages of the living, but I sense she might be younger than me by a couple years.

"I'm Kevin Michaels," extending my hand.

"Call me Tessa, not Tess, please. Tess is for retired cronies, like half of the crowd today. I'm a close call to them, but not yet anyway. I'd prefer to approach middle age with my name intact."

She begins pulling the front of her blouse away from her midriff like picking lint.

"Hella' humid today."

"Tessa, it is," I oblige. "How's business today?"

"Busy as Hades. If it's Tuesday, then most likely the local college lifeguard employee called in sick because I know for sure, he's hungover. Last night was league night. Softball. Because of that, we have few extra staffers today, so I volunteered to step away from boring administration and do a little superficial lifeguard duty. Besides, I can concoct a terrific musk melon margarita. Care to have one?"

I sit up, eager for an explanation.

"You mean cantaloupe? I haven't heard the term musk melon for at least four decades. Actually, it sounds sort of exotic, like a special tropical leaf cultivated for culinary schools or Michelin restaurants."

"So at least I established that you are not from here. See how effective my social skills are?" She winks and shrugs. "This is a fun getaway for me from booking seminars and weddings. Give me five minutes and I'll be your personal escort of the immediate grounds. That is, if you don't mind. I'll even show you where the fifty-and-over crowd skinny dip."

She feigns plugging her nose and submerging with a playful wiggle.

"Sounds intriguing. That's my new scene." I wink back uncomfortably.

"Mr. Michaels, you don't look a day over forty-nine. Now, how about trying some of my magical elixir called the Tessa Treasure or as you prefer to call it, a Cantaloupe Margarita?"

"I'm dying of thirst," I respond, hiking the dog-eared paperback under my arm.

She's totally distracting and animated at the same time. I watch her lock the till and hang out the Closed sign. So much for absorbing myself in this paperback mystery. Tessa wipes the counter with a spare towel and tosses it in the linen bag. I stand and meander from behind the barstool and wait. The throng is an annoying mass of screams and splashes. Moments later she's at my side.

"Just like new. Here." She hands me a frosty concoction. "Be right back." She darts around the corner to the door marked Divas.

She has changed into a one-piece printed spandex swimsuit covered over by walking shorts. The visor is still intact, but the tennis shoes have been replaced with sandals. Tucked under her arm are two clean beach towels the color of faded green.

"Think I'm going to watch you have all the fun?"

She slips her arm inside mine and tugs me along.

"I'll let you know right now that once we finish the grand tour and swim, you are taking me out to supper, preferably off this island fortress. My treat, of course."

I begin to object with an implausible excuse, but she raises her hand.

"Not a chance in Hell you will cancel. Dr. Michaels, correct me if I'm wrong, but I have seen dozens of handsome, middle-aged men pass through this resort over the years. They act like the weight of the world hangs on their every decision. It's either too much work, or not enough family. They haven't been alone long enough to be a person again. Ole's Resort is not a life sentence. It's the perfect place to be someone else for a while."

She points to my forehead and taps it with her finger.

"Those creases are not a result from a high percentage of laughter, are they? You are a serious man in SERIOUS need of a swim in a cool clear lake and you have yet to conjure up any excuse that I will accept."

She looks down at my feet. "I take it you are not from the Midwest by the ankle tan lines. You wear sandals with socks and anyone who begins touring the resort by first scoping out the noise level is looking for solitude. That is not going to happen on my watch, especially on my rare opportunity to sneak out of the cubbyhole office for a day."

She takes off her sunglasses and wipes the side of her temple with the corner of a towel. There are flecks of gray like fine corkscrews through her damp scalp. It's a coin flip, but I believe she's craving a little adult company and escape too.

"First of all," I begin, "it's Kevin, not Dr. Michaels. Most people call me that when they get to know me. Secondly, you are correct. I spend way too much time on my own, so you'd better keep me centered or I might drift off to another chaise lounge or sit next to the laundry room. I do have some dirty shirts and socks stuffed in my duffel. And third, thanks for the lecture, but supper is on me at the place of your choice. I've been to a few resorts over the years and, over the course of a handful, they all look the same. People point me in the direction of the salad bar then give me a pat on the back. Furthermore, I much prefer the hands-on approach, but my social skills are not honed like yours. In fact, I was about ready to settle in with paperwork and the local news, but instead, decided to go create some headlines. I can see it now: *Administrator Saves Lost Camper because of Self-Deprivation and Views the World in Different Light.*"

She smiles curtly and playfully bites the tip of her tongue. I have a cloud of suspicion she's formulating far removed scenarios as her eyes drift past my focus.

"I think you have something, Kevin."

She pats me mother-like on my face with both hands.

"You're such a good boy. Good boy. Now, let me take you down to the lake before your cell phone ruins this floundering relationship."

She was candid and not going to take any nonsense from me. Tessa's stature is way above my six-foot frame mindset and the size of my problems is not going to be an issue with her. I extend my arm and she grabs-on like it's a life preserver.

"Shall we," she mutters.

We walk in silence for several minutes, each still uncomfortably trapped in our privacies. I wonder if this escorted escape is necessary or not. Tessa guides me around the first tee where three silent golfers stand motionless. The fourth player begins his patterned ascent on the ball. Looks up. Looks down. Twice. Pauses. Practice swings. Leans into the ball. Whacks away.

"Whoop."

The ball slices badly to the right and collides with the stern trunk of a Norway pine about one hundred yards downfield, bouncing deep into the wooded outlay.

"Jesus Christ."

"Way to go, Martin!" A chorus of howling laughter and hand slapping follows.

We speed past the furious yellow jacket home base horseshoe pit with spilled barbeque sauce that leads to the country club. Workers are prepping the smoldering firepit with extra flat river rocks and a few coals while others are clamping down the vinyl-checkered coverings onto the picnic tables. Adjacent to the dance floor of polished concrete is the buffet table. Its redeeming grace is the faint aroma of fresh coleslaw and assorted fruit salads veiled in tent-shaped screens. Hundreds of annoying flies scout the area with keen interest. The sugary scent of baked beans bubbles from the skillet.

"Once the lights come on and the cook's smoke canopy takes over, it's a surprisingly good night of fun. You'll see." Tessa squeezes my arm for reassurance.

"Afternoon, Miss Tessa."

"Hey, Tessa."

"Tessa! Are you coming for the bonfire tonight?"

The workers all seem to know her, and I harbor the feeling that I'm the special guest of an extremely popular person.

"I'm part of the fixtures if you're wondering," she confides with a long sigh. "You put in enough years behind the scenes and that prickly voice on the reservation hotline has a face to go with it."

"It's great to work with friends," I add with a smirk. "Most of my acquaintances don't talk back."

She gives me a quizzical look and her lips pucker.

"I'm a forensic pathologist. I'm here to do an autopsy on Ole Olson, the Resort King. The decedent is being shipped and will arrive in a couple days. The two surviving sons have invited me here to stay until then. I get the impression that dear old dad wasn't too high on their list of favorites."

"Between you and me, it was the other way around," she clarifies. "Ole poured out tons of cash to see their ventures sail. But in the end, it was Ole who sailed. I say, good for him. He deserved it."

"This resort is successful," I comment. At the same time, I observe the action in the pool.

"It's taken years to establish a returning clientele." Tessa's mouth forms a thin line. "I'll say this much, there was a period where I swear, they were going to level everything. Buildings, wells, and two-hundred-year-old trees. That land broker is now bankrupt. Thankfully, the BLM stepped in. I got to be honest here. Architects and project managers were flocking like seagulls over a waste recycling center for a piece of the action. Ole's Resort is the name, but at the time, not much else."

Tessa shrugs disappointedly and clears her throat.

"Not all things need change, Kevin. People up here are conservative. It separates them from the city folk. I used to commute ninety miles each day when I lived in Minneapolis. They wanted me to move to Chicago, but I balked and quit. Business suits and airports were dragging me down, my home life suffered, I divorced and became jaded and cantankerous, or so my friends told me. Little did they know about my marriage to a Porsche salesman. He lied to me at home as well as in the showroom and because of him I decided to move back. Coincidentally, it's not unlike old Ole in a way. But that was long ago and we're burning daylight."

She faces me toward the stand of wind-bent pines in the horizon and points.

"Up these hills, about three grinding miles, is a flat rock platform overlooking the lake's south rim. Legend has it that the best answer for tired tourists is only a few minutes of watching the day go by. We can stay longer and bask like your California seals, or step into the clear dark waters formed by the Mississippi. My job never takes me there. I don't even know if it exists, but I'm ready to take that chance if you are."

We had only known each other for a short, non-strenuous, comfortable time but without much fanfare, decide to stuff our towels in a sack and head out. Tessa's hiker stride is killer: long and steady. Nothing about her is lackadaisical. She charges over the rocks and the occasional rotted tree root, never taking a break. I swear she's challenging me to keep up as I trudge behind her, plus it's been a while. My toes feel bunched up in these wool socks and sandals. Every step magnifies the rub between the big toe and this decision. Why didn't I settle for politely telling her no, back at the pool? More than once, I need to duck a bowed branch that juts out and whips at my face. The terrain is soggy and slippery. She points to the dreaded leaf triad of poison oak and uses a long stick she found to stave off red-colored vines.

"Better to be careful," she warns.

I shake my head.

"About two months back, I was stroking my neighbor's longhaired feline. It rubbed up against my bare feet and legs a few times, arching high along my calves. A day later, I was red and itchy. Two days later I blistered up to my inner thighs. Ten days later, and a regimen of prednisone, I jubilantly ceased scratching off the outer layers and popping those infected fluid-filled domes."

"Been there. Done that," she cows.

The last three quarters of a mile Tessa and I single-file through ancient cottonwood and poplar groves, their leaves clattering like baby rattlers. For a moment, I'm gun-shy by the potential of rattlesnakes in the underbrush. But, in time, we begin to level off and she stops.

"You hear that?" She cocks her head, alert, her eyes sweep the panorama. "That must be Sibley's Falls. I've heard if you get close enough, the sound of the water is like a railroad train as it crashes into the rocks. Some people actually thought there were ghost tracks up here."

"I heard that same story as a teenager," I interject. "I used to counsel lost Lutheran children when the island was a Bible Camp. It's like only yesterday, in a sense."

She defiantly places her hands on her hips.

"Kevin, it's not nice to keep secrets from your appointed supervisor."

"Not to worry." I felt like a guilty kid caught throwing stones at passing cars. "There will be a 'rash' more."

"Here, hold on." She grabs my hand. "This might get a little hairy."

The mossy subfloor transforms into coal black slate that shimmers like ground glass goblets. Even Tessa becomes tentative and slows as she gages each rock. The reverberating rush of water ahead has me thinking of those old movies where the earth opens and swallows up innocent children. A canopy of pristine pine trees hovers above in photo album-like beauty and the view temporarily catches both of us off guard. Before we know, our soggy footsteps become water-logged depressions as if walking in sand along the beach. Soon after, we are splashing shin-high with each footfall. The sound ahead of us is like a large engine, roaring at full throttle.

"Let's go," she insists, inhaling deeply, studying the pathway ahead of us.

Suddenly, the lake comes into view as an amazing splinter of blue surrounded by cottages. The sliver widens until we are not able to attach boundaries on either side. We stand at the edge of the falls watching the cascade bubble fifty feet below our teetering feet. The lake's gradual swelling as the rapids drop is a magnificent sight.

Tessa looks to me with giddy excitement.

"There's the magic rock. You're such a Good Boy," tugging at my arm and giggling.

Our mutual coercion has us scurrying toward the knife's edge rock platform. Without hesitation, as if compelled like lemmings to cast away fate, Tessa leaps off the terra firma.

"Waterloo!"

The crystalline liquid swallows her in an instant. When she resurfaces, she is twenty yards downstream spinning and twirling like a fisherman's bobber.

"Yeah, baby," she shrieks. "Come on!"

For a flashing moment, I ponder my Accidental Death and Dismemberment Life Insurance coverage and whether it includes daredevil dives. I tentatively rub my jaw and peer down into the abyss. Are there possibilities that I won't survive? I crouch down and lean over the lip to get a better look in case something impales me or leaves me dangling like the last noodle in a soup strainer. Wrong move. The momentum of the current kicks the soles of my feet from under me. Suddenly, I am airborne, flailing at invisible safety ropes. With no time for either a collective or a creative soliloquy, I yell for my life.

"Oh shi...!"

It isn't Olympian pretty. I'm tumbling in the strong current like a wet handkerchief, my cheeks puckering with grit, shocked from the chilly water, sucking me under and suspended in darkness. I emerge out of the depths slapping the swells and gasping, coughing all at the same time. It must have been quite a sight for the dive judges that fortunately only numbered one.

"Now that's what I'm talking about," screams Tessa above the roar.

I spit frothy fluids.

"I have never done that. It was..."

"Exhilarating? Fun? Far out?"

"More like frickin frightening," I yell back and hear her laugh and whoop.

Downstream, we soon drift into slower and shallower water until I can tiptoe on the bottom. The unknown dive-of-death riverbed is pocked with flat, smooth stones tentatively secured together like puzzle pieces by gravel sediment. Tessa swims past me to the shore until she's standing waist high in the water. She fumbles for her straps, pulls them down to her waistline and turns her back to me.

"I need your help and don't be modest. Gently rub my back. I get an allergic reaction to the tree oils."

I hesitate at first. We've only known each other for a couple hours.

"Hurry up," she scolds me. "I can already feel the itch."

I begin to run my fingers over her lean body from the neckline to the small of her back although she reserves the front for herself in brisk swipes. Her head is bowed as she inspects her chest and each arm. The water's cool temperature creates goose bumps on her tanned shoulders, but I pray that it's all my doing. This illusion of swimming with a mermaid is coming true. My curiosity wanders to her frontside, and whether there will be a need of a professional opinion.

"Now it's your turn, and don't forget your legs," she forewarns.

I shift from front to back and she begins to sweep her icy hands across my waist and pulls down my swimming trunks far enough to place her hands inside and crisscross my faded belt line. In the back of my mind, I struggle with embarrassment and elation, wishing for the examination to last a little longer.

"You need to get a little more color, White Man. Let's swim for the platform."

"I am not death diving again," raising my voice, spittle dripping from my nostrils.

She smiles and glides ahead in bold strokes, churning up small wakes. Treading in this foamy white water is exhausting as I'm well aware of my inept swimming mechanics. She easily out distances me. When I reach the platform, I am totally whipped. My arms are like dead weights and I flop clumsily onto the rock beside her.

"That was great. Thank you so much." She closes her eyes and smiles. "Are you ok?"

"I hated playing Marco Polo as a kid and now, I'm a large fish out of water. My swimming skills are meager at best. Not at all like yours." I sweep moss and grit off my face. "Any more room on that rock for a finless carp?"

"Of course." She pats the flat rock top next to her as if to assign a seat. "This area is for you."

We soak up the late afternoon sunshine for at least a couple hours as our swimwear and soggy towels dry off on this precipice. Sometimes I stand up with my hands on my waist, listening to the loons sing in the distance, and other times I only sit and watch her catnap beside me. Those thin swimsuit straps are off her shoulders again and I steal a peek for rash or blisters. So far, it looks good. She curls up on her side, her backpack bunched under her head as a pillow. Quiet breath sounds come from her lips. I think back how it all began this morning. Much to my amazement work or money has yet to clutter my mind. Here we are, two complete strangers coupled for the day, seeking time away from whatever kept us from visiting this idyllic place. I feel a trust developing between us, someone that I can talk to and like me, a person who has a diploma in internalizing. Whatever we could have in common will have to wait.

When she wakes, we take turns sharing life stories. I tell her that I've been a widower for a couple of years now. She rebounds with a bad marriage and ex-husband's affair. We listen to each other's tales with interest in an informative way, hiding the decaying compassion in our lives. I sense that some of the things she speaks of are bordering on raw, but she catches herself and veers into a lighthearted topic. When we tire of laying bare our souls, both of us contemplate the lake like pioneers looking for cover, evaluating the landscape, searching the shoreline for that place to set up camp. I think back at how her joy bubbled up with that venturous leap, how she lifted my spirit, how much we seem to have in common. But Tessa is far more confident than me, both in the present and the future. She takes life at face value. What will be, will be. Either that, or I'm becoming a poor judge of character.

The sun is sinking beyond the tree level and the pine tips take on a salmon-colored glow. In the light, Tessa's skin tones are like soft felt the color of butterscotch. Her hair dries in frizzled wisps along her ears and temples. There is no tomorrow in the plans. The stars are aligning for me and it's about time.

She sighs, lays down on her back and closes her eyes. The next thing I remember are gentle fingertips slowly combing through my hair. I abruptly sit up, stiff from the rock recline. She's kneeling beside me, glistening in a puddle of lake water that formed between us. Fresh small droplets trail off her earlobes and hairline. My first impression is that she had sneaked in for a dip without her water-logged partner.

"What time is it?" The words stumbling out of my mouth.

"Somewhere near five or five-thirty. We need to get back." She smirks. "You are not much company. You don't talk. You answer even less."

"The same can be said about you," I rebuke. She continues to stroke my head. My scalp's alive with sensations tailing off with each swirl. I look back and ask, "Was I a gentleman?"

"Unfortunately, yes, the whole time, except when you napped. I seem to recall a hand cupping my right cheek about here," pointing to her buttocks. "It was ok, though. Kind of funny."

"I won't apologize, Tessa, and I wasn't asleep. I have to admit, it was kinda fun."

She nudges me in the side.

"Remember, you still owe me supper, but I think we'll go to the Ole barbeque. The food is not that bad. We have some terrific cooks. Plus, I need to show up for business sake. With the brothers gone until tomorrow, my administration duties are extended."

"Sounds like a plan," I respond in my best Midwestern brogue.

Tessa readjusts her cover shorts over those perfect hips, and we head back, encountering stiff onshore breezes and yet, the late day air still warms us like a fall coverup. We eventually arrive at the tree line on the outer edge of the resort and pause. She turns back to me. In the shadows, her features are soft. There is a satisfied sigh as if the pressures of the day have disappeared. Without a second thought, she slips her fingers inside the waistline of my shorts and gives a friendly tug.

"Prime mosquito country is still quiet for the time being, Doctor." She leans forward into me and lowers her voice. "Thanks for a great date."

Officer Perry is still working at the entrance and continuing to politely hand out brochures to a loaded minivan with Michigan plates. We cross in front of a sporty convertible that includes a bickering couple. Their compact backseat is over-stocked with two carry-ons and a large cooler. From the sound of it, they seem road weary. The woman is brunette with alabaster skin and thin eyebrows, her tousled weave is out of control. The male is rather plump for the size car he drives. His graying moustache is pencil-thin, sunglasses perch loosely on the top of his balding crown. He sucks in a big breath and compresses his lips as she banters him. Tessa mutters softly into my ear.

"Lover Boy was here less than a month ago with another weekend prize. God, that brings up bad memories."

The driver looks furtively in our direction, a million miles away, as his date barks on.

"Good luck with that one," whispers Tessa, shaking her head.

I try to change the subject.

"How about if we meet up in an hour? I'll find us a spot at the buffet line. We can continue our planning from there."

Tessa's arms are folded in front. She glares down at the woman and opens her mouth to voice a strong opinion. But she holds back. Her scowl is palpable.

"There ought to be a law against that activity. You know: Go in blind and come out blindsided. Why did we ever come back, Kevin? I was having such a good time."

I place my arm around her shoulders and give her a soft squeeze.

"Tessa, we are old enough and smart enough. It will happen again, guaranteed."

The tap water up here in the lake country is usually full of glacier-age minerals. It has a powdery, metallic taste from the faucet and leaves a lasting film in the mouth. Some places overcompensate with a type of softener salt that deposits a silky residue. As a result, I shower a second time: once with soap and once with conditioner. Still lurking in the back of my mind is Tessa's reminder about the invisible plant oils on our exposed parts. But I think she's pulling my leg on that one. Nonetheless, I am convinced that some sort of rash phobia will haunt me like a bad cold if I stay here much longer. Nevertheless, the shower spray feels extremely relaxing and I unabashedly stand under the showerhead for at least another five minutes.

Coming on the heels of that, I have extra time. Our rendezvous is scheduled for later, so I decide to call the Wasoon Funeral Chapel. Roland Purdy said that the coffin is at the Minneapolis airport and will arrive by late tomorrow. Ole's body is being shipped in a dry ice sealed container.

My initial concern is the untimely thawing. Dry ice is not regular ice. The connective tissues thaw like mush and it takes diligence to get good sections. On the other hand, there is also potential for cold artifact making the soft tissue dissection formidable, like old steaks pulled out of the freezer.

Roland is respectful of my concerns, but in the long run, there's nothing either of us can do. His condescending tone lays the groundwork for the options of embalmed, sealed and not embalmed, or packed in dry ice. The body is to be transported and he will contact me once it arrives. I must have caught him on a bad day at the office. Perhaps he needs an afternoon lake baptism, too. Lose the attitude, Pal.

I know that if I close my eyes only for a few moments, there's a good chance I might doze off. I had a good time today, more than in a long time, and Tessa is the sole reason for my enjoyment. Like Cassie, she's engaging and intelligent, not to mention she won't accept "no" for an answer. I need to reel in my advances because she is not the purpose for being here. Keep it professional. Over the years, I've tallied only one long-term relationship and sense she's more adventurous than I can handle right now. Daydreaming of her swimming ahead of me will have to suffice. Lying next to her on the rocks is going to be a lasting memory. It's a boon to my ego, but this soft pillow feels wonderful.

The nap hour is over way too soon, and I sit up and rub my eyes. Attacking a plateful of ribs and slaw is etched in my brain. At the banquet I discover Tessa carrying on conversation with a group of Asian men all dressed in matching polo shirts and khaki trousers. The art deco emblem on their chest pockets is a new age "Z" with a lightning bolt cutting across the center of the design. Presumably, it's some software business looking to set up shop in the Twin Cities. They stand in a half circle listening attentively to her. Two of them have golfer's gloves stashed in their hind pockets. A short time later, they all shake hands and politely bow as Tessa directs them toward another group of men wearing matching crimson baseball caps with a black spider design.

Ole's must be hosting a technology conference of some sort because the groups I notice are mostly business-types with sunburned complexions. I observe Tessa working the crowd, standing on her tiptoes, waving to familiar faces. She gives me a one-moment signal and heads for the business-suits group making an entrance. One more deal-making introduction requires her attention. We catch up at the chow line. A cocktail waitress zigzags past us and I steal two wine glasses filled almost to the top with red. From its appearance, I expect a soft Merlot, but someone at the bar called it Frontenac. Later, I was told that it's a lower Mississippi river valley specialty. A pudgy, bald man gives me the stink eye because they were the last on her tray. Welcome to the real world, buddy. First come. First served.

"Hey, partner, how was the nap?" She winks playfully.

"It was too brief. Later, I'd like to show you a flat rock with your name on it."

"How about something a little softer next time." She gently rubs the back of her elbow. "Think I dislocated something on that so-called leap."

I step back from her, extending my arms like a large buzzard sunning itself. "Oil free."

"Let's keep it that way," she grins. "It's a good thing we had long sticks. I'm quite sure that was poison oak lurking in the shadows."

She taps me and points out the healthy salad selections. Before long, we're both ogling over the baked beans and franks alongside scrumptious spinach hors d'oeuvres and deviled eggs. The food selection manifests into more tantalizing selections. I drool by the garlic mashed potatoes, fresh trout in a glistening lemon marinade, stuffed pork chops, baked squash with pears and sugared walnuts. My mind is on a gastronomic orgasm. At the end of the table, two chefs are cutting any size thickness of prime rib, the heated au jus collecting on the board is making their glasses fog up. Another pleasant waitress places slices of fresh baked banana bread with chocolate chips on the side of our plates. I load up for a feast like it's my last meal. If that wasn't enough, two attendants arrive, carrying samples of grilled teriyaki Alaskan salmon with tendrils of smoke trailing from the crispy skins. These two young caterers are engulfed as if they are dishing out one-hundred-dollar bills. The feeding frenzy lasts throughout the evening. Those who finish early gather at the bar where bottles and shot glasses line the counter.

What a show. Hearty laughter and more than a few glasses clink in toasts for everything from golf scores to the weather to the perky waitresses. We stand our ground at the corner of the bar. I consumed enough fish to stock a small pond. Tessa leaves me again to fend for myself. A five-piece band kicks up some Credence Clearwater and, of course, everybody joins in the chorus: "*There's a bad moon on the rise.*" After a few minutes, she joins me.

"Not a bad party, isn't it?"

"It's great," raising my voice a little too loudly, "and beats channel-surfing any day. I mean that in a good sense, of course." Clumsy and callus, I let out a long moan, "Duh."

"What you meant to say came out a little backwards. I'll give the three glasses of wine credit. Care to try again?" She holds her tilting glass above my head.

"I sincerely apologize," waffling again for an explanation, fidgeting, altering my stance left to right. "I've spent too much time alone lately and there's nothing else to compare. I am extremely grateful for today, thank you," raising my glass in salute.

She gives me a curious look and raises her eyebrows.

"You are an interesting person, Kevin. No fluff, but there's that manly fortitude dying to come out. This is on my card. I am so appreciative that you stepped in this afternoon. You rescued me, too. The night is still young. There's still dancing and dessert. Pick your poison."

I lift my head in defense. "No more decisions for me tonight, lady. I'm teetering in big ass trouble. Let's grab some dance floor and see where the goodies tray is hiding. Agreed?"

"I'm with you," she beams. "It'll be like the blind leading the blind."

Tessa introduces me to a few acquaintances, like the Carpenters from Stillwater. Their sprightly sunburned faces and Just Married matching wedding rings are the talk of the adoring crowd. Then there are the three obnoxiously loud AVBO employees that are here to "out-convention the whole fuckin' crew," as they proudly exclaimed. I never figured out the meaning of AVBO but didn't really care. This was a hoot. Tessa and I perform a little country two-step and a couple of slow dances. She melds into my staggering frame, sometimes resting her head in the crux of my arm. I draw her close to my chest near the end of the good songs. Sometimes she breaks free to schmooze and I must nestle with my wineglass. The band announces a short break, and the dance floor crowd disperses. The lead guitar player comes to the front of the stage, kneels, whispers into the female server's ear and points in my direction. She nods and winds her way through the crowd in my direction.

"He wants to know if you have any requests. It's last call soon."

"Me?"

She slides a glass of wine to the edge of the tray. "This is on him. He told me to give you a big kiss for helping the brothers. He owes them a debt of gratitude. We all do."

I look back to the stage to get his attention, but he's carrying on with the drummer.

"Thanks," I yell.

He turns back to me and gives a quiet applause. His look is surprisingly soft, but he has a genuine smile.

"Much appreciated. You made my night."

He gives me a thumbs up. "Good dancer."

I slip him a twenty-dollar bill. There's a comfortable warmth on my face.

Moonlight spreads across the glassy lake like a welcoming soft knit shawl. It's the same moon, the same lake, from those timeless years ago with a girl named Erin. Some men ask Tessa to dance and she obliges. Like a jilted boyfriend, my watchful envy begs to cut in, but the reserved practicality bolts me to the chair. I think it's the companionship lost that I most yearn for on this alcohol-fueled evening. Romantic or not, it's a welcome boost to my ego. I have female company again. Someone friendly, someone nice, and I get the impression that she's interested in me.

I had quit the dating circuit a few years ago. Since then, it's been increasingly uncomfortable for me to sustain relationships. Despite the occasional sleepovers, we had little in common.

I have confidence that Tessa and I bond at a deeper level when time permits. But unwanted independence is a scary concept and I fell into it unexpectedly at first. Loneliness became my favorite ally. My time here in northern Minnesota is going to be limited. Living out of cell phones and e-mails is not my cup of tea, but that's the way it is. Crazy. On every budding relationship, I placed boundaries. Perhaps she doesn't want any of this? Am I assuming too much? I might even be fantasizing. Later, the band announces one last song and I stand up to scan the gathering for her.

"My thoughts, exactly." She comes up from behind and tugs at my arm. "Let's go."

The ballad of lost lovers ends too soon. I attempt to kiss her softly on the forehead.

"I'm not trying to be forward, but it seems appropriate with the song's end."

Tessa gives me a responsive hug. The lead singer approaches the mike, yells good night to the crowd and cautions them to walk safely to their bungalows. We get caught up in the shuffle to the bottleneck exit.

"Good night, Kevin. Thanks for a special evening. I must stay with the clean-up committee. Our hired help tends to slack off. You don't have to wait up for me. I'll be here for at least another couple of hours."

Her voiced instructions sound as disappointing as she looks. Her face grows slack and her eyes well up. Fun is over, now back to work.

"Is there anything I can do to help? It must be close to ten o'clock. I'm not opposed to volunteering. I'll stack tables, do dishes, anything."

"It boils down to overseeing the ground's staff, then I have to check our gross accounts. My head is in the till receipts day and night but those irritating phones during office hours are never on hold."

She hesitates, clasping her hands together, giving a half-hearted shrug.

"I'm a little anal about that. It's my punishment for playing hooky with you this afternoon. Get some rest. You have a big day tomorrow and the brothers will be back to give you sly commentary on Daddy Ole."

Tessa impatiently brushes at my arm. "It's time to get to work. I'll see you tomorrow sometime."

She pecks me on the lips and disappears into the dissolving party, directing helpers where to stack chairs and cordially shaking hands of passers-by.

Back at my cabin the ceiling fan slowly circulates the humid air into a sticky swarm. The bed is calling me, I strip down to my shorts and throw on a clean tee shirt. An hour later I am still mesmerized, watching minutes flip off the illuminated alarm clock, and pondering that shared good night kiss.

CHAPTER SIX

My cell phone vibrates, and I fumble for it on the nightstand, knocking the luminescent clock onto the floor. Christ. Where's my glasses. It's only four-thirty. A text from Roland Purdy notifying me the body of Ole Olson has arrived at the funeral home with a subtle hint whether eight o'clock is early enough. He has an appointment in Blackduck with a family later today. Why bother to set the alarm for six-thirty in the first place? I text him back and press SEND. For the next two hours I try to find a comfortable spot to no avail. My pillow has become like a stranger on the bed, preferring to face away in disgust.

I arrive minutes before office hours and watch from my rearview mirror as the hearse van conversion with WFC lettering backs into the mortuary driveway. The morning is already breezy. Tendrils of cirrus clouds smudge an otherwise blue skyline. Ominous dark groupings signify the high propensity of severe weather and bunch like a dark obstructing shroud in the western horizon. Barn swallows swoop low on the gravel searching for small insect parts to devour. Roland hops out, hustles to the back, and opens the rear door. Following his lead, I greet him at the ramp.

"Good morning."

"Long time no see. You sleep well?" he joshes, reaching for a claw hammer inside the panel.

The screeching sound of nails yanked out of a crackling, dry wood shipping container stirs nightmares of shingling old barns, another summer job I eliminated from my itinerary between undergraduate years. Those rickety rafters were so treacherous, plus, I never got past hanging bat-like, gripping a paintbrush under the eaves. Roland forces away the side panels and uses a rag to sweep the loose splinters to the floor bed. Fortified inside this wooden crate, the metallic gray shipping coffin is missile-like. I estimate it to easily weigh three or four hundred pounds and that leaves little doubt the body to be at least two-thirds of it.

We groan our way through the arduous maneuvering of this top-heavy package onto his wobbly gurney followed by a running start and push up the rough-and-ready ramp. His wiry frame sags as he huffs. No way in hell can either one of us do this by ourselves. Roland mentions that there are some plumbing repairs being completed in the back room and therefore, thought it best to divert our delivery from any workman's squeamish eyes.

He cocks his head.

"Some of those guys can poke their hands in poop or crawl head-first under a house to retrieve a dead skunk. But you'd think they wouldn't lose their lunch at the sight of a dead body."

"Not a problem," I tell him. "If it weren't for you, I'd still be in the back of the van with suspended strobe lights and an armful of towels. FYI, I've done my share of digging through poop too."

"That's a funny one, Dr. Michaels. Say, aren't you doctors always serious? You know, working with dead people and all that?"

"We have our occasional moments," I reply with a smirk. "Funeral directors are pretty morose sometimes too."

"Yeah, I guess that's right. It all depends on how you look at it. A week passes and folks either go on with their lives or begin that never-ending journey into guilt. What's it like on your end, Doc?"

He braces the body box against the guardrail with his hip, fumbling in his coat pocket for the office key.

"It's mostly fifty-fifty. Some do. Some don't," I instantly feel the gravity at the back end, my legs spread apart and my shoes digging into the rubber mat. "Final will and testaments usually don't include a postmortem examination clause. To remain politically correct, I let the attorneys handle that."

"Well, I knew Ole better than those two brats ever did," pronouncing it like a German sausage. "He was ok by me. Took time to BS with anyone on the street. Had a seat at city council meetings. He even flipped pancakes for the Kiwanis Mother's Day breakfast."

Roland moans to himself begrudgingly as if introducing another below-average singer in a county talent show.

"Here we go now."

He unlocks the double doors and together we guide the coffin into the parlor area. The ancient air conditioning unit rattles at high speed and yet, there's a trace of lingering humidity, like a bathroom five minutes after a morning shower. I'm dripping like a burst garden hose.

"I'll check the office to see if the paperwork was faxed." He knocks, then peeks into the office.

"All clear. No contractors. Must be another doughnut break." He shakes his head as he disappears into the next room.

The perfumed floral scent of the deodorizing spray is heavy on the citrus side, more like furniture polish: oily and clinging. As for me, fatigue is climbing on board. Road-weary. Too much travel in a short period. Stress. Thanks to the early phone call from Roland, I had a rough time getting back to sleep. A brief nap on that cushioned chair directly to my left would be a perfect respite. Close my eyes for a half hour. That's all I ask. I fight the urge by rocking back and forth on the balls of my feet.

"Here you are," Roland returns and hands me a manila folder titled "Ole."

I take it from him and flip open to the front cover. There's a sealed business envelope with the Wasoon Funeral Chapel logo. I open it to find the signed check and the original signed autopsy authorization that I had faxed a few days ago. Both brothers had crowded their signature, one on top of the other, on the Next of Kin line. Aunt Gail's autograph along with Roland's sat side-by-side on the witness line. The third sheet is a handwritten notification requesting direct cremation immediately following the postmortem examination, again signed by both brothers, and notarized with the official state stamp by Roland.

"Roland, let me give you a hand," making myself available as he pulls the cadaver hoist above our heads from behind the door. He aligns the lift track and produces a bronze key from his pocket. With a click, he removes the coffin padlock, tracks a thin flat blade along the adhesive seal and slowly lifts the lid.

"It's Ole, all right," shudders Roland.

Remnant chunks of vaporous dry ice had shattered the zippered vinyl body bag. From the contact, his skin is chinaware white, like an old statue. The rest of his corpse is as black and purple as an eggplant. The stench of decay becomes intense in the warming air. We both hold our breaths and wince, hoping some ancient African prions have not managed the journey with the body.

Ole's exposed left hand rests on top of a thin fabric, the icy fog rolls out of the container along the rim in vampire-like fashion. Whoever packed the body, ten thousand miles ago, had been conscientious to wrap the head in a towel to reduce mold. Settling tissue seepage outlines the body's periphery and there are dark red chunks collecting at the bottom of the container. My impression is that it's natural puddling from tissue breakdown. Looking at the facial indentation, I surmise that the mouth is agape, perhaps the result of postmortem changes causing that flaccid look. Jaw muscles are some of the strongest in the body. Over time in ambient temperature, livor mortis disappears. A gaping mouth is a Gordian knot, meaning, what you see is not always what you get. On the contrary, if he died in his sleep, or on his back, that's usually a given. The decaying dependent skin on his sides and back of the arms have copious paper-thin blisters the size of soap bubbles that leak murky fluids.

"Well, there you go, then."

Roland motions back from the table and tosses his gloves in the red hazardous container. He slips on his funeral director's dark topcoat and dabs his damp forehead with a towel.

"Give me a jingle when you've finished. I'll be up front doing paperwork. Plumbers might wander in but pay them no mind. I'd like to get Ole out of here as soon as possible. This stench can spread through the funeral home like a ditch fire."

"Gotcha," I said and continue to take external photographs.

"The boys will be coming back to talk about the cremains at noon. That will give you roughly two hours. Will that be enough time, Doctor?"

Roland opens his mouth, then re-checks his watch, waiting for my response.

"Pending any complications, that will be sufficient," I tell him.

"Okay, then. Anything else?"

"I might need some help aligning the hoist over the table. Do you have a moment?"

Roland nods, eyes closed, lips tight, his hands grip the lapel of his suitcoat. He goes back to the disposable glove box and pulls out a pair. A few moments later, we push the gurney toward the prep room door, its standard blue OSHA warning sticker of the dangerous effects of formaldehyde exposure is taped at eye level. Ask any elderly embalmer and he will attribute his longevity to chemicals in a shot glass rather than preservative.

Given that this is a modular, the room is compact like that of an upstairs apartment. There is a porcelain toilet-style sink along the opposite wall, the kind one sees in a hair salon, its bowl discolored by cosmetic red and brown pigments. The tarnished faucet and handles are mid-twentieth century and dulled by time. The original caulking along the framework is piecemeal at best. The prep room table is standard stainless steel with a head block on one end and a rinse hose connected to a floor drain at the other. The overhead incandescent lights flicker and hum.

With some effort, we manage to slip the hoist straps under the body and attach them to the lift. Roland punches the black switch and the motorized device whines to a dull whir, elevating the frosted body from the coffin. He repositions the straps a couple extra times before raising Ole from his bondage. Once over the prep table he slowly lowers the frozen decedent, and the chilled form causes the metal to squeal upon contact.

"Jeez, that was a lot of fun," Roland jokes, brushing his hands up and down against each other. "The poor man must weigh at least three-hundred or three-fifty. You think?"

"Pretty close, I'd say," I surmise, staring at the body. My long, forgotten usage of estimation by the term "pretty" is coming out of hibernation. The Midwestern blood still lingers like a slumbering rodent in a tortuous tunnel.

"Help me get the covering off and I'll take some additional photos."

I check my battery pack and take half dozen shots of our intriguing guest. It's becoming a struggle of wills: frozen wrap versus dead weight. Some portions of plastic shred like paper mache with the slightest of tug along with strips of skin. My educated guess is that Ole had not been placed in deep refrigeration *until* he began to reek.

Ole is as hard as a Popsicle. There's no way in Hell he'll thaw by the noon deadline. I run warm water over his chest with the hose. At least, that will soften him enough to make a midline incision. Other than the discoloration, there is nothing visible on the surface and he doesn't appear at a loss for meals. My best guess is that he weighs around two hundred ninety-five to three hundred twenty-five pounds, excluding the glacial state. His teeth are mostly in good condition. A few aged metallic fillings from the back molars sparkle back at me from the corners of his gaping mouth. Male pattern baldness, bushy moustache, unkempt eyebrows, and coarse facial stubble. The outdoorsy look. A least a hundred or more frozen maggots fill his nostrils and mouth. Ole's hands are working man's: huge fingers and no rings. By stretching the skin, I manage to trace an old appendectomy scar from childhood, based on the faded ellipse-shape. His nails are the color of blueberries: cyanosis, a good sign of sudden cardiac issues. I must pay close attention to the heart and vessels. Look for clots, valve failure, myocardial infarction, and the like. A pesky fly lands on Ole's forehead then departs.

"Bastard. Your Dark Continent cousins have already been here," I murmur, rubbing my numbing fingers together for circulation.

"If you open, they will come."

I pick up my heavy-duty scalpel and elongated autopsy blade -- a

good idea, being that it's inflexible and less likely to become lodged in my unsuspecting palm if I slip. Based on previous experiences, this dissection arsenal can easily become dull, so I line-up a couple extras at the head of the table. With Mr. Explorer in this condition, I'd better keep a few available just in case.

The warming water rinse does the trick and soon I reflect a stiff right and left chest flap, wide enough to use a pruning shears on both sides of the ribs. Snap. Crackle. Pop. Twelve pairs. Rice Krispy-like. I breathe a sigh of relief as to how effortless the brittle plate was to remove. The next phase is to check the pleural cavities. Dark red lakes of frozen fluid surround each cobalt-colored lung and reflect off the overhead lighting. The lung surfaces are diffusely peppered, more than likely, with black smoker's pigment, trapped for eternity with each draw on the cigarette.

Son of a gun.

Ole's pericardium is stretched tight transversely, dark blue and not the normal fatty gray-tan color. A perforation of the epicardium? I make an anterior incision and tease both halves of the stiff sac apart like a wrapper on a juice bar. The cooling has congealed dark red blood clot into a glistening layer surrounding the heart. I take a couple photographs, then gently scoop it out with my hands and carefully place it next to the aspirating tube. There must be at least a soda can or two of red glob slowly thawing in the sink. Ole's heart is shaped like the Liberty Bell with its base four times the size of the apex. Not a good thing to have, meaning more work for the already compromised left side of the heart to push the blood through the body. In addition, there is a thick yellow pad of diet-accumulated fat covering the anterior surface. Cigarettes and fatty food had caught up with his carefree lifestyle. I place my hands under the base and carefully reflect the organ away from the sac. On the posterior portion of the left ventricle, off the septal midline, is an irregular hemorrhagic tear the length of a small paper clip, the original site of the bleed. A rupture.

Ole's heart had given out from an old heart attack. Severely damaged heart muscle doesn't regenerate, but rather, becomes scar tissue. Like a deep flesh wound, healing results in a less vascular, lightly pigmented defect and this is typically easy to single out from healthy tissue with the naked eye. Along with it comes less contractibility and the specific area of injury thins. Picture a slow leaking football that needs to be inflated again, only to discover a soft bulge under the laces.

As a result, the heart loses its muscular tone and gradually enlarges to compensate for the lost contractibility. In this case, Ole's heart got fatter and lazier while his coronary vessels remained the same size, but the lumens became narrower from plaque, resulting in a hypertensive situation. A half-million heartbeats later, the blood supply to the heart diminished to a degree of inadequacy and the result was the remaining healthy muscle competed for oxygen. Eventually those cells also died until there was full ventricular involvement. A breach of the thinned chamber ensued and filled the pericardium with blood until it created a containment pressure to stop contraction.

The bad news is that Ole was in denial. Fatigue. Heartburn. Nausea. I'm sure he convinced himself that those were signs of getting old. The good news was that death for him was sudden and painless. He never suffered. I have colleagues who tell me if there is a choice, this is the way to go. Not particularly my cup of tea, but it leaves the next of kin with clear answers.

In the wake of that I make the noon deadline with a little elbow room to spare. The remainder of the autopsy is straightforward. All the internal organs are undergoing tissue breakdown to some degree. There is a dull red to gray hue in most of them and I'm able to poke my finger through some of the surfaces as if it's Jell-O. His lungs are congested with blood and fluid that had seeped out of the tissues during his last days -- complements of the poor ticker. The organs that require more blood, like the liver and spleen, are also congested and enlarged, the direct default of backflow pressure with a poor pump. Biblical prophets used to practice something called hepatoscopy, meaning to sacrifice a goat or sheep, remove its liver, spread it out on a table, and venture to predict a king's or pharaoh's future.

That wasn't going to happen in his condition. Spreading anything on this greasy cutting board wasn't going to turn back the pages, although he had an enlarged prostate gland.

But that was the least of his problems. Fortunately, the body fat is the least of *my* problems because it had provided insulation, thus preventing further decay, and making dissection of a mostly decomposed cadaver a treat. On the contrary, there might be postmortem cellular artifacts only ascertained with a microscopic examination. I conclude my findings as a myocardial rupture by the circumstances of an old infarction leading to muscular weakening, the eventual rift, and cardiac tamponade. Ole had congestive failure from an enlarged inefficient heart and coronary artery disease. Death was from natural causes. He was respected, so to speak, had a good life, and died before his time. Not everyone has those accolades. I've seen much worse.

I rinse off the tabletop, knot the viscera bag, and deposit it back into the chest cavity. Using heavy duty waxed string I secure the skin flaps with a few loops, melt down the bloody ice chunks with warm water, and run the sink disposal until all the evidence of an examination is history, excluding the putrid air. On my way out the door, I again want to thank Roland who is on the phone at the time. He raises up his hand for me to wait, asks the caller to hold, and covers the receiver with his palm.

"Eleven forty-five. All finished, I see. You find out the answer, then?"

"I'm pretty sure it was heart-related," I tell him. "I'll put together my notes along with the final report. The brothers can get a copy in about a month. Be sure to tell them thanks from me."

"I will do that for sure, Doc," lowering his voice. "I need to get back to this call. It's another late payment issue. Will you be staying on at the resort for a couple days?"

"You know, I was thinking about doing that. I haven't been up in northern Minnesota for years. I'll do some fishing or hiking. Ole's Resort has been a welcoming oasis for me. I'll become a James Dean rebel-of-sort. Reward myself with a mini vacation. The days off I've taken in the past two years can be counted on both hands."

"Good for you." He grins and draws in a satisfying sigh. "When you get back to California, tell that Mr. Dean fella he's invited to stay any time. In the meantime, guess I'll see you around town." The "ow" rolls out of the word as far as it can go without adding two extra syllables.

It was noon and I hadn't had a meal of any substance other than last night. My stomach was growling uncontrollably. The packaged apple bran muffin that I devoured four hours ago from the so-called continental breakfast table was a mere memory. I end up patrolling downtown, scouting for any place with a café sign. Past the filling station at the edge of Wasoon, I spy a local restaurant boldly called the Lazy Bee Café. Drone-like caricatures of contented honeybees sleeping on the outside of a hive are painted onto the picture window. Underneath is a sun-damaged-yellowed menu taped from the inside.

In another era and another owner, my counselor cohorts and I hung out in this same place, drinking Cokes, eating burgers and fries. Wondering if those days still exist, I pull into the vacant space in front and bound out of the car, salivating for that fresh soft bun and an over-cooked quarter pound of ground beef buried under American cheese and tomatoes. Crusty, oily french fries and an iced root beer glass are in my mind, as though I never left the lake country.

I enter in true beast-mode food rhythm, fixated, wetting my lips. The bulletin board is laden with announcements of upcoming farm auctions and threshing bees. On my right are four old style booths with high backs and Formica tops. Burn marks and occasional teen-age hieroglyphics are etched deeply into their surfaces. It smells like heaven is made of fresh pie crusts and coffee. There is a round table where a half-dozen farmers sit in uniform consisting of bib over-alls, plaid shirts, and mesh baseball caps displaying either a Pioneer seed corn company or a Case implement dealer. These Big Tippers were in rapt attention as one of them spouted on about current land prices. This is not John Deere or Harley Davidson turf. One of them pounds the dice cup upside down in the middle of the table as two others lean back, smoking their pipes, waiting for the results. A gray tobacco haze lifts into the ceiling fan.

Four additional circular tables with matching chrome chairs and red cushions are spread out evenly on the non-booth side of the room. A couple of boys, no older than junior high school, are dining on MY favorite meal. One of the lads had dribbled slick barbeque beef on the front of his shirt to the amusement of his buddy. There is the annoying hum of the large, ever-popular, incandescent ceiling tubes. A reverberating counter fan twirls at medium speed near the cash register. From my vantage point, I notice the harried cook, his receding moist hairline bobbing up and down above the divider between the counter and kitchen. Steam bathes his sideburns as he studies the orders on the carousel.

A young lady in apron comes from behind the counter to check the serving lamps.

"Be right with you," she says in my direction with a patented smile. Her nameplate reads "Stella." She is a plump, top-heavy teenager, her half-buttoned, pink cover-up smock is held together by divine intervention. Mousy brown hair pinned back in a ponytail. Stella's roadhouse appearance is more distracting than complimentary.

"Have a seat anywhere."

She points to the first table as "anywhere" and I follow her line of vision, sliding onto the nearest chair.

"Special today is split pea with a half ham salad sandwich." She's poised, pencil in hand, holding the tablet close to her chin, waiting for a response.

"I'm in the mood for a tavern and a root beer."

"Coming right up," Stella says, and pushes past me to the counter, clipping the order on the cook's carriage, grabbing the coffee pot, and hurrying over to the ogling farmers.

"Thanks," I reply in passing and settle back. I had forgotten how few, if any, women ever lunch with their spouses back here. Most of them are home or shopping, but woe to the neighbor who brings his wife into town for a weekly meal. The sad sequel of this scene is back at home. He reads newspapers or dozes in front of the TV. She tries to keep the kids quiet and out of his hair. Later in the afternoon, the same cronies return to the local tavern for a couple of nightcaps and additional social time. The men keep their wives apprised of a limited amount of the daily happenings, where they went, who they saw, and such. On the contrary, these women settle for ice cream cones and tater tots at the local Dairy Queen not to mention packing the innumerable kids in the car for swim lessons and juicy gossip.

At least that is how I remember growing up by slurping chocolate swirls and prodding everything into ketchup cups. Not bad, not good, just the way it was in those days. The culture remains unaltered. Cars and trucks are traded like passing the butter during meals. My mother's sorrow survived my moving away to college although care boxes of cookies made me long for home. Our sixth senses clicked like that.

The café door swings open and the Olson brothers enter, accompanied by Tessa. She wears a starched denim company shirt, complete with logo. The twins had opted for the going casual, consisting of tee shirts and jeans. I motion for them to join me.

"I see you found a reason to stay," Tessa teases and taps the tabletop with her knuckle. I equally match her delight to see me.

"Have a seat. I just ordered," I gesture toward the empty chairs.

The three pull out chairs and gather around me. Aaron tosses his ball cap on the tabletop and runs a soiled hand through his mane.

"I got a call from Roland a short time ago. He said you were finished with the autopsy. What did you find out, then?" His gaze flits about the room never settling on anything for long.

"I can't discuss it until the case is put together with a microscopic examination," I offer up cautiously. "Let's just say for the time being that it appears to be a natural death. Basically, there was nothing out of the ordinary."

"Well, that's a relief," says a sarcastic David, projecting his voice loud enough for the dice-playing farmers to stop and look toward our table.

"Roland says dad was as frozen as a TV dinner. I was afraid he might come back to life once he thawed."

The brothers share a knowing smirk between each other. No love lost in this crowd.

Tessa is sitting across from me listening intently, perhaps conjuring up images of how Ole might have looked.

"Was he that cold? I mean deep frozen to prevent decaying in transit?"

"In this case, yes," I explain. "If there is no other method of preservation, like embalming, then deep refrigeration is the only way."

"Six thousand dollars is a hell of an ice quota. That's the expense for us to ship his body." David pokes his tongue inside his cheek and inhales deeply.

In their defense, I feign surprise at the price although, despite the distance travelled, the brothers got off rather sparingly. I've heard of clients charged roughly double that for cross-country transport. Third world loading docks are not filled with a hoard of refrigeration containers.

"Can we please change the subject?" demands Tessa as she fumbles for the menu stacked between the combination napkin and salt and pepper holder.

"I'm all for that," says Aaron. "Shopping for tractor parts is strenuous. Seriously though, thanks Doc, for coming out to take care of this. We'll get the remainder in a check to you by next week."

"Not a problem. I appreciate your hospitality and allowing me to visit old haunts."

"You used to live up here?" inquires David.

"Actually, I was a youth counselor at this lake when it was a summer church camp. Mostly chasing rich bratty boys off the girl's side of the island. My parents thought it a terrific opportunity given that my interest was sports and theirs was religion. But somewhere between college and life, I got sidetracked. I still love sports, but it's not easy. The competitive juices are still there, but the carton is nearing empty."

I sigh dejectedly like every other ex-jock who's told a woe-is-me story, which is boring as hell to all the non-jocks. The boys nod. Tessa leans back and taps her spoon on the tabletop.

"Stay a couple days extra, Doc. We're hosting a softball tournament this weekend with the local reunion. The Resort team is a little short on talent this year. Playing for fun is ok, but when there's an annual trophy, all bets are off." David leans back waiting for my decision and winks at his brother.

"Hell, Tessa can put you on the roster this afternoon," adds Aaron.

I anticipate this is a tease or a punch line to a joke, but the joke is going to be on me. The big bluff hinges on my response.

"How competitive is this tournament?" I ask, leaning forward, crossing my arms.

"See. I told you he wanted to stay!" exclaims Tessa as she elbows David and gives Aaron a high-five. "It will be a once in a lifetime opportunity, Kevin. Come on. Think about it. A couple extra days' vacation?"

I pause and look up to the ceiling. Do I have any better options?

"I can't think of one lousy excuse why not," Aaron said. He tosses his head sideways to get his oily mane over the left side of his face then anchors his right hand on his hip in a challenging motion.

"I'll need a glove, right-handed," I continue, now feeling drawn into the conspiracy.

"A lefty?" roars Aaron.

"Go buy a new one at Jim's Sporting Goods downtown," David tells me. "He'll get you a good deal. Brand names: *Wilson, Worth, Spalding.*"

"I'll even take you out for a pre-game meal," Tessa gleams and reaches over to squeeze my hands.

"I bet that's not the only pre-game plan," jokes Aaron.

She ignores the harassment and continues.

"Off the island is a classy restaurant. It's not a beer joint, not a café. I told you about it. Called the Trimming Leaf. They serve fresh fish platters, steaks, and pastas. It's been owned by an old immigrant Italian couple for over twenty years. Believe it or not, they even serve some of your California wines, like chianti."

David tries to steer the subject back to the main topic.

"I bet you weren't aware that Tessa was once a fairly good softball player back in college. They wanted her to try out for the Olympics."

"Is that right, Tessa?" I ask, leaning in toward her.

She nervously fiddles with her earring.

"Before marriage, before a padded corporate life, before idiocy. Yeah, I wanted to do nothing but play. I was a third baseman, sometimes pitcher. My batting was alright."

"Yeah, right," Aaron raises his eyebrows and gives her a glassy stare. "All American. We are talking to royalty."

"All American Stupid sounds more like it." She looks intently at him and lifts the glass of water to her lips.

"What happened?" I ask, wanting to know more about her. She places her glass down on the counter and tucks her arms under the table.

"Thanks, guys. I'm sure Kevin wants to hear of my failures."

Her stern comment causes the boys to retreat from their excitement as both pretend to browse the menu. There is an uncomfortable pause that is eventually relieved by the return of the waitress.

"Have you decided?" The smock is now open from the lower buttons. A fleshy navel slit with a metallic gold ring the size of a three-ring binder is in full view. Engraved on it is KENNY.

"Beef commercial," says Aaron, not looking up, "with a Coke, please."

"Me too," adds David, fixating on her belly.

"I'll have the oyster chowder bowl," says Tessa, "and an iced tea."

The young lady refills my water glass and departs.

"Sorry, Tessa," says David.

"Yeah, sorry," repeats Aaron.

Tessa lets out an exasperated sigh. "It's not your fault. I'm a little sensitive. You two can really push my buttons sometimes."

She looks to me with a chagrin.

"It was a long time ago. There's little else that I could have done."

"Next to me, you are as close to a celebrity that this island has ever had," David jokes. "Those lodgepole politicians can't hold a candle to you. It's our way of talking you up. We are damned proud."

"That's a crock," she interjects placing the menu on the tabletop with a SLAP. "You are working my good side for something."

"That too," chuckles Aaron, twirling his soda straw between his thumb and forefinger. "Doc, this woman needs to be dined. She works too hard, and then gets PMS cranky on our asses over lawn mower expenses. Take her off our hands, please. You'll be doing us both a favor."

David high-fives his brother again. It feels like the color of an unripe peach has been painted on my face.

"When do you want to go to the Trimming Leaf?"

"How does tonight sound to you?" she replies, a little overanxiously.

I look up to see the old farmers had paused in the middle of their dice game to check out the commotion coming from our table.

"All right," snaps Aaron. "Mission accomplished."

Was I being set-up? It mattered less. We both laughed at the situation the twins had placed in front of us. The bored waitress delivers drinks in tall, colored plastic glasses. Tessa speaks up.

"Men can be such losers." She places her hand up to her brow in the shape of the letter L.

The brothers yelp with glee. Moments pass, then David asks.

"How about you, Doc? Do you have any family back in California?"

Explaining my widower status has never been one of my favorite things to divulge. Most people react with over-compassion or sympathy. More than likely, I respond the same if wearing somebody else's shoes. But if it makes me uncomfortable discussing it, I back down. On the other hand, they have a right to know.

I turn away for a moment to gather my thoughts.

"I lost my wife during childbirth a few years back and never got back into the social scene. Sort of stuck my nose into work." I stiffen at the thought. "It's getting easier to manage."

A somber tone drapes our table like heavy linen as I continue.

"Now, can we please change THAT subject?"

Aaron and David study me like an alien has landed in their trees. Tessa looks down at the table and quietly rearranges her utensils.

"Hey folks," I straighten up. "This lunch is on me. We all have our problems. You must finalize a funeral so in the meantime, latch onto the good times and let the rest go. How about an Ole Olson Memorial Softball Tournament? Winner gets a big trophy?"

"How 'bout a urinal instead of a funeral with condiments?" retorts David as he readjusts his cap to ride the back of his head. "He might have been our father, but he was no dad. Always gallivanting and living high off the hog. It took us years to get the resort out of the red. Money was no sticking point as long as he used it first."

"As you can see, blood lines run deep for us Olsons." Aaron's knife-like bitterness flies out as if he had been holding back strong emotions. His grin is as frozen as Ole's dead body.

The food eventually arrives. Mine is bland, way below expectation, and I try the Midwestern method by spicing it up with some extra ketchup. Silly me. A squeeze bottle is situated on each table. Between gulps and sips our fluxed agitation eventually subsides. We fought over the bill even though I insisted on paying. I sincerely like them and want the boys on my side if need be. I might need them again.

Tessa caught a ride to the café with the brothers, but they were not returning to the resort. I offer to give her a lift back to work for which she willingly obliges. We walk out of the café and toward my rental.

"Well, that certainly offered up an interesting meal," she says with a sarcastic grumble.

I switch on the car, turn left at the first stop sign and onto Lakeside Highway.

"Those boys grew up without a father figure and I say they've been doing all right despite it. When I speak to clients like them, the mothers dominate the conversation. The male children are merely that: childish. They act immature as if seeking a sort of melancholic reprimand from their dad."

"Any plans for later?"

We watch an older couple crossing the street in front of us. The man guides his wife by the elbow. She has a hitch in her stride which causes her to grimace. On her free arm dangles a purse while a walking cane supports the weaker leg.

"Got to put together these case notes, then do some dictation. Check my messages even though I prefer not. Why?"

"I thought you might like to drive up along the north shoreline. I'm part of the volunteer fire service and it's my job to check fire trails. I'd feel more comfortable if you came along because it's pre-winter bear foraging season and they chase anything that moves."

"Ah, dinner times two," I quip.

Tessa looks in my direction and I sense today's luncheon had unsuspectedly dipped into a troubling past. On the drive, she becomes quiet and sullen, sinking in the seat and resting her head on the back. Something catches her eye on my side and when she turns, I notice she's been tearing up. Words unspoken keep my unnerving concentration on the road.

"I need to get away for a little while. Please come with me."

"Of course, I will," and pat her on the arm.

We hit a snag of construction traffic as we approach the resort. From the looks of it, Ole's boys did good as the resort is truly becoming state of the art. To compete with upscale metro areas, there's a conference center with separate housing. Wireless connectivity and off-season upgrades are advertised online. There are pictures of smiling couple's with wine glasses and business-types in suits shaking hands near a podium.

The flagman allows us to continue. I park at the registration office.

"Thanks for lunch. I owe you." She lets her head fall back onto the headrest and sighs. I'm drawn between gratitude or relief. Lines of stress are forming on the sides of her closed eyes.

"You'll get your chance later," I joke. "Get back in there and sic 'em."

Some of the oak leaves drift across the driveway as brittle yellow remnants of summer's passing. It's only August and fall knocks on my vacation doorstep. The acorns are smaller than expected for this time of the year, exploding under the weight of my tires in front of the cabin. I switch off the engine and reluctantly pull out my cell phone. A female recorded voice informs me there are no new messages. That sympathetic electronic robot will never know how relieving those words are.

Cooled breezes abound off the shoreline and fan me through the car's interior. I lean my head against the backrest and recall the wheat harvests of my youth. My job was to unload the grain truck while my uncle combined. With a juicy foxtail between my teeth and a cold can of pop, I was made in the shade. My uncle's tree-trunk forearms were covered with military tattoos, the blood veins as roped and blue as the embedded pigment. I often wondered how he got so strong. Only three years in the Army, but a farmer for another forty. He'd puff on his Winston's, the smoke clouding his weathered face. It was his style to squint as he spoke, and it reminded me of those Hollywood celebrities in black and white movies. Those were the days.

In time, I doze off in my seat thinking about him, about Tessa, and about the smell of sun-warmed grain on a humid August afternoon.

CHAPTER SEVEN

As the ancient ice floes receded from this country twenty millennia ago, the landscape became as gouged and blemished as an adolescent face. Further north, the rockier basins developed permanent scars where the channeled water remains cold and dark to this day, and the pungent smell of algal bloom is virtually non-existent. Non-human global warming intervention formed the lakes and forests. Modern science has predicted earth is between glacial ages. Unfortunately, there is no frost on Tessa's right foot. She's pedal-to-the-metal. Rumbling over dirt trails. Whiplashing her rider. Motion sickness floats in me like a drifting buoy.

Our truck takes us from the primitive loam and sandy shoreline to sheer cliff-like borders in a matter of miles. The pine forests are still unspoiled, except for an occasional discarded beer can or plastic water bottle. Further into the hilly drive, large trees still present in full canopy, blocking out the sunlight from the mossy and moist groundcover on the forest floor. A few evergreen spurs had tried to form within a pinecone drop zone, but they grow spindly without the ultraviolet support.

Tessa explains to me how she checks the under-branch dryness of the needles for the detection of heat stress.

"So far, so good," she summarizes and brushes damp earth from her palms.

We hike at least a three-mile loop, occasionally stopping to manually test the branches by bending the needles, looking for toothpick conditions.

"A couple of years ago it was an unusually dry year. The ground was a tinderbox all summer, but we survived it without a single blaze. Some say it is global warming revisited. Others, like the old school believers, call it cyclic. Your thoughts?"

"Luck," I answer flatly, staring off into the reddish-brown patchwork.

Our trip continues in the truck on a graded fire trail, but within miles, it's a bucking bronco. My knees bang on the glove console and I grip the hand rest to prevent flying headfirst through the windshield. In due course, all that transitions as we unload the four-wheeler from the truck bed. I must cling to her waist like a marsupial as she dare-devils over and around tree roots the size of power poles. At a rise she cuts the engine and rests her arms on the steering column.

"Listen."

The forest is alive with crackling treetops, gusts, and the faint screeching of noisy territorial jaybirds.

"Better than any song, I'd say."

She closes her eyes as if to contain this contentment and covers her mouth as if to keep her thoughts private.

"The only time I saw trees like these was up here at church camp," I tell her. "There was no time for spiritual interpretation when all you wanted to do was kill a couple kids. This is absolutely beautiful."

"Yep," as she offers up a Ms. Sunshine smile, lips pursed, eyes closed.

Tessa suddenly sits upright and strokes her throat, no longer smiling. "There was a missing female counselor years ago. People thought she was a no-show or runaway and had a troubled home life. Were you around when she was here? Her last name was Garner."

"It was Erin Garner and, yes, I did know her. Actually, we worked the same camp." I lift my visor and rub some flecks of dirt or gnats out of the corners of my eyes. "I had a huge crush on her. We were teenagers. It was a month or so later that I found out she went missing. Anything ever become of her whereabouts?"

"That was about the time I arrived with my new fiancé," she replies, making a choking noise in her throat. "It was the talk of the town, but it also raised some fears of a killer in the community. You can imagine how things can take off."

"The mystery is still unsolved as I understand," I add. "We were close friends and I always had hope that she was found in some nearby city. Guess that never happened. Sometimes I think back and wonder if she was the rationale behind my becoming interested in forensics. To this day I am still filled with guilt that I was not able to join in the search for her, nor able to do anything to solve the mystery."

Perhaps. Possibly. Maybe. Those were the futile words of hope - - not forensics.

"You were sixteen," Tessa chides. "Don't beat yourself up over something of which you had no control. All the time that has passed, it's foolishness to think otherwise. You have a life, a career that gives people peace of mind, and an admirable attitude even though you doubt your instincts sometimes. Men are like that. Funny, I feel like we've known each other for years. I only wish we had met in some other time before our lives were tossed off-track. Things might have been different."

I'm at a loss how to answer and turn away.

"What would you have me do?"

Tessa lets out a huge sigh.

"The west ridge needs to be checked and that will take about fifteen minutes by four-wheeler. No need to get off the trail and hike it. I'd love to take a swim beforehand. You can dine me, and I'll grill you."

She cocks her eyebrows at me, waiting for my response.

"Lady, I'm all yours. Let's get going."

Our inspection ends and we backtrack to the north gate entrance where we load up the four-wheeler. Tessa jams the truck into gear and careens around slow tourist traffic until we're at the south entrance of the resort. For the second time in one day, I hang on for dear life. She's emphatically showing off her driving skills, but I promptly get the point. The first in a series belches form in the back of my throat. A tap on the horn to move a wandering pedestrian and she whips in next to the equipment barn and switches off the tired engine.

"Meet you at the clubhouse in fifteen minutes? Do we have a deal?" she asks, smiling, holding still as if in anticipation.

"Deal."

It isn't Club Med, but rather more like Club Medicare. Groups of so-called *mature* adults sit around the circular glass top tables in very modest swimwear for their age. Some have the workings of a genuinely nice tan, especially the golfers with their bone white feet. Nevertheless, the atmosphere is jovial with hearty belly laughs and periodic clinking of champagne flutes.

We arrange our towels alongside the steps, then bask under the late crystal-clear skies. Like our excursion two days ago, both of us take a couple laps before plopping down on the warm concrete. Tessa's outdoorsy lifestyle complements her good shape. An eye-catching, sexy gold toe ring glitters on her right foot which, for me, fits my independent impression of her to a tee. A college-aged waiter wearing a beige Ole's Resort tee shirt, swimming trunks, and leather sandals asks for our drink orders and brings back two tall screwdrivers garnished with slices of orange, peach, and a cocktail umbrella. So delicious. I go from sipping to chugging.

Tessa smirks. "Little thirsty?"

"What's in these? It tastes like an Orange Julius on steroids."

"It pays to know the help," she coos with a slurp from the straw. "Like the movie, *Cocoon*, there's a fountain of youth in every swig."

The table of retirees next to us cackle at a delivered punch line by a balding man.

"Ever think about retiring, Kevin?"

"That specific topic will usually come up when I'm filled with self-pity," I respond, looking down at my empty hands. "My short answer is 'not really.' After the death of my wife, there was an interval when I needed to give myself a swift ass-kicking. I was so remorseful and hopelessly abandoned that work kept me focused. I had to relearn how to live."

I sit up and lock my hands around my folded knees. There are no boisterous cannonball challenges, no stick figure brats whining for attention while their starlet moms chat away their time, and no days-old sunscreen film in the water. On the contrary, it is a tranquil reverse from yesterday. We have entered the world of guests topping off another day in paradise.

"Do you have any idea how long it's been since I've lounged with anything other than a dull book or even worse, case notes?"

"I get the feeling you do ok by yourself. If you're trying to conjure up sympathy, don't bother. My dates over the past decade have been more like assignments out of a private charter school. You know, the more you have, the more you pay. Quantity does not mean quality."

She rolls over onto her stomach and stretches until her lower spine pops.

"Ah, that felt good."

She crosses her legs and lies flat.

"Any children?" I inquire with self-doubt bringing up this topic.

"Couldn't. Can't. I had an acute case of endometriosis in my late teens, followed by laser surgery, scarring, and infertility. About the time I was in my early thirties, my lover-boy decided marriage to me wasn't fun anymore. We'd argue over any and everything until he moved out. I eventually filed for divorce. He, we, had not saved nor invested. We had a re-modeled two-bedroom house outside of Duluth. That sale pushed us into the upper wage earners come April fifteenth," she says with a hint of cynicism, then continues.

"Like you, I sweltered in my losses. I had to get out because there was nothing left. There was an ad for a nanny back here in Wasoon, but little did I know that an argumentative old man was trying to raise two foul-mouthed, spoiled twin boys. Guess who? He offered me the job but basically let me call the shots. I compiled a monthly expense account and he'd write the check. Mr. National Geographic kept his distance, usually in Africa. When the boys turned twenty-one, it was play money." She giggles. "Sort of like nuns in a pickle patch."

"Nuns in a what?" I look at her in disbelief and laugh uncomfortably.

"Ole paid for anything they wanted clearly to keep peace. It was anything and everything when the checks arrived. I tried to contact Ole, but he never returned my calls. He kept sending money, spoiling them, spoiling the relationship. He was not a doting father. He preferred to draw a distinction from fatherhood. I suspect he accidentally fell into the category of father-figure and it aged him. Early on, the brothers were his exact clones: arrogant and constantly getting in fights. God, it was annoying. I threatened to quit, but I was under contract until their twenty-fifth birthday. It was not until the cash flow dwindled did the boys begin to understand what kind of father Ole was to them. My hope was that the family attorney's suggestion to sell the resort for big cash caught on, but the brothers wanted something glitzy. I think you can see where this story is going?"

"You get the resort refinanced, become property manager, and sunbathe with lonely male clients on the side," I answer with a knowing look.

"Right on," she responds dryly. "So, between that and my significant other wanting to try new material, I soured on a big cartload of futures."

She pushes up on her elbows and sips her drink through the straw.

"Good drink, isn't it? Plus, this confessional is a hell less embarrassing."

"Hey, it wasn't meant to go that far, Tessa."

I look down at my sunburnt feet. Michaels, you stupid idiot. There's a stagnant pause as if we had opened-up beyond the limits of comfort.

"I need another drink," she grumbles and looks away. "Those people are having way too much fun."

"Tessa, this resort is your baby. Those people over there are your successful rewards. No one else has the know-how to run this business. Give yourself some due credit. I know the brothers appreciate everything you've done."

"They're my babies," she replies. Her look is flat, the smile has waned.

"Money only creates limited satisfaction. I don't earn nearly enough. Others in the laboratory business are easily in the high six figures, and I usually don't get paid up front either. I work with clients who deal with grief first, funerals last. It's a tough business, but I believe in it and that belief goes a long way. As I see it, there will never be enough to retire comfortably on my salary. But somewhere, an airliner is dedicating a window seat over the wing in my memory with a plaque."

Tessa rolls over onto her back and places her hands behind her head like a pillow. Bright sunlight bounces off her mirrored glasses and, for the life of me, I can't tell what she's thinking. Legs straight. She taps her feet together. Lips pursed. Something.

"I need to cool off." In an instant, she sits up and reaches for her towel. "A purge, Kevin. Come on."

We have the pool to ourselves. The older crowd is content to socialize and ignore our laps and sulking.

"Any poison oak rash?" I ask between lap-labored gasps. "My fifty-meter show off freestyle is pathetic."

"None. I expected nothing less. Good job, Doctor. You still have the flair."

The drink was decreasing my inhibitions as I sneak a look at the outlines of her small nipples that were becoming more evident inside her sleek swimsuit. She is very agile in the water. Her rounded thighs fare effortlessly with aquatic kicks and barely needs to tread in place. Not at all like the middle-aged bum who was trying to keep up with her.

"Forty years ago, someone said similar words to me in the back of the chapel. That was Erin Garner, the missing counselor. I was enamored enough with her to believe anything she said. We had a brief spin on that teen-age love train. I grew up fast after that. Being here revives those memories."

Tessa slides in closer, cornering me along the steps, her citrus breath on my cheek, and her cleavage is pressing softly against my arm.

"Some memories are good to keep. That was your first love. When it's done correctly, it's filed in the good old retention bank."

There is a sudden gust, and the paper plates are carried from the tables into the water. The disconcerted guests vault out of their chairs to capture the few left on the pool's edge. Pieces of cake dissolve into red and green surface sludge.

Tessa laughs. "Don't worry. It's the most exercise they'll have all week."

"I hear you," and surprise myself by kissing her on the lips. She grabs me by the arms and pulls me into her chest.

"Thanks for listening, Kevin. It's been a long, dormant summer. Despite it all, I'm looking forward to the winter season. We sponsor all types of conferences to cross-country skiers and the snowmobile set. January is the perfect time to be up here. It's quiet, cold, and very snowy. The summer seasonal sticker shock has receded and there's a good month or two of deep snow, the kind you wish for as a kid. It's that ugly, icy meltdown period between March and April that gets under people's skin. Check it out sometime."

"You mean to have me carouse with other irritated customers?"

She offers up her most stern look. "Here I use my best sales pitch and you still don't bite. This laziness is affecting your senses."

"I'll admit that 'lazy' is not in my immediate vocabulary but definitely is something I can get used to," I respond with an over-the-top, easygoing smirk.

We lull a good hour. The temperate midday warmth is allowing us to spill more than baked beans on our past lives. She tells me about two miscarriages and one misfired marriage. She has no living parents, had surgery on her left knee for a torn meniscus back in college, and fears developing osteoarthritis down the road. Her hands throb all night from keyboarding and, most importantly, she loves a margarita after work. As she continued talking, her pretty smile reflects, in my opinion, a made to order set of teeth, although she is self-conscious of old molar fillings and covers them up by unconsciously dabbing the corner of her mouth with the napkin.

It's easy to see she longs for a couple hours each day outdoors doing PR. She tells me it takes the starch out of the mundane business of maintaining a resort. I picture her standing at her office window on stormy days, nose pressed against the pane. She's comfortable with being single, although, I'm sure, the eligible candidates line up along the wall waiting for their turn on the dance floor.

Her hairstyle is short and practical. Other things are more important than preparation. Contrastingly, I have known other women who haven't changed anything from high school cheerleading days, including hair color. Like some of the ladies up here, they had become trophy wives, stay-at-home moms, or never had a career to fall back on despite an education. Even at fifty, they want to look closer to thirty. For them, the fear of aging or losing the best part of their twenties is unbearable. But children don't want their mothers to act like them. Odd. In the teenage suicides that I've been involved with, it became the stark nature of the loss that compelled parents to reexamine themselves in a total new light. It literally took the tragedy.

I overexposed myself to Tessa, but it's a good thing. I haven't felt this relaxed and trusting in a long time. What the hell was I thinking by kissing her? That was a little over the top, emotion-wise. Better rein in those ideas, ice down, and slow down.

We track down a couple of abandoned Adirondack lounges at the far fence and claim them by draping our beach towels over the back rests.

"You mentioned the girl counselor, Erin Garner. Was there ever any news on her disappearance?"

Tessa is wearing large-rimmed sunglasses and a visor. She tilts her backrest down and allows the sun's warmth to do the rest.

Meanwhile, I sit forward with my drink.

"I kept thinking that someone either saw or heard from her by now. Missing person cases get lost in courthouse boxes. Maybe she died of accidental causes in the woods rather than the inevitable criminal theories. Somewhere, someone knows what happened."

The buffet cart is wheeled out, draped with linen whites, the wine glasses clanking in the holders. Resort-types stand in anticipation as the maître d' positions it alongside the cocktail bar. The first feathery wisps of clouds dim the once glossy reflection. A tourist bus motors onto the driveway heading toward the registration building, its brakes screech into a slow halt, and the pressurized door opens with a *whoosh*.

"Perfect timing," Tessa narrows her eyes and props her fist under her chin. "The clouds come in and it's suppertime."

She stands beside her chair and gathers her towel.

"Tell you what. Being that you're an interested party, how about supper first, and if there's enough daylight, we take a drive out to the other side of the island. The area has not been redeveloped yet. I'm quite sure the girl's cabins are still standing...occupied by mice and such."

"I am a bit curious," I declare and take a moment to push my sunglasses up my nose, "unless you prefer to stay here."

I point to the feeding frenzy of the Fabulous Sixty-Plus Foragers.

Tessa smiles. "When it's free, you had better look out for the stampede."

Dinner - - or as it is coined up here, "Supper" - - at the offsite restaurant is superb. The main course, a fresh walleye, pink in the middle, is adorned with plenty of flavorful fat that's been baked to perfection. Besides the basic under-cooked potatoes and lifeless asparagus, the overall presentation is way beyond my expectations. We share a fruity two-year old Mississippi River Frontenac from Red Wing Estates. Short growing seasons don't allow for many tannins, like California. This wine is not something I am used to. It's sort of on the sweet, unfinished side, something amateur winemakers dawdle in at first. I try not to act snobby, but it's barely palatable and has me wishing for a dark, ice cold Lager instead. Percentagewise, the other patron tables I notice either have beer on tap or fancy brewery bottles.

Luckily, Tessa suggests that I bring a light overcoat. According to weather predictions, a typical late August cold front is approaching. The open-air restaurant seating is nothing elegant, with checkerboard tablecloths and comfortable cushioned chairs with padded armrests the main decor. A scrumptious peach cobbler doused in caramelized brown sugar and oatmeal, accompanied with strong decaffeinated coffee, rounds up the evening. We are two contented companions. Over Tessa's shoulder is a spectacular view of the lake and pink sunset beyond the city lights of Wasoon. When the bill arrives, I gladly add extra tip money. I pay double at home for this same meal. Tessa's complexion is rosy. Her lips are upturned in a smirk.

"How is the wine?" I inquire.

"I'm not sure. Shall we order another bottle?"

We opt out of that decision but on the way to the car I cradle her arm as she covers up in a cardigan. We pause to look at the ever-darkening sky.

"This storm comes with strong wind, no doubt. We are way over-due for a soaker."

Midwesterners live and breathe weather. They only watch tele-vision to confirm their known suspicions that those rectangular swathes of red indicate a potential for severe systems.

"We don't have to go, Tessa," I explain.

"It will be fine. We'll do a look-see." She squeezes me on the arm and gives me a condescending maternal pat. "There are only a cou-ple hours of daylight left and you have me interested also."

The pre-storm breezes kick up creamy foam along the lakeshore drive. Between strong gusts, my rental straddles the modest bike lane stripe as if on a tethered line. Tessa sits silent in the passenger seat, but I know she is helping me steer with her imaginary wheel.

"There will be some serious leaf and pine needle detail at the resort tomorrow," she clicks her tongue as a broken-off elm branch sails past our windshield.

I interpret her remark to mean that this escapade might not be a good idea tonight. We eventually slow, then pull onto the roadside to watch the blustery developments.

"Tessa, I don't want to put us at risk. We've been driving about fifteen minutes. Let's call this off. It might get worse."

"The next turn-off is ours," she replies, leaning forward, head up, and alert. "Once we get inland it won't seem as bad. We'll be protected."

"Yeah, but only until the rain comes at us in torrents," I add, tilting my head from side to side, sorting out the options if we get trapped out here.

"Not to worry, Kevin." She points. "Okay, here we go."

Gray-black thunderheads creep and morph across the sky, their full underbellies warp into other enormous shapes of precipitation reservoirs. I remember well how a tornado demolished our farm and left the barn and granary a splintered woodpile. The whole family, excluding my dad, huddled in the basement, me on my older sister's lap. The ozone-moist humid air intermingled with the smell of canning jars, dirty clothes, and mice. Out of respect for the home-site, my father had decided to ride out the storm on the front porch steps. When the storm passed, he calmly opened the trap door and walked down the ancient steps.

"It's over," he stated rather glumly. Not a tear of loss, but a deep sigh of relief that we had survived. I never forgot that moment of family closeness. He hugged my mother with one arm and the rest of us each received a brisk head rub with the other. This little curiosity excursion is one of those nights as well.

"Stop here," she instructs me. "It's over the hill a few hundred yards."

We get out and fix our eyes upon the pathway in the graying shades of the towering conifers. There is still a faint evidence of the original walking pathway, morphing into a narrow deer trail. Plentiful seedlings had rooted in the packed soil over the years. Tessa and I weave through the groves, sometimes pointing to decaying wooden signposts that hang from tree trunks by one peg or nail, the painted words long ago leeched out from aging. It leaves me to wonder if this might have been the girls' escape route when the boys raided their camps following prayer sessions.

In the dimness, a sextet of single-story cabins eventually materializes, camouflaged in the overgrowth. Except for the window frames, the buildings are virtually invisible. A miniature funnel of leaves darts through an open space between the pump house and the main cabin. Tessa covers her eyes from the swirling dust and opens the screen door of the nearest unit where a rusted padlock secured the door jam.

"Looks exactly like a couple years ago when I last checked," she said.

"Looks the same to me too, the last time I checked forty-five years ago. Even the padlock looks to be the same."

We walk around the property noticing all latched doors in both the front and back entrances. It's too dark to see clearly inside through the grungy panes. I feel a need to explain.

"The counselors had a walled-off bungalow that separated them from the plebe's bunks. Each unit had a toilet, a modest sink, curtained shower stall, and the world's coldest concrete floors. The chill crawled up to my ankles sometimes."

She closes the screen door.

A vivid reminder on how I had once complained about Erin's icy toes even as we sat along the moonlit shore, it was as if time was inert out here. I picture those caddy young ladies forming alliances against other roommates. Erin used me as a sounding board on occasion. She complained how undisciplined they were. Daddy's little girls.

"I'm satisfied."

We gather our belongings and make the way to the original trail. Tessa stops and points.

"As long as we're here, I want to check the pump house if it's unlocked. The water hydrant is supposed to be still usable in case of fire. I'm sure it's not potable anymore, though. You'll have to wait for a drink when we get back. Too bad, we should have brought that extra bottle of wine."

All at once, the island resonates with an explosive clap of thunder directly overhead. I grab her hand and we rush to the watershed ahead of marble-sized hailstones. I force the door open, popping the rusted hinges off its track. A division of marching soldiers might have been louder as we scurry inside. The ongoing deluge traps us from making a practical race for the vehicle. Rain pours off Tessa's brow in huge droplets, my fleece jacket is becoming saturated, the cold-water seeping into my bones. I'm beginning to feel quite foolish about ignoring the ominous weather.

"Sorry, Tessa. This was poor planning."

Her denim coat is holding up much better than my covering, but her khaki shorts cling to her tan thighs like wet paper towels.

"Hey. I'll take partial blame. I got you to drive," she inserts. In between the intensifying hail and thunder she shouts, "What do you want to do? Wait here or dash for it?"

I anxiously scan our interior surroundings. A couple of old-fashioned garden rakes, a shovel that was still caked with red dirt and plenty of black widow spider webs at face level. We stand on the elevated concrete platform and I struggle with a few futile pumps with the lever. Momentarily, the spout burps and gurgles a bucket-full of dark, putrid water.

"Needs a little priming, but at least it's still working," I assure her, standing aside as the dribbling ooze splashes on the wooden platform.

"If only my previous dates acted the same."

She gives me a bemused smile.

Tessa removes her drenched coat and snaps it a couple of times, sending a mist onto the wall beams.

"I can't get any wetter. How about yourself?"

"I'm too cold to care, right now," I tell her. "Let's stay for a little longer right here. I feel like a teenager trapped on a desert isle, like a *Survivor* without the tribal council. We can opt for a dash to the road or give it until things lighten up a little."

"And if it doesn't?" peering under her raised eyebrows.

"Well then, there's nothing like a little campfire without either the camp or fire," I gesture to her pockets. "You don't carry a flashlight, a cell phone?"

"Nada. It's back on the car's seat. I thought we wouldn't be gone that long. Remind me to practice saying 'no' when we get back."

I spin her around to face the door and begin to give her a brisk back rub.

"Hot shower, hot chocolate, and definitely more of this," she moans.

"Sounds like another deal," I reply.

Outside, the hail subsides into a virtual spray that obscures our view beyond the tree line. The cabins setting dissolves as we continue to watch from our entrapment.

Tessa asks, "Were you happy here, Kevin?"

She arches her back like a satisfied cat into my kneading.

"It was okay, I guess. That was my first interaction with leadership roles. There were some advantages. I met some nice folks during the summer. As a matter of fact, people that I never got to see again still drop me a Christmas card."

I point in the direction of the farthest cabin on the right.

"I believe that was Erin's. At least, I think so."

The rain flies at us in horizontal planes as if buckets were being tilted into a large fan. Stunted elm yearlings bend to the ground at the doorsteps from the gales.

"It was so long ago," I shout, "but like only yesterday after seeing this again,"

Tessa takes my hands and crosses them around in front of her chest.

"It's all right. Memories can be a comfort. I never attended anything like this. But my older sister did, and she said the same things: endless summer now ended."

Tessa studies the trees and pathway, then looks back to me. She bites her lip softly. Her brows are wrinkled.

"Does anyone know we are here? I don't suppose you had this all planned?"

"I'm notorious for convincing pretty resort managers into abandoned sites." I draw her close to stop her shivering.

"Actually, it's not a bad idea," she giggles.

We chuckle at our silliness.

"Hey. Do you see that?" says Tessa directing my attention to the cabin I thought was Erin's.

There is a faint yellow glow reflecting in the window, soft and weak, like a candle flickering through the dusted glass. I halfway expect to see a search party coming down the lane looking for us.

"I'm not sure, Tessa. Like a lightning flash, or something like that. It's hard to tell if we are seeing anything at all in this weather. I'd say it's coming from inside the cabin. We checked all those doors and they seemed secured and unopened for some time."

From our secluded spot the light slowly fades but reappears near the bunker's quarters.

"Our eyes are playing tricks on us, Kevin," she said. "When we get back to the resort, I'm going to notify Security to check these places for any break-ins. There have been a couple of transients lurking in the woods north of Wasoon and I suspect this is an element of their migration route. It won't surprise me to find them using these shelters to hide and grow pot."

The luminescence gradually dies out, leaving us temporarily blinded by a near-by bolt of electrical energy. The smell of ozone is close, remarkably close.

"Enough of this," shouts Tessa. "It's way too romantic for me."

She drapes her jacket over her shoulders and steps out in the dreary quietude.

"Coming? Dear?"

The storm's energy propels us, dodging whiplash birch branches and projectile pinecones along the trail. I fumble for my keys. At the same time, she yanks open the passenger side door and nose-dives in.

"I must have left the car unlocked." She looks puzzled. "That's not like me. I habitually lock everything up here in the wilderness."

"Who is going to find us out here?" I question, still digging into my pocket for the keys.

We pull out, spinning on muddy slurry until the tires grip the asphalt. The windshield wipers sweep the fallen needles as she fiddles for the defrost button and fan. The drive up here was expected to be short and simple, but instead, we encountered unmet expectations and solitude. She unzips her coat and unfastens her seatbelt, drawing her legs up tightly to her waist.

"Keep driving. I'm so cold."

"At least some of this night was worth it," I stutter, but can't stop shuddering. "I'll help you check out those cabins tomorrow if you want."

We ride in silence, the storm slowly passing us to the east. Her puzzling thoughts seem secluded in a darker chasm that I wasn't allowed to view.

CHAPTER EIGHT

A s if last night's storm never existed, the morning lapis sky lights up my room. Branches lazily sway from occasional gusts. I dropped off an absorbed Tessa at her truck and headed for my cabin as the storm howled on and on. Although relieved that we managed to get back safely, I was still a little disappointed that a potential passionate-laden course went off track. I lied awake, hearing every new hour 'Ding' on the nightstand clock. By four o'clock, my eyes throbbed from lack of sleep. Our social was sensual and auspicious even though the trip to the cabins churned with unease and reserve.

Feeling guilty for abandoning my business, I place an errant call to my message board. There is a second-opinion inquiry for a recent suicide that's been cleared by the coroner, and two calls for previously done cases. The last message is from an attorney in Texas who had tried to recruit me in the past for expert witness testimony. My cajones aren't that big anymore. He won't be receiving a response.

Of all the upscale things that I usually never do, I order room service breakfast mostly to avoid catching Tessa at the buffet. I had crafted a now broken vow not to hole-up in a motel room and eat, thinking it was better to force myself to see and be seen. But seclusion got to be a good habit and it kept me from LSRS: Lost Spousal Retreat Syndrome. A grief counselor suggested this to me. The excuse of Ole Olson's autopsy report hasn't been working to my satisfaction.

I am in the bathroom brushing my teeth when I hear the screen door rattle, and a quick rap.

"Going to spend all day in there?"

It was Tessa, one hand on her hip, the other holding the door open. She notices the splayed-out paperwork on the desktop and clicks her tongue.

"Looks like you are back to work early."

"Thought you might be too busy this morning," I sermonize. "You know. Cleaning up from the storm and such."

"Scare you off last night?" she asks as if calling my bluff. "What's for breakfast? Blueberry muffins or fresh cornbread with links?"

"I went for the muffins," answering, rubbing my hands together. "Back home, the berries are mutant, the size of large marbles from over-irrigation. People like them that way. Up north, the fruit is tinier with intense berry flavors. How can I resist? Care to come in?"

"Okay. I need a little break anyway."

She steps in and closes both the screen and cabin doors behind her. I push aside a sofa pillow and for her to sit.

"Anymore coffee in that pot?" She picks up the spare mug on the tray.

We split the remaining morning brew. I suspect there is something else percolating as she slowly stirs some powdered cream into the mixture. A vociferous blue jay assails my windowsill in front of the porch, noisily claiming this territory from a spellbound gray squirrel under the oak tree. Suddenly, the animal leaps onto the side of the tree, a fat acorn jammed in its mouth. Tessa laughs.

"Those two go at it all the time. I watched that same episode yesterday. The bird never relinquishes until Mr. Bushy Tail disappears. In the spring, that jay literally attacks the groundskeepers."

She hesitates, her voice is unusually flat and monotone.

"Are you that provincial, Kevin? Are you still holding on to your possessions? Do you have any acorns that can't be shared?"

"Not any more than usual," defending myself, fidgeting, clearing my throat. "If you're concerned about my being a widower, there are some tough periods like vacations, holidays, or even nights. Some things won't, nor can't go away because it's safer to store them and let the jaybird remind me who's the boss."

"I can appreciate that logic," she takes a long sip of coffee. "In the long run, all that remains are a few empty shells." She places the cup down and clenches her fists. "Shit. Pardon the French."

"Let it out, Tessa. You're still connected to your sister and there's nothing wrong with that. I see an assortment of that in my line of work, too."

She places her mug on the platter and sits forward.

"Kevin. I want to apologize for how I treated you last night. It was sophomoric and rude. I wasn't aware that seeing the girls' cabins would affect me so much."

She clears her throat and pauses.

"I haven't been honest with you lately. Those counselors, like yourself, took on a huge responsibility back then. Some had never been away from home, let alone, a lake. They had bratty, pubescent girls dumped on their laps and weren't remotely prepared for the responsibility. I know. My older sister told me all about it, Kevin. My older sister was Erin. Erin Garner."

I must have been totally sanctimonious not to see the resemblance. Sitting across from me is Erin's sister. Erin had never mentioned any sisters, let alone her home life. Tessa: Robin-egg-fragile. Now I was beginning to understand.

"I had no idea," stumbling for the right words. "I'm sorry if any of my crass comments hit home."

"Nonsense, you are the perfect gentleman, always tactful, always concerned. Tell me, is there anyone like you back on the farm that needs a little companionship?"

"Fortunately, that fruity, Scandinavian, vena tarter mold was shattered years ago," I joke. "Tessa, how can I help?"

She holds up her cup and gently blows away the steaming vapor. "I have never missed a day without thinking of Erin. Now, it's going on a lifetime. What happened isn't as important as where. She either died accidentally a long time ago or was murdered. Crucial leads and interest have scuttled their course with both state and local authorities. Lord, it's been thirty years or so."

She pats my knee.

"I think that my marriage break-up had something to do with this depressing infatuation of finding my sister. In my dreams, we are grown up women living only a driveway apart. I envision myself a spinster, of course, but she has four daughters and the youngest is attached to yours truly, Aunt Tessa, like glue. We do all sorts of fun things. Isn't that silly?"

Her eyes glisten, a solitary tear forms at the corner and she rubs it away from her cheek.

"Not at all," I add empathetically. "The relationship is still attached by love and blood. It's normal for you to feel that way."

I stand up from my chair to sit beside her on the sofa as she quivers and buries her face into my chest. After a few minutes I grab a couple of napkins to wipe her face. Outside, the same annoying blue jay screeches.

"That damned bird sure knows how to kill the moment," she pouts. "I was thinking about proclaiming something risky."

"It's best to hold that thought for later," I said. "Are you going to be alright?"

"If you asked the brothers, Aaron and David, I haven't been normal for at least twenty years," she chuckles. "Sometimes, when I'm overworked, or depressed, or both, they will take me out to lunch or play a trick on my hard drive at the office. By then, I usually come out of the funk. It was my stupid mistake for the need to see the cabins. It was better off to stay here. That trip was idiotic."

"Hey, listen," I cut in. "I have a few extra days available. Let's say we do a little fact-finding trip. Are the local sheriff's people friendly? I mean do your charms work on them as well as they have on me?"

"There is my reproachful cousin deputy. Sometimes I fear the entire town is interbred to some degree."

She scoots forward on the cushion, her eyes widening, a grin spreads across her face like a child opening Christmas presents.

"That will have to do," giving her a fist pump.

Years ago, most of the county sheriff's departments took over jurisdiction of anything outside the city limits, thus eliminating the constant battle over whether a city police officer chasing a suspected drunk driver out of town amounts to county enforcement. I used to laugh when the local newspaper was delivered. Amidst the who visited whom for Sunday dinner were two columns of weekly incidents. The city police and county sheriff report usually balanced each other out on print. But the line was drawn on reasons that account for an arrest. The city police cited. The county officers arrested. The police had breakfast with the farmers. The sheriff patrolled the doughnut shop. Ticky-tacky reporting by a biased news editor favoring the locals over the county Gestapo.

I usually worked with the county and rarely had a problem with body releases or death certificates. The "both hands in the cookie jar" mentality sometimes resulted in delays with autopsies over the years. Invalid toxicology reports can be a legal hassle in the course of time, and a hasty acquittal for those overzealous defense attorneys. I want to reassure Tessa that I won't stir up additional issues between the two organizations.

Outside, the scuffing sounds of chaise lounge chairs cuts short our intimate discussion. I hear the chatter of kids and parents setting up for the first swim of the day. From the weather reports, storm clouds are expected later today.

"When do we start?" Tessa is eager, hands clenched together, eyes wide and unblinking.

"How about after a couple of eggs and a bagel?" I said pointing to the room service tray.

"Excellent idea." She anxiously scoots closer to me and takes the butter knife and jam. "I am starving."

Three-quarters of an hour later I am waiting in Ole's Resort company truck during which Tessa jogs into the office quarters. In a fleeting moment, she's back and hops into the driver seat, smiling and fiddling with her office key ring. According to her, Paige, the Intern, is to handle the phones and scheduling. Paige is a recent university graduate student trying to learn the ropes in hotel management with this summer job. I recall one of the brothers mentioned her name either at the funeral home or at Bee's. We drive away satisfied that resort life can do without Tessa's supervision.

The downtown stores are opening for business. Most of the cars that I noticed yesterday are again in front of the same café where we met the brothers. So much for healthy lifestyles when only barbeque beef sandwiches and soft drinks are at the mere taking. I must admit that this escape from my vigilant dietary habits is rollicking fun. How do these people eat like this and live so long? This has always been the medical mystery. If it were me, I'd be a full-blown diabetic with high blood pressure. In fact, they might be, but they sure know how to enjoy life. I promise my cholesterol-laden blood vessels a cleansing trail run later.

The sheriff's sub-station is located roughly a mile outside the Wasoon city limits next to a farm implement dealership. Work trucks with large trailers, pickups, and even a few Harley's stack up along the curbs. There is a single patrol car in front of the sheriff's office as a second unit reverses out. Tessa and the driver, a mustached burly redhead, exchange polite nods.

"That's my 'let's keep our relationship a secret' cousin. My mother and her younger sister never got along in the wake of Grandma and Pops deaths. His name is Jonah, like the Biblical Jonah, although this is true role reversal because Jonah is built like a human whale."

His eyes are deep-set, and his large lips form a wet oval as he wheezes. I thought there was a weight restriction as opposed to a weight requirement for deputies. The veins in his neck pop out like large worms with each exhale. His officer hat perches on the top of his head Laurel and Hardy style.

"It will catch up to him sooner than he thinks," I remind her. "Diabetes, heart disease, amputations, and sepsis."

Tessa looks up to me with a puzzled look. "The last thing you said. Septics? Like septic tank?"

"No, sepsis," I explain. "It's a bacterial infection spreading through the blood stream, raising havoc by increasing body temperature that eventually affects the pumping mechanism on compromised patients. Blood pressure gradually drops, and the heart goes into arrhythmia. Doorknob-dead, as they say. Think the opposite of anti-septic and you'll get the idea."

"That's rather blunt, don't you think?" She turns to face me; her lips are upturned.

"Blunt, but true, young woman," I tell her. "Who else can help us in the station?"

"Let's see if Nick Lundgren is actually working today," she mutters. "He's a regular enforcer of our resort during his days off, ogling the bathing babes, calling it security detail. But the only thing secure is the deadbolt on the restroom door. We can't prove it, and yet, our insurance premium has taken an occasional pricey hit on lost or missing items of value. Here's the scoop. I think he pilfers the loot and pushes it off in pawnshops around the area. I'd love to catch him in the act someday."

"Well, let's see if we catch him at work," I smile, looking down my nose over my tinted glasses.

A soft alarm bell signals our entrance. The substation office consists of two main desks, a reception area with folding chairs, and a glass-walled interrogation room in the back. There's a kitchenette on the left where two officers are chatting next to the coffee machine. Both are moderately overweight, and each has a trimmed moustache with bushy sideburns. The Bobbsey Twins. Their short-sleeve uniforms display the county emblem above their badges. Neither acknowledges us initially, until there's a loud horselaugh from the taller one. Then, they both look to us as if we've rudely stepped into their space. It is near lunchtime and I presume by the empty receptionist chair, that these two officers are responsible for that duty until she returns. The shorter one with dark hair studies us and recognizes Tessa. He wipes his mouth with a napkin and comes over to greet us.

"Tessa, what brings you here? Not another missing men's watch, I hope." He smirks. *Lundgren* is stenciled on his lapel.

"Hi Nick," she counters. "This is Dr. Kevin Michaels. He's the doctor from California I told you about. You know, the autopsy on Orvil Olson?"

"To be sure," extending his meaty hand. "Nick Lundgren, Deputy Sheriff. I'm duty-bound to also add Wasoon County, but we have such a largely unpopulated region that most of my time is spent here at the substation."

"I understand," I tell him. "Where I come from is mostly retired or rural, much like here."

His look is vacant, as if trying to imagine an unpopulated California. I get that expression all the time and I'd bet money that his next comment is either about quakes or fires.

"You know that the West Coast is doomed to break off into the drink someday," he warns. "You picked a hot and humid time to visit, Doc. It's expected to climb into the nineties by the weekend. That ought-ah' charge up the thunder bumpers. What can I do for you? Want to do some fishin'? I can sell you an out of state license."

"Thanks," I interject. "That is a very tempting prospect and I used to fish when time permitted. But now, it's mostly fishing for clues."

"I hear ya. Seriously, we got some of the best walleye hot spots you can imagine. World renown according to *Block and Tackle* magazine."

He puffs out his chest and draws in his gut.

"Nick," Tessa butts in. "I've been telling Kevin, er, Dr. Michaels, about how Erin disappeared years ago. I know how I bugged you in the past, but I got over it. I truly did. But we went out to check fire trails yesterday and came upon those old broken-down girls' cabins on the east side. It got me thinking again."

Lundgren's demeanor dampens, and he begins rubbing the back of his neck.

Tessa points. "Now don't give me that look again, Nick. Dr. Michaels is something of an authority in forensics. I want him to read the files with me."

He pauses to thumb-rub his ear then lets out a huge sigh.

"Tessa. It's a cold case file and we have nothing to follow-up. The last time you inquired was about two years ago. You had watched a program on that forensics cable station. I spent the next three weeks interviewing old camp workers and chasing down truly dead leads. It was totally frustrating and futile. I re-boxed it all and put it in our storage facility."

He nervously rubs his arm. There is a flush in his cheeks.

"I know you mean well, and you are more than welcome to go over the files once again with the Doc, here. But don't get your hopes up. We have no updates."

He drags out his desk chair, plops down, and grabs a tablet.

"I'm going to give you another authorization form. The storage unit is near Hipp's Grocery. You know where that is. Look for the blue iron gate directly south of the parking lot."

Tessa nods. "I remember seeing that gate and never knew that sheriff's files were stored there. Isn't that a little insecure?"

"Not much that happens here gets anybody too excited," the deputy reacts, leaning back in his chair, tugging on his tie. "We needed to free up some departmental space -- either that or someone loses an office. You'd be surprised of the number of boxes. Like I said, it's hard to get fired up over dead issues, err, I mean..."

"I understand, Nick. No offense taken," she tells him.

"Okay, then. Here you go." He hands her a piece of paper. "Better call first. Alice isn't always available to open up because she works part time at Lucy's Hair Salon."

Tessa tosses me the truck keys and we eagerly load up and drive away. Tessa's demeanor is obviously uplifted. As for me, I'm cautiously supportive, like stepping onto a patch of black ice. I've learned the hard way that situations don't always fall into place. The city lunch crowd is meandering in line outside Bee's Café, checking out the menu, waiting to be seated. Some obvious tourists are milling outside the shops, window-shopping. They are easy to spot in their printed shirts, golf shorts and sunglasses. No toothpicks dangling from their mouths. No jeans. No interest in blending with the clientele. Loafers.

I notice the twins, Aaron and David, coming out of the café. David spots us driving by and delivers that patented, passive head bob. He's stopped by a girl roughly his age who is passing by. Aaron waits a step behind and digs into his pocket for his cell phone. Meanwhile, the girl nervously runs her index finger back and forth through her charm necklace, listening intently. Once again, David, the charmer, has a rapt audience.

"That's Paulette Johnstone. She works for the catering company that we sometimes employ for weddings. Good worker. Pretty. A little flirtatious as you can see."

Tessa opens her mouth to add more commentary, then holds back with a concocted smile.

"Probably looking for a little attention," I said.

"Like we all do at some time or another," she adds. "It's funny to be on the observation end." Tessa's looks back as we pass by. "That ingredient of my life seems so long ago. I don't remember ever being that way."

"Thanks for shooting down my best efforts these past two days," I scold her.

"You know what I mean, Kevin. It's that first time learning the sexual ropes, getting a boy to notice you, then keeping his attention long enough to see him again."

"Works for me," I surmise, "but go ahead and keep digging your hole."

Hipp's Grocery is set in from the street with a modest combination gravel-asphalt parking zone. A pimply-faced bag boy busses the empty carts that rattle and clatter.

"There it is, I think," Tessa points at an iron gate adjacent to a recycle service center.

I signal and wait for another gravel truck to pass. The grocery store extends lengthwise to the storage facility and we pull into the nearest space.

"Good timing, Doctor. Look." Tessa calls my attention to a curvy middle-aged woman wearing a haircutter's smock. Her coif is spiky, salt and pepper, with exaggerated dark sideburn whips that curl toward her cheeks. She chews gum opened-mouthed in pace with her stride, each leg swings outward with effort to give the impression of a parading penguin. A half-smoked cigarette dangles in her hand.

"Let's grab her before she collapses," I joke sarcastically.

"Shh, here she comes," whispers Tessa.

Alice takes one last drag and flips the butt onto the pavement, taking an intentional step to crush the smoldering stub, but she misses by a good shoe length. She comes to Tessa's side and leans in.

"Hi, Tessa. I'm on a break and got a call from Nick. He asked me to open up for you at the storage locker."

The remnants of her inhaled cigarette smoke trails into our faces leaving the vehicle's interior a filmy gray.

"That's right, Alice. I want to look at some old files on my sister's case." She adds, "This is Dr. Kevin Michaels from California. He's a friend visiting the resort."

"Howdy," I say, extending my hand in front of Tessa.

"I hear that it's pretty hot and dry out there. The news is always about fires and quakes."

Her eyes narrow and she gives me a fake smile. The West Coast must be as alien as Mars to these people.

"We get our share of hot, but it's not that bad," I entertain in my best defense mode. "All summers are dry. It only rains in the winter months." Don't scold or lecture. I remind myself. "It was a good time for me to get away."

"I'll say," she rejoins, her expression is soft, spiritual. "This is God's Country."

I reflect on how ironic that God's Country is protected by unrelenting, blood thirsty mosquitoes and mind-numbing humidity. Not wanting to push the envelope, I add, "I'm not a stranger to the lake country. I used to work the old church youth camp back in the day."

"You mean you knew Tessa's sister, too? Now that's a coincidence. She was a couple years older than me, but I remember her. It's such a sad story. I never found out anything else about her." Her voice trails off, staring straight ahead, focusing on nothing.

Tessa interjects. "Look, Alice. I'm on an extended lunch break and need to get back to the resort. Is there any chance I can get that file pretty soon?"

"As luck would have it, I have the key." She dangles the ring near her puffy face and points.

"The last time Nick sent me in to retrieve a box was last Spring. He's notorious with wild goose chases and dead ends. As I recall, to the far left I found the sixties and seventies. They might not be in any order, but the decades are pretty much intact. I wasted the noon hour digging around for nothing."

She shakes her head, looks down the street, then back at Tessa. "Good luck. I'll unlock and take the key with me. I need to go into Hipp's for some cigarettes, but I was told to stay here. If you finish, you know the drill. Put the pad lock back on."

She looks to me.

"It's nice to meet you, Dr. Michaels. Hope you're having a good stay."

She gives me a quizzical look as her cell phone chimes. "That's Nick's way of checking up on me." She pulls it out of her smock pocket and toddles away.

"Well, let's have a go." I begin to open my car door and Tessa does the same.

The rail gate crawls on screeching tracks. There is no alarm system. Neither are there any motion detectors. This is a plaintiff's nightmare. Inside, the storage unit is standard-sized. There are rows of gray metallic shelves fitted for office boxes but cluttered with some cardboard files and other office property such as typewriters, ledgers, and desk lamps. It brought me back to old hospital morgues where tissue containers had been permanently displaced with withered, mummified remains barely immersed in decades' old fixative. Some of these boxes, though, are in mint condition as if shoved or slid into the musty darkness for later filing. The stench of rat urine permeates from the rear of the room. I find a light switch and flip on a dimming small wattage bulb above our heads.

"This ought to be hella fun," Tessa chides. She crosses her arms in front and rubs her upper arms briskly. "Remind me to double shower when we get back to the resort."

"You won't have to be reminded. I'll be waiting."

I shove boxes aside to make a pathway toward the pre-determined era. In the back space are plastic office crates of padded manila folders and large zip lock bags containing such items as clothing, combs, and even a couple ancient handguns with wooden grips. A boy's mangled bicycle is suspended from a two-by-four stud by a large nail, the front wheel bent in half. I'm hard-pressed not to believe the potential degree of domestic violence is being kept secret in this quiet community. Although identifying any or all absconded evidence might prove demanding, it speaks of the details that are held for further reference, no matter how minute the safeguards.

I hold my breath and squat next to the boxes pushed under the first shelving units. Out of pure luck, these are the ones we've been looking for. Unfortunately, they are in disarray. Some of them face outward with legible case numbers whereas others are unlabeled. This might be quite challenging. Misfiled or misplaced, even missing. All three possibilities come charging at me like startled rats escaping a flashlight beam.

Some boxes have been shelved with their labels facing to the back. Others are crossed out with a black Sharpie and relabeled with handwritten numeric. If this discrepancy on any other cases make their way to court, the defense attorneys will have a heyday. Gathering my bearings, I kneel to read the labels on the second shelf from the floor.

Moments later, Tessa yells back to me.

"How's it going? Pardon me if I don't seem too anxious to join you."

"Still looking," I call out, shoving and lifting boxes aside. "I think I've at least hit upon the correct era."

The acrid foulness of mice droppings is encompassing, and I cover my mouth and nose in hope of a protective psychological barrier. With my other hand, I push the boxes and use my arm to clear away the unkempt ledges looking for that elusive "Garner" label.

Success. A boot box with her name and case file #66-206. Kicking up a layer of settled dust in the shuffling and sliding it toward the light has me feeling like a fireman during a second story rescue.

"Hurray," I yell out. "Here's a box with Erin's name on it. Is there anything else?"

"It's been years since I last checked. There used to be a zip-lock gallon plastic bag with her comb and a few hair berets. They might have placed all the items in the one box to save space."

"I didn't find anything like that down below, including the top shelves." I hold up the last box to my face. "Nada, I'm coming out."

With the small box in both hands, I hustle out through the shadows to meet her. She is flipping through old files sitting in the plastic office crates by the open gate.

"Look, Kevin. Here's a ledger from September of the year she went missing. There's no record of anyone taking a call for a missing person, but that might be in another book. Why I imagined this was going to be so easy is beyond me."

She blows dust off another book and wipes her hands on her thighs.

"I'm in about the same boat," I said. "Some outdated hospital storerooms I've seen keep records boxed like this too."

I place the salvaged box down in front of her. "Be my guest."

She reads aloud. "Garner, Erin #66-206."

Her shoulders curl forward as she cups her hands over her mouth and deeply sighs.

"All the times that I've been searching, it never gets easier. I'm sorry to drag you into this, Kevin. I truly am."

"Hey. It's all right. If my assistance gets us over another obstacle, then this will all be worth it. You are welcome to have some private time. I can step outside for some fresh air."

As if opening a precious gift, Tessa gently lifts the cover and sets it aside. Slowly, she begins to bring items out of the box and spreads them on the cold floor: a coin purse, a set of car keys, a hairbrush, an address book, a few bobby pins, and a wallet-sized photo album.

"This is what they recovered at the scene. Her belongings were dumped on the car seat and the car was later sold to the hardware owner's son who eventually totaled it. All we have left of my sister is right here."

I pick up the wallet and thumb through the first few sheets. There is her class photo which I remembered receiving, except mine had a hand-written, heart-shaped design on the back with the words "Never Forget Me" in the center. Back in the camp days, Erin wore her hair pinned back and scarfed, but in the picture, her hair is straight and long. Her eyes smile back and my throat swells thinking about her loss. The backside of the holder is her high school identification card and the school stamp. Next is a medical insurance card with the flip side being her driver's license. There is a folded dollar bill on the very next sheet. Pasted on the backside is a family photo.

"Is this you?" I ask, handing it over to Tessa and pointing to the curly-haired girl seated next to Erin.

Tessa stifles a weak gasp.

"It was Easter Sunday. Mother always dressed us alike because we were only a year apart. Maybe she'd wished we were twins."

She pauses to study the images.

"Look at that mop of hair on my head. That's certainly a long way from graying, and short."

She takes the insert and carefully teases out the photo.

"From now on, this belongs to me," she said sternly. "Boxed up for years. It's time to show them off again."

It brought back lost memories of how Cassie died: unable to breathe, tachycardia, organ shutdown. Three months after her death I, too, packed all her belongings to give away and stuffed photographs too painful to review into empty shoeboxes. The last time I went into my attic, the stack was still there, covered in dust and dead moths. I, too, had buried the person and stashed the life into storage.

"What about the sheriff?" I inquire. "How come he won't release this particular box to you?"

"Sheriff Carlson died about five years ago. There's no interest in this case. It's still on record as open because he never got around to filing it as 'Closed.' Things change slowly here, Kevin."

She opens her purse, brings out a brown wallet bulging with credit cards, and carefully fits the faded photo in an open slot near the back.

"Let's leave. It's too discouraging. There really aren't any more clues to chase."

She stands and brushes off her knees.

"Each passing year doesn't get any easier. I've prepared myself hundreds of times for the worst news even though it's been decades. Remember when milk cartons had pictures of missing children on the back side? She was one of those. Here's the kicker. Erin was allergic to dairy products. How peculiar is that?"

I lock the gate as instructed and step out into blinding sun and welcoming fresh breeze. There's not much theft around Wasoon, and it's not surprising if these random cars are unlocked with keys still in the ignition. Seatbelts are for show within the city limits, so a cop doesn't ticket you. What's the point of securing a storage facility containing legal documents? I fire-up the truck expecting to head back to the resort, but she insists on making one last stop.

"About two miles out on Route 52 is a memorial plaque for my sister. It didn't seem right to have a tombstone, so we asked the county to construct a small billboard, with a nameplate in her honor. Only local events are advertised on it. You'll see."

The warm gusty wind forces the rental into a sideways skid and if it weren't for the narrow, painted bike lane, we'd ride the grassy edges on this banked curve. Treetops undulate at our passing. An old farmer is valiantly puttering on a late-model John Deere tractor, pulling a rake load of dried ditch grass while holding down the top of his cap with his hand. There's a hint of freshly mowed alfalfa, reminding me of stifling dairy barns bunched with manure-crusted cattle, their tails whipping at the pesky bot flies. This lifestyle is so humble and original by way of comparison to my life or to when I was growing up. Back then, it all seemed so much like work.

Tessa signals me to slow down and I notice the billboard that she mentioned, stained white by pigeon droppings, the aging wood frame stands yellowed and dried.

"Pull in and we'll walk," she instructs.

I slow to allow a grain truck to zip past.

"This will only take a minute or two," she informs me as if she were distributing coupons door-to-door.

"Take as long as you like," I remind her. "It's important to let her know that we still care."

Tessa holds her visor cap snuggly onto her head and steps out. We dodge potholes and trample over marble-sized cockleburs that embed the soles of my cross trainers like Velcro. That shoe inventor never lived up here before fame. Dried foxtails are beholden to spear seedlings into any type of sock. In a minute we solemnly stand at the scaly wooded structure supporting a metallic plaque with the inscription "In loving memory of Erin. She always wanted to tell us something."

I look to Tessa.

"It's like an amusing reminder," I say as I lean over to pull out the speared weeds. "That's how I remember her, too. She kept us all on schedule."

"That's the point, I guess," she replies, her head droops, her chin quivers. "This is where I learned my organization skills. It was my idea for the quotation. Do you think it's corny?"

Another semi rumbles by and honks. Tessa waves.

"That's Vincent Bode, the trucking magnate of Wasoon County. He wants to marry me in the worst way, and I can't fight him off much longer. Believe me, I've tried. We both have this ticking biological time bomb. Vincent is always bragging the third time is the charm. It's our little inside joke."

She stoops over and pulls out a green foxtail head, nibbles on the soft stem between her front teeth, and looks forlornly down the road at the distant truck.

"Vincent is on the fast track: fast trucks, fast cars, and faster woman in every city. He guarantees me an interesting lifestyle. I'll grant you that."

Tessa hooks her arm through mine.

"Isn't lake life fun?" reflecting on the plaque, meditating. "It's a damn miniature soap opera."

I hear a meadowlark's throaty territorial call and catch it gliding along a nearby fencepost where it alights and then lifts into the gales. Before long, it's twenty yards away finding another post to rest on. Cotton ball-shaped clouds form mountainous shadows over the land and race across the fields.

"And that's the end of this story," she laments. "Walter Cronkite used to call it that way."

"Erin's story is still unwritten," I remind her.

"I don't know where else to turn. There doesn't seem to be a direction. I deeply appreciate your coming along with me, but I can't keep you from your work any longer."

"Tessa, Erin was my friend, too."

I have the urge to tell her how much I care, but instead, I hold back to allow us this private moment.

"Tell me once again where she was prior to the disappearance. Perhaps something will click."

"Well, she was just off work. She clerked at Hipp's Groceries and had called to tell mom that she 'll be home in about an hour. She needed to buy gas and collect some college prep materials from her friend, Norma. She drove a used Ford Fairlane, our Uncle Billy's. He's been dead for decades. That piece of junk digested both gas and oil in equal parts. Anyway, that's all the information we had. The filling station's attendant, Ray Perkins, remembered seeing her because she was waving to him."

Tessa softly bites her lip, internalizing, holding back an emotional flood.

"I could tell you that's the end or create a story about how Ray had a criminal past like they sometimes do in the movies. The fact of the matter is that Erin is still missing."

"Where is Ray Perkins these days?" I inquire.

"Up here, you work all your mundane life at some trapped job, then retire." Her voice trails off. "There's an unwritten rule that you will eventually become nursing home bait, ready or not. Poor old Ray worked at that filling station up to a couple years ago. The mailman discovered him stroked out behind the counter, paralyzed on his left side, unable to speak. His family placed him in the Vet's Home over in Red Lake. He's Sioux. Sixth generation. Red Lake is an Indian Reservation."

I receive constant convalescent care inquiries from next of kin who call when irrational and litigious. I try to explain that an autopsy cannot accurately address standards of care although I'm certain the burdening care was questionable. That last comment I never dare reveal to them.

"So, you're saying it's pointless to see him?"

"Not pointless, but pretty much a waste of time," she replies. "Human leads dwindled down to nothing years ago, Kevin. It's so frustrating. You are looking at the most interested party." She spits out the withered grass stem, but the wind blows it back in her face. "Damn it!"

She sits back onto the grassy slope. The ever-present breeze combs the tips of green into horizontal planes. I move in next to her, give her a gentler squeeze, and wait for her to relax. Whips of feathery cirrus clouds sweep above us like an artist's stroke.

"One thing for sure, I'm getting an abundance of hugs lately," she said wearily and rests her head on the hillside.

Ten minutes later we trudge back to the company truck. I open the passenger door for her to hop in. An energetic horn blast comes upon us from behind like the unsuspecting fire engine siren in city traffic. A large semi-truck slows to the wide of the road, the air brakes squealing the giant rig to a halt. The man she had acknowledged moments ago grabs his cap from the dashboard and exits the cab.

"I knew he couldn't stand the competition," she moans. "Be nice and don't chew him up too badly. Save his untrusting, toothy smile."

Despite his wiry frame and with biceps as thick as my calves, trucker Vincent Bode struts toward us.

"Hey, Tessa. Are you out doing some bird watching?"

His face and sleeveless arms are the color of dark maple syrup, bulging veins cord through both forearms. His face is wolfish with a high forehead and deep-set eyes. Vincent's jeans are faded and thinned beyond modesty as, I'm sure, he relishes. He closes in and stoops down to meet her at face level.

"I'm Vincent, Tessa's fiancé. We haven't worked out the details yet, right darlin'?"

He extends his hand. His vice-like grip is alpha male type.

"Right," Tessa beams. "Vincent, this is Dr. Michaels from California. The Olson brothers asked him to do an autopsy on Ole."

Vincent chortles, shrugs, then straightens and places both hands in his pockets.

"Old man Olson agreed to this? I mean, an autopsy. Isn't that where you gut them like a deer? What's that supposed to tell ya? Hell. You can't bring 'em back."

"Some people want to know," I tell him, feeling my body posture becoming a little rigid.

"I used to spend summers here as a teenager at the Bible Camp. Tessa is giving me a little tour."

"That must have been some time ago," he says with a tight expression, not fully committed. "The camp has been closed twenty years or so, I guess."

I look over to Tessa who is shifting uncomfortably between the two of us. Vincent and I are a far cry from ever being pals. Crusted bedsores come to mind.

"Before the twins were born, the resort was known as Ole's Fishing Shack," she clarifies. "From then to the present is like day and night."

"I'll say," he harrumphs. "We get a batch of high rollers through Wasoon these days. It's a little too uppity for my blood, but I do like the Country Club. They got good music on weekends, not to mention to-die-for margaritas."

"See. I told you," Tessa taps me on the forearm.

Vincent chuckles. "If you are not a drinking man yet, by the time you're finished with her, you damned will be. Those two brothers are the cause of sundry immemorable nights for me."

I check my watch. "Tessa, I've got to get back to check my voice messages. In the meantime, I'll take you back to the resort."

"That'll be great," she says, picking up my signal. "Thanks."

"Well, it was nice meeting you, Doc. I got to get back on the road myself with another grain delivery. I'm heading to the harbor for a delivery of seed corn, but I'll be back by early morning. It's a quick turnaround job. You take care, Tessa."

He tips the bill of his cap toward her and saunters back toward his idling Peterbilt. Once inside, he slowly maneuvers back onto the road. Two horn blasts and four downshifts later, my neighborhood competition is already a quarter mile away.

"He's awfully nice," I entertain, leaving myself open for criticism.

Tessa was not paying attention, but instead was fixated on a Meadowlark resting on her sister's plaque behind us.

"I'm sorry. You were saying?"

"I said that Vincent was a good guy. He's a little too reserved for you, though. Are you with me again? Earth to Tessa?"

"Yes. I guess." Her glumness is obvious, and she shrugs her shoulders.

"I grew up with the Bode clan. Vincent is a year younger, but he's never changed. Believe me. Ever. The Bode's were always truckers, so it's not unusual at all to see Vincent follow the plan."

"It's not all professional courtesy, if that's what you're thinking," I remind her. "I don't go around embracing my clients on a regular basis. That's bordering on sexual harassment to some hierarchy."

"Am I considered a client, Doctor?"

"It's more like the other way around," I said. "You have an open compassion for certain things that others think trivial and I'm totally envious of those qualities. My life has become too superficial, not cynical, but in a sense, more skeptical. I've spent way too much time plodding from case to case, city to city, looking for more layers of decay to hide under."

"You're lonely, aren't you?" she sighs. "Me too."

My previous work travels often brought me through rural areas such as this. There are country highways, pickups with camper shells, motorcyclists without a care in the world, people pulled off to the side taking selfies, hikers with backpacks thumbing for a ride, wildflowers galore, grape vines...and now, here I sit, like one of those tourists on a grand trip.

To the west the sun pokes out from behind a large cloud mass like a curious stranger in the next room, and I can immediately feel the instant warmth. I begin to straighten loose strands of Tessa's hair from her face and forehead. She is dozing, the fatigue of her sister's loss holds lock on her soul. There might be no new answers but, if that happens, do I play a role in the outcome? Surrogate or substitute?

Overhead, more cumulus clouds are re-grouping into rumbling gray-blue masses. If by chance, humidity and summer are not dissipating yet. This country is so beautiful. The frenetic push for buds, then germination, then seeds, all taking a brief vacation from their duties. The calm before the storm, cycling year after year. Erin's timelessness is like that shaded peak overlooking the lake that Tessa and I enjoyed.

These past two weeks, I, too, have been feeling fatigued, both physically and mentally. It's because of the travel, but I can't rule out a little depression coming on again. The signs are there: insomnia, lack of appetite, a pounding migraine behind my eyes, uncertain about casework details. I mentioned to Tessa about the need to check my voicemails, but that isn't true. Not only is the languid sunshine warming me, but it also feels as if I am running a low-grade fever, leaving my joints stiff and sore like I had been bounced off a three-story building. I always keep in shape on the road by over-exercising and I consider my immunity levels are typically good, except for an occasional flu virus. But three weeks ago, I traveled to Midland, Texas, at the request of a bereaved family who lost a son. Conversely, he had lost them. Mental issues. Runaway. Living in homeless shelters. DOA.

When I first saw this emaciated gaunt young man, he had been deceased for at least five days. The family had exhausted their efforts for a coroner's investigation. The county eventually declared it a natural death. Then I got involved. His father signed the authorization and I agreed to do the case. The funeral home where the body was held in refrigeration had allowed me to use their prep room on a late Friday. I nearly missed my connecting flight, was late on arrival, and had lost directions to the funeral home. The director was pissed. We hardly said ten words to each other. Mentally and physically, I wasn't even close to being one hundred percent.

The decedent's brief history was easily foretold. Unshaven with bold, dark tattoos on both arms. I knew for sure the creases of those heavily pigmented areas held injection site scars. They left him as is, bagged and sent him to the funeral home where I set up shop. Copper studs adorned the multiple piercings: both nipples, the tongue, and earlobes. I suspected he was Gothic and gay, but the family never opened this delicate topic. His father was the esteemed high school principal and city councilman. Discussion was out of the question.

Frothy blood-tinged bubbles exuded from the decedent's nostrils; a characteristic sign of pulmonary edema brought on by sudden cardiac failure. His upper torso was the color and tenseness of ripening grape skins and his cherry-colored corneas bulged beyond the edematous eyelids. According to the report, he was headfirst, sagging halfway off a urine-stained mattress. To make matters worse, he'd regurgitated and passed out from alcohol poisoning.

About an hour into the dissection, I noticed a pinpoint red spot on my latex gloves. Damn, I must have nicked it accidentally. I ripped it off and discovered the puncture site from which my life was dribbling like a leaky kitchen faucet. AIDS. Hepatitis. MRSA.

I feverishly milked my hand to bleed and raced to the sink and soap dispenser. Rub. Rub. Lather. Again. Rub. Rub. Lather. Fifteen minutes later, the bloody water in the basin became faintly pink, then clear. How? When? This was all a pointless matter of importance now. Without knowing, I delivered myself a death sentence, living with a chronic condition of fevers and prescribed medication for the duration. Succumbing to eventual liver cirrhosis, or even cancer combined with immunocompromised pneumonia.

I was in denial and didn't report for a titer check until the following week. The waiting agony consumed me like starving mosquitoes. I'd have to sell my home to afford proper care and insurance won't cover the mounting hospital costs. My neighbors will avoid me. What do I tell Tessa?

Yesterday's message stated my test results are still pending. Can I come in at my earliest convenience to draw more blood? To me, that meant failing the exam. I clearly knew the risk potentials. In a grim sense, my outcome was a carbon copy of all those families that I've tended to in the last thirty-five years and the past was catching up to me.

When Tessa and I had returned to the truck, I sneaked into my pocket when she wasn't looking, took out the packet of aspirin and popped the blue capsules into the back of my mouth to swallow. Just battling with some unsuspecting midwestern bugs, I tried to convince myself.

CHAPTER NINE

On the ride back to Wasoon, Tessa's head falls back on the headrest. It doesn't take but a few minutes for her eyes to close and she is out. The recent flood of dashed hopes, the pent-up guilt and loss are all too familiar. We pass the local Dairy Queen and I turn in. A little chocolate swirl will help ease the pain. I kill the engine and wait for her to wake. She jerks at the sound of a slamming car door and bolts up.

"Lunch?" I ask.

From across the street, we watch a couple of young girls in an endeavor to play tennis in the blustery weather. Most of the game consists of retrieving netted balls spiraling toward the neighboring court as if magnetized with each gust. There are medium-sized cracks in the asphalt along the baseline and the sagging net defines the degree of importance Wasoon city places on public recreation.

I felt an opportunistic loss for these two girls, knowing that to the generation preceding them and following them, tennis is near the bottom of the entertainment totem pole. But with some instruction, it can be more than a social pastime. Their meager rallies toy like a game board where an arrow is spun and then a plastic figure advances until the ball needs to be picked up again. Court time is a foreign term. Each girl grips the racquet handle in the middle and flails with soft lobs to get the worn ball back into the other court. I have this nagging urge to rush over to their rescue, if only to give them a two-minute lesson on net play and not destroy rural images of Wimbledon any longer.

I am beginning to feel better. The aspirin kicked in and my lethargy has dissipated. We sit on top of the picnic table under the perfect shade of a buckeye tree. The hazy, golden gaffs of daylight are like faded outlines of our shapes in the concrete platform.

"Do you play any sports?" she asks through a lick and frozen mouthful.

"I do a fair share of middle-distance running and biking to keep in shape. It's hard to get involved with team sports, not to mention that my work takes me away from local events."

I lean back on my hands. "It's passively boring at times, but I'm not the Country Club type. There aren't enough hours to dedicate in practice, much less finding like-minded souls. Besides, you've already seen how terrific a swimmer I am."

Tessa offers up a guilt-free smile, the first one today, and a lingering cat-like stretch.

"I was only using one leg, Captain," she wisecracks. "Some chickens swim better than you."

"Well, at least I achieved the rock," I remind her.

"That you did, I must admit." She hesitates. "When are we going back?"

"Looks like I have some free time coming up," I respond. "Do you have any plans?"

She finishes eating her cone and wipes her sticky hands and lips in a fluid movement, her voice is light and energetic.

"Pick a time. I'm entertaining a client. Yours truly. Chalk it up to business expenses."

Her eyes become slit-like as she bunches up the napkin. "I know why I like ice cream so much. It relaxes me. I love smashing the soggy cone with my tongue like a kid."

"You said it. Like a kid. Somehow, I'm going to have to teach you some manners."

Suddenly, the Wasoon Funeral Chapel van whizzes by on the highway heading east out of town, the windows rolled down. It's Roland wearing a dark blue sportscoat.

"There he goes for another pick-up," she motions. "Roland always wears that coat when he has to recover a body. He says that it's his lucky jacket...economically speaking."

She hands me an extra napkin.

"I hear that Priscilla Jennings has been ailing. She is one of the original Wasoon Daughters of the Revolution. They sponsor a host of charitable events each year: Tuesday raffles, Christmas crafts, Spring auctions."

"It sounds a like the Soroptimist's Club where I live," I remark.

"They have tried in vain to recruit me, but I don't feel old enough yet," she replies. "Is that cruel? I mean, baking cookies? Hosting teas? Monthly meetings?"

She pretends to hold an imaginary demitasse to her mouth. "That was more Erin stuff."

"It's closer than you think," I joke.

Tessa needles me in the side.

"Thanks a lot. You're a big help, old man."

"Point taken," I laugh, defending my ribs and vulnerable mid-section from further attacks.

I lean over and kiss her in a moment of weakness, but the impulse is strong. I taste her warm chocolate breath on my face and my hand cups her chin. Please don't let this end too soon. But there's still guilt, and I need to own up about my infection concerns.

"That's one more thing I like about ice cream." I dab the corner of her mouth.

"This is not a professional courtesy in the slightest," she coos. "The next time might be, though. Better be careful how you receive them."

"I'll be waiting hopefully," I respond.

In my mind, we had skip-stoned into another phase of this relationship, seemingly necessary, but not out of necessity. I can't say that there's any reluctance on my behalf. From the beginning, I have been attracted to Tessa. She's outspoken to a tee. Her exuberant demeanor toward patrons was Cassie-like. She is a step-into-a-crowded-room-and-there-she-stood beauty for me. More than that, it's like a mid-air collision with my slow to evolve paper kite emotions. I am vulnerable, admittedly so, but available and terminally alone. That seemed to be my perfect combination until now.

"If you don't have plans for this Saturday, I'd like to invite you to a wingding at the resort. It's an all-class reunion for the Wasoon High School. I suspect that a measurable group of locals will be there. Perhaps even a few from the Twin Cities will show up."

She tugs on my shirtsleeve.

"You will be my official escort."

"Well, I am available, and I am staying nearby. But I've been to one or two of these in the past and been subjected to the fact that no one brings his or her respectively bored spouses. It's that high school mentality conglomeration. The old cliques get together and fabricate lifestyles. First boyfriends go through the wonder-ifs. I felt uncomfortable at my wife's twentieth and vowed never to put myself into that situation again."

We stand and walk to the truck. I open her door and contemplate how situations like this can go south in a hell basket.

"I guess my insecurity got the best of me then. But if you're in need of a male escort, I'm all in."

Tessa laughs. "Gee. Your reunions sound like fun. This will be a Sunday picnic by comparison."

I decide I need to shed some light and exorcise an explanation.

"Stupid me. I got into a shouting spiel with my wife at the open bar. My level of alcohol, and believe me, I was shooting down champagne like Pepsi, stoked me to let her know about who I thought was fast becoming an overfriendly male classmate. Earlier, I learned that he was divorced. Twice! The Dick acted the role to a tee by charming a group of her female friends. He was in his element. I wasn't introduced as her husband, but I managed to slur out a few drunken words saying we were happily married. Ha. Ha. The more they cooed and giggled, the angrier I became. I was fueled like a jet fighter. Long story short, we argued until we arrived home. Two weeks later, she went into premature labor, became toxemic, and died."

Tessa listened attentively and placed her hand on mine.

"I was an undivided ass and have never forgiven myself," I said. "She told me to grow up. I argued there weren't a handful of men in that room that had yet to grow up, myself included. At least my rants were legitimate, or so I tried to convince myself."

Tessa tosses her waste into the trash bin.

"Don't stop now. This is getting interesting."

I exhale loudly, reliving the frustration, reliving the incident, reliving the aggravation.

"She insisted on staying and would catch a ride back to the hotel. I felt like excess baggage. The whole scene was so insane. I sulked the entire evening at the bar."

Tessa briskly rubs my back as if to reassure me that it wasn't my fault. "Hey, partner. You won't be on the receiving end of any repercussions like that in the village of Wasoon because most of them will retire by ten o'clock. Parking zones for fifth wheelers will be totally full for the weekend. They'll be loading up with Seagram's Seven and Screwdrivers beginning at noon. You will see more men with hair on their upper lip than on their heads. Women will starve themselves for two months in advance of D-day. It's a genuine hoot. By the way, I'm presently single."

I had calmed down and began to massage my forehead.

"I apologize. You really got me wound up."

"Totally my fault," she apologizes. "Let's change the subject."

"Okay," I said. "How about lover-boy, Vincent? Does he have territorial dibs on you."

"That's what he thinks," she eases back. Her response is like shifting a cycle into cruise gear. "Vincent's domain and mine don't collide. He's all talk. Trust me. It's a trucker's talent."

She sits back in the truck, and I gentlemanly draw the seat belt across her lap.

"Thanks," she adds and grabs the fastener.

"The answer to your original question again, yes, I'll be glad to escort you. Any specific time that I should expect you?"

"Be ready by six-thirty," she instructs. "People up here don't like to eat late."

"Meaning…" I asked, waiting.

"Meaning food is a priority over booze. They want to be fed. You saw how that turned out?"

We pull up to the main office building and I help get her attaché out of the car. To my surprise, I now have a few good things going my way and no overt animosity from the brothers for the autopsy. The diagnostic results are going to be conclusive, there is a woman who's interested in me, plus, I have a date. Take it slow. This is a learning curve. Also, my febrile lethargy is subsiding, which is a good sign, unless I am entering a latent phase only to spike a high temperature later. Today, that issue isn't going to stalk me.

I walk back into my bungalow and notice the stack of requested medical records had arrived. Someone from the front desk must have placed them on my desk. Earthbound again, I am reminded of my initial reason for being in Wasoon and without delay sort through the top few sheets of medical and clinical history. This chore brings up nothing out of the ordinary. Unfortunately, I'm distracted. My thoughts keep drifting back to Tessa.

Was meeting her as random as it seemed? This whole area summons memories like textured pages of a book. I am being drawn to the hospitality of the people, neighbors with their patented hellos, truckers honking greetings, even managing to kiss a total stranger. I sure hope the opportunity presents itself again and again. I'm not fighting nostalgia, but rather, succumbing to homesickness.

"Screw it."

Like a teenager with nagging homework assignments or prodding parents about my private life, I close the files and walk out the door. If my days in little Wasoon are pre-measured, why am I waiting to be spoon-fed? Too much time is being spent answering other people's concerns. Let's test the curative powers of this territory.

In a matter of minutes, I'm standing outside the cabin door, cinching up the drawstring on my trail shorts, and stuffing a five-dollar bill and cabin key in my hind pocket. I trot past the bocce ball court with a show-off-style, pick-up-the-pace jog, then past the tenth tee and the resort perimeter. In another two hundred yards, I am hustling past the security gate a little winded, but not going to let any of those *old* people notice. The paved bike lane out of the resort is wide enough, but I prefer to stay on the gravel edge. The packed stones pulverizing beneath my shoes sound more like the approach of a marching infantry. Black bear and wolves beware. Rabid human on the loose.

Coming from the opposite direction is the Wasoon funeral van with the ever-present Roland. He gives me a courteous nod but doesn't slow down to talk. I hope dear old Roland isn't making a house call. At the first turn, I veer right onto a fire trail. Nothing but trees ahead as far as my feet will take me. With Norway pine groves lining the packed granite, I suck in the scented beauty and allow my stoic self a smug smile. Ten minutes in and I stop at a ridge-way clearing, the sweat purging out of the deep furrows of my forehead. I hunch over, my panting pounds in exaggerated gasps. Slow down. Remember, you need to follow the same route back. In the distance I can discern one of the roads Tessa and I had traveled yesterday and to familiarize myself, I decide to head in that same direction. My comfort zone is like a one hundred eighty-degree turn. Hardpan sandstone and fallen tree stumps are no match for my stamina. It's probably psychological, but nonetheless, any physical signs of an impending malady are as physically absent as that frozen strawberry fruit bar I had been fantasizing about for the past twenty minutes.

On my round trip back to the resort, I pass the deputy's vehicle parked at registration. First, it was the funeral director, now it's the deputy. Happenstance? I decide to walk in and inquire with Tessa. Deputy Lundgren is leaning over the counter taking notes on a small yellow pad. Tessa happens to be on hold with a phone call and signals me to come over. Lundgren acts aloof and fiddles with his pen.

"Yes. That's right. About nine o'clock, after cocktails and supper. Her husband noticed that the door was unlocked. No, not that I know of. This weekend's school reunion festival. Hold a minute, please?"

She cups the receiver.

"Kevin. One of our tenants is missing. Her name is Darlene Gabbart. She came up from St. Paul for the class reunion. I'm talking to the Lake County Police right now."

Back to the caller.

"I'm sorry. You were asking?"

Lundgren says, "Nice old gal. Class of 67. I'd comment on her spiciness, but that's an understatement. She had a potty mouth. Some of the things she called me. Can't say I didn't deserve some of it. Most people wouldn't think that she was an ordained Presbyterian minister. Guess this reunion was a spiritual vacation of sorts."

"What did she look like?" thinking that I might have seen her.

"Well, I'd say she was heavy set, but that might get me into a boatload of trouble." He pinches the cap's visor on the top of his head. "To be politically correct, let's call it two twenty-five plus."

I feel it incumbent to oblige him with an uncomfortable smirk. Dilated capillaries web his cheeks, eyes glassy and bloodshot, he habitually licks the inside of his lips. The obvious morning hangover still in its drying out stages.

"I don't mean to be caddy, Doc. This resort has at least ten reunions of some sort each summer. There's usually at least one idiot that's MIA who eventually calls us to report they're fine. And they are usually surprised that anyone cared enough to call us."

"But you still follow-up on these cases, I'm sure," I blurt out, shifting the casual conversation to a pointed thought.

"Obviously," widening his stance and giving me an arrogant chuckle like he wasn't going to have me tell him procedure.

Tessa disconnects. "There is no APB yet. Let's give it another six hours. That will be a full twenty-four. As far as they're concerned, it's best to wait until it becomes official."

"That's not very reassuring," I forewarn. "I guess my logic is hospital emergency-based."

"I can appreciate your concern, Doc," Lundgren adds. "We're not spinning our wheels. Chances are she is around somewhere, unharmed, taking a stroll, and lost her way."

"Who came up here with her?" I ask.

"Her husband, Carl," Tessa replies. She nervously taps on the countertop. "Word like this can become dour gloom in a short period. It could put a damper on the weekend festivities. Mr. Gabbert just now went back to his cabin to check his cell phone for messages."

The deputy gathers up his pen and pad.

"Well, let's leave it at that, then, Tessa. Until further notice, Darlene is not missing. Keep me posted."

He speaks into his collared intercom.

"This is Lundgren leaving the resort. Stand down on the missing persons. Check the local Quick Stop at the outskirts of Wasoon and the security guard at the resort entrance. Get back to me. Folks want to know if Mrs. Gabbert has been seen. Do you copy?"

"Ten-four."

Lundgren leaves us standing alone.

"That wasn't very helpful," I tell her. "It sounds as if we're overly worried."

Tessa looks up.

"I get a little fretful with these older people. They save all year for this special weekend and it doesn't take too much for them to be dissuaded from coming back next year."

"I hear you," I said. "The deputy seemed too impersonal."

"You saw him when he's practically sober," she tacks on. "Out of the substation, he's plenty personal."

I watch as the deputy and Roland speak to each other outside for a few minutes, then get into their respective vehicles. The Wasoon funeral van leaves empty and is followed by Lundgren. Seconds later, the driveway is invaded by another busload of visitors. The first passenger out is an elderly man in golf attire: Bermuda shorts, polo shirt, visor, and sunglasses. He lugs a carry-on in one hand and secures an empty plastic cocktail glass with the other. Two cackling women wearing printed floral Aloha shirts and shoulder strap bags follow.

"Let's hope this happy fellow is distracted and he doesn't see the town's funeral director and constable drive off," Tessa says, inching closer to me, as the twenty-some passengers descend upon the guest registrar.

"Are we still up for this?" I ask. Checking my watch.

"Absolutely," she quickly speaks up. "We'll hike up the complimentary beverage minimum to two. It will be all right."

"I'm available to help out if need be."

"Thanks, Kevin. I appreciate the offer. We'll keep them dining and dancing. Most people will never know. Besides, I'm praying Darlene will show up for last call."

"I hope to be in my bed long before that," I tell her bluntly.

"Who's dating whom?" Her eyebrows rise.

"Well, you never told me which 'Class of' I'm supposed to represent."

"When you mull about the crowd, select anyone with matching hair color to yours, then add ten years. That will put you in the 'Honest' category."

Tessa points.

"Let me clear up something, I'll see you later. By the way, did you find any interesting new trails on your jog? I watched you disappear off the grounds a couple hours ago."

"That was an exhilarating run," I said, thinking back. "I got on some familiar roads from yesterday. Join me next time."

"I'll pedal. Thank you very much."

In any capacity, the last two days have not been my usual routine which means I've had the opportunity to think outside the box. I survived without a phone call or text, and life went on. Imagine that?

Back in the cabin, the shower felt refreshing as the diluted delta of red-brown dirt rinses off my legs and swirls into the gurgling drain. I thought I heard a knock at my cabin door.

"Yes? Be right there."

I wrap the towel around my waist and open the bathroom door. The screen door rests on its trip-lock, but I can't recall leaving it ajar.

"Hello?" I call out.

Only the annoying jay outside screeches. The room becomes

suddenly dimmer as if the curtains were pulled closed. Seconds later, the boom of directly overhead thunder rattles the knick-knacks on the decorative shelf above the television stand.

"Jesus Christ!" I yell. "People get used to this?"

Even as a kid, storms have always frightened the hoolies out of me. It's more foolish than actual but the expectations manifesting into these funnel-causing beasts always get my rapt attention. The so-called weather experts aren't to be trusted even if they are selling us on their presentation. But these damned spontaneous thunderstorms can detour a normal person's comfort zone on an unnerving, divided course. To think about the potential destruction, no matter how much or how little, festers in the back of my mind like a root canal gone bad.

The once placid heavens open with a rush and marble-sized hail pelts my roof. I watch with disbelief as it bounces off the hood of my rental car like the sound of a heavy metal drummer playing Taps. Every direction I look is oppressively shadowed. To me, the resort looks like the prime target, a ground zero.

Pine branches fall onto the drive like zombie raptors shot out of the sky. Those lingering skeptics are darting to shelter with their towels covering their heads against the deluge. It's a Norwegian Hell storm taunting those stragglers who wander the shimmering links. Believe me, it's just the beginning, without the least trace of doubt. The only thing separating me from disaster is this skimpy towel. A figure sprints frantically toward my door and I hold the door open and signal.

"Get in here. Hurry."

Tessa flips her raincoat hood back.

"The power is temporarily out. We got word of a body found on Fire Road Thirty-five. That's one of the trails you and I checked. Want to come with me?"

I suspiciously gander at the crush of rainwater making visibility outside, or anything that was once visible, dissolve into a faint image.

"Does it rain like this every fricking day?" I shout over the deluge.

"We're in the most humid portion of summer," she yells back. "Everything is damp and green. Jet streams dip out of Canada and the Dakotas dragging any hint of moisture and molding it into these huge prairie onslaughts."

"That's not very comforting, Tessa."

"Call it poetic justice for living up here," she smirks nervously, her eyes dart from the doorway to my waistline.

"I'd like to call it something else, if you don't mind." I wrap my arms close to my chest as another blood-curdling explosion of thunder ensues.

"I love you, too," she laughs and points. "You're losing your towel."

"I'm *using* my what?"

"Your towel," she aims a pointed finger at my belly. "Please get some clothes on or the invitation is off."

"Let's call it a rain-out," I shout. "I don't think it's safe or sensible for us to head out this moment, don't you?"

She turns to inspect the dissipating view out the screen door, evaluating, pondering. "Looks like I'm stuck here until further notice like Lundgren said. I believe that's fruitless."

The bathroom light flickers once, then goes out. Outside, the entire grounds become dark, as if on a timer switch.

"For once, you listened to me," I reprimand her as I go rummaging through my suitcase.

"Don't bother," she said and shuts the door behind her. "Got any more towels?"

In a ravenous, sweeping motion, an instantaneous unconscious reaction, I capture her in my arms, and we tumble crossways onto the bed. Like a teenager, she fumbles to open her blouse and unstrap the front of her bra. I struggle to remove her galoshes and wet socks. We combine our cravings, pulling her trousers and panties down to her knees revealing a dark triangle of pubic hair. There is a resounding rumble overhead as I anxiously begin to trace her nipples with my tongue. She curls her arms around my neck as I unknot my towel and press on top. Tessa arches beneath me and I feel for the small of her back to support the inviting lift.

Her eyes close and she offers up a small gasp. I push the pillows off the bed and wait for her to remove the last of her clothes. Her scalp is damp, and the nape of her neck has the intoxicating scent of spring lilac. Her body shudders as we entwine. She trembles and then lets out a soft moan. I surrender in a deep lingering kiss that draws our thighs into a rhythmical spasm like that of a racing scull. Tessa presses and whimpers weakly into my chest as we ransom ourselves to the shameless energies. Feverishly lustful. I have the desire to give everything, share everything, be everything, and she responds, inhaling quietly, grabbing for the sheets, and throwing them over both of us. She shivers in my arms and I draw her close until we both collapse into slumber. An hour later, we awake, and I follow her to the bathroom. We shower together, the soft soapy spray trails off and, for the moment, cleanses the emptiness out of both our lives.

CHAPTER TEN

The suppressed concerns of the missing Darlene, then the deflating discovery of a body, create an apprehensive overtone amongst the staff. Paige sits in front of the registration counter staring glumly at the computer. By the time Tessa and I board the sheriff's cruiser and drive away, there's a small somber gathering at the resort entrance. We ride in silence knowing that the worst possibility is to come and yet, somewhat hopeful that this is merely a case of mistaken identity. Perhaps it's a deer or wolf mistaken for the shape of a human. I recall a poster on the café window warning of poachers. Maybe it's someone who decided to take a break and accidentally left a jacket on a fallen tree. Think positive and prepare for the best-case scenario. This isn't doing any good. There is a light flutter in my gut. I place my hand on her knee and softly squeeze.

She looks out her window, not in tune to me, but acknowledging my presence with a soft grip. Hard to believe that only hours ago we were skin to skin, immersed in each's desires. I sense our busy lives are on the rebound again, never accounting for how much we take for granted. Love, hardly. Sex, less than occasionally. Companionship, rarely. We can't allow anything first-hand to come up for air. I ponder where we've been and where we're going as if we're being reprimanded for having these feelings. In turn, Tessa's signals equate to me more than an elemental need. In my defense, I remember fondly the cabin's power outage, and the subsequent call on her cell phone that had us both scavenging for our clothes.

"This is the fire road, Deputy," she points.

Lundgren exhales loudly and slows upon command. "What's wrong with that one?" pointing.

"It's full of potholes and erosion. Dr. Michaels and I were up there a couple days ago. Take my word for it." Her tone is sharp. "Lundgren, it's my job to keep people safe. You are in the same boat and not vice versa."

"Ten-four," he responds impassively and slowly shifts in his seat.

The remnants of the blustery downpour abound. Bent branches dangle precariously from their trunks and muddy rivulets shoot past us over the narrowing road edge. The car's defrost blasts warmed air to the backseat leaving me near the point of motion sickness. The rain has settled down, but the deputy keeps the distracting windshield wipers on high-speed with an annoying rub-squeak-rub-squeak.

In my mind, I review how to handle the potential situation so as not to get in the investigator's way, but reassure that proper procedures are still maintained. It has been more than a few years and my expertise at crime scenes is a little rusty. The photos and close-ups of the decedent come first. Collecting soil samples, recording liver core temperature, the presence or lack of beetles and maggots harvesting the decaying remains are second in line. Specific types of insects indicate how long the body might have been there, depending upon environmental factors. This is not to be my responsibility tonight, and I thought it better to back off for now. Let them handle it. I'll support Tessa in whatever capacity she needs.

Earlier in my room, she explained to me that the coroner's office is on call if and when necessary. I told her that was a good idea. Jurisdiction comes first. The rest of the investigation will stick to identification of the body. Based on the chilled reception at the sheriff's office, I have a skeptical feeling these local authorities are more territorial than the big city departments who review cases daily. This is the local's time to relish in the dimming spotlight of notoriety.

The drive takes roughly twice as long due to the inclement weather and the frustrated Lundgren loudly announces our arrival to the dispatcher.

"Looks like we're here."

Tessa scurries out first, hiking up her hood, as I stand alongside the passenger door awaiting my assignment, if any.

"What am I going to do, Kevin?" she asks, her voice shaking, her eyes watering.

"If you want me to check it out first, I will. Otherwise, I'll go with you. The damage is done, and attention needs to be placed on eliminating other causes, if any."

The three of us stumble along the saturated path, leaving deep, muddy imprints with each step. The mass is a human body slumped over the trail's edge facing down, its head nearly submerged in muddy water. The first responders were busy setting up a perimeter in the runoff. A flashbulb suddenly illuminates the area as the sheriff's photographer begins taking photos at various angles. In that split second, tinges of red combine with the slurry at the decedent's bloody mouth. Another picture is taken, another photo flash competing with the lightening in the distant skies. The disposed body, from torso to the head, is illuminated from the contrasting electrical energies as the diligent investigator moves down the slippery slope with strobe and a tape measure. He begins to take additional photos.

Tessa and I stand motionless watching the dogged photographer continue with close-ups of the torso. Lundgren intervenes, coming up from behind us.

"All indications are that it's Mrs. Gabbert. How she got up here is anybody's guess." He hikes up the collar of his raingear and shudders. "But she sure knows how to ruin a good night's sleep."

A little dark humor is not unusual in the coroner's office or law enforcement in general. It comes with the territory. Death scenes still need to be analyzed, but the actual death is not as important as the how it had become a potential crime. That's the coroner's duty. All joking aside, I think back on how I was reamed on the witness stand once, for smiling.

Not wanting to raise insult over his sovereign domain, I speak up, hopefully to regain a perspective.

"Is there anything out of the ordinary? I mean, suspicion of foul play?"

Beside me, Tessa covers her mouth.

"Nothing that stands out yet, Doc. We've been thinking that she was up here hiking, got lost, and then the storm caught up to her. She might have fallen, hit her head, something like that."

He turns, his face is tight, his eyes narrow, looking directly at me past the brim of his hat, as if I'm stepping on his toes, questioning his procedure. How dare I?

"It was dumb luck that a couple of hikers were heading down this ravine. We won't eliminate any alternatives, Doc."

"Has her husband been notified?" asks Tessa.

"I think Officer Patrick is on that duty presently back at the office," Lundgren informs the two of us, but continues to glower at me. He steps back and hawks up a phlegm ball from deep inside his throat, expelling the mucous bolus onto the watery trail beyond the trees and, at the same time, scrubbing his hand over the front of his face.

"Anything else you want to ask? I need to get back to work."

It was a signal to either leave or shut up, but Tessa was not intimidated.

"Look, Deputy, I am the manager of Ole's, as you very well know, and I'll stay out of your way. Give that authoritarian attitude a ride. Despite of how straightforward you might think this plays out, I've got clients that don't expect anything less than perfection, complete with personal safety. If I find that this was not a natural death, I'll have hell to pay, and you, Deputy Lundgren, will have a ton of paperwork to explain. I brought Dr. Michaels with me because in these matters and perhaps, just perhaps, an extra set of eyes is how to pursue an investigation."

She rests her palm on the deputy sheriff's shoulder.

"After all, we have hordes of seventy-year-plus visitors hiking on their own, five miles outside the resort during a thunderstorm."

The chastisement was too much for the blushing deputy and he backs off her stronghold.

"I apologize, Tessa. I have a couple other things going on right now, but I'll try to not let it interfere with the investigation. We'll get it right, down to the autopsy, if need be. Count on it."

"Count on me watching from the wings, Lundgren," she said, poised like a cornered feral cat.

I sense her body sizzling with disgust.

The tempest is not lessening as Tessa presses her rain slicker hat on the top of her head. I shove my hands into my coat pockets opting out of giving her a comforting hug. The tension between local law enforcement and the two of us is arcing like the sagging high line wires of command on this soaked hillside. I hesitate to answer back with suggestions for fear of overriding any decisions in the making.

"I'm not here to step on your toes," I tell him. "Don't change your routine on the account that I happen to be visiting. All I'm saying is that if you need a second opinion, feel free to ask me."

"Roger, that."

He was speaking into his collar connection.

"I'm sorry, Doc. You were saying?"

We're ushered toward the idling cruiser by the Assistant Deputy, without any fanfare, and told to wait inside. Tessa is fuming.

"Lundgren is a major pain," she mutters, crossing her arms in front. "I only tolerate him because he provides security to the resort. I even think we are related in some primitive sense, through uncles."

I snap out my drenched cap on the floor mats. "He's showing off to me more than you. Lundgren wants me to know my limitations in his territory."

"I suppose you are right," Tessa agrees. "But that doesn't alter the fact that he can be such an ass at times."

"On the contrary, I think he is fearfully respectful where this case might end up if the County is called upon to add punch," I add.

"He's worse than the two twins combined, Kevin." She holds up her cell phone. "Better check-in with the resort and be sure no one else has contacted Mr. Gabbert yet."

Tessa tilts forward as if to physically get a better signal.

"Hello, Paige? It's Tessa. The reception is poor. Can you hear me? Yes. It's Tessa. The body might be Mrs. Gabbert, but not until an identification is complete. Is Carl up to talking to me?" She cups her ear to the receiver. "I can't quite understand you. Please repeat." She looks at the message screen. "Shit. The phone is dead."

I fumble inside my coat pocket for mine, but it is gone.

"Sorry. I must have left mine on the nightstand, next to the towels." Tessa guardedly smiles.

"Enough said on that topic, please. This cruiser could be bugged."

Moments later, Lundgren taps on Tessa's window.

"I'm about ninety-nine percent positive that the body is Darlene Gabbert. She is wearing a plastic wristband with her name and 'Class of 67' on it. Do you want me to notify the coroner first, or do we contact the resort?"

"I lost connection with the resort about five minutes ago," she said. "Before going any further, let's be sure on the identification. Give Roland a call soon. He will be absolutely furious to drive up here tonight in the van."

"I'll try on the short-wave," Lundgren yells over the wind. "We should think about moving her away from the gullies. Her body can wash away. Do you agree with that assessment, Doc?"

"That's a good idea," I holler back. "If there was any evidence as to why she was here, it's all downstream by now. Better to retrieve her with some dignity intact. At least that's my opinion under these circumstances."

"Roger that," Lundgren says. "My bet is on natural rather than accidental right now. There is a deep cut on the inside of her lip, like a trip or fall and her heart gave out under the strenuous hike."

"But that doesn't answer why she was up here," Tessa adds. "Were there any tire tracks or footprints?"

"Not sure about that, considering the weather and all," Lundgren said. "Remember that the resort offers these mini tours for the guests. Perhaps she got off the charter for some artsy-fartsy thing and missed the ride back."

He sweeps his arm over the terrain, then rubs his jaw.

"This is not far from where the four-wheelers pass. These packed trails are being hit hard tonight. My guess is on big time erosion by tomorrow."

"This time, I'm on your side, sheriff," she says. "I'll check on those tours tomorrow. Follow your procedures to expedite this grim situation. I'll vouch for you if need be."

"Thanks, Tessa. I'd appreciate that."

She rolls up the window and looks to me.

"I feel terrible about this, Kevin. Somebody's mother is going to end up in the funeral prep room; caked with mud and gravel, blood coming out of her mouth, hands all scratched up. Then her husband arrives to identify the body who was, in a few hours, about to laugh with classmates, toast good times, and sing the class fight song. It's hardly fair how age doesn't become the aged. High school was the best measurement of their lives and this reunion stuff is important to them."

"I couldn't agree more," I said. "It is still a good idea for at least a Deputy Coroner to have a look-see. Trauma to the mouth can be a vague indicator of how she ended up in the trail."

"You think there's something to the blood in the mouth?" raising her eyebrows, tilting her head in my direction, hinging on my response.

"Well, I never got a good look, thanks to the sheriff. All I'm saying is that being as exact as we can by eliminating the options are always the best policy, even in the north woods."

Suddenly, there is another flash of lightening and she recoils.

"If this investigation team doesn't have considerable practice or, as I sense, a lack of familiarity, there's no harm in having the County Coroner come over. I only want the truth."

"We all want the same answer," I respond. "Lundgren acts as if this is small potatoes, but Mr. Gabbert needs to be dealt with respectfully. Sometimes, even the tiniest detail turns out to be an asset."

Through the windshield I watch a silvery moon crest in between gaps of thunderheads. In that eerie glow upon the vehicle, I am reminded of science fiction movies where a mysterious spaceship shines a solitary beam onto the ground. Suddenly, there's another reverberating clap above us that vibrates the car hood. Too close for comfort. A bolt discharges on a large pine tree, splitting it like a Paul Bunyan ax felling a forest. Tessa shudders and clutches her throat.

"Don't even think that I'm not scared, Kevin. No one gets used to these giant storms."

"Let's say we head back to the resort rather than get washed away?" I suggest. "We can have Roland give us a call after he picks up the body."

"Sounds good to me," she nods abruptly.

The treacherous ride back to the resort with Lundgren at the wheel lacks an ounce of precaution. His skids around potholes are all for show, but Tessa keeps her mouth shut. This midnight monster weather-beater is loaded to the hilt. No doubt, more tree damage and debris will be strewn around the resort. Each of us are keen to the squad car's radio announcements of road closures and power outages. The winding road down to the valley is as black as a city hearse. Not a yard light or car is visible. Tessa checks in with the resort and is relieved to know that the emergency generator is working. The City of Wasoon has some fallen trees near the high school. The downtown water tower with the big W is overfilling and looms as a threat due to the soggy conditions. All passersby and curiosity-seekers are warned to stay away from its base.

"Can I drop you both off at the resort?" Lundgren asks, glowering.

"Thank you," Tessa exhales, her thoughts scattered in short responses whereas I'm relieved that we survived the trip down the mountain. "I need to see how the tenants are holding up. But a refrigerator-sized Valium that the customers can lick like a Popsicle at the counter would be most welcome."

"I'm all for that, Tessa," chuckles Lundgren.

He is more reverent now that the issue of remains is being addressed. He nervously rubs his chin with his gloved hand.

"Once again, I apologize for my conduct up there. The whole place is unsafe tonight, especially the woods. We had a bull's eye target on our back for lightning strikes. You saw how that tree was roasted."

"You called it correctly, sheriff," Tessa reassures him. "Thanks for your concern."

"Roland is on his way to pick up the body as we speak. One of the Deputies is waiting for him on the site. He'll have the dear old woman back at the funeral home in no time. I hope the road holds up, otherwise there will be some unique rafting stories."

"Like the River Styx," I concur, internalizing an annoying sigh, not trying to generate any additional disdain over his behavior.

"Who?" inquires Lundgren, his voice raised and squeaky.

"Never mind, Deputy," says Tessa. "See you tomorrow sometime."

Back at the registration building, some of the guests assemble near the fireplace, hands in pockets, cupping coffee mugs, darting looks. Two of the elderly men attentively stand when we enter.

"Was there a body up there?"

"Is it Darlene?"

"Is she dead?"

The bombarding questions come at us from all directions. One query feeds off the other until we are surrounded by the gathering group. Tessa attempts to calm them.

"We've had a power outage and are now on auxiliary generator service. Please, don't further compound things by speculating what may or may not have happened. Yes, we located a body that requires positive identification and that's all I'm going to say about that right now."

She looks to me.

"Dr. Michaels has been kind enough to accompany me to the site and he thinks we allow the authorities to take over the role of making sure the deceased is properly handled. The storm has created quite a mess, as you can imagine. We're going forward with the weekend festivities, nonetheless. Don't let this hamper your celebration. Your classmates would expect the same treatment."

"What about her husband? Where is he?" The question arises from someone in the back of the group.

Tessa looks up with direct eye contact to the inquirer.

"Mary Jo. Let's wait until things settle down. By then, I'll be glad to answer any further questions."

She addresses the assembly.

"Thank you all for your diligence. Please prevent those worries from becoming fears. I will be sending complimentary gift boxes to the suites tomorrow."

She takes my arm and escorts me to the back office. It appears the crowd is still a little disheveled, but she offered reassurances that we all share the same concerns. In the back of my mind I hope they aren't expecting me to become involved. After all, it's best that I keep to myself, as far as Lundgren is concerned.

"I thought you handled that well," I said as she closes the door behind us.

Tessa walks around the desk only to collapse in her chair. Her mouth forms a tight frown and tears begin to trickle off her reddened cheeks.

"You can't imagine how awful it feels to lie to those lovely people. They hinge on my every word. How can I stand there and convince them that tomorrow will be better?"

"You said nothing wrong," I let her know. "You comforted them more than anything else. That whole group therapy collective is exactly the correct response. None of them are prepared to expect the unexpected. They had planned this getaway months, maybe years ago and the death of an immediate friend is too sudden to grasp. Imagine all the fearful tales they harbor, then we walk in to calm them down."

The office air is stuffy, like an attic's stairwell, and my rain slicker smacks of the dampness and mildew. This is my first opportunity to check out her workplace. Amongst the ledgers and calculator on the desktop rests a picture frame facing her area. I pick it up. Two teen-aged girls hamming underneath a rustic door frame, arms draped over each other in a friendly embrace, that telltale smile of obvious siblings. Erin is wearing a green plaid bandana. In contrast, Tessa holds a black comb over her upper lip like a moustache. I give it a closer look.

"It's the last picture we took together. Two weeks later, she was gone." Tessa gathers her arms under her sleeves and withers in the weight of despondency. "That was taken at the entrance to her cabin, the same one that was locked a couple days ago."

"You both looked quite happy."

"We were good friends as well as sisters. I'd bounce off crazy ideas at her all the time. Erin was my sounding board about life, the perfect husband, money..."

I replace the picture to her side of the desk and stand back from the desk.

"What's next, Tessa? How about getting some rest? Roland will be calling soon."

She opens the pencil drawer and begins rummaging.

"Somewhere in here is a copy of the guest list for the weekend. I decided to keep it handy just in case. Emergency or not, I need to know exactly who all our guests are." She pauses. "Here it is."

She holds up a stapled set of papers and begins flipping through them until settling on a specific one.

"I want to be sure that Darlene and Carl's names are on the list. Looks like their home phone number is still a Saint Paul area code. He used to be a school principal back in the day when Wasoon was a snowmobile town. She served the local Presbyterian congregation as a deacon. That was around the time I was a senior in high school."

"Good thinking," I tell her, while leaning forward to scan over her outstretched arms. "That takes care of the second most important piece of information that authorities will want. Small town folk care about each other and need to arrive at an understanding. It's payback based on their original roots."

The urge to come over to her side and offer a comforting hug is tempting, but like her, I am drawn into guilt and morose, the same way it was when Cassie died. Helplessness. Unavailable. Unable to right the wrong.

"I want to spend more time with you, Kevin, and relive how we were in your bed earlier. But right now, I need to sort out these accidental issues prior to Lundgren calling. Can you understand how important that is for me?"

"Of course, I do," I respond, empathetically. "You take all the time you need. In the meantime, I'll head back to my cabin and await your call."

She pushes away from her chair and stands as if our meeting here is over. We say our goodbyes on mutual ground and give each other a stiff embrace as if we're nothing more than acquaintances. Even though I understand her situation, the brush-off feels impersonal after our time together.

"Lately, I seem to be always apologizing, Kevin. I need to focus on the resort. You're not distracting me, and it's not Darlene Gabbert either. Erin has been on my mind. The memories peak. I feel responsible. I'm to blame. I'm the onus. That's why I try to stay away from the reunions. I had a school of friends and classmates who knew her. Sometimes I get the feeling that all the glances and whispers as I enter a room are indirectly because of her through me. I'm not being paranoid, am I?"

How can I tell her the truth? I still get the same impression from people who were friends with Cassie and me.

"It doesn't go away easily," I tell her. "We are doing it to ourselves. We interpret it as sorrow when what we should focus on is compassion. People mean well but during times like this, they don't know how to react."

"They loved Erin and yet, I can't be her replacement. She was stronger in various ways and I feel overloaded with two personalities." Her eyes begin to water as she drops her head. "I'm not good at acting."

Tessa is begging to resolve an amenable piece of a multi-mosaic puzzle that has been lost or accidentally discarded. It gnaws at me the way she's berating herself. This isn't the woman I met a few days ago. Diving fearlessly into rapids or unashamedly brushing the poison pollens from my back. She's grown sullen, muted from happiness, storing away those attributes that are her uniqueness. She's wearing her discouragement like a hooded jacket.

I lift her chin and softly kiss her forehead.

"As soon as Roland calls, let me know. I'll drive over to the funeral home and wait for the husband to arrive."

"Thank you very much, Kevin. You're wonderful. I'll make it up to you. I promise."

On the walk to my cabin, I see the Lundgren cruiser. Surprisingly, Mr. Self-Important has enough common sense to keep the flashers off. He reaches for his hat and rain slicker in the back seat, then struts into the lobby. Maybe it's me, but I'm forming doubts that the power struggle over the Gabbert woman's death is over.

CHAPTER ELEVEN

The last two months of Cassie's life was filled with unremitting turmoil. The fresh energy that she brought to intimate conversations was soon-to-be overturned by poorly received arguments by me. I contributed it to depression, a life in tatters. She was getting fat and her Artic blue eyes were offset by the downturned smile that complemented that limp salt-and-pepper ponytail. Disease can do that secretly, too, and I knew something was not right. Being pregnant was not favorable for her. I came to believe that if she had the chance to do it all over again, this wouldn't be a tough decision. She stopped sprucing up or wearing fashionable maternity clothes. Without make-up she looked even older and preferred to wear sweats around the house because nothing else fit. Weekend open house agendas for the realty business were the only times she dressed up. She would, matter-of-factly, peck me on the cheek and hoist her leather portfolio bag to the side of her baby bump and march out the door.

I was selfish, bordering on egotistical, always seeking new career choices. The few successes I encountered in the private sector weren't received well with a relegated stay-at-home soon-to-be dad. In my opinion, Cassie misunderstood my issues. She insisted the fuss was petty at the expense of her pregnancy. I escaped by spending more time gabbing away with neighbors because they had a friendly ear. The silence behind our closed front door was a moot reminder that things were about to get worse.

Most people in this Sierra-sheltered lifestyle left you alone except for the prattling mailman, or the widowed Jewish lady with the orange hair and the ever-yipping poodles, or the snoopy neighbors peering into our backyard. This demographic covers a wide range, but we feigned a good job of appearing like a happy couple in public and not like the strangers that we were becoming. I brought Cassie an abandoned tabby from the pound to keep her company when I was away on cases. Not a trained house cat, it autographed our new leather sofa on multiple occasions with annoying claw marks and even shredded the bottoms of our new linen curtains. My frustration with the cat mounted, but Cassie was protective, saying that it had separation issues. But in the long run, it was a blessing the day kitty ventured onto the street beyond our drive. I never told Cassie that I buried it in a rock pile down the lane from the mailbox.

I was the world champion at burying things. As a child, my pet cemetery was not exclusive of my family's dog. Roadkill that I dared to sneak home out of the view of my father was given last rites. Pancaked bird carcasses and skeletons were buried in unmarked graves in the grove.

When Cassie raised her voice at me, which was periodic, I felt as meager as some leftover ground squirrel remains that I had decided to shoot at with a disintegrating rifle bullet at three hundred yards. That was the beginning of my downfall into forensics.

Why we argued was irrelevant. She was unhappy, unemployed for the first time in her life, and worse, she was drawing near middle age as pregnant, a trifecta all the way. What was I thinking? I narrowed it down to within a couple of weeks where the conception might have taken place. Either it was a weekend getaway to a cohort's wedding, or it had begun with a second bottle of pinot grigio from our vintner neighbor's stash and ended with a lasting hangover for the whole next day.

I decided early on that this baby was not mine. I was away too much. More so, how was it literally conceivable that we were about to have a baby? Science was betraying my clouded judgment like a Judas. Didn't I learn anything in medical school? The law of averages usually sides with the winner, but I had become the loser once again. Picture a blessed-perfect couple having a newborn enter their lives: the planning of the baby's room, baby clothes, anticipating the birth. Now replace that image with two adults who should've known better. One of them is clinging to a thread of self-confidence after losing a malpractice case, and the other is a well-renowned commercial real estate broker easily making three times her spouse's salary on commission alone. Moving to the hicks and living off minuscule contracts from being a hired gun for the bereft was not going to pay the bills.

Topping that off is a still unlivable cabin I had promised to finish a decade ago. I was too proud to have her share expenses since it was I who insisted on the holding of demolition. I was a doctor, for god's sake. Big-headed, self-important, and all that. Then there was that issue with the temporary loss of my state license to practice medicine and a trailer load of shouting matches. She'd sulk about in the silent kitchen with a never empty glass of wine or cocktail. Meanwhile, I distanced myself in casework, but all in all, it felt like being on the Most Wanted. Looking back, the litigation was a brutal blow to my ego.

Fatherhood isn't the issue, but rather the lack of a father figure. Most of my cases were on the East Coast. Cassie became sullen and quiet every time I called her from an airport. I think she felt the baby provided the missing ingredient to our relationship, something her prior husband refused. That idiot made it clear that the two mistakes of his first marriage crash wouldn't transpire again. She stuck herself deep into work until I came along.

I came from the same situation, but a different location. I was not very adept in dating and enjoyed the company of only a few women. Most were squandered away by my lack of interest or dedication. It seemed that for weeks or months at a time I was hot to trot, but at age thirty-nine, I needed to grow up fast for my own sake. I knew it from when Cassie and I met at an open house near the Tiburon Lagoon neighborhood.

Cassie was a no nonsense, shoot-from-the-hip type of person. Business first, and always riding herd to reach her aggressive goals. Small talk wasn't her cup of tea which came as a big surprise when we slept together. Later, it became superficial confession time. She let out that the sale and commission went to that same loser she divorced less than a year ago. As for me, I was merely consumed with all manner of coincidences in the battle for second place.

It was as if we latched on to our personal bruises and waited for them to scab over or eventually disappear. We didn't have to look that far to prove we weren't meant for each other. Handholding, dancing, even small talk seemed forced. Showing a flicker of affection in the wake of a shouting match was a struggle. Still there was something that kept us going and that was loneliness. It was a temporary fix for the addicted-to-work crowd. We were not able to share the affections that both of us desperately needed. If we discussed anything about our day, I held back. If she tossed out a mundane comment like, "It's Sunday. We should be doing something special," the agnostic in me retorted. "What's wrong with staying home for a change?"

But I wanted to say, "Why is there a frickin' need to be out in public when we're both perfectly content not talking to each other?"

So, we attended a few services at the community chapel. I wasn't sold then and, for certain, still passive on the whole gambit. It stirred bad memories of growing up watching my parents quarrel. But I wanted to stay in tune to her feelings because I knew exactly from where the source of my disgust arose. Yet, I was relentless.

Both my parents died in a car accident when I was eighteen. They were driving to visit me at college for the first time and got broadsided by an eighteen-wheeler. The day of their funeral, I was pissed. Now what? My Aunt Norma raised a ruckus at the gravesite, chiding the kids for not being respectful. My sister's six-month old baby daughter whined through most of internment. Certain chairs up front were reserved for next of kin, but that didn't stop her from claiming a seat facing directly in front of the matching coffins for all to see and hear them. The pastor, bless his soul, led us in prayers and hymns, constantly coordinating when the mourners should sit or stand. To the final say, Aunt Norma always wanted to be the center of attention, even at someone else's funeral. No way was I going to relive that.

I ended up living with my grandparents where religion was roughly hewn into my being like canvas patchwork on used coveralls. Work presided over fun and studies reigned over sports because Grandpa preferred the farm report. I gleaned my emotions in petty crime novels and hand-me-down Playboy magazines from classmates. Girls were classified as "sluts" or "chicks" amongst the guys and consequently, I felt uncomfortable around either one. No dances, but plenty drinking, especially in undergraduate school. This was how I had become a dysfunctional adult.

Any follower of Freudian psychology can savor these beleaguered sticking points. My concern is where I rank Tessa right now and that's undeniable. I hate myself for it, placing her on a mental graph chart. I am used to connecting with families injured by death, not by illness. They want me in a different capacity, not a substitute, but rather a cure. I can't guarantee that Tessa will appreciate my absolute interest in her if I get involved with the death of Darlene Gabbert. The way prosecution had stripped me raw under subpoena left me as insecure as a batter facing a major league baseball pitcher. I want very much to help, but do I jeopardize something deeper? If I step beyond the mixture of love and guilt from past failures, then what?

I need to bring up that accidental puncture wound prior to my testosterone rush. To some degree, I might have placed her in harm's way and that is totally irresponsible. While I mastered contriteness to inform all my previous co-workers how important it is to approach cases as potentially hazardous, how can I exclude the most important person in my agonizingly dull life? To play devil's advocate, I had even written journal articles about the safety fears in the morgue and how they can be reduced by accounting for the elimination of potential errors. Who was I trying to kid about my blunder? The court was right by taking away my privileges. I needed to be taught a lesson.

The odds of Tessa contracting hepatitis from me are negligible. Nonetheless, they exist. I was symptom-free until two days ago. Considering all I had been through it seems quite odd that I'm looking on the positive. Surely, this isn't my Midwestern pessimism coming to the front, where I was taught there was either too much or not enough to go around. I eventually convince myself to get another blood test at the local hospital in Wasoon this morning to play it safe. At any rate, Tessa has a right to know and I'll take my chances with any ensuing wrath.

As rapidly as the storm's advent had devoured the landscape last night, the low-pressure blast from the heavens subside. The shower's blustery residue swirls through the exfoliated oaks, and the waxy cottonwoods again begin their constant cackling. I take off my rain slicker and give it a strong whip. There is a woman's body being wheeled into the funeral home at this very instant. Fingerprinting will leave grey-blue ink stains on the tips, and the gravitation of lividity to the dependent soft tissues will define the final moment. Morgue refrigeration can only halt the degradation so long. Like old tomatoes, the corpse softens, the fluids leach, and the answers diminish. It's time to dismiss those negative thoughts. It's time to circumvent that mysterious bleeding site. It's time to step up. I have the answer.

Back at the cabin, I pull out my cell phone and call the Wasoon County Coroner's office. There is endless static on the hold line. A recorded voice tells me I'm being connected to the on-call officer.

"Deputy Jaffery." The voice is business-like, monotone.

"Deputy Jaffery. My name is Kevin Michaels. Dr. Kevin Michaels. I'm staying at Ole's Resort outside of Wasoon."

"What can I do for you, Doctor?" His question is more like a directive to continue.

"There's a body of an elderly woman found on a fire trail outside the resort's grounds. For the time being, no indication of foul play is under consideration, although she was discovered a long way from the resort. From my brief time examining the body, I didn't get the impression that she's physically able to hike up three or four miles of boulders and fallen trees. This woman is rather stout. She has a gash in her upper lip as though a trip and fall had taken place. There's a big runoff near the location of the body, and it was my suggestion that the sheriff's deputy move her unless she slides down the ravine. They took some pictures, though. I am a board-certified forensic pathologist visiting friends up here."

No more sugar-coating for now. I wait for his response.

"You say, up at Ole's Resort, outside of Wasoon?" The way he asked, delayed, I know he was writing down my story as I spoke.

"Yes, that's correct. I guess I'm calling to notify you in case communications break down because of the storm." I am not about to lead him on a deputy-lynching if need not be.

"Where's your location?"

He is silent. There is the clatter of keyboarding.

"Deputy Lundgren dropped us off back at the resort, and I'm in my little bungalow right now. Do you have a medical examiner or a coroner? I am willing to step in and offer a second opinion. My medical license is valid in twenty-four states. Minnesota is one of them."

"Thank you for offering," he laughs quietly. "Most of our actual crimes are comprised of bar brawls and spousal abuse. Let me get your phone number. Michaels, is it?"

"Yes, Dr. Kevin Michaels. Lundgren is well-trained, but I don't think his procedural investigation techniques are ready for this. Of course, the whole issue is easily explained if a witness comes forward. Knowing how these cases can drag, you had better be aware how it might turn out."

"I appreciate it, Doctor. Can I get some more information about you? If I may..." There was the muffled sound of a keyboard again being attacked with vigor.

"I'm staying at the resort. I am a private pathologist called in by the family of Ole Olson. I completed a postmortem examination on him a few days ago."

"Do the twin brothers still own that place?" he asks.

"Aaron and David employed me to perform the autopsy," I tell him.

"Was there a cause of his death, then?" The subject of concern leapfrogs to another topic as he glosses over. Bored stiff. All day at his desk playing twenty questions about fishing licenses. Sneaking a call to his girlfriend. Brushing the uneaten cookie crumbs off his desk.

"I am not allowed to say, Deputy. This is a private matter." I am anxious to have someone else tell him about Mrs. Gabbert.

"I see," he says, back on track. "Well, I thank you for the call. I'm going to contact our dispatcher and see if she's heard anything from Lundgren. I want his version and the status of the body. I'll get back to you and we'll go from there."

"I'm merely making myself available," I reassure him. "Please keep me informed, and thanks for listening."

"Copy that," he responds. "In the meantime, you're staying at Ole's with this cell number?"

"I am," I tell him, feeling as if the interrogation is about me. He wasn't interested in the deceased. "Will you keep me informed once the coroner is contacted?"

"That, I can do," he said. "Let me follow-up first on this with Deputy Lundgren. Ox before the cart, you know," and disconnects automatically.

I look at my cell phone wondering if I had blown a golden opportunity by jumping to illogical conclusions.

I switch on the television to check for weather updates. Radar indicates that the storm is tracking to the east in an owl's wing fashion over at least three counties. No doubt the seriousness won't be tallied until tomorrow.

I look intently at the bed where Tessa and I had been lying a few hours ago. How can she ever trust me again when I confess about the needle stick? My indecisiveness was the crumbling block of my relationship with Cassie. Standing here recalls how Tessa had yanked up her slacks as I hurriedly threw the blankets in place and tossed the pillows on the headboard. That was subtle, like hiding an ostrich Easter egg in the center of the lawn.

There is a message signal flashing on the resort phone on the nightstand. I dial Front Desk and wait.

"Ole's."

"Yes, this is Dr. Michaels. My phone indicates I have a message."

"One moment, please."

I scan the room for other evidence of Tessa's surprise arrival.

"Doctor, there was a call from Erin. She left no return number.

Our phones have been down for some time. We lost the ability to replay the voiced messages. I'm afraid you can't hear it."

The remote falls out of my hand like a hot iron, bouncing off the nightstand and crashing onto the floor. My jaw tightens. I'm being watched.

"Erin? Are you sure she said Erin?" I question.

"That's the message. Nothing more." She continues. "Like I mentioned, we can't replay, so I wrote it down. I hope that's all right. Get her number if she calls back, okay?"

"If she does call again, please get in touch with me right away."

Everything will be all right. Don't panic. I'm certain it's just a mistake. She might've gotten the name mixed up with someone else. Perhaps another person named Erin from the message service? I feel weightless, light-headed, a witness to the conversation from the cabin's ceiling above me. Tessa is playing a joke. I need to be careful about asking her, though.

"Thank you, Doctor. Good night."

CHAPTER TWELVE

The next morning swoops in like a famished barn swallow on the cricket hunt. My sandpaper-scratchy eyes throb and there is a pounding in my head. I roll over to the side of the bed and struggle to sit up. The blankets and pillow lie in a heap on the floor next to my trousers. My effort to sleep was fruitless. My throat is dry, and there's a dull ache in my shoulder. I continue to have those damn recurring nightmares where I'm late for appointments or walking into offices that dismissed me after the malpractice fiasco. Even worse, I'm looking for an opportunity to right myself by doing piecemeal cases that everyone complained about, but never wanted to claim. Suicides. Auto accidents. Stillborns. Lately, those nightmarish ideas appeal to my assembling guilt complex. How to atone for the past transgressions? I shower and throw on loose fitting slacks and a tee shirt, then order in for breakfast. It arrives cold and the coffee is so bland that I open the front door and toss it out on the grass. An hour later, Tessa calls.

"I informed Mr. Gabbert about his wife. He was walking into the buffet for a cup of coffee and chatting with some of his classmates at the bar. The poor man had no idea where she was. He expected to find her in the lobby near the reception table which is where they usually would meet up."

That is exactly the way my clients are caught off-guard. Most are innocently minding their own business when someone, a little too solemn looking, strolls up to their house and knocks.

"Tessa, I'm sorry that the responsibility fell on you. It's not your call. In this circumstance, it's the county's job. Don't beat yourself up. I'm sorry you got caught in the middle."

"Well, it's done, and he mustered enough bravery to thank me," she responds in a business-as-usual tone. "I have some other news, though. Before you go down to the funeral home, our buddy,

Lundgren, wants you to come to the sheriff's department. He has a few more questions."

"Am I in trouble of some sorts?" inquiring like being scolded, wrinkling my brow, raising my voice.

"I don't think so," she answers. "It's more about the details he could have missed. Least, that's what he told me."

"Why didn't he contact me directly?"

"Lundgren is afraid of you, Swami. You are smart and handsome. That's a threat to any wholesome boy up here. Don't you know that I'm your medium?"

In my mind's eye, her Cheshire grin is forming.

"If that's the case, why are you not telling me in person?"

"First, I'm swamped with Darlene's fretting classmates. Secondly, Wasoon Tribune wants plums to grow out of apple trees with an overdue deadline about the weekend's events. And third, we need to keep our distance, if only for a little while until the pollen settles."

"That's an interesting way to put me on the back burner," I said, feeling as if my new affection is strung out on a clothesline.

I tug at my shirt collar and watch a fly land on my breakfast plate and settle on the butter knife.

"I'll agree to anything you say, but some things are only temporary, please."

"Something lasting begins with patience," she answers, leaving me unable to come back with a quick response.

On my way to the rental car, I encounter the harried brothers, Aaron and David, unloading about two cords of freshly cut oak logs from their truck onto a flatbed trailer. Some of the smaller pieces are leafless dried branches that snap like pencils when tossed to the pile. David's headband is wringing with sweat as he takes off his leather gloves to wipe his brow. Meanwhile, Aaron has walked around to the passenger door, reaches in, and turns down the booming radio volume from metallic to an easy-listening, top forties decibel.

"Hey Doc," Mr. Leonard Skynard yells out to me. "We're getting the incendiary devices for tonight's big finale. You must have been snoring up quite a storm last night. Most of these fallen limbs are out behind your cabin."

So that was the ground-shaker I felt around two o'clock as I was about to shut down.

"I thought that was coming from the neighbor's next door," I told him. "I was out with Tessa. You heard about the Gabbert woman?"

Aaron adjusts volume again.

"Darlene Gabbert? That was her?" His mouth opens. "She was the nicest lady, but the meanest Sunday school troll I ever had back in grade school. She always remembered my name. Constantly grilling me. How's your father, Aaron? It's so good to see you, Aaron. She never got the two of us mixed up."

David hops down from the truck box and hikes up his trousers.

"I'm sorry that Miss Tessa and you had to find her like that," he said. "Guess she must have fallen or something. Least, that's Lundgren's opinion."

The payloader rumbles past us, driven by one of the motley landscape employees I had noticed yesterday. From his ragged appearance, he might have had a night not unlike my own. He signals to the brothers.

"Jimmy must be in more of a hurry than usual. He hasn't even had his mid-morning beer yet," Aaron chortles.

"That's what happens when there's a death in the family," David answers.

"Death in the family?" I ask. "He knew the Gabbert lady?"

"We are all related up her in some fashion, Doc," David counters.

"And some are more related than others, if you know what I mean," says Aaron with a snort. "How are you and Tessa getting along?"

Inside information is easy to come by up here, I thought. The company has spies in the walls.

"She's been a big help to me, and I hope to return the favor somehow."

"Tessa can rule a tight kingdom," Aaron adds. "She's fretting over Mrs. Gabbert being up in the trails."

"Yeah, that can be pretty scary in the night." David cocks his head toward his brother. "Remember about a year or so ago when that trail bike was discovered? We never found an owner. It's still stashed away somewhere in the work shed."

I remember seeing a crumpled bike in the storage shed downtown when Tessa and I searched for Erin's belongings.

"Folks say it was that runaway kid's from Thief River Falls. Others claim it was stolen from a church garage sale in Bemidji. I still think it looked like the Christiansen boy's. You know, he was found a week later in that old camp well."

"Where's he now?" I asked.

"Dead," David stated flatly. "By chance, Tessa happened to be up checking fire trails at the old church camp and leaned over the well shaft. Next thing, she's screaming on the phone to Lundgren that she thinks there's a body in the water. He claimed that fishing out that kid was like scooping a bowl of stew with a wooden spoon."

"Good one," remarks Aaron. "It's lunchtime and you come out with an assorted menu delight." He leans back. "We are not trying to joke about it, Doc. It's our way of dealing with things."

"I understand," I tell him. "It must have been quite a shock to have another body show up so soon."

"We don't get used to people keeling over. Some things are unexplainable while others are plain stupidity." Aaron looks down the driveway toward the payloader. "We better go over to help the hired man to stay on his good side. He's our big stick for the tournament. You still considering coming out for the game?"

"That is an all systems go," I answer like a NASA engineer.

"Good," says David. "I want to see how a lefty swings the bat right-handed. That's one of the weirdest things I ever heard."

"Catch you later, Doc," Aaron yells as he walks along the muddy tire tracks, remnants of the wash-out from last night. David goes behind him off-track, making his own soupy shoeprints.

I continue toward the office but decide against it. Allow Tessa some space, like she requested. As I reluctantly slide in behind the steering wheel, the humidity and heat escape the rental car's interior as if blown out with a fan. On the passenger seat is a sealed manila envelope next to the damp baseball cap I wore. Tessa said she was going to bring me some information about the Gabbert's. Perhaps she had accidentally dropped it on the seat last night. Odd. We weren't in the car last night. Was there a reason that she avoided me? I flip it over. There is no writing on the outside, and it feels as if something soft or delicate is inside. I invert the envelope and pour out its contents onto my lap. It's a green plaid headscarf, like Erin's from the photo. Maybe Tessa had kept this as a memento and meant for me to see it later. But how did this end up in my car?

As expected, vehicles are backing up at the security gate entrance. Purdy directs them toward the registration office and rechecks his clipboard. It's only eight-thirty but according to the bulletin board, the weekend is to begin with a golf tournament. With all the resort improvements and road construction it appears some of the duffers are arriving late for their tee times. Cars move slowly along the semi-circular drive near the clubhouse. It goes without saying the escorted golfers are agitated and hop out of the still-moving vehicles, hustle to the back, and flip open the trunk to retrieve their bags. Some cars have fun-loving foursomes with beers and cigars. I hear them crack-up over something as their cheap cigar smoke wafts in the still air. These poor bastards in their polo shirts and plaid shorts. At the end of the day, all the whiffing at the ball and making a couple pars, will be the source of abundant storylines.

If I were arriving late at Ole's today, I'd be impatient too. Road crews halt drivers with the yellow warning *Slow* sign as loaders with front-end scoops motor down the single-lane path. It's easy to justify that this resort is not transformable without extra manpower. The landscapers were called on their days off, grabbed their tools and put back to work. It's a circus of rakes, shovels, and trash containers loaded down with anything that once was airborne. I shake my head in sympathy.

Downtown Wasoon is so busy that it takes me a *whole* minute to find parking in front of the sheriff's office. The absurdity is that back in California the ability to pull into any space might require a couple laps around the building. Two Deputies I had not previously met are walking out and I move aside to allow them space. Inside, Lundgren is on the phone behind the counter, but he acknowledges my presence.

"State highway is gutted, you say, Frank?"

He unconsciously pads his right hip holster.

"Well, we'll send a cruiser over to help you cross the river. It might take an hour or so to get there using the back road, but that's our call. I can't believe you still have power. Most of the east side of town is out. MG & E has been going like fifty to get people hooked up. You understand there are other emergency priorities, right?"

I pick up a gun safety pamphlet from the counter and skim to the highlighted words, *Permit to Carry a Concealed Weapon Application.* Lundgren presses on with Frank.

"Listen. I've got a visitor, but I'll get back to you soon. Talk to you later."

Lundgren hangs up and slides his gun belt higher on his hip.

"Hello, Doc. Thanks for coming."

He vigorously scratches his scalp as if there is an irritating bug in place.

"Old Frank has been bugging me for the past hour or two, calling every twenty minutes looking for the road crew, asking if they're still chugging coffee and dunking doughnuts."

I smile. "The elder statesman has a point, Deputy. He's missing out on the Bridge tournament at Ole's. You saw the traffic. I never imagined how big these reunions could be."

He nods and casually rotates his left shoulder a couple times.

"Last year was my thirtieth. Some of the rascals I ran with then are still the same bozos. Between horseshoes and softball, I was a wreck. Hauling drunks to the clink or arresting punk-asses who tried to put a spin move on me as I applied a shoulder with handcuffs. High school reunions can take their toll"

He motions to the desk behind the counter for me to come back and have a seat.

"I got a call from the County Headquarters this morning and they want to send out a coroner to have a look at Darlene. It's a good idea, but I got the feeling that it was more than a suggestion. Are you the instigator for sending those hounds on my scent?"

I sit forward and stutter through an explanation.

"I meant no harm, Deputy Lundgren. I was mainly looking out for you. Attorneys, county or state, can be major hinderances to the truth and love to carve small-timers, like you and me, into judicial morsels. If something, anything goes wrong, they'll be on your doorstep with a subpoena." I tap the tabletop with my knuckles. "I like it here. I like the way people take care of each other. It would make an interesting story on how the county looks on the state's jurisprudence, and vice versa."

Lundgren ponders that for a moment. There is a tightness in his face that soon relaxes. He looks up to the circulating fan blades above us. His eyes have a red tint, like an apple dulled by too much sun.

"Are you sure you are not protecting Miss Tessa, instead? I can handle it if you say 'yes.' She was awfully nervous last night. Usually, she can brush these instances off like bothersome mosquitoes, but I got a feeling her rudeness to me was sprayed-on with a hose." He leans forward, face to face, exhaling a fruity-Danish, strong-coffee breath. "Has she been that way with you, Doc?"

Tessa is a determined woman. Overall, he's correct.

"I only met her for the first time a few days ago. You saw us touring the city and she drove me out to the memorial plaque she had erected for her sister, Erin. I think the anniversary of Erin's death is coming up and that's bothering her to a degree."

"Well, I'm a big boy, Doc. If she wants to chew me out, let's say that I deserve it. As I once heard in a song, she needs a little less talk and a lot more action."

He gives me a once over, but I'm sure he's thinking lower.

"Yes, I do, Deputy, and yes, I was up in that same area earlier. But the answer to your next question is no, I didn't see anybody else, and no, I don't have a criminal past."

"Hey, don't get defensive, Doc. I was about to point out that that trail is old and hard to find without going into the woods. It's one of the original packed paths during the church camp days. It was told to me by one of the boys that you were once a counselor up there and you knew Tessa's sister."

I want to circle back to the purpose I was called here although this cold case still festers a little. Right now, it's Tessa, first and foremost.

"I apologize," I retreat. "I have become the new mother hen. Tessa is going above the call of duty as the Resort Business Manager. She works hard. This is a risky business that needs to run smooth. Do you agree?"

"I've been watching her handle this business for the last ten years, Doc." He presses the buzzing button on his two-way radio collar. "You are only a visitor. Let's try to get along till you leave."

"I don't have a problem with that, unless you have any objections," I interject.

He stands up, an indication our meeting is over.

"Inside is official business. Outside this door is your business."

He escorts me by the arm and holds the door open.

"Good to see you again, Doc. I'll hook up with Tessa and you at the reunion."

I stand in the doorway weighing the pros and cons. Meanwhile, Lundgren returns to his desk and sits. This meeting has gone against my conscience, more like suspicions, topped off with a dose of caution. Tessa reminded me more than once that I am intimidating to the gentlemen folk, but I thought I was blending in well. A visit with the funeral director, Roland Purdy might be the ticket. He might need my help.

A large municipal work truck is oiling down the Wasoon Funeral Chapel grounds with a sticky-watery substance. Gravel and dust are any merchant's biggest enemies, but the last one who needs this is Roland. With the summer season on the home stretch, these gouging rains can take every remaining pebble downstream from the city outskirts, leaving the surface eroded like a County Fair racetrack. Road and street repairs are a never-ending pain in the ass. I decide to pull over, my fat tires sinking into the clay pack. Roland's van is in front of the florist delivery door.

The combination oily stench of hot liquid tar and truck exhaust can defray any potential customer from deciding on a loved one's service until a better day. There's no way to avoid the unctuous substance and I tiptoe like walking on fire to the side entrance. Roland is about to open the door when he spots me.

"Dr. Michaels, what brings you here?"

He wears a stained plastic apron over his shirt and tie. The long white waist strap is knotted in the front on his spindly frame.

"I was finishing up with Mrs. Gabbert. You missed the coroner by minutes."

"So, the county sent a representative?" I inquire.

"Correction. It was a deputy-appointed official, not a Medical Investigator. More like a Decedent Affairs person. That's the type of people we get up here in Wasoon, being that the county is so large. It might take a day or so to get someone of importance."

He pulls at the cuffs of his rubber gloves and they come off, inside out, with the sound of a nipple being yanked from a dairy calf's mouth.

"Will there be another visitor from the County?" I ask.

"Only if there is a need," he surmises, inspecting his hands. "Usually, they go back to headquarters and re-hash the slim report with the higher-ups. If they feel a need, we will be notified the next day. In the meantime, I'm free to embalm and prep the body for viewing. I was over and done with her last femoral. All the routine toxicology and blood work were completed by the lab crew last night. They're on twenty-four-hour call. Those folks cover three or four counties in this sparsely populated region. If the deceased is from out of town, I have to connect with the family and decide my next move."

He swats at a fly with the pair of gloves but misses badly.

"Mr. Gabbert was very cooperative. He even selected an outfit in which I can dress her. He wants it to be like her most favorite time: the reunion. I won't say no to him. Good old Darlene will be wearing the Class of Sixty-Seven banner over her chest like a contestant in a beauty pageant."

I envision all her friends offering condolences to the bereaved, wearing cheerleading outfits and football jerseys. What a send-off. I wonder if the church organist is preparing to play the class fight song.

"Did she have any children?"

"She has a daughter in Arizona and a second one in Texas," he answers. "Both are ministers, like she was. Darlene preferred to stay in Minneapolis rather than retire to the heat."

Roland chuckles. "Folks were getting into the reunion until this happened. With the banners strung all over town and the event's brochure handed out at the café, a death dampens the activities for the rest of us."

"It gives pause to contemplate the inevitable," I tell him.

"I'll grant you that one. It's like nightfall, or better yet, like trying to induce fixative into Darlene's neck veins. They were as hard as sinew. Nearly plugged with plaque from old age, but you already know how that is."

I consider the potential of embalming fluid squirting all over the neck, table, and floor.

"Bad vessels, you say?" I inquire.

"Constricted and calcified," he goes on. "There was some soft tissue hemorrhage as well. Not much, but enough to wonder if my cannula tore into the jugular by accident."

Red flags sail over my common sense like contrails from a jet. Postmortem hemorrhage is not feasible, but vascular hemolysis can occur at any given time.

"Do you mind if I take a look? I might be able to figure out if there is a secondary vessel that you could use to get infusion."

"Be my guest, Doc. I still have her on the table drying off."

He leads me into the prep room where the aging exhaust fan blows loudly overhead in a vain attempt to keep decaying odors at a minimum. The pale nude body of Mrs. Gabbert is lying on the metallic gurney, the drain hose attached at its base, leading to a flush unit. Her rotund shape is elevated from the surface by a head block under her neck and two additional blocks suspend each forearm to draw the excess liquid away from the upper torso. Roland had applied an initial layer of rouge on her cheeks, but the lower lip is puffy. I notice the subtle bruising on the left side of her mouth.

"Good job on the prep, Roland," I tell him, leaning over her face, inspecting the blushing skin tones from the tinted embalming fluids.

I'm getting used to calling everyone by their first name. This was initially an uncomfortable reply, but now I consider it rude to address them any other way. Prosecuting attorneys often use that ploy to get on your good side. Then come the lies and accusations. Anything to rankle you.

"Thanks." He peers over my shoulder. "She needs an additional base layer, but I'll wait until you're finished, if that's okay."

"I'll be only a minute," I forewarn him and shake out a couple of gloves from the box to put on. Doing so, I bend in for a closer look.

The embalmed tissues are firm as I palpate above the incision for crepitance or crackling that might indicate a hyoid bone fracture. A common mortuary string holds the skin in place right of the throat where the jugular is located. I casually rub the base coloring away from the right side of the neck. The pasty caulking is not quite dry and its residue smears like cheap latex paint. Because the pink tinge in the embalming fluid can obscure tissue damage, looking for trauma is tricky. Roland had perfused adequately. Dissection and further cutting on her is something I'm not going to undertake.

"You say there was some concern whether or not the main vein was patent?" I'm directing the question toward the body as if she might give me the answer.

"Well, all I can tell you, Doc, is that everything felt a little spongy, as if blood had seeped into a false channel or cavity. I became a little concerned that it was my fault. Next of kin are most comfortable with that 'just sleeping' appearance."

He hesitates.

"Sometimes, I want the body to look alive. Got to sell the job as well, you know."

"I understand, Roland. You do good work."

"Thanks," he sighs.

My fear of being caught by a county officer with my hands illegally on the body; how do I explain that?

"I can't be one hundred percent certain of anything without using a scalpel and peeling away the layers. Were there any comments from the deputy or coroner's assistant about the neck?"

I begin to palpate the back of the neck and other side of the skull.

"He didn't look overly concerned. I can tell you that." His voice becomes territorial, defensive, as if the Gabbert body was still his responsibility.

"That's alright, Roland," I begin. "They were making mental notes at the time. I do the same thing when focusing on the death."

He pulls a clean white bed sheet out of the counter drawer. "Well, if you're finished, let's cover her up. Between the dust outside and flies in here, there's enough to worry about without making up corny conclusions. Leave that to the authorities. Don't you think so, Doc?"

"Yes indeed," I agree and step back as he unfolds the sheet.

Outside, the diesel truck motors to the back side of the building near to the ramp door. I hear the dry, rocky gravel unloaded and come to realize how close we were to the door accidentally blowing open, and the entire construction world witnessing the two of us hoovering over a body. Curiosity-seekers come in all shapes and sizes. I recollect how some of the most notorious bar room stories I'd ever heard began with the sneak peek of a dead body, and a morgue attendant with blood smears on the apron as the door accidentally opened. I appreciate small funeral businesses like this who still give a personal touch to each client.

"If you need me for anything, I'll be staying on for a least a couple more days. Tessa has invited me to be her escort at the prom, err, I mean the reunion."

I tap Roland on the arm.

"Will you be there?"

His stance stiffens.

"There is always a get together of some sorts up there. The summer is filled with meetings and tournaments. A town like Wasoon needs to be playing up to these gatherings all the time. We used to have community-only gatherings. Pass the welcome baton to the next sorry-ass resort. Least, that's how I see it."

"How do you mean?" I ask.

"Well, we have mostly locals at these doings, but some city folk come into town driving new cars every year and throwing down a measly two-dollar tip to the waitresses. It's as if they are rubbing our noses in their successes just because they left Wasoon. I tell you, Doc, I, for one, rejoice that the high-rollers are gassed-up and back on the road."

He drapes Mrs. Gabbert and draws the edges of the sheet snug under her limbs.

"All the other merchants feel roughly the same except for the convenience shops and filling station. They act like they still live here in their minds. I see them take advantage of the sporting goods shop, trying to Jew down the price of last year's golf clubs because they're not the latest technology. Other things, too. For instance, they poke fun of the Bee Café. They ask, 'How can a dump like this still be serving the very same fried food at those prices?' and what not. They joke about everything they grew up with, like the most recent farm auctions, baseball schedules taped to the windows, who caught the biggest walleye."

"Don't sell your little village short, Roland," I tell him. "There's no need to be resentful of your fellow classmates. Egos are like balloons at a birthday party. For instance, at my medical school reunions, the reception room is diluted with over-inflation and that's not clearly on the dance floor. I stopped attending them years ago."

Roland chuckles and shakes his head.

"I ought not be unloading on you like this. It's alright in the short run, but I long for the days when Wasoon was mostly farmers and fishermen who kept to themselves, like when the church camp was still open. Now, that was fun for kids and parents alike. It was something only Wasoon had and even the Twin Cities newspapers placed ads in the Sunday editions. We were unique in that regard. The ministers force-fed Bible stories on us, but we found new friendships from kids we grew up with, not out-of-towners. That was my idea of a vacation." He huffs. "We were not gearing up for a busload of geriatrics."

He escorts me to the entrance ramp.

"I guess I'll be there for a short while," he concludes with a *poor me* attitude.

"If I see you, the first drink is on me," I said. "That's rationale for being a good guy."

"Thanks, Doc."

Back in my motorized sauna called a rental, I hastily crank the air conditioner on high and pull away from the oncoming road grader followed by a tar and oil packer. How I ever became used to this is still a mystery. Freeze your ass in the winter and live on canned sodas all summer. Was I the only one that had sweat glands the size of grapefruit?

My cell phone vibrates, signaling a missed call. It's the phone number from the reference lab I used for bloodwork. My test results are in. No, I bet it's worse. There's going to be another delay. I can't suffer through any more agony. My heart pounds and my neck feels tight. I exhale deeply and hit the call back button.

"This is Dr. Michaels. I see I missed a call from this number."

I never get used to disheartening news, board exam test scores, or jury verdicts. It never sits well at the end of the day. Like my Midwestern brethren often promised: if you wait long enough, something bad is bound to happen. Was I feeling a tinge feverish or perspiring out the verdict? How about my headaches and stiff joints? Is my irresponsibility with Tessa going to carry over to our relationship? I close my eyes as the executioner places me on hold.

"Dr. Michaels. This is Ruth Austin, head of Dynamics Laboratories. You sent us a second blood specimen a few days back and I wanted to give you the test results, if I may, over the phone. Are you free to discuss?"

"Now is as good a time as any," I respond, watching the work trucks and passing cars. Wishing time would speed up.

"Very well," she said. "It looks like the surface and core antigens for Hepatitis A and B are negative, as well as C."

My thoughts are jumbled. "Thank you."

Total disbelief and relief.

"I had other blood tests taken at the same time. About those?"

I need clarification, the meaning of the report, and not have to milk the answers out of her, especially the portions that are usually highlighted with asterisks as 'above normal.'

"Good news on the other viral studies, as well. All are negative. Congratulations, Dr. Michaels. I take it you had quite a scare during an examination?"

Tears of relief well up in my eyes, not knowing whether to cry, smile, or say a prayer of thanks. There is a sudden giddiness and I flop back into my driver's seat.

"That is an understatement," my voice rising. "It felt like a pin prick. But worst-case scenario, my concern was on high alert."

I'm sure she has given very glum results to other candidates in the recent past. I catch myself closing my eyes and covering my mouth. If ever I needed some welcome news, this is it.

"I can appreciate the risks you take in your business. We all work under stressful situations, even in the best of conditions. People always say that the risk of contracting either AIDS or hepatitis is extremely low, but I'll gladly trade places with those nay-sayers any day."

She pauses to suppress a sneeze.

"Excuse me. Air-conditioning and respiratory bugs mix rather well in the summer."

"Sorry to hear that," I empathize. "I'm calling from northern Minnesota. This appears to be ground zero lately for crushing humidity and big thunder bumpers. I sometimes think the drone of refrigerated motors does little to quell the heat. Television weathermen are a pain in the ass, too. We hinge on every syllable as if we're all doomed."

"We are in a sweltering hot period, also," she adds. "The only way to cool off is with a big storm. That, my friend, is long overdue." She pauses. "Work or pleasure?"

I close my eyes and think of a lake water swim. Tessa naked in my bed. It seemed such a long time ago that we sat upon that flat piece of marble and watched the day disappear.

"I was called to perform a private autopsy on a local celebrity of sorts, a lake resort owner, pseudo-treasure-sunken ship hunter. His shipmates hadn't heard from him for a couple days and I venture the smell of death was strong in his berth. The family is questioning how it happened. Fortunately, the people up here are very cordial and straightforward. I'm beginning to appreciate it more each day."

"Well, I've never been out of Utah except to visit my mother in Grand Junction, but I hear from others who have been to the Midwest that it's very relaxing. Perhaps I need to get away more often."

"It's working for me, Doctor. Like you, I've had the exact problem for years. Any family?" By the friendly sound of her voice, I feel a kinship between two overworked souls.

"My son is in high school. In his words, he's a big time senior next year but still doesn't know where he wants to go. His father and I are a dull cog on his chain of fun as he refers to it. Sometimes we come on like gestapo interrogators. At least, that's the impression he leaves with me. How about on your end?"

"No family. I'm a recent widower and not particularly good at using free time. Mostly, I work and try to stay busy," shortening my responses, shortening my excuses.

"Well, have a good stay, Dr. Michaels. I hope these results allow you to relax a little. If you have any questions in the future, please feel free to contact me. Goodbye."

"Goodbye and thank you," I answer back, but she had already disconnected.

Percentiles of good news are still below normal, but these outcomes are the perfect answer. The Wasoon funeral van silently rolls by, its dark windows unreflecting. Everyone has a place to go except for myself. Even the dead have appointments. My thoughts roll toward Tessa and how I nearly subtracted years from her life. Stupid. Very stupid. Seeing the cellular destruction firsthand isn't anything like the lasting impalement this malady bestows to not only the patient, but also the survivors. I need a cold shower to purge.

My internal clock is signaling that it must be around the lunch hour as I pass through the downtown district toward the highway leading to the resort. That was the best news all week. How about celebrating with a snack? I make a quick stop at a small family-owned business off the main drag called the Blue Mound Deli. Upon returning to the resort, I resolve not to punish myself in the cabin, except to review autopsy notes and hope to casually check on Tessa to see if there's anything she needs. I have been fraught with malpractice guilt over a moment of extended desire and without delay want to exterminate those concerns. She will never have to know, will never have to decide her future with me. Twenty minutes later, I grab the paper bag with a fresh Reuben deli sandwich with chips and two sodas off the passenger seat and hasten into the lobby of Ole's Resort.

"Hello, Dr. Michaels," greets the cheerful intern. "If you're looking for Ms. Stevens, she's not here." She stuffs a magazine under the lip of the daily ledger. "There was a call from a caterer in Roseland. Something about being late, or staffing, or something else. She huffed out of here in a hurry, I'll tell you that."

She sits back attentively, drawing her legs beneath her on the seat.

"Is there anything I can do for you?"

"Delivering lunch to the hungry staff," I regroup and set the sandwich bag on her desk. "Have you eaten, yet?"

"Thank you. Thank you very much," she gushes as if opening a surprise Christmas gift, scuttling the wrapping, and beaming. "Wow. This is ten-times better than my peanut butter and jelly."

Daintiness, however learned in college, is out the back door once she's into the second chomp. A couple more bites and slurps from the root beer, it's as if she hasn't eaten for days.

"Is this from the Blue Mound Deli? It's been quite a spell since I've had a sandwich from there. Dr. Michaels, I hope I'm not embarrassing myself too much."

I bring up a stool and sit across from the devouring princess careful not to be overwhelmed by the carnage.

"How is the internship treating you? Does it meet your expectations?"

"Pretty much," she dabs her mouth between swallows. "Ms. Stevens, Tessa, can be a little bossy, but I'm learning so much about the business. The good thing is that this will be perfect for my resume once I finish my senior project in the fall. Hopefully, some hotel management headhunter will find me here in Wasoon. It's a stretch, but I'm trying to get my foot in the door at Plymouth Century Estates. Are you familiar with the Lake Superior region up north? That community is developing into a getaway for the Twin Cities people."

"Everybody needs a place to call home," I warrant. "Some only need more bedrooms and chandeliers. Come to think of it, a fair share of them have been my customers or clients over the years."

"This place is nice, but too low key for my taste." She tidies the front of her resort smock.

Replaying the situation in my mind, anyone I have been in contact with this week in Wasoon treats a crisis in similar manner with a tinge of sarcasm. She re-wraps the remaining half of the sandwich and tucks it back into the bag.

"College students need extra brain food, besides a trashy summer novel or two," I smile. "It's yours. I had a huge breakfast."

"Thank you very much," she says. "I was beyond hungry."

"You know, there are some things for which Wasoon is famous besides energetic college coeds."

She smirks.

"I get the point, Dr. Michaels. My friends and I are always looking for a way to trash this little place and I sincerely apologize. Please don't tell Tessa."

"It's not necessary," I shake my finger at her. "My impression is that Wasoon forgives. Townsfolk will be waiting for you."

"Exactly, Dr. Michaels. I'm afraid to waste my time and money by looking elsewhere. This resort internship is a terrific steppingstone to something better. But the boys suck."

She slouches back in the chair.

The melodic chime of someone opening the front door cuts short our banter. Another elderly couple enters, this time wearing Hawaiian prints, wide-brimmed straw hats, and wheeling neon-colored luggage.

"Back to work," she smiles cordially. "I'll tell Ms. Stevens that she missed you. And thanks for the lunch."

The confinements of my cabin under shadow my need to resolve something nagging in the back of my mind as if I had walked into a closet and forgot why I went there in the first place. In a matter of moments, I hike back to my rental and head to the other side of Wasoon City. Ribbons of heat bounce off the pavement ahead of me. I manage to direct the vented air conditioning on my face and in a matter of a few miles my shirt feels like a slimy alien clinging to my back. I strain forward over the steering wheel. Perhaps someday I will get accustomed to most everything I hated about summers up here.

CHAPTER THIRTEEN

O n the wide array of non-paved roadways I've experienced on Indian reservations, this is the absolute worst. The Red Lake Convalescent Home and Care Center is a beacon for the rundown community of paper-thin shacks and twenty-four-hour convenience stores that push cigarettes and liquor. The car shocks sound off like miniature detonations with each dip and pothole. Although this division of the city offers a pastoral view of well-fed grazing cattle at the forest line, the sharp contrast to barb-wire fence lines and rusted farm machinery is a stark reminder that those days are gone. Decades gone.

I slow as a group of ragtag juveniles fling a frisbee onto the street traffic in front of me. My heart races for that classic moment of trepidation we've all experienced: the sudden burst of a little brother or sister racing to join them. Oblivious to the street traffic. Blind to anything but the fun. To the left, an elderly woman is gathering bed sheets and flannel shirts that flap in the breezes. She yells something inaudible at them. The boys giggle and vanish into an unkempt side yard. The open garage door from which she came out harbors a chained-up pit bull that charges at the straggler. Saliva and canines. The woman continues to collect the laundry as if deaf.

The Center has a front grassy yard displaying a statuesque angel standing guard in the middle of a fountain, holding a sepulcher. The building itself is a single story, red brick box. The only defining character is the semicircular corral of aging Norway pines with the central focus leading to the entrance, much like an institutional hotel. An elderly landscaper in bib overalls carefully prunes away the last wilting blooms of summer roses. His working partner is a thickset Native American teenage girl in straw hat and wearing a protective headset. I watch as she rides the lawn mower in brisk laps around the brick wall. Other than that, there are no other signs of human activity. By the time I arrive, the nursing personnel are preparing residents for either social activities or naps.

The entrance doors draw sucking vacuum from the weather seals as I grip and pull at it for leverage. The characteristic Convalescent Home has all the earmark smells of antiseptic alcohol. Loose stools are masked by astringent floral deodorizers that bombard me with faded images of my mother's final weeks. She had been convalescing after an accidental fall that led into terminal unconsciousness. Floor fans loudly hum and face outward through the doorways like electric sentinels. Televisions in the private rooms are turned up extra loud to annoying game show audiences. From this viewpoint I notice a spate of open wards revealing senior citizens in varying stages of dress, or undress, their aged pallor is like delicate china. Some sit in the Lazy Boys beside their railed beds. In one room, a woman is busy realigning tattered cards and get-well letters on a dresser top. A sullen, elderly man is seated next to the window, scowling. Nurses stroll up and down the corridors like security detail. One of them pushes a wheeled dispenser of medications and paper cups and knocks loudly on the door frames to announce her arrival.

With no one to greet me at the nurse's station, I continue to wander the dimmed corridors, pausing briefly at each room to check the name plaques placed in the metal slides. A wafer-thin nurse in a pink smock politely smiles as she scurries past without an ounce of interest. In one room a feeble woman carries on a hushed conversation to an empty bed. Across the hall, I see a dresser display framed with family pictures next to the 'cord of life' emergency switch that dangles on the bed railing.

I always explain to my clients that an autopsy doesn't address standards of care. Only the anatomical findings are listed in the final report with a cause related to the death. Over the years, I've encountered both grief and acceptance in unequal portions. It resides within these walls, too. Generally, places like this are the last resort and not an Ole's Resort. Forgotten and existing in shaded rooms, even dimmer with forty-watt bulbs, the residents, however the care, become accustomed to their surroundings. It reminds me so much of moles in a subterranean hole, pushing mounds of soil to the top, only to burrow deeper into despair.

In due course, I arrive at the tee-shaped corridor and hesitate. Down the left wing what looks to be two female medical personnel in teal-colored smocks stand outside a doorway conversing in hushed tones. One of them covers her mouth while the other co-worker frowns. The speaker stops to greet me.

"Excuse me. You can't come down here at this time. We have a departure."

She smiles politely.

"I suggest that you check in with the front desk and they'll be able to help you. Right now, we're waiting for a call back from the funeral home."

Her voice is raspy like the sound of stepping on pebbles in a cave. A pastel cigarette holder protrudes from her chest pocket.

A skinny pink-smock nurse steps out from the room and draws the heavy door closed behind her. Looking to her workmates, she speaks.

"That will do for now. Has Roland been contacted?"

"Yes," the taller one replies, then scrutinizes me. "Perhaps I can help you. Who was it that you are visiting?"

"It's been years, but I wanted to pay my respects to Ray Perkins. I used to know him back when I was in high school," I lie. "If you can direct me to his room, I'll leave you to your duties. I'm sorry for your loss."

"You said Ray Perkins?" Her eyes dart to the other women. "Are you a relative of some sort?"

"Not really," I explain. "I happen to be staying at Ole's Resort and wanted to say hello. I'm Dr. Kevin Michaels, a friend of the family."

Her mouth forms a perfect O.

"Then we are sorry for your loss, Doctor Michaels. This is Ray's room. He died sometime this morning after breakfast. I'm surprised, too, on the account that he ate everything. We helped him to the bathroom, and he was bathed. We thought he was taking a siesta when the housekeeper stopped to tell us. He's an invalid, you know."

"I understand he had a stroke that left him paralyzed on the left side," I reply trying to create more feedback. "Had he been sick?"

"Not any more than usual. His heart vitals have been checked daily and breathing sounds were normal."

Aspiration pneumonia. Older people often have trouble swallowing and can regurgitate bacteria-laden gastric contents into the larynx and trachea where it seeps into the lungs with colonies of toxic killers. It is the common cause of death in bedridden, convalescent patients, along with sepsis. My guess is either that, or age-related cardiac failure right off the bat.

"The summers are not easy on our residents and it's unusually tough this year with all the humidity. Our air conditioners are running twenty-four seven."

"I can appreciate that," I tell her in accordance. "There's nothing you can do about the weather. At least he was well-cared for and comfortable. Thank you for everything. By the way, did he have any family?"

"No one immediate," the door closer responds. "He was the last of the Perkins in Wasoon. One brother died a few years ago and Ray never married."

She stares at her empty hands.

"We lose a share of residents who have no one that seems to care. They are not only sick and old, but terminally lonely. We'll gather his personal belongings and have it shipped to Goodwill or something. That dear man, Roland, was barely here earlier to pick up Rosie Peterson's death certificate. Ray missed an opportunity to ride share the ride with someone else in need."

"I hear that the city council set up a care fund for him years ago on account that he was living on a meager retirement income and Medicare," interjects the speaker.

"Yep. I heard the same thing," adds the door-closer accenting her Scandinavian descent, folding her arms in front.

"Well, he was more of a family friend," I explain. "My parents brought food to his apartment above the filling station for holidays and sorts."

These stories are becoming easier, although there was a general hint of truth.

"If there is anything I can do, please contact me. I'll be at the resort a few more days."

"Thank you, Doctor," they reply in unison, polite and caring, an unending dedication and servitude to the forgotten.

Nostalgia is becoming my worst enemy and I'm not getting very far in the search for clues or answers to Tessa's concerns. My soliciting skills are out of touch. Again, I happen to be a day late, an hour short, or not even on track with the people of Wasoon anymore. Erin's soft voice circles the back of my mind like a glider catching updrafts. I long to spend more time with Tessa, but is that because she reminds me of Erin, or do our two empty vessels need to be refilled? Why the headscarf as a reminder? Unexpectedly stuck in lake country limbo, the people of this community are far ahead of me in these aspects. I had hoped that Ray Perkins remembered Erin, but that was wishful thinking. By the time I get back to my cabin, Tessa will be back from wherever. I, most certainly, require a little company and positive reinforcement.

CHAPTER FOURTEEN

By the time I return, the resort has undergone a major change. Colorful streamers hover over the barbeque pit welcoming the various alumni classes. Each banner is unique and displays a specific class year. It's easy to tell the spirit of competition between graduates is going to be the highlight. School colors of emerald green and autumn gold abound. Women are wearing logo tee shirts and mascot visors. The gents all seem obliged to be carrying around one of those complimentary padded beer holders with their graduation year stenciled on the sides.

Long lost classmates hug and point at each other in surprise all while the caterer's staff scurry to reset tables and line up chairs. The fun-loving alumni are oblivious to their activities and the lost serenity outside my cabin is now a sea of cackling ladies gladly enjoying their free time away from children or spouses, or both. Chirpy guests hoist plastic champagne flutes toasting everything from the Lazy Bee Café to the ancient Dairy Queen where Tessa and I shared ice cream yesterday.

I check the pestering cell phone attached like a vestige to my belt. There are no prevailing messages to hound me. Thank God for the North Country where I can use the flimsy excuse of poor connections. For what it's worth, there's nary a note from Tessa either. I half-way dreamed of catching her sitting on the edge of my bed going through paperwork. With all the merriment at the resort, my cabin is the perfect hiding place from the emotional traffic outside.

What to do? A free day is filtering through my grasp. I feel like the out-of-place ogre standing in the wings at a beauty contestant's acceptance speech. I begin rummaging through my carry-on and my file of autopsy notes on delinquent cases. Out of guilt, I let out a huge sigh of discouragement. An hour into this suffering, I tip my head back, mutter a few F-bombs, and close it. This is as far as I can go with it for now.

My knee joints scream from yesterday's trail adventure and dragging out the cowboy best seller that inspired me at the airport is a total waste of time. Besides, my chosen seat from yesterday is presently occupied by a boisterous nineteenth hole golfer. I guess my membership card to that club hasn't been issued yet.

The phone rings and jolts me out of self-pity.

"Hello?"

"Hey. It's Tessa."

"Where are you?" I ask, an embarrassing hint of whiney desperation seeping out of my voice.

"I'm on my way back from Bemidji. We had a catering crisis."

"I was told that at the front desk," I add. "Your college intern, Paige, devoured a Reuben sandwich I had gotten for you."

"Sorry," she continues, the connection is peppered with static. "I will be back in a couple hours. Are you still up for a reunion date tonight?"

"If it's any indication how the evening will materialize by looking outside, then it is a tentative 'Yes.' Supervision will be necessary, of course."

I hear her chuckle.

"Is it that bad?"

"For good measure I predict some periods of welcome silence will be had by all tomorrow morning."

"I hope that doesn't extend to present company," she teases. "I want to continue where we left off, if that's all right with yours truly?"

"I'm on the same page. What do you want to consider first: the thunder or the shower?"

"I was thinking more on the line of supper followed by a dance or two," she chides. "Let's not jump to any conclusions how the rest of the night is carried out."

"Roger that," I answer. "By the way, Ray Perkins passed away this morning."

"How did you find that out?"

"I was on my way to visit him, mostly to see how he looked and if he remembered me. But I was a few hours too late. As I was told, the housekeeper alerted the nurses. They thought he was taking a nap."

There is a stagnant pause. Are we disconnected? Then, she speaks up.

"I knew this day would come, but I always held out hope. The staff never indicated to me that his health was declining."

I respond. "It looks to me as if he was a minimum care client. Roland was on his way to pick up his body when I arrived. I'm sorry, Tessa. I know you felt a kinship through Erin and him. I guess it was truly time for his system to give out."

"Give out or not, I'm still not going to give up, Kevin. I always felt he was the last living clue. He knew enough to talk about my sister. Sadly, that is not the case again. Is it possible that no one saw her besides Perkins?"

Her frustrations keep surfacing and I feel my presence has something to do with that. Tessa is anxiously waiting for the drawbar of doubt to be lifted. I dare not tell her that these issues are more like am Amtrak not taking any more passengers. She'd eventually learned about the old man, but thanks to my big mouth, it's another millstone.

"Don't consider it futile, Tessa. I know it's easier said than done, but answers are still out there. We need to find an opening. Think about other places to check out. I'm here for you as long as you need."

"Kevin, you have gone way beyond the call. I love that you are staying by me through all this, but you have a business to keep alive and I don't want to be in the way of that. Like I told you. All the doubts, the rehashing, the sleepless nights and yet, fat zeros are the only result. It's not to be."

I hear loud electrical discharges emanating from the receiver, like giant rats grousing through a box of newspaper.

"This connection is getting worse. When can I expect you?"

"Around four or five at the earliest," she answers. "The crackling is not as bad on this side. I can hear you loud and clear, but this storm could pack some punch. All in all, it's just added fluff for the big shindig. Don't worry. You'll be in good hands all night."

I yell into the phone that those hands better be warm, but I don't think she hears me as the bell tone "beep-beep-beep" flatly announces that we have lost our connection.

"Hello? Tessa?"

There's nothing but the irritating grainy inaudible clatter on the other end.

Outside, I hear raucous laughter as if someone is either pushed or has fallen into the pool, followed by applause.

"Whoa!"

I peek out from between the blinds like a nosey neighbor. A saturated gent clings to the edge, his hairpiece is the color and sheen of turpentine and flops to an abnormal length on the side of his face. His eyeglasses precariously dangle from the bridge of his nose and he spits water like plastic mermaids at water theme parks.

"Way to go, Harry."

Harry. That's the least of his problems. Hairless is more appropriate. A fellow alumnus with a sunburnt pot belly sticks out a plastic cup of beer which Harry gladly grabs and chugs. High school class reunions bring out the worst in the men. They should sign irresponsibility waivers to be read during the last will and testament. I should be so quick to judge. I'm acting like a nosey, twice-divorced widow living next door, the curmudgeon poking her nose out the peephole. I hope other available medical personnel are on call if something worse takes place. With all this craziness, anything could happen.

As if a weather switch is turned on, the wind kicks up and pushes the towering pines tips to bow. It won't be long until the mornings in resort country will be a crisp forty degrees. Classic Indian summer is waiting offstage. Tessa is distracted with multitudes of more important issues for me to get in the way, yet I am very appreciative that she takes the time to call me and check in. That's school-boy crush material and I begin to develop an escape itinerary in case she hasn't.

Another ring on my room phone and I answer.

"I knew there was something you wanted to add to the night's gaiety."

"Err, hello? Dr. Michaels? It's Roland Purdy, the funeral director in Wasoon?"

"Sorry, Roland, I was on the phone with Tessa and ..."

"I understand, Doc," he adds. "That woman can tease the life out of you and cut you off in an instant. I guess she gets that from being around those annoying twins. They're always trying to get the upper hand, you know. Your cell phone won't allow me to leave messages, so I took a chance that you were in your cabin."

"I never thought of that," choosing to sit in my recliner as he talks. "I venture to guess there's some truth to her pseudo-sister-brother relationship. What's up?"

"Soo-doe what?" his questioning voice is raised, curious.

"Pseudo...never mind," I say collectively. "How can I help you?"

"Well, I understand you had gone over to the nursing home to check on Ray Perkins. Looks like you missed the midnight train to Georgia. Nurses told me you were there."

"Yes. That's correct. I had some spare time and wanted to see if he remembered me."

That version of the true story was easier to streamline, plus it keeps Tessa out of the immediate picture.

"How long had he been dead?" he asks.

"I never got to see him," I reiterate. "The medical staff were closing off that portion of the facility to visitors when I arrived. They told me you were there to pick up another body and had to come back. Lucky, it wasn't rush hour."

My attempt at 'corn humor' sounds empty and crass.

Roland doesn't skip a beat.

"I have no trouble with you being there, Doc. Is there something I can help you with? I have Mr. Perkins here at the mortuary. You can take-a-peek again."

He pauses.

"The county has cleared the death as Natural Causes, so they won't mind, I think."

I won't second-guess the authorities in northern Minnesota. It might obstruct future opportunities for business.

"Do you have something in mind, Roland? Do you want me to request a second-opinion observation of some sort?"

"All I am saying is that you are the only person I know with any forensic training and I consider you a friend on a professional level. I'd appreciate some advice on these matters. Sometimes, I don't believe all the X's and O's are capitalized. The county does a cursory check-off and onto the Wasoon Funeral Chapel gurney they go."

He chuckles.

"Before they can make another decision, I flush the vessels with embalming fluid and aspirate the gut. A formal dress or suit is given to me by the family. I cut the seam from the backside, select a coffin, arrange for a service, and send out the bill. It all is a little simplistic if you ask me. I've been doing funerals for around thirty years. I'm becoming a little jaded, but you could clarify it as plain leery. Old age and death always have to be the one-two combination."

"You're sure that Father Time isn't catching up with you, Roland?"

"No not yet," he defends. "Dealing with the business of death has its drawbacks. Let's just say that I've been watching a fair amount of those crime shows on TV. It gets me wondering about how things like this can happen in cozy Wasoon. You understand where I'm coming from?"

Poisonings, smothering, and strangulations. Not in Hometown, USA. Clients often ask me about the state-of-the-art technology that can capture offenders, like those on the recently popular CRIME SCENE, a hot new syndicated investigative journalism show. Visualize silhouettes of hardscrabble men wearing wife-beater shirts, racing in slow motion from houses. Talk about sexism or racism. The tabloids have nothing over televised programs that popularize these fools. I venture a guess at this unsolved crime happening in Wasoon forty years ago to someone I knew. Has my return churned up the gossip pond?

"Roland, I don't think giving second opinions is a healthy thing unless I'm called upon to testify. That's dangerous ground because there are slick attorneys lurking, exactly like the criminals they are defending. They're only trying to construe excuses to get their clients exonerated. Believe me, I've been there."

"I'm not suspicious of anything, Doc. In my own way, I'm trying to put one and one together to get three, even though I know that leads to a cartload of trouble. Someday I'd like to tell you about the time a family chewed me out over the wrong dentures in their Grandfather's sew-together lips."

"Like I said, Roland, I'll be here if you need another opinion, but sleuthing around is definitely not a good idea. There is an all-school reunion for the living. Let's try to focus on that instead of the recent losses. Don't you think that's a more pleasurable approach?"

There's another loud 'kersplash' outside my door, as if a large boulder is being dropped from a two-story building into the deep end. Is it too late to change my question to Roland? I don't want to treat gashes with cadaver tape tourniquets.

"I hear noise. Are you at the pool, Doc? Sorry, if it's your day off."

"No, I'm just closer than I need be. Listen, I'll talk to you later. Thanks for calling. I appreciate the respect you have for me."

"It's nice to have someone to talk with about these things. I'll see you later tonight."

A true Midwesterner will internalize this to the grave and it's a good thing that Roland and I keep our guards up for the time being. Human error is the worst client to defend in court. A large knot simmers in my gut. I begin to think back on my world that caved in no more than a year ago. How ironic that I fall in the same boat. Suppress. Stew. Bottle up. The malpractice trials. Death of Cassie. The death of Erin, not to mention a careless fling with a sharp scalpel.

Northern Minnesota is not going to get any greener this year. In a matter of a few weeks, the weather patterns will begin to resemble a colorful palette of rusts and scrambled egg yellows. I remain locked in the dead zone where there is no request or desire for a second opinion. Some things are unchangeable and yet, Tessa is on my mind. She's been good for my spirit and I hope that the feeling is mutual.

CHAPTER FIFTEEN

The alumni team coach's glower is wavering as he tosses a weathered right-handed fielder's mitt in my direction. I sit on the corner of the dugout bench watching the men warmup by playing catch or jogging to and from the right field fence. I expected to be a fill-in or DH. My head isn't in the game. It's only a cordial invitation. Right?

"Doc. Why don't you take third base?"

By the simple laws of reasoning, the only idiot that's sober and playing the hot corner is me. I'm clamming up like hopping on a roller coaster without rails. With each batter on the left side of the plate, I take a baby step backwards and by the fourth hitter, I'm standing on the edge of the outfield grass. My first reaction to every swing is a grimace, a flinch, or a blink. Any shot in this direction explodes off the bat like a self-guided missile, line-driving over my head or in the gap between Aaron and myself.

So far, these guys can crush any toss at will. For the first two innings, anything coming to the left side of the infield through the hole, or not, is relegated to Aaron, playing shortstop. He has amazing soft hands and smoothly brings the ball up out of his glove and whips the throw to first like a semi-pro. I muff my first attempt and clumsily trip over the bag on a disparaging lunge to catch a foul ball.

As we enter the fourth inning, sportsmanship is being discarded with deliberate speed by both teams. A friendly game is but a moot reminder and has taken on a hostile demeanor. There are fewer beer coolers in the dugouts and the teams hustle in and out as distinct as the bold chalk lines.

No love is lost with the scorecard standing at 10-7, us in favor, thanks to a couple of fielding errors by their second baseman who laughs it off much to the irritation of his teammates. Deputy Sheriff,

Jonah the Whale, saunters to the plate, painfully obvious to me that he intends to bring a reckoning in his own matriculating manner - - schooling alumni on how this game is to be played. An infielder is either going to have a ball cannoned through his chest, or the community water tower had better expect a collision with small white satellite in a few moments.

As if orchestrated, a cotton-ball cloud, the size of the lake itself, casts an ominous granite grey shadow over the playing field. Jonah flips a bat into the chicken wire backstop fence and unzips his sports bag. He slowly brings out a copper-colored club and begins to practice swing on the edge of the dugout. That weapon easily costs three hundred dollars. Boys with their toys, some motorized, some aerodynamic. Some are sporting WMD's.

Aaron signals to the left fielder who is favoring the left-center gap, to back up a few steps and guard the foul line. He gives me a fleeting look of helplessness and chews on his lip, his own version of last rites, and takes a cautionary step back from the imaginary landmine I'm to guard. A Gypsy moth glides past his line of vision and he swats it down, then stomps it flat.

"Move up a little, Doc," he orders. "I'll take the deep shots. You cover the short angle in front of me. Okay?"

"Roger that," I reply. He's suggesting that I become the sacrificial lamb. Age before beauty still exists in the ranks. I feel like a taxidermy buck's head and gawk at the pitcher.

What ever happened to the Co-ed Invitational Tournament? Big mistake for passing by the larger diamond first, acting a little too casual for my own good. Women are invited to participate on this field, but I'm certain that the competitive history prevails and there is an indelible requirement to perform at the highest level. The hell that I stepped into is sixty feet away, aiming his bat toward deep center like a programed Daisy Cutter missile, leaving no remnants of life in the wake of impact.

The 'ping' of the bat in the adjacent field jolts me out of my trance and I gander to my right. A deeply tanned outfielder wearing a tight-fitting halter top careens to her left, cutting off a line-drive base hit, where-upon she scoops it up on one hop and wheels it to the cut-off second base woman. I exhale and slouch. I used to be able to do that, too. Say your prayers, Michaels. Hey, batter. Please leave my appendages intact, replete with that ever-shrinking sack between my legs. Is everyone up here that damned athletic? My feeble 'I'll watch' holds less ground than a sink-hole next to the poor Gabbert woman's body.

Jonah steps into the batter's box, tightening his grip, sticking his chin up and out. His manhood won't take walks. It's slow-pitch. His alumni tee shirt of '06' stretches over his biceps like slick nylon hosiery. Tomorrow there will be a front-page headline: "*Deputy Sheriff hometown boy does well. Looks to get laid on a frequent basis, and hits blinding scud rocket at rookie third baseman. Funeral plans pending.*"

Come to think of it, sobriety is not such a good idea right now because I sure can use a shot of something strong to take the edge away. Other routine grounders through the legs and dropped Texan-league bloopers have been laughed-off thus far, but I feel a need to repent my errors in a big way.

The first pitch intentionally is lofted and hangs twelve feet before dropping deep into the strike zone.

"Strike one."

Jonah ignores it like an annoying gnat. A swirling breeze kicks up dust devils behind the pitcher's mound as the ball is side armed back to the pitcher by the catcher. The fragrance of grilled hot dogs from behind the home plate fence invades the tunnel of terror and mayhem I'm about to witness. Tranquil innocence, my ass. Fading sunlight pokes a hole through the cloudy barrier like a voyeur hovering around home plate and the backstop. This hitter is a 'must out' because he carries the eternal risk of ridicule, especially if I'm involved. Where's my old high school pal, Brandon, when I need him?

Jonah scowls and tilts his head back as the second pitch lands on the lip of the plate.

"Strike two."

Two bad pitches. Not strikes by any rule book. He widens his stance, wets his lips, and leans in to devastate the next offer anywhere close to the hitting zone, miles wider than mine can ever be. My first at bat ended abruptly with the first pitch. I topped a weak grounder to the second baseman who taunted me by cocking the ball until I legged it to first for an easy out.

"Shit," I growled and scuffled infield dirt all the way back to the dugout where I sprawled in the corner like a pouting tee-baller. Finally, the centerfielder came over to give me a fist bump.

"Don't let him get under your skin. He does that to everyone."

I hunch over on my toes, my glove tip dragging on the ground in front of me, awaiting my destiny as the pitch is delivered. I can't use the out of practice excuse any longer.

"Whhoock!"

It's the distinct sound of two unequal solids meeting in a mid-collision and allowing momentum to determine its outcome: Physics 101. The centerfielder is on a reverse gallop during which the rest of us stand dumbfounded by the ball's trajectory, an arcing bomb that will easily land three hundred feet away from this universe. I watch Jonah lollygag around first. He doesn't perceive there might be a play on him. Guess where's Ground Zero? To my surprise, the racing young fielder chases down the ball and cocks his arm back to fire a laser to shallow left center where Aaron meets him and cuts it off. Jonah is steaming past second base toeing the inside corner and kicking up little pieces of clay and gravel with his cleats.

Oh, damn.

It's like glancing into a rearview mirror and seeing a semi-truck unexpectedly bearing down on me. He's closing the distance between the two of us at the speed of sound. There's a wild-eye scowl stretching across his face, his fists are clenched and his arms pump like pistons with each stride. Aaron rips the relay out of his webbing and launches a one-hundred-foot rope in my direction.

"Catch it, drag it, put the fucker out before he touches base," I overhear the catcher yell out.

I widen my stance in front of the bag and prepare for eventual impact. Blocking this human freight train won't be necessary because I am not going to be able to stay continent, much less put a tag on. The ball takes a skip hop in front and bounces into my chest where I pin it in the webbing. The burly deputy is airborne into a headfirst dive as I sweep my glove across his broad backside, summersaulting over the top of him like a drunken gymnast, and face-plant onto the compacted gravel beyond his cleats.

Bam. Bam.

Much to my surprise, the ball is secure in my glove and my ankles are still attached to the rest of my trembling frame. Somehow, I have heroically robbed Jonah out of a triple. I stand, gladiator-style over the fallen lion, astonished, relieved, amazed. My mouth is open wide enough to trap large moths or small birds.

"Wow!" Aaron yells as he races toward me. "That was one righteous-bitchin-frickin play. Way to go, Doc. You saved our sorry asses."

Jonah groans, his abdomen rides the bag like a flattened saddle, his cleats have left two elongated skid marks an inch deep in the base path.

"FUCK!"

He spits a wad of dark tobacco juice in the direction of my shoes, hunches over, then slowly rises and gives himself a "standing-eight count," like a weary martial arts fighter in the third round. Aaron yanks the ball out of my glove and around the horn it goes. I slowly survey my frame for anything obviously out of place. Super Batter also rights himself and heads toward the dugout silently dusting off his knees and elbows. Someone hands him a can of beer and he guzzles it in three swallows, letting out a reflective belch over the humiliating situation. No afterglow praises for him. Meanwhile, my head rings in loud voices not heard ever since I was twenty-five and hungover.

The rest of the game is a battle of egos and errant gusts. Routine fly balls sail into the night lights like dancing white gulls only to fall short or land in front of the charging, frustrated outfielders who are an alcohol-fueled step slower. More beer cans are opened, and fewer empties make their way into the trash receptacles. The littering is like carnage at a tail-gate party. By the fourth inning, my confidence and comfort zone are on the same page. I strut along the dugout fence, eager for another at bat. I tilt my head back toward the pitcher and hit a liner over his outstretched arm. For that, I was rewarded loud yelps from my teammates, but was left stranded on first base. Jonah never gained any extra humility either. He did rake a ball down the right field line for a stand-up triple. Standing aloof on the bag, he avoids any eye contact with me, but I oblige his efforts with a high-five. The next batter whiffs and dribbles a ball in my direction. I charge, picking it up barehanded, and whip it to first for the out. Their last rally is thwarted without much leftover fortitude and we end up winning 12-10.

Back at the resort, I am ushered to the chilled keg by my Braveheart teammates where a plastic cup is thrust into my hand like a trophy and I gratefully lean forward to receive the golden elixir from the dispenser. Aaron steps out in front of the hoard and begins to applaud. The other players follow suit. I feel my face turn bright red and hoist my beer to the sky. Afterwards, we talk up the game, discuss general local baseball, and 'dis' Minnesota's perennial losing Twins. They all grew up together and I am welcomed into the clan like a lost classmate from another state. It feels good to belong, an honoree of some sort. Some of these boys can still play a mean game of softball: steady fielding, selective hitting literally anywhere, anytime. I'm sure summer recreation leagues up here are antagonistic every night, encompassing the occasional weekend tournament qualifier for higher state rankings. We had our share of sun today, but the rosiness in the noses and cheeks indicate an ensuing alcoholic buzz.

I catch myself laughing a little too loudly at off-color jokes amongst the virile male-pack who are not the usual multiethnic stereotypes from my hometown. These third generation German, French, Icelandic, Scandinavian lads are as diverse as regular versus diet sodas. I prefer to think of them as folklore, the way they kid each other about family background. North or south Wasoon? Catholic versus Lutheran? Which of the women still have moustaches? These contrived stories are significantly better than the reminiscent high school day's fiction that reunions can generate. I think about my high school pal, Brandon, and how he'd fit right in.

Grilled hot dogs are passed around and I'm famished, grabbing a handful of chips and salsa as an appetizer. When in Rome, act like a Roman. When in Wasoon, act like a native. I insist on being called by my first name, but that proves a thorny issue with Aaron and David. They introduce me as "The Cutter" and eventually, the dragged-out, technical explanations give way to farfetched legends. It's not important anymore who I am to them. Forgetting any inherent transgressions that are hounding me is a welcome relief.

We all have a closet full of tall tales, but not this weekend. My new teammates are considering a rematch tomorrow. It's more like a fantasy league where images become fuzzier with each swig. I giggle at my insobriety that lingers like a condescending relative who refuses the hint to leave. My voice is bubbly. I'm tossing out compliments everywhere and holding my arms out wide as if to hug the whole world. I should slow down and pace my drinking self, but none of the others seem to be as loaded as I feel.

"Hey, Doc," slurs my new-found friend, Jonah. "You know, I might have taken you out at the shins if I wanted to."

He sank half a beer in two gulps and wipes dribble from his mouth. Snorting. Laughing. We exchange knowing looks.

"I'll give you that one," I tilt my head toward his direction. "A lucky catch and tag. You slid right into my glove."

"That's a load of steaming horse manure," retorts Aaron, now holding two full beer cups. "Doc, here, has played some ball. You saw his moves at the bag. Your big fat ass can't hustle anymore. Too much stud farming if you ask me."

"Watch your manners around the deputy," roars David, who has stepped up from behind me. "He's loading up on liquid ammunition as we speak."

"Yeah, watch it," the deputy whines. "I know I brought my badge along in one of these pockets," fumbling clumsily into his chest pocket. "Never mind, it's back in the truck for safe keeping. I guess I have the night off."

"Most of your nights are that way," adds our team's pitcher, a lit cigarette dangling from his tight lips.

"Damn straight," says the centerfielder who began that calculated throw. God, it seems like only minutes ago.

"Contrary to popular beliefs, not all the action takes place at the cheerleader camp in Pelican. Try to date women your own age, whatever that is."

"Bullshit."

"Bullshit is right," adds Aaron, toasting the group.

"Let me bartend for you both," I interject, trying to detract from the chest thumping. I take their cups and stumble away, once again hoping that my dwindling emergency room skills will not be called to action.

The filtering shade provided by the tall cottonwoods overhead creates mobile shafts of orange-peel sunlight. The picnic area is strategically set up for loungers or players or other attention-seekers tasting and talking trash. I am hoping that Tessa arrives soon. I need an opportunity to self-brag, poke my chest out, and present a wide smile.

"I was told that Tessa is here with the new caterer," Vincent Bode comes up from behind, surprising me as if he was waiting for the right moment to spring, keeping me off guard. His cologne clouds the air. Pungent. Spicy. Over-applied. A noxious film. The kind that travelling pharmaceutical sales reps wear.

"Folks have been complaining about the Tompkin's Food Service for years," he shouts over the crowd. "At the least, their hot dish isn't too spicy, but the meat is always undercooked. No one likes that California cuisine up here. It's strictly meat and potatoes. Everything else is fluff with Western dressing if you ask me."

Vincent wears pressed new black denim jeans with a banded

collar cowboy shirt. His gold belt buckle houses the emblem of a rumbling eighteen-wheeler leaving a lingering trail of exhaust from the overhead muffler imprint. The stylish ostrich-leather boots give him an extra three inches of elevation.

"Tell her I'm waiting for my dance. We always kick it up surprisingly good at the resort."

He clicks my plastic beer cup and brushes past to hit on a couple of younger coeds who are joking with the caterer lad holding a pitcher of margaritas. I smirk, thinking back to a similar theme of how I met Tessa a few days ago.

I notice that cliques are forming early near the buffet tables. Any graduates within the past decade still dress fashionably modern, as if they hopped out of last year's Pomp and Circumstance. In contrast, couples from earlier decades giggle and waggle. They blend with any crowd but seem to prefer gathering around large tables where a few reserved chairs have been draped with light coats or shawls on the backrests. There's a good turnout from the geriatric graduates too. Two much older women with walkers and matching jackets sit next to the memorabilia display, garnishing golden banners across their chests. I am feeling as out of place as a clown at a funeral. It reminds me how I once performed a second opinion postmortem on an exhumed body. The elderly decedent was a lifelong hospice volunteer, and her final request was that she be buried in her colorful Goodwill costume.

Mr. Talkative, Security Guard Perry Brown, weaves through the guests and stops to chat.

"Hey, Doc, quite a crowd, don't you think?"

He scoots next to me and pans the gathering like we are on television facing an imaginary camera.

"Where these women came from is a mystery. We never had that many good-looking girls in high school. To be honest, some of the faces don't even look familiar. I wonder if they might be at the wrong reunion party. There's another hoopla at the club house across the lake tonight as well."

"How about checking ID's at the gate?" I grin while at the same time toasting my teammates passing by. "That's the perfect place to get acquainted."

"I had yesterday off," he adds. "I went to Duluth to hit the mall for some new threads and a haircut."

He extends his hand beyond his receding hairline and rubs his moussed crew-cut.

"Got to look good for the ladies in case I get lucky tonight."

"I hear you."

I go along with his chitchat, trying to look interested in his testosterone flush.

"There are plenty from which to choose. You might have a tough time settling for just one."

"It's never stopped me in the past. Once the uniform comes off, there's no telling what level I might be called upon to offer protection."

He hikes up his trousers with attitude.

"There's Deputy Jonah honing on some undeclared property. I think I'll mosey over to offer some security detail. By the way, I hear you had quite a day covering third base for the home team. There's talk about making you an honorary alumnus for the annual game."

"Beginner's luck," I pretend. "I might need a few more grounders next year and certainly will bring my own glove just in case."

"Good talkin' to you, Doc. I'll see you around."

He disappears into the female throng.

Feeling a need to dilute some of the tap beer, I meander over to the salad bar that is still being organized by the new service personnel, grab a small handful of miniature carrots, and begin munching away. Alice, the hairdresser, scoots alongside me. She is wearing a dark polyester smock with matching capri pants and white leather sandals. Very out of context from her day job.

"Hey, Doc. You're a sight for sore eyes."

She gives me a condescending pat.

"I hope it wasn't too much trouble in the storage facility. I told you that it's hardly opened all year. Crime doesn't pay in Wasoon."

"Tessa asked me to help her find her sister's belongings. You are right, though. It is quite musty in the back, but we lucked out. Thanks for opening it up for us."

"Not a problem."

She jerks her head and slurs into a throaty drawl.

"Have you met Gail Nevers?"

She steps aside and the aunt from Rochester emerges from behind her rounded frame.

"It's nice to match the voice with the man, Doctor Michaels. I take it you're enjoying the stay in Minnesota? Cheers."

She tilts a plastic flute of blush wine to her lips. Her eyes are large and amazingly mink brown. Her hair is long with ginger-colored bangs that are both alluring and dated. Delicate hands complement her full-figured body.

She closes the distance between us. Her all-school reunion tee shirt has a few barbeque stains spattered on the front. She tilts her head back but catches me peering at her chest.

"In case you're wondering, that's the result of food prep. Tessa went in search of new caterers."

"Cheers," I reply and toast both ladies.

"Thank you again for doing the autopsy on Ole. They won't admit it in public, but I do think the brothers miss their father to a degree, and not because of the monthly checks."

"People I have spoken with consider him a local philanthropist," I add. "The resort is a true give-back to the local economy."

"That's for sure," she nods. "There will be a private service tomorrow at the funeral home, then internment at the cemetery outside of town. You are invited to attend. The boys adore you."

"I'll give it some thought. Thank you, Gail."

She scrunches up her nose and sneezes into her napkin.

"AHH CHOO! Excuse me." She reaches into her purse. "Still have a bit of a summer cold. In and out of air conditioning is a way of life up here."

Dabbing her nostrils with a Kleenex, she continues.

"I knew Darlene Gabbert from high school, too. Reunions and

funerals are not supposed to mix. She would have enjoyed seeing all this compassion."

"You were raised in a good community," I console her and scoot in side-by-side as the buffet table is being attacked by the early birds. "The locals have a way of taking care of their own."

Gail eyes me curiously.

"Doctor Michaels, there's a good chance your true roots are emerging from hibernation. Do I detect a sense of melancholy in your voice?"

She had me. No Cassie. No Erin. No Tessa. I clear my throat.

"This is about as close to a family reunion that I've been in easily twenty or thirty years. Everyone is happy to see each other and only a handful act as if they are still clinging to old crushes like medallions. Present company excluded."

"Are you finding Aaron and David to be how you expected?"

She lifts her chin, her arms folded in front of her breasts.

"I can appreciate their upbringing," I tell her. "They have a wonderful support system with your help."

She blushes.

"Ole, the father-figure, was more of a personal loss than they go on about. These young men literally resided in the principal's office during their 'wonder' years in school. Wondering who was fighting whom, swearing at teachers and all that."

She takes in a breath. "Parents complain that administration is sending the wrong message to the entering students. Ole's off-the-cuff learning tactics were by reaction, not by example."

She straightens the front of her wrinkled top and adjusts her sagging neckline. A woman's voice from the gathering behind us yells her name. Gail acknowledges with a toast of her flute above her head, then looks back to me.

"He was gruff, unsociable, and full of it. A perfect combination for the gossiping crowd. Because of him, sugar cookies and coffee became the main staple of the Lazy Bee Café. Folks saw him drive by and the negativity spread like wildfire."

"I wasn't aware of their darting past indifferences," I respond. "People have treated me as if I'm part of this community."

"That's because they like you, unlike some of the others. You don't hear the comments some of our dear neighbors have construed about your presence. Nosing around the Resort like you own it. Why is a snooty doctor from California cutting up a beloved icon? Blah. Blah. Blah."

She takes another sip, but I'm distracted by lingering wafts of honeyed barbequed beef ribs.

She explains. "If it isn't for my support, crusty Deputy Sheriff Lundgren has you tapped for speeding and illegal parking. He wants you gone."

Just then a group of women push their way to the front where we are standing.

"Gail Nevers. Is it really you?"

A slight woman in her fifties is holding her hands to her cheeks in astonishment. Her corsage is the soft color of whipped butter. There is an embroidered name, Wilma, over her left breast pocket. Both Gail and Wilma scream in joy and the other three women give little applauses eventually joining in the group hug. I back away in my least embarrassing technique and slither toward the Exit sign.

A slender, comparatively younger gal wearing urban-style denim jeans tucked into camel-skinned boots corrals me.

"Not so fast. You forgot two things. First, your name tag and year of graduation. Second, and most importantly, you forgot to ask me to dance."

I'm whisked out to the floor in front of the stage in between a midst of a dozen or so couples. Brenda, as her nametag reads, guides me to a clear space and embraces me in a close stance. Arched eyebrows with a trace of glitter, luxuriant black hair, a distracting dimple on her chin, and voluptuous. How you say, it's what the Doctor ordered.

"I was about to..." I stammer.

"Hush up," she whispers into my ear. "I'll let you get back to your mommy after a song or two. I'm Brenda, Class of Moonbeams. I know all about you, Dr. Cosmos," she chuckles. "You might be from California, but I know a Midwesterner when I see one."

She presses her ample breasts into my chest, our thighs are molded like fitted two-by-fours. As if choreographed, her head goes directly onto my chest without passing goal and I am locked in for take-off without an escape hatch.

"I manage a bank down in Thief River Falls," the words oozing out of her mouth like hot lusty gel. "It's mostly car and truck loans for the younger farmers who are having a hard-go as more mega mergers take over most of the available land. B & B's are the new quick buck. How about you?" she asks and nudges closer, pressuring the small of my back with her flat palm.

"How about myself what?" I quiz with nervous reluctance.

"Are you a bed or breakfast man?"

Her pencil-thin eyebrows and her sea green eyes are like sabers slicing through my wilting resistance.

"This might be our first in countless upcoming reunions," she offers up a devilish blink.

I am convinced she is looking for other "firsts" tonight.

Trying to regroup, I tell her, "I received a missed call message and was about to dart back to my cabin to answer it. Wait for me. Be patient. We can continue this dance later. I'm thinking of purchasing some land in the Lake country. Hopefully, there's a good connection who you might know to refer me to, or some foreclosures to recommend."

"Brenda, darling." He curls his thick forearm around her slim waist and rolls her away from me into a snug face-to-face.

"Vincent Bode, Class of No-Class," she says averting his gaze and clutching her wrap.

"Right on, Babe." He removes his hat and genuflects. His hair is thinning, but nicely painted red. "The last time we saw each other, which I recall was this past Tuesday, that outfit was draped in the closet covered in plastic." He chuckles to himself and lowers his voice. "On the contrary, you left nothing hanging on me. Dangling? Yes. Hanging? No."

The local band swings into another tune from the rocking eighties and Vincent releases his waist hold on her, takes her by the hand and twirls her into a double spin.

"That ought to remind you of something similar."

His upper lip curls into a leering smile. "Doc, here, has a house call. Let him go. I'll keep you warm 'til he returns. Is that ok with you, Doc?"

I give the Napoleon-esque trucker a grateful pat on the back.

"I'll be back as soon as I take care of business. Thanks, Vince."

Brenda laughs and yells out to me as I walk away. "Say hello to Tessa when you see her. Ask her if she remembers me catching her making out with that auctioneer at the softball tournament last year in Cloquet. Pretty artsy-fartsy gang bangers if you ask me."

"Do you have anything else to add?" It's Tessa to the rescue. She's wearing a floral-print blouse, blue jeans, and a pair of heat-seeking looks for armament.

"Brenda the Bitch Queen has short-term memory. She is correct about one thing. It was an auction, but it was *her* ass that slid under the gavel. I was completely there for the resort. You know, donation, fundraiser." Tessa snickers, then says to the bank manager: "Your bank is all about giving back. Right, Brenda?"

Vincent and I are accidentally nudged in the back by the food cart as a tuxedoed teenager hustles across the walkway.

"Hey. Watch it." Vincent spits out as if he is defending a territorial shrine. Always the gentlemen to the end.

"Come on, Kevin. Let's get some fresh air. It's suddenly quite stale, even outside." She securely grips my elbow. Looks like I'm a Wanted Man. This is the second time in a matter of minutes, and I don't want this moment to end.

We head upstairs and stand at the railing near her office. Through her body language, I know Tessa is critiquing the antics between Vincent and Brenda on the dance floor. She sighs heavily and folds here arms across her chest.

"That was like a high school cat fight. No one is aging gracefully tonight. I'm sorry you had to step into it like that. She has never combined coming of age with depth. Brenda is a one-person act. Her stage is a queen-sized bed."

"It's alright," I add. "I enjoyed your rescue moves. It lent respectability to being a Wasoonian for the night."

"Who is she trying to kid with that sleazy outfit? I guarantee that most of that advertising is not hers."

Tessa strokes her throat like there's an irritating itch.

"It's been a stressful week and it's still not over."

I begin to gently knead her tense shoulders. She's battling fatigue. A long sigh ensues.

"I'm not bullet-proof. This is not the average gathering, Tessa. The list of events since I arrived is death, autopsy, missing, and more death. Tack onto that my poor timing and your sister and we have a movie in the making."

She slowly rotates her shoulders and tilts her head forward. On the ground floor the disco ball is aglow and the strobe flashes across the ceiling. In the darkness, I discretely lean forward to kiss her softly on the nape of her tanned neckline, but she passes it off.

"Not in front of the *children*," she mutters and leads me through the sliding door into the office.

The room is comfortably cool and quiet. There are no annoying hums of fax machines or phones. She pulls out two of the cushioned rolling desk chairs and offers me a seat. The outside lighting through the blinds transforms the ceiling into a collage of wavy grays and whites. Tessa crosses her legs, rests her arm on the desktop and drums her fingers. From my viewpoint, the gloom is gaining control of the rushed lifestyle she has been chasing for a few days now. But this has been her comfort zone. This is a familiar role. Despite it all, her feminine outline is soft, like an old hazy black and white photograph. Her form-fitting jeans accent the athleticism and the rolled-up sleeves on her blouse give the impression that she's ready to go a couple rounds with you-know-who. She stares right through me and I wilt as if a large bullseye has been placed on my forehead.

"Give me a couple more moments exactly like that and I'll be ready to enter the crime scene again," she sighs. "That Brenda hit a sore spot. She's the whys and wherefores that my marriage to Mr. Volvo Salesman went south. If you haven't figured it out, that so-called auction to which she alluded was the beginning of their affair. They pawed at each other in front of me, like racehorse breeding stock roped to a stall. It was so disheartening, Kevin. A bona fide low point in my married life."

She buries her face into her hands.

"I'm getting through it fairly well, but I was hoping not to run into her tonight, at least not when she's cupping your butt. Don't you know better by now?"

"Tessa," I begin. "Nothing you saw was intentional. She hooked me. I was in the wrong place at the wrong time."

I place my hand over hers apologetically.

"I don't even know the woman. Her story is written all over those painted lips. Why do you think Vincent was so willing to round up his zippered troops?"

I'm exasperated and attempt to further explain.

"Let's draw up some lines of trust here," I affirm. "You need not feel betrayed by me. As you can plainly tell, I'm trying. Mind you, it's not because of Erin as much as it is about us."

Is now the right time to confess to her about the blood scare?

We both fall silent. Best not to get defensive or air out any differences. That's the easy way out and it could cause more harm than good. Tessa has every right to act jealous. I've been fraternizing with the enemy, both the human type and the viral form. No matter how covert Brenda's scheme was, I still feel guilty as if Tessa's life's decisions impact everything. Downstairs, there is another gleeful shrill. A missing classmate from the yearbook has unbelievingly transposed in-the-flesh. It was all too close to the actuality of Erin's loss. Reunions mostly suck.

Tessa speaks up.

"You mentioned a headscarf to me late last night that you suspected I might have left in your car by accident."

"Yes, that's right," I respond. "It looked like something Erin wore years ago when we first met. It was in that photo we found in the storage facility. Is it as a memory token or am I wrong about that?"

"Well, it wasn't me," she says flatly. There is a rising color in her cheeks. "I never saw the scarf. But Erin had a habit of wearing those colorful ascots during the summer. Folks struggled to tell us apart in high school. I preferred to don a baseball cap because my hair was usually cut short. Do you still have it?"

"It's in my very own Ole's Resort cabin. I'll let you see it if you behave and apologize for that brawl mentality."

Her eyelids narrow as she stands, facing me, offering her hands. I'm yanked out of the chair.

"Partner?" she cooed. "You go right ahead and put that keepsake in a safe place. If I ever have a need to bring a little reminder of Erin back, I'll look at you."

She pecks me on the lips. I fight an irresistible urge to darken the blinds and lock the office door for about twenty minutes. The storm of a couple nights ago affords the same furious background, but I'm sure we'll manage. Tessa allows me to draw her into a lasting hug. Suddenly, there is a knock on the door.

"Miss Tessa? Are you in there?"

The petite inquisitive voice is Paige, the Intern.

"Miss Tessa?"

"Yes, Paige, we're in here," she calls and dabs away the lipstick from my lips. "Hold that thought," she instructs me. "I'll be right back."

She opens the door. Paige knuckles are raised to knock again. Her mouth forms an inquisitive 'O.'

"Sorry to interrupt. Aaron saw you go in this direction and thought you might be up here. Your 'Safety Net' was how he described it."

She notices me next to Tessa. "Hi, Dr. Michaels."

"Hello, Paige," I respond.

Paige focuses back on Tessa. "Well, we are having another slight problem with the caterer's hook-up to the LP tanks near the food service unit. There's not enough pressure for them to fire up the extra grills. Looks like we're going to by-pass the water heater for the time being if that's all right. The twins said this is something common with the old gas lines underground."

She pauses for a response from either of us.

"Welcome to Resort Trouble-Shooting, the Novice's Edition," mocks Tessa. She flicks her eyes upward and grabs her lightweight coat behind the door. Looking back to me she says.

"So, Michaels, am I going to see that scarf or not?"

"I'll come along, be the invisible third hand, hold the plumber's wrench, tap the pipes to release the air bubbles, and then, I'll show you."

"How about retrieving both of us a couple of wine coolers instead of getting in the way? It's a little too cool to skinny-dip. I'll shut down the entire evening's activities. No one will even care."

I can feel my face redden.

In the interim, Paige blushes uncomfortably.

"I'll get Aaron."

We re-enter the throng. From the boisterousness and yelping, it's notching up to another level. Just as I suspect, someone who missed the thirty-year graduation get-together suggests a popular Village People medley. Soon, everyone crowds the dance floor in jocular renditions of disco. Rhythm wise, some are better than others. In my opinion, practicing in front of the bedroom mirror has done wonders to the self-reliance, but some of the acrobatic attempts are awkward and look physically dangerous. Elvis left the building long ago.

Tessa pulls my head down to her level and yells into my ear to look for either David or Aaron. I understand the immediate need for the mechanically inclined and leave them to fend for themselves. Meanwhile, Lundgren is leading the single file parade with his left hand sitting on his hip, throwing his right arm down below the left of his waist, then repeatedly snapping it back up. Admittedly, he is spectacular: very retro, very movie-like. Others tag on his lead, but not quite as flamboyant a delivery.

The ladies, including Brenda, sans Vincent, take their turn in the folly. Brenda effortlessly squats down halfway and hops on her toes like riding a wild stallion as the men appraise her every move with whoops and hollers. With that distinct image securely fastened in my left brain, I slip through the hoards and back to the keg where I find David, his head bobbing to the beat.

"Hey, Doc, what's up?"

He was preparing to hose another cupful but stops short.

"Tessa asked me to find you," I explain. "There's something about the LP gas line and the grills..."

"Oh, fuck," he exhales, while a deep frown materializes. "That happens twice a month throughout the summer. This fall, we *will* get that re-plumbed."

His jaw clenches, and he scratches the back of his neck as if he is trying to decide whether to hand-deliver two freshly poured brews or come to Tessa's rescue.

"I'll take over here," I said rescuing the spigot from his hand. "They're over by the pit."

"They?" he questions.

"Paige and Tessa," I explain.

A grin, the size of Lake Wasoon, skirts across his face.

"Awesome."

For the next half hour, I am resigned to barrel-tapper and chief brew dispenser with neither a lagging nor lack of customers. It became the made to order job in this conglomeration of reunion wannabes. I am introduced by my teammates to other reunion-types. One of them is a petite woman from Iowa who still practices OBGYN out of Storm Lake. Like me, she doesn't feel comfortable near the dance floor, although her spouse is relegating himself as the new Travolta with some of his 'temporarily single' classmates. Music and drinks, the fuel of fools. In this frenzy, anything is possible.

David never does return, but Aaron passes the word along to me that some "cosmetic" plumbing needs to be done in haste. With this information, I decide to disengage myself and see if Tessa needs further help over at the side station.

When I arrive, she is kneeling beside David, holding a flashlight directed at the main gas meter as he bangs on the valve with a plumber's wrench.

"Crappy old valve is corroded shut. I'm sure that was our local plumber, Paul Sawyer, jawing away with the preacher about a half hour ago."

Shaking his head, dejected, lips compressed.

"I'm afraid to do much of this without some surveillance from the guy who built this contraption in the first place."

Tessa looks up to me and explains.

"Paul is the maintenance contractor we use. I sent Paige for him."

I tentatively look at the frenzied crowd. "You know with all these people smoking cigarettes, it's not a good idea to open up gas lines in the first place."

"I'm with the Doc on this one," echoes David. "One shower per day is plenty for me."

He looks to Tessa.

"Let's get the charcoal pits fired up and have an old-fashioned dinner."

She takes my extended arm, pulls herself up beside me and looks for something to wipe her hands on.

"That sounds like gold, boys. From the celebrating around us, anything edible will pass inspection if the liquid fuel in the keg doesn't run out. Great idea, David. Let me get some of the busboys to help you."

"There you go, Tessa. I'll take care of the rest. Get your beautiful kisser splashed in all the photo-ops for the Resort's sake. If they want to complain, have them come see me." David is also looking around for something to wipe his hands on.

"I'll grab us some hand towels and be right back. Don't touch anything."

I shake my finger at her. "I can't leave you alone for one minute, then all hell breaks loose."

Tessa grins. "Nothing but trouble from the time you arrived. But you seem to be practical enough to survive this invasion. Have I told you recently how much I'm enjoying your company?"

"Either I have a short memory or have been locked in a coma. No. Is there anything else you want to tell me?"

"Oh, if by chance you haven't noticed, or if Erin wasn't in the picture," her eyes glisten and her lips tremble, "we're both forty years older, not smarter. Let's leave it at that."

It's ironic how life stands still despite the fact that people maniacally disco dance in front of you. I am feeling the music and the beer is giving me a Wizard of Oz Lion buzz. Before I know it, the dance parade materializes, and Tessa and I step out to the center. Lundgren finishes a knee-slide across the slick linoleum as if he were the star of Footloose and stops in front of Brenda the Body. She gives him a sexy sashay, kisses her index finger and places it directly on his lips. The other women in line clamor around him like lionesses after a kill. He arches his back and palms the floor behind his heels as she cups her mouth and lets out a shrill "OMG! How are we going to follow that?"

Not missing a cue, I raise Tessa's arm and spin her a couple times and continue down the middle like two tango dancers in a hunter's crouch, only to rise and re-spin her at the other side. The crowd cheers madly and my inner Fred Astaire takes a deeply grateful bow.

We say our goodnights earlier than I anticipate. Tessa, always the giver, offers to stay late but insists that it's not intentional. She explains about resort responsibility and how abandoning the new caterer isn't appropriate. It's not my call anyway, although I insist on sharing clean-up crew duties. Empty beer glasses and dirty dishes are collected and piled in large bins. Mr. Clean is working full-time, and I must give kudos to the new people taking ownership of their new duties. Stealing a contract is going to do wonders for their business, not to mention their pocketbooks. It's worked for me countless times over the years.

Tessa walks with me to the exit gate. "This won't take long, Kevin. I promise." She slips her arm in mine and gives a gentle affectionate squeeze.

"The last time I heard that from you, we were on a hillside hike," I chide her. "It's getting to be a nasty habit."

"You know how compulsive I am about the business. It's my baby." She kisses me on the cheek. "Go to your room, Doctor Michaels. Sweet dreams and thank you."

Sweet, they are not. My room is stifling and still, as if the last molecules of fresh air have been sucked out by a large exhaust fan. I feel like I'm being swallowed-up by my mattress. There's a humming, whirring vibration. Burned flesh. Nothing else smells like it. Something's not right.

Growing up as a farm boy, I strongly remember the electrical blaze in my uncle's hog barn where two hundred pigs perished. That noxious odor of decay swept across the valley for days until a handful of thunderstorms raced through and, in its wake, left a breeding haven for the mosquitoes. Fortunately, the stagnant, soiled waters ran downhill past our house and snaked through the barnyard leaving rivulets of a fetid brown-green muck, a foot deep in places. That was the worst year ever and I can smell it again.

Something presses up against my side, something moving, struggling, and as hard as I try, I can't free myself. I raise my hands to cover my face, scrape against a lid, and begin to pound on it. Hollow and soft, like cardboard, like a cremation carton.

A couple men are shouting. There's the whirr of a large fan or engine, followed by hammering. My hands tingle. There's inaudible yelling, arguing, and pounding. Suddenly I'm jostled, the feeling of being hoisted or wheeled. A deafening roar. More full cries of horror. More thrashing.

Hhhaaallp! Hhhaaallp!

I hear a woman's delirious voice. I can't move. Our bodies rock into each other, then apart with each shift from the outside. More shouting, more hammering, more jostling.

Whoomph!

There's a sensation of being dropped and the crackling sound, like a fire. Then the distinct odor of burning wood envelopes me. A brilliant light appears at my trapped feet. Suddenly, there's violent thrashing and kicking and nearby, someone howls in pain.

Hhhaaallp! Hhhaaallp!

The person flails as I watch a large flame form over its head. The mouth opens and closes, fighting for oxygen. Then the fire engulfs the frantic form until there's no more, only muscle and bone and ash.

"Kevin. Wake up."

"What the hell?" I shout, my hands in front of my face.

"It's me, Tessa. I've been trying to revive you for a couple of minutes. You were in one heck of a nightmare."

She dabs my forehead with a washcloth.

"No more shots of tequila with the boys," she warns. "You are drenched."

My body trembles and I struggle to sit up. Dizzy and disoriented.

"Give it a little more time, Doctor," she says. "I'm a little concerned about you. How does this feel?"

As she continues to massage my scalp, I'm chasing the ghosts who seal wooden containers shut with hammers and nails in advance of rolling them into the incendiary closet. Images of Roland and myself in the funeral home orbit my brain like pestilent satellites.

"Tessa, when did you get here?" My mouth is dry. It hurts to swallow. The nightmare is still vivid.

"We stacked the last of the patio chairs and washed down the cement a half hour ago. I went upstairs to lock the proceeds in the safe, check the security system, and sneaked across the property only to find you feverish. You were rubbing your face as if your hands were pinned crossways on your chest."

I move my numbing wrists back and forth.

"I must have fallen asleep for a few minutes with my hands in a crazy position under my chest. I awoke, but trouble is, that damn thing was so vivid. It's not worth describing for fear of it ever existing."

Tessa helps me to sit up.

"This had nothing to do with refusing another dance with Brenda, did it?" she smirks. "Stress can compound those revamped feelings or emotions. School reunions attract unused brain cells like ants to a picnic. The fabricated stories are certainly more exciting than reality. Three-fourths of the people here tonight are on the same page, but not to the extent of nightmares. But Kevin, your door was unlocked. Any excuse for a house call, Doctor."

"I doubt any of the dancers were being cremated alive," I said adamantly. "There's nothing unusual in the water?"

Tessa tilts her head and gives me a silent look. "Is there anything you need to tell me, Kevin? I get the impression your life is more complicated than you let on. Take more time off. Spend a couple days on the lake in a houseboat or stay in a secluded cabin away from here. I can arrange for a personal chaperone."

"Just the thought makes me fantasize." I look away. "But seriously, I've had a handful of recent issues to deal with, although they seem to be resolved."

I lay a hand on her cheek.

"Remember when you wished to have met forty years ago? I'm developing a crazy teenage crush on you."

"Spoken like a true teenager," she smiles, inhaling deeply and holding it for a moment. "Between the soft cone at the local drive-in and this, I'd say we have a few options. Any of them come to mind?"

Tessa dissolves into my embrace and I spend the remaining dark hours listening to her breathe deeply, unabashedly kissing her as she burrows into the crook of my arm. The moonlight enters the room like a secret lover, leaving its glow on the bed. I am eternally grateful having her near. I give her an endearing squeeze, but something about that horror pushes my revival button. Was this malaise part of a latent virus or is there a crack in the Wasoon secret armor of decades ago?

CHAPTER SIXTEEN

The next morning ushers in a preview of typical fall weather. There is a pre-wintery chill in the air topped off by a light spattering of cirrus clouds stretching into the entire horizon. No one takes this for granted in the north. The deluge of heat and storms, it's expected as gospel. The foliage is beginning its 'show-off' stages with a hint of oranges and mahogany in the leaf's veins. Bolder native weeds and the once seeded grasses with blood red chlorophyll are gearing up if for only a week or two. I'm overwhelmingly sentimental that another summer season is assessing its remnants with the threat of a cloudburst. At least, the academic weather forecasters are predicting it, providing they have an updated copy from the National Weather Bureau to read in front of their television monitors.

Tessa rustles on her side of the bed but I manage to embrace her in a deep-waist-never-let-go grip, my forearm brushing against the undersides of her breasts. Her sighs are loud, dreaming in anguish, fidgeting, fighting against a dark force. When we finally are both awake, she scurries to the bathroom. The dark tan line on her thighs and backside are well-suited to my sore eyes. The nightmare is but a faint memory. I join her in front of the bathroom mirror and affectionately tap her on the butt as she brushes her teeth.

"Thanks for last night."

She reaches back to touch my forehead. "You don't feel feverish, like last night."

As I shower, she soaps my back in lathering swoops. The cool tile is like an ice pack on my feet.

"I must have been out of it," I said. "It's not hangover-like, but more like a comatose grogginess. Even my joints are stiff. I must have slept like an unwound grandfather's clock."

"Think about what I told you last night, Kevin. Think about getting away from this resort for a couple days, but don't go too far because I still need you. All this extra stress piling up inside, I wouldn't doubt you're coming down with something you inhaled in that musty storage locker. That's possible, isn't it?"

I lean back into the rinse and surrender to the nozzle spray. The complexing distraction of last night is a persistent swirl of soap and lather into the drain.

"If you ever want to talk about it, I'm here...not always in this situation or with a soap bar in my hand, but you already know that."

"I will," I tell her, "and thank you for waking me last night."

"It was more like three hours ago," she scolds. "If anything, go for a ride today and get rid of that damn cell phone. Visit some old stomping grounds. If need be, call me on my cell and not the resort phone."

She scoots in closer and puts her arms around me. Her eyes are wide and glossy.

"Supper is at six o'clock sharp."

"Roger that."

I give her a peck on the cheek and watch her sneak out of my cabin. When she leaves, I gather some day-trip items, fire up my car and spin out. On the way, I half-salute the slouching Security Guard Extraordinaire, Perry Brown. The lingering smoke of barbequed meat wafts in a breezeless haze. I roll down my window and inhale. Pine and barbeque sauce. Not overly cautious today, I jam my foot on the accelerator and fishtail off the resort grounds in front of a honking flatbed truck.

I decide to drive some spirited off-road gravel fire trails, the kind I had noticed the other day when Tessa gave me a tour of the girls' cabins. My driving skills are on overload, aggressively gathering speed in the straight-away like a treacherous Mexican desert cross-country race and slowing only when the single lane morphs into a packed fire trail. In one smooth descent, a blue jay drops out of the evergreen canopy in front of me like a Walt Disney movie, gathers up a large dead flying insect in its beak, and lunges onto a lower branch on the other side of the road. I wasn't half that skillful yesterday on the softball field. With every shot at me, I backed off, lifeless, like a dead insect waiting to be scooped up. Better to stick with scooping body fluids in a morgue.

This road has its own demonic personality. A left bank in a rain-drenched pothole buries my front tire and I maneuver around a tree rut, the size of a railroad tie. Poking out of the sandy-loam soil are countless aged and shattered dead branches as if a large tree house is being renovated directly above my machine. Soon, I am whisking past a funneling slide of obscure hardpan that is still misshapen from the last storm. I appreciate how a fire crew and Tessa can recognize and identify the exact road to take when they all look the same to me. In theory it isn't that much different from an autopsy when I am handed a blurred photograph from a scowling plaintiff attorney.

"Could you tell me what this is, Doctor?"

Reinterpreted, that insinuated: "In your experience, do you consider this normal?"

"What's normal to you, Counselor, is more like the implied question."

On and on, it's a sensational cycle of who's zooming who. I shake my head and suck in a deep breath. Up ahead is a once-familiar wooden sign. I downshift onto the narrow lane of the girls' cabins. This must be another road to this side of the island. Not a bad idea to check out the pump house water clarity again as a favor to the resort staff. Downpours expected later in the day don't necessarily translate into a spotty shower. Once the sky spigot is opened, there's no telling how long before anything can turn it off.

It's interesting how these building sites seemed so formidable so many years ago. All those young adults and prepubescent females scampering about as if each moment were measured by the staff. Mostly forgotten, the unit of cabins is now like driving onto a cluster of war zone encampments that have been shuttered and teetering into a pile of termite excrement. I track down the most favorable place to park and shut off the engine. I dread the thought of the car's hot oil pan or muffler igniting a grass fire.

The sun is slowly climbing above the tree line, enough to draw gnats and mosquitoes out of the stillness for one last shot at a blood meal. The swarm around the hood is like an insect relay machine and I decide to leave the windows cracked as the idling engine disengages to a dying quiver. So much for tune ups and high-priced octane gas.

I step outside and am greeted by the musty scent of fallen pine-cones that jogs my memory of every shed and garage from my days as a 'ward' of the church camp. There was always something that needed to be dragged out, hosed down, wiped clean of black widows, or utilized as some sort of contest or sporting event, not that it mattered. Even the basketballs were worn and flat. My dad always reminded me to bring along my old sporting supplies: a cracked wooden bat taped on the handle, a second-hand fielder's mit, and a football that was laced together with leather shoestring, the kind that spirals by spinning them nose down on the grass.

But in the world of haves and have nots, it was a minor compromise - - because there was always Erin. She beat a run down between second and third base, she out swam any of the other so-called swim team. She out-did anybody or anything. Like Tessa insinuated, this is the exact purpose that I ended up here. This clatter is an audio filter, away from the sounds of lament and remorse. Get on with my life. Let her go. I pinch the bridge of my nose, squeezing my eyes shut, trying to divert the vivid images.

From a distance I can see the pump house door is still padlocked shut although the rusted hinges insecurely hold the cover in place like a well-used three-ringed binder. There's no need for a forceful entry if it remains fastened. Besides, we tested it only a couple days ago which was a good sign. How about that flickering yellow light in the main cabin, or was that my imagination? I head in that direction to check it out.

The news that nearby farmer's land had been raided and crop seeds deposited here by local animal scat is still evident. The shaded walkways lead me to think other critters have found it safer to settle on barren spots of clay and stone as well.

Constant reminders of decay and desiccation slow my progress as I warily high-step over those nagging, infection-laden, thorny weeds. There is an intense insect-buzz alert as they assault a varmint. Scavenger flies circle in columns as I guardedly approach, wildly waving my cap back and forth in front of my face. The swarm is situated in an open patch of wilting long bladed wild blue lilies that bend from the animal corpse. The furry remnants of a small mammal are splayed out, its dehydrated skeleton collapsed days ago from the developing states of disintegration. Now all that remains is a leathering hide and its telltale striped black and white hair. Skunks.

A muffled scratching sound arises from alongside the main cabin's wall, digging or burrowing like a rodent and I tentatively step back. In my mind, a skittish retreat is not a loss of manhood. Not in the mood to encounter a rabid animal of any sort, I step lightly around to the rear of the building where there's a raised cement platform. I recollect decades ago, wrenching my back by stumbling off the edge into the darkness during a patented escape from Erin's room. Both of us were thankful that the visiting church clergy cleared his throat loudly sooner than later. That was his signal for me to clear out and I was fortunate to leave with my shirt all but buttoned. Erin giggled as she clasped her bra and hiked each cup into position.

"Hurry," she smirked and pushed me out the screen door. "I'll see you at breakfast."

But I was ducking behind the low-lying bushes trying to tailor my sight to the darkness.

"Pastor Williams. I'll be right out. Please have a seat," she calmly called through her bedroom door as if nothing happened. Ironically, it was a scheduled preparation of biblical devotions for her Christian charges. We both got caught up in the moment and forgot. Mini-prayer sessions rotated from the boys' side of the island to the girls', every other day, seven-thirty sharp. I had miscalculated, thinking that tonight the boys' armor could withstand another round of Lutheran blameworthiness.

And now, here I am again, standing on the doomed step and having my own little mental get together. Something is scratching on the other side. The fear I carry is not age-specific and this jaunt through memory lane in an abandoned cabin leaves me in a state of unexpected unease. Worst case scenario, there's that smell of decay again, and with each gasp, the strong stench permeates my nostrils as if the vapors are becoming a solidified residue in the back of my throat. Despite the years, dissecting and gagging exist on the same page. Perhaps portions of the carcass have been dragged into a safe zone to be savored by something larger. I recall Tessa mentioning that these buildings have remained unopened for years and a land developer had placed a bid on purchasing acres up here for more lake home sites. But the actual staking of the property is not even in the planning stages yet.

I grab the handle and swing the door open. To my astonishment, along the wall is a tidy cot, exactly how us counselors were to leave the cabin once our seasonal stay was over. My mind is in time warp zone. Is it possible someone lives here, or am I seeing things? No left-over potato chip bags or beer cans, but proof of a recent visitor exists. As generic as this setting appears, things look quite comfortable. The nightstand is placed next to the right side of the bunk bed and a plain dresser aligns against the wall. The private bathroom stall, sink and shower are spotless. Clear water drips into the basin. *Drip. Drip. Drip.* A used bar of Irish Spring soap rests on the sink's edge.

If I'm the only sane person, then where the hell is Erin? Where is that sad smile? Those emerald eyes? Where's Erin? Suddenly, a pounding throb wells up inside my head that transfers like a roller coaster ride to my chest and I fumble for the folding chair by the door entrance. I'm not old enough for this. This is only a short excursion, not a terminal trip. Tessa listed her requests: a brief getaway, don't check voice mail, and visit some old stomping grounds. But it's all too familiar and this room looks like my own cabin. Have I been drugged?

I check my pulse, going through all the recognizable stages of a heart attack. A tad high, but not fibrillating. I've read EKG's in medical charts that were ten times worse, but those were not mine. My mind scurries for a morsel of semblance as I pull out my cell phone and scroll through my Contacts searching for the resort number. God, it's taking a long time to connect. I'm not able to pick up reception out here. Hang up and try again. Busy signal. *Beep. Beep. Beep.* High-pitched. Like a fax dial tone. Slow down. Got to remain calm like I was taught in med school. Try again. There's absolutely no way my body is going into rigor in this room. I'm not entering lividity without a free-for-all. There will be no gray-blue discoloration and no wheeling me to the coolers where the drawers glide out and they slide you onto a stainless-steel tray. No one is going to evaluate any gravitational settling of any of *my* liquids. Not anything like that.

I hear a faint dial tone, but the connection is scratchy. The battery power must be getting low. Mental note: no cardiologist is going to map anything of mine. Screw the backless hospital gown. Screw it all.

"Ole's." That must be Paige.

"Hello? Paige? Can you hear me?"

"Hello? Ole's Resort, Wasoon."

"Paige. It's Dr. Michaels. Is Tessa available?" I plead. My voice is choked with emotion.

"Oh, Dr. Michaels. I can barely hear you. Are you looking for Miss Tessa? Yes, I can find her for you. Hold on a moment, please."

Click.

She's well-trained and efficient, I must admit, but being placed on Hold raises my blood pressure. I begin to rub circles on my pounding chest as my other hand trails up to my throat to press on the jugular vein. No ramrodding throb, no cosmic faint murmur either. Most ER docs call it a 'scare' unless the blood tests prove otherwise. I am beyond healthy, damn it!

"Kevin? It's Tessa. Where are you?"

I hold my breath. The sound of her voice is reassuring like a rescue from a deep well.

"You won't believe it, but I'm planted on a kitchen chair in the old girl counselor cabin we visited a few days back. It's spotless. The furniture is arranged like company is expected sometime soon."

"You are where?" her voice raising in disbelief.

"I'm in the girl's main cabin...on the other side of the island."

Feeling a need to explain, I continue.

"Like you told me, I got in the car and down the road I went. By coincidence, I came upon the backroad entrance. It's all weeds and saplings, but this room is spic and span. Remember that yellowing glow we noticed in the window when we got caught in the storm?"

"Kind of." She hesitates. "How did you get in?"

"The door was unlocked," I tell her. "No forceful entry, if that's what you're wondering."

I resume.

"Long story short, I became curious and went inside. By the way, there are skunks living underneath the floorboards."

There was a calculating pause on the other end. I had caught Tessa off guard.

"Tessa, what do you want me to do? I can contact Lundgren and have him stake it out unless you prefer to handle that assignment."

"I'm in the middle of negotiating with the terminated caterers right now, Kevin. It's a little too complex for my brain at this moment. You think someone has been using the cabin as a shelter?"

"Right down to the shower and sink," I take in her questioning. "The water is still hooked up."

My phantom chest pain has subsided. The monitor hook-up apparition with hairy ER residents fresh out of training will have to wait for a more appropriate, life-threatening admission.

"When I get a chance, I'll ask around the resort. Perhaps there's a plausible explanation. The land developer came by to test the water table, or the fire crew is doing the same thing."

"Or," I barge in, "you have a free-loader transient hunkering down until winter sets in and the entire island goes into hibernation."

"That is a remote possibility, Kevin," she says. "It's so odd. We were there and checked the pump house. How is that building?"

"Looks to be intact," I counter. "Door and hinges are intact."

I slowly assess my surroundings, looking for anything else that Tessa knew about. The Comet-like cleanser bleach aroma is strong and being that it's already the month of August, there is only a little pollen in the air. This side of the island always got hit hard by thundershowers. Erin teased that the excuse for her flushed complexion was an allergy. She complained about the detail that the boy's side had the best shade.

"When do you expect to come back?" Her concern is not concealed in her voice. I check my watch.

"Within an hour or so. You might not be aware, but I used to be able to identify animal tracks rather well. I'll nose around to see if any other signs crop up. I can reach you on the cell phone if needed, correct?"

"If not, leave a message with Paige," she replies. "She'll be able to find me. Be careful out there, Kevin Michaels. Wild animals carry all kinds of diseases. Both the humankind and the neighborly-friendly black bears are free range foragers these days."

"Don't remind me," I respond and check my pulse. "I'll be ok."

Recalling how the light was discernable from the pump house, I stand and cautiously step over to the window and lift the shutters to a direct view. Sunlight sparkles off the galvanized roof like a pebble dropped into a crystal-clear pond. In contrast, there is a leaden gloom in my chest of the shadows. Come to think of it, I entered this cabin through the front on occasions, not that my sneaking in from the back was without purpose. Where are you, Erin? Off the radar like that?

My eyes flutter as bile forms in the back of my throat. A sigh of relief. Still no lingering pain in my chest. In front of me is this peculiar rusting doorknob that I believe leads to the girl's bunkroom. The wood paneling is loose, and the framework is brittle-dry. There is a faint scraping sound beyond the door, a hurried scratching, and digging. Rodents on the move. Nails or claws? In a couple more yanks, I'll know. Is this where you've been hiding all these years?

"Hey," I shout, trying to stir up any furry beast with sharp teeth and claws.

Suddenly, the door gives way and I stumble, and out of nowhere, there's a *Swoosh*, then a *Whoop*. My head jerks like a tether ball on a short rope and I feel my face smashing onto the old linoleum floor.

It's becoming so familiar. Prep rooms have icy floors like this and most smell like detergent, but none of them spin freely like this one. Blurry, dullness, senseless, bottomless.

CHAPTER SEVENTEEN

"**D**r. Michaels. Can you hear me?"

Far removed. Murky. The words echoed in a hollow space. Who's Dr. Michaels? Why the yelling?

"Dr. Michaels. You have to wake up."

Constant. Megaphone-style. Earsplitting. The volume controls are funneling through my skull. Someone's face is close to mine. I seem to be floating or spinning toward a level beneath them. Stop yelling. Stop with the exploding voice grenades. I begin to resurface. A slow-motion ascent. My head whips to the side. A slap. How? Where?

"Dr. Michaels! Dr. Michaels! Still no response, Chief. We might have to E-Vac him soon."

The yelling continues and I fight harder to speak.

"Hang on, Chief. He's moving his mouth. He might be choking."

I exhale and gasp at the same time. The Chief's voice speaks up.

"These woods are super dry. Looks like we're going to lose the cabins. This whole side of the island will be ash in about ten minutes."

"Yeah," I murmur with a raspy tone and try to swallow. The smoky taste of incinerated timber coats my mouth and throat and I hack, strangling in mucous.

"That's it, Doc. Try to breathe. Don't pull on the tubing. It's oxygen. Take it easy and slow."

My eyes sting and tear-up.

"Where am I?"

Bewildered and befuddled, my mind races and my head pounds.

"No need to talk right now, Doc. We are damned lucky to find you. Thanks to Paige and Tessa, we located your cell phone signal through GPS. This here is Fire Chief Rawley and I'm..."

All at once, there's a loud crackling, exploding sound as a nearby building collapses and succumbs to the flames.

"Look out!" Rawley exclaims as the EMT grabs and drags me headfirst onto the uprooted land near the front wheels of my rental car. The incendiary heat imparts an orange glow reflecting off their helmets and I strain to see the ember cloud mushroom above the once cleared girls' cabins fifty yards away. The entire site is quickly becoming blackened kindling. Firefighters scurry with portable flame retardants to kill the billowing ember remnants. At times, they disappear into the carbonated fog as if drawn or sucked in by the flame, the combustion is a giant molten monster towering over the treetops.

"Damned lucky, I'll say."

The Chief bends over in front of me. "Miss Tessa told us where you might be. She said you were going to check the buildings for break-ins."

His nose and bushy salt and pepper moustache are moist from the tight shield fit and the rest of his face is covered with soot. Good thing. This might have led to considerable lasting pulmonary damage. He continues to rub one of his bloodshot eyes as if there are small foreign particles irritating it.

"I'm sure glad you were still in your car. Things may well have been worse had we dug you out of the cabin over there." He looks back at the girls' main cabin. "These buildings should have been razed years ago when the church camp was discontinued. I presented that option to the county, but they preferred to do it the hard way."

His voice trails off as he wipes his lips with the back of his hand.

"It takes only one idiot to ruin these once beautiful landscapes and dissolve them like sugar in water."

My memory is slowly falling into place. I struggle to sit up and ask, "I was in my car?"

"That's right, Doc. You were slumped over the steering wheel, like you were exhausted or passed out."

The EMT pulls the respiratory mask off my face.

"There's a huge knot on the back of your noggin." He touches, then presses the spongy left side of my skull.

"Hey."

"Sorry, Doc," he apologizes. "This has all the signs of a delayed concussion. You probably staggered back to the vehicle, then passed out."

"We need to talk, Doc," Rawley advises, looking downward over the bridge of his nose, "as soon as you're able."

The mere sensation on the back of my skull brings a sudden surge of dizzying nausea. I scramble to my side and gag.

"Take it easy." The EMT secures an oxygen mask on my face again. "Being a doctor, you should know all the symptoms."

"True, but I never thought it'd happen to me." My rasping voice strains as I yell over the roar toward Chief Rawley.

"Was there anybody else? Were there any other bodies?"

I think of blackened corpses coiled in a fighter's stance, the tendons and connective tissues withering under the extreme heat, and joints being baked into a permanent flexed state.

"This breakneck fire is too intense to evaluate," he hollers back. "We'll let it continue to burn for now." He points to the hillside.

"Our main objective is to secure these acres. If it marches toward the other side of the island we're doomed. There is less available water over there and I'm not for being on the defensive for much longer. When we bring in the air support, the county wants a journal-full of explanations as to why we can't contain it with only ground support. You can appreciate how that goes over between those assholes and us volunteers who are risking our lives."

In the smoke and haze, his ghostly appearance becomes more familiar-friendly. I acknowledge with a slow nod. To my surprise, he's the pitcher for the other team in yesterday's softball match.

"It's a hell of a way to end a reunion weekend, right Doc?"

In the scorching gloom he forces a wry laugh, surmising the hopelessness.

"As hard as it is to earn a living up here in the winter, there are still opportunists who will take any advantage. No disrespect, Doc, but in my mind, visitors aren't always welcome."

If only some of my clients had that fireman's mentality. The EMT elevates my head and offers me a squeeze bottle.

"Have some water. Take a drink...slowly."

I oblige, but my parchment requires plentiful gulps. Soon, I'm chugging.

"Doc, this is the good stuff. There's ample more in the cab, but I think you better slow down. All that smoke might force you to upchuck again."

Far be it for me to disagree with his orders. I hand back the empty canister.

"Thanks. I needed that."

The once magnified throb in my head recedes and I attempt to stand, illogically thinking that vertical orientation will take away the initial spinning in my brain. I stumble back. Fifty yards away the flaring natural furnace is growing in leaps and bounds. I had the good luck to survive. Overhead, I pinpoint branches from the treetop becoming instant torches.

"These buildings are crazy dry," the Chief surmises and puts his retardant gloves back on.

"This is ridiculous," the EMT shouts back. "We need to utilize that fire trail soon. Otherwise, we'll be trapped like fools."

He carefully grabs me under my elbow and lifts. "Here you go, Doc. No time for anymore evaluations. Can you walk on your own?"

The three of us retreat, dragging the fireproofing blankets in the grit behind. A shower of cinder balloons above our heads as the intense heat swirls with the breezes to form a glowing funnel. The EMT yells into his collar microphone. The two of us hunker down at the explosive sound of the collapsing structures.

"Brings back some very strong memories." He crouches down and frowns. "Three tours in Mosul."

"How about my car?" I ask.

"We're trying to secure the road as quickly as possible." His reply is abrupt as he studies the inferno.

"First things first. We called for a Cat and water truck. They should get here any minute now. Once they give us the green light, we'll go back and get it out of there, provided the steering column and metallic paneling aren't melted away."

I am on pain overload. My brain feels as if it had been punched through its weakest point and trying like hell to push out from under the scalp of my temple. My face feels flash-burned from the heat. I stand beside my rescuers and their vehicle as we watch the flames frog leap to another vacant building. If memory serves me, that was the tool shed where we once stashed beer.

Whoomph!

I cover my eyes to the stabbing heat. My singed face smells of smoke and retardant. Malicious fire-bombing is the perfect description. One timely, small explosion sets off another, and then another until the entire building site is aglow.

I yell above the flaming roar, "How did it all begin?"

He tugs up his jacket hood and shrugs it off.

"Any number of ways," he glances around to see if others are listening.

"Natural, man-made, or accidental. Take your pick and consider yourself lucky this time."

My guess is unproven. The only evidence available is my bruised skull plate.

"You're bleeding again. Let me get you clean gauze for that wound."

Crimson liquid drips off the side of my face, down my arm, and trickles onto the back of my hand. I press my head on my sleeve and blurt out, "I'll be ok. Let me help you do some salvaging."

"Doc, you're only wearing jeans and a tee-shirt. Where is the logic in becoming an honorary fireman?"

"Not thinking about my current uniform," I answer. "You found me in the car? I mean, was I leaning back or forward? To the side or passed out?"

They ignore my questions and focus on our more urgent predicament.

"Jesus, it smells like a petroleum factory. That storage shed must have contained some old canisters from years ago." The Chief turns to me and asks, "How do you picture this going down, Doc?"

My first job out of college was an Autopsy Assistant handling formalin tissues and sewing up cadavers. That was well ahead of OSHA-type regulatory agencies placing a leash on hazardous waste disposal. I boxed and carted the old discards down to the hospital blast furnace and practiced my "limb tosses" into the glowing grids. If my mother only knew how I supported my med school expenses.

"I think my nose is too plugged up with soot to be sure," I answer. "By the color of the smoke, I'd say some oily residues or such, like you suspect. Do you bring out forensics on cases like this?"

"Hell, no," he snorts. "This ain't no television special. We are volunteers putting out fires. Sometimes Duluth will send a newspaper reporter with a digital camera, but you'll read it two days from now on the back pages. This is Wasoon: retirements and reunions."

He checks his watch.

"I tell you what. If you feel up to it, I want some feedback on your purpose out here."

I cough and wheeze. My chest is aflame. Trying to gather accurate storytelling and not speculating may be considered by some a hoax in an unwanted assignment.

The medic unloads a helmet, then grabs a portable BP monitor and PFT machine. He quickly straps the helmet on me and doesn't stop there.

"I want to take your blood pressure and check your breathing. Now, I know it all sounds a little lame, but every victim receives the same treatment, unless there's no pulse. You don't mind, do you, Doc?"

"It's part of the protocol." My voice crackles. "Only, I usually receive the pulse-less ones."

I extend my arm toward him.

"Tessa took me on an unexpected scenic drive a few days ago. I explained to her that I once counseled up here when I was a teenager. It was all remarkably familiar. We checked locks and the pump house.

The water smelled stagnant, but the pump still worked. Not much else to say. The stop was all of five minutes, and then we were gone."

I observe Chief Rawley listening in as I continue.

"She said that sometimes vagrant hunters sneak into the quarters for shelter. By chance, I was touring the back roads today and came upon this side of the island again. As a favor to her, I thought a second look might be a good idea. There seems to be a host of thunderstorms passing over."

The stoutly EMT unwraps the cuff and places it on my bloodied upper arm. The constriction begins as he squeezes the bulb.

"How about the main building?" Rawley inquires. "There was a shovel outside the rear door."

"That was probably me. I door seemed to be ajar. I picked up a shovel that had fallen over and placed it against the frame."

"Was the door opened or previously padlocked?" he queries, still rubbing his reddening eye.

"I remember going in and seeing pretty much a vacant, well-kept room, as if some cleaning-up had been done. Not too musty. No smell of mice or rodents inside."

The allusion of attorneys asking similar questions springs out like a ghost in a closet and I reel in my explanation.

"All looked to be unusually tidy. I called Tessa to tell her where I was. She took in the information, but I don't think it registered because she was focused on last night's caterer mishap."

"She has been stressed. I'll grant you that one," the medic adds.

"Anyway, I closed the building. There was no padlock, though. Next thing I know is that my head throbs like a son-of-a-bitch, you're yelling at me and trying to place a mask over my face."

If that explanation were any less-detailed, I'd be in the slammer for arson. I attempt to deflect more reasoning as to why I was here by gingerly rubbing my sensitive scalp.

"Does the County have a lot of intruders up here?"

Both men looked at each other as if to decide which one will speak first. On the background pathway, the water truck pulls up and one by one, a handful of firefighters leap off with axes and spades. The leader crawls on the ladder device and hooks the hose extension to the top rung. The driver sticks his head out and bellows orders to the man at the hose crank. Despite the chaos, they collaborate in a feverish, but orderly pace.

"We get our share, but law enforcement is lax when it comes to the island. I guess they think the isolation and containment is sort of a dissuader rather than a persuader, if you know what I mean."

The medic grins.

"Anyway, it's likely something like a medium-sized branch or one of those giant, rock-hard pinecones might have fallen from above as you were on your way to the car in sort of delayed reaction. It knocked you senseless enough, but you still stumbled on, like a robot, to sit down inside. That's where we found you over the steering wheel."

He points to my rental sitting at the edge of the fire line, partially covered in soot.

"Like I said, it's a good thing your phone is still on. Tessa was quite frantic when we notified her of a smoke sighting. Generally, we will high-tail it to every fire, but this time, the urgency was warp-speed."

An odd comparison, I thought. Between the fishing and farm reports, and now Star Trek science fiction. That shovel alongside the rubble is the only clue to another visitor besides me. It's a miracle. The smoldering is losing some of its intensity and, hopefully, those soldiers in flame retardant jackets and leather gloves will get the upper hand and save the Valley once again. Perhaps the tinder still holds other clues. Whoever is trying to cover up the evidence might not be that successful after all.

The opaque grey smoke-filled sky darkens into a fog-like consistency as they suppress the oxygen-depleted fire with foam and water. In a matter of thirty minutes or so, the whole incident goes from a bleak hellhole to molten ash: old wood, older memories, caught up in the vacuum created by a struck match. I need to find an equal balance in knowing and sequestering in the back of my mind.

CHAPTER EIGHTEEN

Following my medical evaluation, I collapse on the edge of the tailgate in delusion as to how this whole situation happened. The firefighters are scurrying about in preparation to evacuate, and inside my pants pocket, my cell phone vibrates.

"Hello?"

"Kevin? Thank God you're alive. I've been worried sick."

"Tessa, yes, I'm fine. I have some first-degree reddening, but it doesn't appear to be that bad right now. Those firemen who saved me are first class. I will forever be indebted to them."

I stifle a hoarse cough.

"Sorry about the cabins. Everything is still a blur."

"That's nothing to worry about," she says. "Those buildings were like cardboard, ready to ignite."

"Well, there's still something unusual as to how it all began," I remark.

"Are there any other bodies? I mean..." She hesitates.

"Just because your newest best friend is a pathologist doesn't mean you have free rein on the body count," I remind her, although those same thoughts linger with me like a bad toothache.

A firefighter from the water truck is driving my rental as the caravan heads out of the perilous area. The EMT slows our vehicle as another volunteer lurches off to extinguish a mini fire along the roadside. Anything with a remote possibility is suspect. My skin feels hot but doesn't appear burned. There's no blistering and that is a grateful sign. I stroke the singed hair on my forearm.

"We are stopping along the way to put out matchstick versions. Fire Chief Rawley is seeing to it."

"He is a good Crew Chief," she says. "Somehow, there's always a responsible sense of urgency when he's around. Too bad the negative press will override the activities of this weekend."

The fire convoy is moving again and this time into an open standing of green saplings. This must be another of the recently honed fire trails back to civilization. All eyes are on the surrounding hilltops looking for other signs of smoke. The road snakes for the next two or three miles before I'm able to see the depression of the valley floor where the resort rooftops stand out like flattened green stones. Residual wisps of firepit log smoke rises near the country club. I surmise this specific road is not an easy Sunday drive, yet secluded enough to be unnoticed, unless someone steps on your escape plan. For sure, someone was using that cabin, either to live or hide and I happened to be the lucky S.O.B. to flush him from the scaffolding.

"When are you coming back to the resort?" she asks, with anticipation in her voice.

"We're making our way back now," I tell her. "No longer than a half hour or so, depending upon other smoke signals we might locate. You told me to get lost, but look how it turned out?"

"This is not funny, Kevin," she admonishes me. "The dice are not rolling my way. I need a little support from the hired hands."

"Point taken," I apologize. "Let me get back and clean up. It sounds as if the Chief wants to talk to me."

"They said you were 'passed out.' Were you unconscious?" her voice rising in disbelief.

"Something like that. They said I was slumped over my steering wheel. I have a bump the size of a pheasant egg on the back of my skull."

The lingering dullness magnifies into a simmering headache, flipping painful throbs back and forth like pancakes on a hot griddle.

"I'll check in at the ER sometime soon. It might be a mild concussion," repeating the EMT's choice of words.

"First, I try to drown you, and then you try to knock yourself out." Her voice quivers. "It's all too much for me right now. I feel responsible."

"I guess we're coming into some sort of full circle," I tell her. "From now on, I'll be extra careful off base. How's that sound?"

"Perfect," she sighs heavily through the speaker.

My clothes reek of smoke and wet ash sticks to my boots like syrup. Whoever had sneaked up from behind and clobbered me was serious about keeping that little cabin stay a secret. Still, there's no apparent need to have me suffocate in the smoke. No way did I wander to my vehicle and pass out in the driver's seat. Like Tessa had warned: be careful. There is a conspiracy brewing. A disgruntled employee is trying to get even.

We stop several times to do spot checks. By then, it's late afternoon. On the way back, one of the drivers yells out, "What's for dinner?"

The other riders give him a resounding "Lazy Bee!"

I can't object given that they saved my life.

Based upon my insistence, we do not go to the Emergency Room for a check-up, but instead, opt for the café. My treat. The hamburger I order is cardboard chewy and overdone. All told, the meat is far beyond the patented barbequed, smoke-filled flavor advertised on the menu. Nonetheless, we chow down with diet Cokes and peanut butter Rice Krispy bars as if it's our last meal. We spend little time talking about the fire in the woods. For the most part, it's better suited for becoming ancient history. Everyday existence takes precedence. There is the lament of men's softball league winding down, state fair coming up, and who's going to the Garth Brooks concert in Duluth next weekend. Most of their opinions are a consensus, as if voicing another viewpoint forms a rift in the brotherhood. Over the years of volunteering, they've developed into a tight unit. That's why they became firefighters in the first place, and that's why they're good at it.

I hold kidding in high esteem. It's to help me take my mind off a near-death occurrence. I see my reflection in the café window, drained of color, a patina of ash in my hair. They continue to poke fun at me, and 'Doc Casper' is my new nickname to them. The adjacent booth of elderly farmers gives up serious dice time to come over and add their two cents about the Wasoon situation.

"Darn reunions stir up the atmosphere with all kinds of extra smoke and dust," the man in the striped bib overalls comments, snapping his fingers. "I hear that heavy air like that can make a thunderstorm more intense."

I offer my uncertainty about the weather with a shrug and jokingly add the only time I'm not bit by mosquitoes is during a rain shower. That doesn't go over too well, or they don't get my sense of humor. The old man deadpans me deep into my chair as if to remind me that his knowledge is supreme and I'm a mere visitor. I didn't want to initiate an argument, so I decide to back off from any further comments.

"Yeah, that's possible," adds the driver.

"You can say that again," is the whooping chorus from another fireman as he slaps another cohort on the shoulder.

Smart ass Michaels. Be grateful to have another bite for that pie hole mouth of yours.

My rental receives a still-drivable evaluation by the fire chief, and I eagerly vault in it for the jaunt back to the resort. I have a choice of either cleaning up first or checking in with Tessa at the office, not so much to draw attention, but rather to find out if the firefighters know anything significant. The chief should have more input now. At the time, his main concern was to get the hell out of there before we all perished.

As I expect when I arrive, Tessa is diligently distributing verbal orders to everyone passing within earshot. A true multi-tasker, she signals and points, and signs forms handed to her all at the same time. Other times, she stands resolute with arms crossed and shouts instructions. I catch her looking up in surprise.

"It looks like you've crawled out of the barbeque pit. Are you going to be alright?"

"It's all on the surface," I argue. "A little scrubbing and I'll be good as new. How about yourself?"

She looks at Paige, turns and gives me the once-over, then lowers her voice and makes direct eye contact.

"Luckily, the fire was put out as soon as it was. We're having serious fires this summer. Thankfully, the only damage out there was to the building site. There is nothing of any value, except memories." She looks to the side of my face, scrutinizing.

"Let's get you cleaned up, Doc."

She takes my arm by the elbow.

"It's not good business practice to see the employees bringing their work into the lobby. It might give visitors the wrong impression."

"You always seem to be hustling me off to one place or another."

I cough some dark phlegm into my borrowed emergency room face towel.

"This is nothing compared to some of my better days."

"Well, you are still under my tutelage as far as I'm concerned," she prompts, displaying a rosy grin, plucking at ash particles off my shirt. "I don't want to be the spoiler, but if you don't want to take care of yourself, I will. And no bubbly throat clearing in public, please."

Tessa sits on the edge of my bed and waits as I shower off the grime and soot. The fire's heat and smoke has left me a little wheezy and the irritants give me a croaky voice that gargling won't take away. For the time being, I'm like an active member of the Smoker's Union but my respect for the firefighters is paramount.

"Tell me, once again, about the girl's cabin."

"In my opinion, someone is playing house," I answer. "But it's all academic now. We can't prove it."

I gently rub the shampoo over the painful spongy knot under my scalp, a stern reminder that I'm unable to recall all the details. Watery crusted blood dissolves into a puddle and swirls into the drain. Had I been so stupid to accept the scratching sounds were not vermin of the human version? Through the semi translucent shower curtain, I see that Tessa is standing in the bathroom doorway facing me.

"Something's not right, Kevin. We were only up there a few days ago. You think someone has been using the premises in those woods all this time?"

The last of the grime washes away. I turn off the faucet and grab for my towel.

"Here," she says, pulling the curtain aside and handing it to me. "Get dressed. We got some errands."

In a matter of minutes Tessa throws the truck into gear and, once again, I end up jostling along in the passenger seat. In no time we are off the resort property limits and back onto the coarse fire trails leading to the scene of the crime.

"I'm going to take us to an old, abandoned taconite mine shaft that was converted to a through-and-through hiking trail about ten or fifteen years ago," she yells over the engine whine. "It's only about one or two hundred feet from entry to exit. Most people aren't aware of its existence, and we don't advertise it because of vandals and pranksters."

I envision bat-infested guano crumbling from the rock ceiling and putrid water leeching off the interior walls.

"It's the only other means of sneaking up to the cabins. How I know this, you ask?" she pauses to tilt her head toward me as she bobs her eyebrows. "We Christian girls used to go up there and smoke joints."

She grips me by my elbow. "This is all confidential, you understand."

"Of course," I mutter, my hand clenched to the door handle on this roller-coaster ride of death.

Trees whistle by, their branches whip the fenders and side panels like large praying mantis clawing to get inside and devour the passengers. Where did she learn to drive like this?

"What's the hurry?" I yelp as another thick, low-riding branch whacks my door.

Tessa grins and continues to follow the road with her eyes.

"Show-off," I mumble.

The countryside opens like flipping a page in a new book. The conifer clearing is quite evident. Spindly shoots of aspen protrude through the hardpan and I'm soon aware that we are in some sort of reclaimed mining experiment. Most of the taller twigs hold sway, leaning into the direction of the sunlight, keeping that portion of the road especially lush. In contrast, the other side of the road is stark, like a control burn attempt from a previous fire. Only a few decades ago this landscape was so vital. Then came the days of bulldozers and excavation shovels unloading porous rock-fuel into giant truck beds for the trek to cargo ships stationed at the port.

"Must have been quite a sight," I mention to Tessa as if in passing. She nods.

"I remember our parents taking us up here when Erin and I were still in grade school. We'd stop on the east side and watch them dig and unload for hours. My dad admired the enormity of the project. He constantly reminded us how iron came to be in virtuously everything we used or neglected. Waste not, want not was like an indelible tattoo in our brains."

The deep earthen scars from decades of abuse are all that remain of a by-gone era. Some of the hills are eroded with tall weeds while others are made of giant granite boulders pushing out of the ground like primeval rock landslides. Decades old earth mover tracks are embedded in the clay and limestone.

"What about this mine shaft?" I inquire. "Aren't we now driving in the other direction from the cabins?"

"True," she responds. "This road encircles the erosion and riverbed. The only other alternative to the civilization below is by helicopter. It's a long shot, but I want to be certain."

She touches me on my sore thigh which causes me to flinch, but her driving is distracting enough.

"I haven't been up here in years," she reminisces. "Back then, there was no road. I know you're still a little sore, but here we are. Trust me with this decision."

She smirks.

"I have a good feeling about you being a pretty decent guy under that stern exterior. So, don't let that senseless pessimism that we have in our DNA poke you in the forehead."

"I'm with you on that one," I tell her, but my mind is on an unexpected rise in my malpractice insurance premium. "We have to be careful, Tessa. Someone could be watching us tootle around up here as we speak?"

"That's why I picked the company truck," she says. "There are always hikers and campers on the island. At the resort entrance, we remind them that the company trucks are the lifeline in case of emergencies. When they see one of these, it's patrolling and not spying."

She firmly grips the steering wheel with both hands.

"Hold on. The next mile or so will be a little rough."

"As if I don't already know." The sarcasm drips out of my mouth as I draw my legs together and clutch the elbow rest.

The overabundance of ruts and gullies are doing wonders for my lingering head throb as she careens around tight corners. Regardless of the conditions, Tessa is zoned out and heavy-footed to a point. The truck absorbs most of the road shock, but a rickety county fair roller coaster comes to mind.

"Look over there," she points. "Tell me when you see a dark hole. That's where we'll enter the cave."

"Great..." I mutter.

"What?"

"I said okay!"

It's useless to argue. Who am I to give her suggestions?

"Will it be tree-covered, or an open hole?" I ask. Worry is gnawing at me like glowing embers.

Her response is direct as she deftly maneuvers around a large pothole.

"Within the shadows, it'll look more like a large gaping mouth. You know, like one of those faces of devils on marble sculptures in front of museums or churches. Boy, us young ladies made up some scary stories. A couple hits from the joint and a malt chaser does wonders to the inhibitions."

"Rock? Folk? R & B?"

"Janis Joplin was dead, but Erin used to love that music." She drops her voice to a reflective soft response. "I sure miss her."

There is only enough room in my mouth for one foot and I offer up an understanding pat on the arm.

"Sorry."

"It's alright," she replies. "Over the lost years, I have sprinted into my share of doubt and dead ends, too. But in my heart, we still need to try. I feel that the resort is counting on me somehow to rescue it from this dreadful weekend. Can you understand my concerns?"

"Yes, and I appreciate your efforts," I struggle to find the right words. "I see a depression over there. Is that the right spot?"

She downshifts and looks past me to the right.

"I think that's it, Kevin. Good work."

The opening is not obvious from afar. It's puckered into the rocks and overgrowth, like an inverted hairy navel on a giant's abdomen.

"How in the world did you girls know about this? I'm guessing we are at least three or four miles from the cabins as the crow flies."

"We usually got free time on Sundays," she replies. "After going for ice cream one afternoon, we hiked on a different route back to the church camp and discovered a cavity in the hillside. We squeezed through the opening to find a narrow footpath leading to a wider cavern where we could sit and enjoy our secret beverages. Exploring our new hiding place, we were thrilled to find the end of the cave opened to the back side of the camp. The new tenants arrived around supper time and although the hike back to camp was still long, it gave us time to straighten out and sober up. Not too Lutheran-like, was it?"

"You were still impressionable and pondering your faith," I reply, shaking my head. "I used my free time to study the catechism."

"Yeah, right..." she drops the comment like flicking a piece of lint.

We stop below the ridge. She reaches under the seat and pulls out a pair of tattered gloves. From behind my seat, she grabs a combination shovel-spade.

"Here. You'll need these."

The hike to the opening is a steady climb for about a quarter mile from the gravel road. There is a faint smell of sulfur in the air, like gunpowder residue at a shooting range.

"Do you detect that odor?" I ask.

She looks back.

"Peculiar, that smoke from someone's fireworks prank last night got trapped on the valley floor. There's not a wisp of wind today."

I'll go along with that unusual answer, being the well-versed urban doctor that I am. Tessa is far more adept with the activities, and I don't think twice.

"Mining has been shut down for a quarter century or so. They used to dynamite the shale surface overlying the rich veins of iron below. The big hauling equipment rode the mountain, tethered by cables until the roads were level."

She grabs a backpack from the truck bed.

"We often would hear the booming explosions throughout the island...even vibrating under our feet on occasion. It was a struggle for those screwed-up teenager girls who lost faith in the Bible Camp system."

She brushes my arm.

"Let's go."

I draw in a short breath, my mind searching for ideas on how to circumvent the situation, hoping it will all work out.

"Tessa, please tell me again why we're doing this."

She stiffens.

"I want to follow-up on my intuition, Kevin. This is the only other way I can think of where someone can sneak up to the cabins without being noticed. Trust me. I'm responsible for this resort. I need to know if and how anyone is able to get in and out of here and, unbeknownst to me, live in one of the old cabins."

Low lying shrubs and grasses cling like mutant vines to the rocky landfill as we skid and slide a couple of times. But for the most part, the trail appears narrow, deer-like, and well-used, traversing the incline. In five minutes, we stand in front of the Volkswagen-sized opening.

I rub the back of my aching neck, tentatively responding to a foreboding that I'm certain is preplanned. "Let's make the correct decision this time."

Tessa hesitates, glares into the darkness, rustles in her back-pack then offers an extra flashlight to me. Her voice is steady and low-pitched.

"From here on out, it's solid ground. Not to worry, Kevin, there's a gradual bend in the cave that does not allow us to see the other opening until we're about fifty yards inside. I'll take care of you."

Hellbent. Risk-taker mode with precise movements. Any budding management team would pull their eye teeth to have her. As for myself, I'm more than content to watch from a distance but she's driving me to the edge like a soldier living on adrenalin. Uncertain. Tense. Skeptical.

Our first few steps constitute strewn slivers of shale and crushed pea gravel used for footing when the mine was still active. The dank herbaceous scent of wet moss and groundcover is overpowering. Gradually, the hollow-echoing sounds from our hiking shoes bouncing off loose rocks is replaced by muffled footsteps as we walk deeper into the cave entrance. The temperature is like that of a church social basement but cooler and with a touch of humidity. Condensation cascades down my neck as we progress into the unknown. Tessa extends the flashlight and sweeps over each dripping wall.

"It looks like we're in luck, Kevin. The recent rains are still leaching off the stones. It's a good sign for our valley water table."

She faces me. "Have you noticed that there are not any wood beam supports in here?"

That's the least of my concerns as I glance back to the entrance, a mere ten yards away.

"Cavernous fungi and spores aside, I'm more concerned in the tons of aerosol bat guano we're going to inhale once the batteries die."

She clicks her tongue.

"Not everything is a working laboratory. It's surprising that you lived this long thus far."

This is a maiden voyage for me, my first trip into a cave. I still have inherent claustrophobia from when my kid brother covered me with a heavy blanket, then sat on my chest. Any form of hyperventilating in front of her is pointless. Where is she taking me? Did teenage girls think this was exciting? I guesstimate we are roughly thirty or forty yards into the mountain side when she stops and holds her arm back onto my chest.

"Odd. I can't identify the passage we used through to the other side. It's all so dark."

She continues with the beam until she comes upon a mound of rock and debris, some of which are the size of small implement tires. The honed-out walls are collapsed and block our path. Only a dim lit sliver of light pokes out of the top surface layer, so faint that I can't trust my eyes. I hope her bat-like instincts come to a quick fulfillment.

"It's a cave-in of sorts," she summarizes. "After all these years, this once-infallible hiding place has met its end. My theory of someone sneaking through this cave to get to the back side of the camp is shattered."

She uses her flashlight to scan above and beyond my head. Our backlit shadows glide over the glistening ore, like bizarre stick figures on a granite easel. The dripping room-sized vault produces a continuous dampness on the precarious geology. Suddenly Tessa grips my arm.

"Look."

Poking out of the crumbling floor is a shattered, ovoid white globe: a human skull. I cautiously move forward. The jaw is disarticulated, and some front teeth are missing. There's the telltale sign of a stellate cranial fracture over the left orbital ridge. Blunt force trauma. I have seen it hundreds of times and can say with certainty that no one survives this sort of injury. Self-inflicted or accidental, this is an untimely death. We inch our way, careful not to disturb any other boney remnants. My morbid first impressions are of imminent dread; has Erin been located?

I imagine her coming up with friends or by herself purely to get away. Not a healthy scenario at this moment and I don't want Tessa to hear my assumptions. I right myself and swallow hard. After a brief examination, it's enough to identify an initial anthropometric overview that this is a young female. The maxillary grooves are less pronounced, and the remaining incisors are too small for a man.

Tessa huddles behind me, her flashlight hand trembles.

"It's not Erin, is it, Kevin? Tell me it's not her!"

Her voice borders on hysterical, holding one arm tightly around her stomach, trying to steady herself.

The obvious answer sits on the edge of my tongue, but my lips are sealed. I lean away, trying to avert her pleading look.

"No one can be certain who it is, Tessa," I say to her. "Hopefully, we can get the proper authorities up here to examine and remove the remains. Have there been any reports of people missing in the past months or so? I only mention this based on the findings."

"Maybe there's some identification buried under the rocks," she clutches my arm.

"That's on the table, but I'm afraid we might unearth some structural support in the process of digging. It's not a good idea for us to contaminate anything. Like I said, we need the authorities to do their investigation. Remember, we're a long way from the resort and phone service is not good up here. Let's head back to the truck and call the sheriff's office."

In all honesty, I believe we've discovered Erin's corpse. This was a Counselor's hideaway. Once again, my mind searches for an answer of how she got here. It's no leisurely hike up this mountain, and likely not an easy trek to or from the other side of the cave either. She needed to get a ride from someone who knew about this hideaway. Was it a hiker or another Counselor? How about an out-of-town worker at the mine or perhaps a friend scouting a new trail? The long, emotional, ponderous climb both Tessa and I are tethered to is relentless.

CHAPTER NINETEEN

Knowing that the skeletal identification results might take weeks, I consent to a little time off from the case per instructions from Tessa, a reminder that the mystery might have come to a sad ending. For the past hour I punished the rented Santa Cruz hard tail mountain bike through some single tracks on the outer boundaries of the resort until pausing long enough to catch my breath and look up. The sky is poking through the evergreen canopy, filtered with soot and haze, the trail is powdered in ash. Even though I had applied ointment to my arms and covered them with gauze, my burn marks continue to speak in harsh tones of irritation and rawness.

But my mind is elsewhere being that my unforgiven curiosity has been my demise thus far. This inherent pursuit.

Erin.

Tessa.

Each name counter-grips part of a tethered rope that is my heart. Days from now, I will be back home in California, or flying out to God-knows-where for another case where, once again, scrubs and exam gloves will be the formal attire.

Dissatisfied, I press my shoes into the pedal straps and guardedly lean into a sharp incline. Tufted strips of saplings growing out of the crevices kick shrapnel-like shards of granite pieces from the tires at my calves.

Slow down. Idiot.

I ride the hand brakes to a slow stop until the ground levels. Morning shadows cool the air to a point that biking idiots like me can exercise and not exorcise. The ground is covered with pointed obstacles like stubble on a man's chin. I hear pine trees crackling as they bend to neighboring tips in the subtle breezes. Overhead, serpiginous contrails of two military jets crisscrossing in maneuvers are the only other evidence of human interaction.

Earlier today, the cave was closed off as they removed tons of boulders and gravel, mostly by hand. The Superior County Coroner's Anthropological Unit sent two technicians to sift through the remains. Tessa and I had remained vigilant the entire time watching from along the entrance site. Strobe lights gave the cave an eerie semblance of gothic murals in museums. Unfortunately, the angel, Gabriel, wasn't present and there was no roll call - - only the occasional vocal instruction from the lead investigator and acknowledgment from the local excavator.

We watched as the cadaver bag was requested. A junior investigator appeared and deliberately unrolled and unzipped the black vinyl sack. The tractor was turned off and a moment of respectful silence was shared. Soon after, an additional coroner investigator arrived and faded into the entrance. I am aware that their function is to gather identifiable pieces of bone and fabric carried out by the various assistants in five-gallon plastic pails. Once out of the cave, lids were handed to them and they closed each container with an authoritative SNAP.

A somber Tessa sat on a nearby stump, shoulders drawn, and knees drawn tightly together. I sympathized as best I could by scooting in close. We both wrestled with which of the alternatives was more satisfying: recovery or remorse.

Back at the rest stop, I check my wrist for a residual racing pulse. Satisfied that it's falling back to a normal rhythm, I cinch up my gloves and tighten the strap on my glasses. So much for regret. The first push off the pedal once again reminds me that burnt skin is quite unforgiving. I power through each stroke trying to forget the excruciating pain in my calves. Years of autopsying charred people was never rewarding. The cadaver's hands form "death grips" as muscles contract from the heat. The jaw muscles also contract, and the mouth is agape. I can feel their terror and sense their doom as flames consumed them. Up until a day ago my existence had been measured on the short cycle, too. In frustration, I silently join in their bellows.

Upon arrival at the resort, it's business as usual. Landscapers continue to rake the fallen pine needles, teen-age valets in their green bowties and blue jeans stand attentively at the circle drive podium. There's the occasional shrieking from someone launching from the diving board, and mid-day shadows cluster around the cabins like late embarrassed arrivers at a wedding. The soft breezes are not as humid as yesterday. My entrance screen door is ajar with a daily newspaper lodged into the jam.

SKELETAL REMAINS FOUND IN OLD TACONITE SHAFT

Bold-faced headlines such as those are not easy to ignore and I skim the story for any realistic or intrinsic details. The writer gives credit to the responders who were out on a fire trail assessment without mentioning names. Fortunately, nothing is written about the body identification although back home in California this story would come with potential photos of missing people. As is the custom, those snapshots are dated to a point that any facial resemblances are obscured.

Cleaned up and re-salved with ointment, I gingerly walk over to the dining hall for breakfast leftovers still warming in the buffet pans. Ceiling fans undulate over the hall in broad hypnotic swipes. The lunchtime dishes -- macaroni, tuna, and Jell-O -- are scooped-up by the grousing guests who evaluate every pan as if it's their last meal. I huff under my breath. Pick something and move on.

Tessa enters through the side door connecting the office to the fellowship hall. She wears an Ole's Resort uniform, and her hair is bunched in a short ponytail. She wears earrings the shape of little gold cabins with pierced blue stone inlays. Her smile looks forced as she passes through the dining hall. She stops to converse with a cheerful older couple. I watch as she tries to avoid contact with another group. She soon notices me with tray in hand and approaches.

"There's a better selection in the galley. The cooks are hoping to phase out this brunch menu by 12:30."

She politely tilts her head to a trio of elderly women who side-step the busboy as he dresses up the salad with garnish and candied walnuts. The three anxiously wait for his departure and move in for the kill.

"I'm good. Thanks anyway."

I lean in. "How are you holding up? It's been a couple days."

Tessa's fatigue is palpable. Her eyelids are puffy. I detect the smell of liquor.

"It's been a battle, Kevin."

She rests her hand on my arm.

"Somehow, this resort life isn't as peachy as I willed it to be."

I allow her time to ponder, and she continues.

"Erin was twice the sister that I could ever have been. I try to emulate her in so many ways. That hole in the mountain, the darkness, the crumbling rocks...."

"We still don't know for sure if it's her," I interject. "Let's keep hope on the Front Page."

"I know. I know," she counters, hoping to stop the internal bleeding, busying herself by checking her cell phone for messages.

"If you need some help around here for the next few days, I'm available. My flight plans have changed. I want to spend more time in Resort Villa Land, that is, if it's okay with the HR Department."

CRASH! TINKLE!

A food tray explodes onto the floor and utensils skirt under the counter like pucks on ice. The trio of meandering ladies gasp, then burst into giggles, pointing accusing fingers at each other. Other patrons in the nearby tables flash their condescending expressions at the silliness. The teenage male water server races to their aid with a towel and kneels to remove the debris.

Tessa gently squeezes my elbow and says, "I think I know exactly where you can be used."

Lifeguarding is the last thing I expect Tessa needs me to do. As for this day, it's the world of wheelchairs with umbrellas, decades-old hoists, and soggy towels. The crowd consists of a dozen or so semi-charred, semi-glazed senior women wearing sunglasses the size of ski goggles without a care in their private little world. Colorful swimsuits that were once stored deep in bedroom closets blossom like spring flowers in pastels and various black patterns from stripes to dots. There are plenty of scoop necks along with freckled cleavage. Technicolor sandals and brilliantly painted nails abound. Various concoctions of wine coolers in tall plastic glasses stand like attentive soldiers on the side tables.

"Tessa told me that you are a doctor?" The comment comes from Gloria, the middle-aged banker's wife.

I'm aligning a stack of clean beach towels on the shelves behind the drink counter. Her neighbors stopped clinking toasts to listen. I'm on stage. Coppertone and bebop. The diving board rattles and launches another customer into the deep end.

"Yes, err, sort of," I explain, trying to not act too dismissively. "I don't treat patients or have a clinical specialty."

"Are you a surgeon, then?" asks Joyce, the Everything-Is-Funny Giggler as she dabs her face with a soggy drink napkin. She shoulders alongside Gloria, scooting her chair next to the table.

"Not exactly," I say. "I conduct death scene investigations. Autopsies."

Usually, that takes time to settle in, but their reactions and the fact they've been drinking for a couple hours, leaves me with two options: Towel Folding 101 or Shock TV with the Pathologist.

"Well, there certainly has been a lot of that going on lately," retorts Abby the Gabby as she is known to her tea-totters. Wearing a large Panama hat, arms folded against her chest, she defiantly clutches an iced drink in her left hand. That hand rests directly on top of her ample breast exposing a large, clustered diamond wedding ring. Her accomplices nod but I'm distracted by the matching yellow hairband in those wavy blond locks, pulled so tight that her crow lines have become tiny white slits. She waves away a fly buzzing in front of her face.

"Health situations can pop up anytime," I explain. "I've seen heart attacks at weddings, strokes following a big meal, and people without any symptoms of cancer succumb to the disease who were merely strolling in their backyard."

The concierge busses in a large tray of melons, grapes, and assorted cheeses.

"In other words, it can happen anytime, anywhere, and without explanation. Don't let the fear overcome the fun."

The ladies turn to see Wilette, another one of their cohorts, move in closer toward us. A few moments ago, I had overheard her bragging in earnest to be of royal Hawaiian descent to a group of outsiders, but she is by far the fairest of them all. A white artificial plumeria, perhaps the only one within three counties, is pinned into her salt and pepper beehive-do, above the right ear, signifying she is single and looking for love. Her linen shawl is wrapped under each pudgy arm. Her nails are manicured and bright green. She steps forward and continues.

"And the body in the cave?"

Her tone is short, harsh, and accusatory. I thought I had left the attorneys back in the Cities. Two passing blue jays screech on the fence. She takes off her glasses to watch, then lingers for effect by turning side-ways to me. She wears a heavy application of luminescent eye shadow and heavy rouge. I hope it's waterproof. Two hours into the first day on the job and Wilette has me cornered without any aloha in sight.

"The investigation is still pending," I begin. "It might be weeks before we know anything. I'm not part of that but I was one of the poor souls who happened to come upon the remains. We need to remember not to be swayed by newspaper headlines. Missing Persons is involved as we speak."

The grilling felt like an interview outside the courthouse, barring the dark suits and flashing cameras.

"Well, I certainly hope this gets resolved pretty soon," she adds. "There are a group of us that have been coming to Ole's Resort for years. It's hard to believe there's a killer amongst us."

"There is NOT a killer, Wilette," Gabby Abby opens her mouth to add criticism, then stops short. "Let the County take care of it. How about us taking care of ourselves at the same time? Hey, Ladies of the Reunion. Anyone for another spritzer?"

With that said, there is a unison cheer. Wilette retreats to her chaise lounge not before trapping a younger couple who were minding their own business. She stands and nods in my direction. I know they're gossiping by the mocking laugh all three are sharing. In all actuality, I am a little older than some of these eye candy brides, but it still feels like a buzzard has begun to pick at my bones.

To avoid the spotlight, I quietly hustle drinks and efficiently replace wet towels. My anal-retentive mind continues to line up the patio chairs in the least obstacle-like fashion, yet somehow, mysterious forces seem to move them every fifteen minutes. It feels good to be busy and not dwell on the potential negatives.

The latent summer sun casts long shadows over the west side groves and there's a hint of autumn nippiness. Earthen tones of dry soil beds along the fence offer contrast with the emerald blackberry bushes and flowering myrtles. I smell the tangy fragrance of aged, seasonal, geraniums in the half wine barrels near the gate. This time, neither the angry bees nor wasps are in attack mode. The ladies are having a blast thanks to my doting ways, and the thank-you's are in abundance. It's the alcohol talking and the bubbly remarks flow like freshly poured champagne. We are beyond the polarizing past and into the eminent present. It's for the best.

Later that night I stroll the grounds past the athletic fields and fire pits. From the gathering present, it looks as if the men and women activities are separate. Men sit close to the rustic fire, smoking and drinking beers. The women are as loud, sitting at the picnic tables with their iced highballs or white wine. From all appearances, the aspen-smelling hardwood and cigars all seem to be ignited at once, leaving a grey hue that hovers like a large cloud over the main assembly. The aroma of sorts is intoxicating to anyone associated with camping. I recall how my dad spent eighty percent of his life on a tractor seat or in a barn, ten percent at the supper table, and nine percent with us kids hitting grounders in front of the house. The remaining one percent was when dad had the heart attack and died. That doesn't count.

"Larry, you are such a pompous ass. Par is a golf term and, rightfully so, not your profession. Come to think of it, pastime is even a stretch."

"Bag it. Clubs are farm tools in your situation. A garden hoe comes to mind..."

"Golf is a mind game requiring the capability to think."

"How about you *think* on this?"

It all degraded after that. Boys will be boys. Two men drag a washtub full of beers on ice toward the seated crew.

"Look what the cat dragged in?"

"Here, Kitty, Kitty, Kitty."

"Meow." Larry spits out of the corner of his mouth into the flame.

There are nine men playing hit and field under the lights on the diamond. A pitcher in blue jean cutoffs lobs balls to a shirtless batter in knee-length khakis and cleats. Three outfielders shag flies and relay them to either a left or right middle infielder who rolls them toward the mound. There's a *ping* from the bat, and the yellow tournament grade softball carries like a silent cannonball in a beautiful arc toward the fielder. There's the muffled sound of a catch. I hear the buzz of moths and beetles in a frantic orbit of the fluorescent lights. All this is my favorite form of ear candy.

"You up for a few pitches, Doc?" Vincent, the trucker, holds the ball above his head at the mound, a cigarette in between his lips, the ash coiling like a fat gray worm.

"No thanks, buddy," I explain. "I'm still a little beat up from the fire," pointing toward the crusting strawberry on my knee.

"Gotcha," he nods. "That body thing in the cave was the clincher."

He squints through the smoke. The creases around his temples are trench-like.

"Any word yet on who it is?"

The level of concern is growing like freshly watered weeds in a field of corn. When word trickles down to the locals, it's a matter of time until even the neighbor might be guilty.

"Nothing yet. Maybe later."

He signals to the batter with his gloved hand in the air.

"Ball up."

The batter crushes the next pitch on another rope, exactly like a couple nights ago. The left infielder leaps in vain as the two jawing outfielders hightail and sprint as it crashes off the fence.

"Holy shit, Earl," yells Vincent. "Save that for the tournament."

Being midweek, activity at the registration office is basically nil compared to this past weekend. As I walk past registration, I catch Tessa's intern at the counter. By estimation, nine hours into this shift and her uniform is still undaunted. A thick barrette secures her hair as she looks up and gives me a weak smile. Summer struggles to surrender in the North Country. The western horizon is now the color of ripe grapefruit and the landscape is coated in shades of purple and grey. Another perfect August day is coming to an end.

I check my cell phone messages. One from the County Coroner's office in Grand Rapids questioning me about the condition of the body before moving it. No rush, but please call back sometime.

No rush? Right.

Too late for today, but first thing tomorrow I will follow-up.

Later that night, the anxieties resume in full air raid and my mind starts to run the video. Autopsies are lined up in cities hundreds of miles apart. I enter a morgue only to discover the body on the table still alive and trying to crawl off. I call for help to secure the emaciated old man from falling. There is a web of still-attached body fluid collection bags and catheters that clatter when he rustles to escape. The prep room has no electrical outlets, and a swinging propane gas-lit lantern is suspended over the morgue table. This lighting is too dim for me to read the name on the wrist band. Serpentine shadows glide across the body. The blood tubes are cracked in the stand and the sharp edges point upward toward my extended palm. The gurneys are double stacked with bodies already dissected and sewn shut. But I can't recall if it's my doing or, am I an assistant? Sutured skin incisions are ready to pop like strained rubber bands.

I jerk awake, trying to focus. Hundreds of crickets and a solitary owl sound off outside my door. Then, there is complete silence. All at once, large raindrops, singularly, then occasional, begin to rattle the windowpanes. It's the makings of a hailstorm. A tempest presses against the framework and I fear a tornado will soon materialize.

Someone opens the screen door and steps in as the booming thunder pounds against the cabin walls like a giant with large, balled fists.

"It's a torrential downpour out there. Can't you hear it?"

Her green slicker is shiny from the wet, her hooded face is shaded, motionless. She is standing at the doorway, waiting for me to respond, water pooling at her boots in oval black outlines.

"Kevin. Care to go for a walk? Like old times?"

She remains motionless. Draped in that dark wet coat. An opened umbrella in her hand. She reaches out.

"Let's go. It's our time."

There's a flash of lightening and the room erupts in a veiled yellow glow that illuminates her face. Sunken cheeks. Gunmetal skin tones. Eyes pinpoint and red, like lasers. In the mist, her hands are upright and open. The crumpled green headscarf that she used to wear is like an offering to me. "I have saved this for you. It was your favorite."

There's another flash from outside.

"Go ahead. Take it."

Thunder rolls across the valley like a giant bowling ball and pins the agitated air molecules against the vibrating walls. I hear the gate slam and giddy voices of women, some shrieking, some laughing, some cackling hen-like.

"Erin," I stammer. "How are you here? Where have you been?"

I sit upright and pull the blankets away from the bed.

She stands motionless like an inky statue.

Outside, the storm arrives in forceful torrents. The windowpane rattles, the drops are super-size. I struggle to sit up as the screen door sails open and bangs against the abutted jam.

"WHOP!"

Erin has disappeared but my emotional power switch continues to flash. The springboard clatters. There is the sound of a cannon-ball-like splash followed by yelps and cheers.

"That was definitely a TEN."

"Gloria is the Champion."

I hobble to the doorway. My legs are raw and the gauze wrap from my shins has unraveled. I brace against the screen door framework and gaze outside. Dark water foams against the sides, sloshing over the coping, and tidal-waves the slippers and towels into and under the chairs and tables. Swimsuits lie in disarray along the fence in a saturated mound. In the water, buoyant naked pearl bodies bob with the new eddy of forces. Breasts and feet float to the surface like heads of large aqua serpents searching for food.

Abigale the Gabigale has dolphin-like skill, easily gliding between Wilette's floating arms and Joyce's open thighs. Martha is the quiet one and doesn't participate but prefers to stretch out on the step. Her thinning wet hair is in disarray and she gathers the loose ends and hooks them behind her ears. Another flash casts an eerie glow in the cabana. Martha's nipple rings are small yellow orbs as she leans back against the edge in full display, eyes wide and glowing.

These fearless retirees challenge every thunderous display with a boisterous "Yeah!"

The larger the splashes, the louder they got. Someone who the group named Perky Paula tosses a floatation ring into the water and the straddle is on. Wilette manages to secure it under her waist, her ivory butt surfaces to the delight of all of them. Awkwardly, she flips upside down and comes up spitting and coughing to shameless applause from the audience. Like nude parachutists leaping from the belly of an airplane, the platform empties, some free-falling, some holding their nose, some vaulting off the side on the deep end, some of them jiggling, and all of them giggling.

"KERWOOSH!"

I glance at Gloria as she submerges and begins to glide beneath the wading legs. In one graceful push, she slowly steps out and zeros in on me. Her physique is mind-blowing flawless: lithe and muscular. I'm mesmerized, totally trapped in the moment. Muscular arms, flat stomach, equestrian-pointed hips, she stands unabashed. There is a golf-ball-size, rose tattoo on her inner left thigh with a thorny stem that horizontally leads across her navel to her right hip. Is this the same woman that I bantered with no more than twelve hours ago?

"Hey, ladies, look who has come to join the party?"

The jamboree begins to chant.

"Kevin!"

"Kevin!"

"Kevin!"

One of the women stands next to Gloria, then there is another, then there are two more, then the pool is empty. They promenade toward my door leaving a small river from their dripping bare bodices. Overhead, another brilliant flash of a blinding electric arc floods the scene. The tallest fir tree near the registration building explodes as if a celestial warning is being broadcast.

"CRACK!"

The tree top sizzles and splits into uneven halves. It's as if a monster arrow had bulls-eyed on target. In that micro-moment, the women freeze, their hypnotic mission short-circuited. The startled leader, Gloria, jerks her head in surprise and looks to her cohorts. Wilette glowers and brings her hands up to her parted lips.

"Well, what are we going to do now?"

In that secluded moment, the wind, the rain, and the gaggle are at peace. Paula modestly holds her arms over her breasts. Abigale awkwardly covers her crotch with both hands. But Joyce maintains her challenging stance and gropes Wilette's behind.

"To the loch. All of you are a dithering bunch of out-of-date tuna cans," someone shouts.

"Aye, aye, Captain," rejoices Paula as she cups her front with both hands and presents them to the onlookers. "No argument here."

"Let's spawn," Gloria shouts above the silliness, displaying a wide grin as she playfully pinches someone's bare behind.

As if there is a new mission, they race for the water. I fear of their revisit at my doorstep, dragging me with them where we all end up sizzling from a cloud of voltage. White bottoms with tan lines bounce in the flashing darkness. Human-like zebras are loping wild in the Serengeti of this Wasoon resort.

CHAPTER TWENTY

The next morning is cool and breezy. Last night's storm had sucked in northern Canadian air like an opened door. With little fanfare, a flock of geese hover above in final approach lakeside. On shore, the "*put-put-put*" of trolling motors is a constant irritation. In addition to that, a quarter mile out, two turbo-powered jet skis roar like Harleys towing wakeboarders to their doom. Acrobatic maneuvers aside, the tether rope tension is propelling these hapless young men in tight circumferential whips, leaping with facile movements fifteen feet above the choppy surface. I stick my foot into the bath-like temperature shoreline. There is the combination murky smell of late summer algae and boat motor combustion. Nearby, two seagulls fight over a rotting sunfish carcass.

I can't decide if I am hungover or sleep deprived. That midnight exhibition is still crystal clear in my mind. I've witnessed unexpected and unique experiences during my stay here but retelling this story is the topper, and the sorceresses would evoke the Fifth if questioned. I could be wrong, but I suspect their husbands have no clue.

The puzzling element for me was the Erin apparition. Is that nightmare conjuring up another round of guilt?

All in all, the daily resort routine is typical. Scheduled activities have not yet begun for the up-and-at-em retirees. The valet boys are driving golf carts in succession along the shaded stop. I decide to forego the irritation and drive to the County Coroner's office in Grand Rapids.

Population-wise, the town is a larger version of Wasoon. The revived city supports a couple upscale strip malls with notable chain restaurants and grocery stores. Still, the dominant preference vehicles are jacked-up four-by-fours and my rental is easily a hood shorter than the majority. I drive through the downtown portion with my window down. It's mid-morning and the aroma of fresh baked pastries and espresso shops are jumpstarting my hunger. Since the last time I was here years ago, the offspring boom of stop lights have soared to a total of FIVE in the three-quarters mile or so. The main buildings are still brown brick, but instead of apartments, the new shops' second floors are now investment companies or lawyers' offices.

The coroner's office is on the south side of the city limits in a clinic-style, stucco complex. There is a shush of traffic in this area of town. Large signs direct me to parking. The front reserved spaces are for clergy, handicapped, and police vehicles. A slender mustached man, built much like Vincent, is walking out as I drive by looking for a vacant space. He multitasks his cigarette pack and the cell phone and eventually fumbles the phone to the pavement, which leads to a frustrating expletive outburst. Another woman in surgical scrubs and wearing the fabric head cover follows him out and dodges his sidewalk obstruction. With diligence, she digs in her bag for sunglasses and coordinating cell phone. It's a comedy of dueling looks, the strained smiles, the bright sunlight. Batman and the mole woman outside their comfort zones.

I take for granted that Northern people are mostly unemotional types and to be fair, I still bear resemblance to them. In the past, this form of expression has caused me some criticism from co-workers and attorneys alike. Even if this were a call with the winning lottery numbers or from another lover, the level of excitement would be the same.

Once inside, the quiet air conditioning sets off the working atmosphere. The reception desk is manned by a twenty-something gentleman wearing a white County-emblemed polo shirt and khakis. His nameplate reads Andrew Kvistad, the perfect Norwegian name to match his auburn sideburns and gangly frame. To his left, the computer monitor screen reflects in his glasses as he studies and jots down notes on a pad. I notice some phone numbers circled in red ink. With his free hand, he picks at a crusting shaving scab under his chin. Soft blowing sounds emanate from his mouth.

I tap on the counter.

"Excuse me. I'm Doctor Kevin..."

"Yep," he interjects. "We have been trying to reach you by phone, but our systems are out of whack from last night's storm. It's getting a little frustrating on this end."

He has a flushed appearance and wrinkled collar. Overtime's worst nightmare. He pauses, then adds, "You can call me Andy, or Andy K., or A.K. It's all the same thing."

"That answering service lost my connections too," I tell him and lean inward toward his desk space. "I understand the Coroner wants to talk to me about the body?"

The young man tidies the desktop and opens the top drawer, shoveling post-its and pens into the void. I take note of yellowing sweat stains under each arm and his oily forehead complexion. There is the smell of cigarettes and musky adolescent cologne in the air. His ears stand out like Great Lakes mussels, the right ear lobe is pierced and holds a small metallic cross. He nervously drums the desktop.

"Affirmative. It says that you noticed remains in a cave up alongside the Wasoon Resort. Is that right?"

"In the right place at the right time," I clarify. "The Resort Manager, Tessa Stevens, and I were checking out smoke trails in the air. We drove the fire roads toward the old taconite diggings. Unfortunately, we came upon this abandoned mine."

I don't want to explain any further to the Assistant about missing persons. The back door behind the counter opens and a heavy-set, forty-something man wearing a black nylon windbreaker with the County emblem on the left chest pocket pushes past us. His tinted glasses are block-framed like the Irish rock star, Bono, and are typical law enforcement black. Carrying his cap by its bill in one hand and a leather attaché in the other, he renders quick work of acknowledging us with a nod.

"A.K. Sup?"

"Impeccable timing, Spence. This is the Doctor who discovered the body."

He extends his calloused hand. "Spencer Smith, County Coroner. I prefer to be called Spence."

He has a busy smile and thin lips that curl up on the edges. From his unhealthy bulk, I judge his daily stressful routine to be far from humdrum. Isolated counties like this generally utilize outside contractors to perform examinations of the few violent crimes beyond car accidents and suicides. Even though he might be six feet four, he hunches and meets me at chin level.

"Damn Vet wants to put my prize Malibu down and it's pissing me off."

He tugs on the lapel of his coat.

"She's been with me through thick and thin."

"Racehorse? Grey hound?" I ask.

His head jerks back in disbelief.

"Jet ski."

As if I'm supposed to know.

"He wants to charge me forty-five hundred for the engine and another bundle for the hull."

To a certain extent, my background with water toys is a garden hose with nozzle.

"That sounds a little steep," I add in support, as if I own a marine drag machine.

He draws in a large breath, measures his response and chortles.

"No shit, Sherlock."

He has the dead-eyed affection of a feeding shark. Better ease off the pedal. Spencer's mood is sending out a strong signal.

"When you said 'Vet', I assumed it was an animal."

He lets out a wheezy chuckle.

"That's Arne, our local motor sports repair shop. Big time skier and full-time BS-er. We joke that he gets more service calls than the veterinarian. Somehow the name stuck. But I tell you what, the bill he sends makes me think twice about euthanasia."

"Here are today's reports, Spence," says Andy. He hands him a small stack of folders. "On the top is the 'Cave Remains.'"

"Thanks," he replies and jams them under his arm. "Follow me, Doc."

His office is unexpectedly uniform, like walking into a model home. There is a modest desk with a captain's chair and two padded visitor's chairs facing inward. Piles of papers and folders are spread out like puzzle pieces on the busy desktop. Everything else is either neatly stacked or lined up on the bookshelves behind his chair. There isn't the anticipated smell of old coffee cups in the trash or stale air from closed-door conversations with dark-suited men. The room has a plain and simple window facing the street that rattles as a cement truck rumbles by. The photo gallery consists of two framed pictures. One is a young man's high school graduation that includes his parents. The second is of that same man, a few years older, standing in front of the hull of a small boat.

At the time of the first photo, he was the spitting image of his father: husky, same no-smile, same height, and the same lack of embrace that I'm getting used to seeing up here. On the right is his mother, wearing an unassuming hat and dark-framed, old-fashioned glasses, clutching her bouquet in one hand and a Bible in the other. Easily a head shorter than her son, she has an uncertain glee for the momentous event, or was it a loss of connection?

The other photo is of Spencer kneeling in front of a gargantuan jet ski with his hand resting on a huge trophy. In this shot, the smile is from ear to ear.

"Is that your Baby?" I ask.

He stops his settling into the seat motion and gives me a quizzical look.

"That's her," he said glumly, quietly answering back. "RIP, I guess. Here, please have a seat," pointing me to the vacancy in front.

His eyes dart over to his desk phone. "Finally, a few minutes without that damn blinking message light." He sinks back into his creaking chair and groans. The deep wrinkles on his forehead relax.

"I'm not so sure today is going to be any better. We have a three-car pileup with fatalities up on Highway 27. Top that off with a botched robbery at the Kwik Stop out in Northome." He grins. "The suspect was shot in the ass by the clerk as he blew through the front door." The smile fades. "Now this."

He takes the top folder and opens the front flap. I give him a couple moments of silence.

"Has there been a preliminary report from the autopsy yet?" I ask.

Deep in concentration, the verbal request doesn't connect, as if he is not hearing me. He closes the folder and replaces it on the desk. Leaning forward on the armrests, he begins.

"The body was in bad shape, mostly scattered bones. Nothing recent either. There were a few threads of material, like denim or wool. Whether it's men's or women's is uncertain at this point. Report calls it carnivorous artifact from a large mammal like a bear or wolf. DNA is going to be a pisser because of the timeframe and bats love to adorn the ceilings of dark, protected spaces."

He sets the paperwork on the desktop and rotates it toward me.

"Our famous hometown mascots are everywhere, excluding car washes, but I can be wrong about that too. The Wild Wolves. Mind you, this report is still pending."

I pick up the forms and scan the pathology summary at the bottom. Analogous to the Death Certificate in style, the findings are listed sequentially from main to incidental. In this case, skeletal remains are unidentifiable without teeth or hair. The coroner's office has a major issue that might require a lengthy list of missing persons, which likely will include Erin. The overhead air conditioning kicks in with a whir and a few pieces of lint shoot out from the vent like a dying cough.

Spencer looks up and pats his belly and points at the vent.

"As you can see, it hasn't been used much this summer. I wear this coverup to hide my lard ass."

"What type of animal artifact does this suggest? Teeth marks? Gnawing? Bone scattering?"

"That's the puzzle, Doc," he answers and takes back the folder. "Like I told you, it's not unusual in this situation to ever know. Poke holes. Puncture holes. Even something like some sort of metabolic breakdown after death."

He pushes away from the desk and stares out the window. His sun-damaged complexion is reddish, and his cheeks are flecked with freckles from countless years of wearing caps down low over the forehead. Small beads of sweat form like glistening mini domes on his sideburns. Once again, I'm invisible in his space. His concentration is unbroken, even from the annoying large construction trucks back-up warning signals. To make noise, I skid my chair closer to the desk.

"I'm receiving at least ten calls per day from families who want to know if that body is their lost relative. It's a stuck response on my end. I tell Andrew to keep it close to the cuff and don't let out any frickin' information, but sometimes newspaper writers will call pretending to be related. Boy was I burned on that one when I investigated a case fourteen years ago south of Superior, along the Canadian border. Ream me once, but never ream me twice."

He blows out a big sigh to collect his anxiety.

"Now I'm getting fired up again. First, it's the Malibu, and now it's you."

He looks back to me. "Sorry, it's not meant that way."

"But it rhymes," I grin. "We are brothers from another mother, Spence."

I stand and we shake hands. Mine dissolves in his giant mitt, like a human to a superhuman. I hope he doesn't crush it.

"Keep me in the loop," I invite. "I'll be staying on for a couple more days in a consultant capacity only. If you get into a bind, I know of some good connections that might help you out. It will only require a racing jet ski and a life jacket, plus, of course, a lakeshore cabin. Do you have any ideas?"

To my amazement, the drive back to the resort through the construction zone is effortless, as if the work is in accord with my visit. I think of Spencer's frustration and how it's manifested in hopelessness. I plug in my cell phone and check messages. None. Great.

A few miles down the road I spot a couple of bikers, male and female, in matching magenta bibs and helmets, fixing a flat along-side the road. The slender woman wears mirrored sunglasses and stands beside the upright black Trek. Her fellow rider squats over the downed bike evaluating the tire seam to the rim. This non-event will be an exaggerated campfire story somewhere tonight. As luck would have it, ruptures are the main course up here, like Ole's big heart. Things once considered safe and smooth, over time, erode and can garner sharp edges. On the passenger's seat, Erin's green headscarf mushrooms from the rolled-down window air, rounded like a full sail on a white cap lake.

CHAPTER TWENTY-ONE

The memorial service for Darlene Gabbert is scheduled for three o'clock. The resort entrance displays a large, framed picture of her in, it's safe to say, the most recent family photo. Looking closer I notice several of her relatives have been cropped out, leaving the focus of her husband, Carl, and her in an embrace. By the expression on her face, I gather that Darlene was a happy soul and full of life. She was wearing the typical Sunday's finest: high-waisted, floral-pattern dress of this culture. Her smile reveals a front row of perfectly straight teeth. Dentures, I presume. Mr. Gabbert is hugging her in an uncomfortable stiffness. It appears to me that the happy occasion with the two of them in the center, was forced as they squint with half-smiles into the sun.

People are filing into the adjacent conference room where they're greeted by two of her classmates seated at a receiving table, each wearing baggy Class of '67 matching polo shirts. There's a Guest Book alongside a donation basket filled with dollars and cards. She was well known locally, because it appears most everyone I had been introduced to thus far in Wasoon are in attendance. Deputy Sheriff Lundgren is in uniform and accompanying Alice, the beautician. He secures his hat underarm as he guides her by the elbow. Alice's hair is cut short with a faint hint of yellow-orange highlights. She still maintains dark mascara and rouge accents and wears a similar set of the resort's gold cabin earrings that I had also noticed on Tessa. Her attire is a modest linen poncho over a tank top and dark pants -- quite a contrast to the loud salon smock she wore outside the storage facility a few days ago. Lundgren acknowledges the seated women as Alice signs the Guest Book.

Next in line is Stella, the café waitress, escorted by Aaron and David. Despite my first impression, these gents clean up quite well.

Aaron wears pressed denim jeans, a Western shirt with bolo tie, suede sports coat, and matching boots. David is a yuppie version of his brother, fashioning an indigo blue sports coat, white open-collar shirt, khakis, and loafers. I notice the female college interns manning the beverage table near the doorway, but ogling David as unobtrusively as possible. Much to my surprise, Stella is striking. Clearly a beauty hidden from view behind the apron and menus, she smiles easily to others and runs her hands through her hair for attention and soaking up complimentary adulation. I catch myself trance-like. Her form-fitting autumn-colored polyester skirt, egg white blouse and a scarf are a hit.

Being a memorial service instead of a funeral, I see no men in dark coats or women in black dresses. I felt ill at ease with only an extra dress shirt and windbreaker packed, but no one seems to pay any attention to me anyway. The gathering is more festive than not. Roland Purdy told me at the funeral home that Darlene's body is to be shipped back to Texas at her daughter's request for burial in a family plot next weekend. Open caskets can often take the 'f-u-n' out of these functions and the resulting tone evolves from dark and somber to relief when the lid is closed. Nevertheless, I can't forget about her "spongy" larynx that I palpated in the funeral prep room. My concern is dual. Had the investigator noticed it, or was it merely from the elements? At either rate, that ball is not in my court, per se.

Just then the man of the hour, Roland Purdy, comes out of the conference room, dressed in funeral-black, quietly shaking hands with the brothers, offering a friendly hug to Stella. He distributes folded service brochures to seated classmates and friends.

"Thank you all for coming. If you'd please have a seat, we'll get underway."

The folding chairs are filling up and the latecomers will have to end up standing. There's some shuffling and muffled coughs, then the room quiets down. Carl Gabbert sits front and center surrounded by the aqua mermaids who tormented me the previous night outside my cabin. Others I am introduced to by Tessa are somberly selecting chairs a couple rows deep. I take an open seat near the back, next to Paige. We politely acknowledge each other as I gently squeeze her hand.

"How are you doing, Dr. Michaels?" digging in her purse for tissues.

"As best as can be expected, I guess," eyes fixed toward the front. "How about yourself?"

She pauses.

"I registered both her and her husband on Friday. She was so looking forward to this weekend. Old style glittery jewelry around her neck. Class colors. You know. High school stuff. Most of the resort is composed of Wasoon folks. Even I was getting into the festivities and I'm not from around here."

She places the celebratory gift rose on her lap.

"It sure was surprising why she was on that fire trail," she dabs the corner of her eye.

Not sure how to answer back, I look down and open the memorial brochure to browse. The obituary portion is basic, only offering home residence, occupation, survivors, and of course, years of birth, graduation, and death. The same entry-way photo is shown on the front cover, and *You Will Be Missed* stenciled in bold lettering underneath. Despite the inclement weather we suffered through this past week, today is an Impressionistic placard of cloudless blue. There is a soft, warming breeze out of the northwest. For the time being, there isn't that bolstering roar of a speed boat ripping offshore. Indeed, there is hope for this godforsaken country.

For the next three-quarters of an hour, the local Reverend, who also wears a polo shirt with high school décor, offers condolences, a couple prayers, and introduces Darlene's visiting classmates to the group. He asks them to stand. At that request, at least fifteen or so, mostly women, including a lesbian couple in matching blouses and punk-style haircuts, stand to soft applause. The service is concluded by a group chorus of the high school fight song and "How Great Though Art." Roland Purdy reminds the group to sign the Guest Book and take some cookies and beverages offered in the lobby.

"That was nice," Paige concludes, her eyes shining. "Let's hope it doesn't put a damper on the rest of the weekend."

"It won't," I reassure her. "She'll be remembered fondly in conversations all night. If anything, there might be a swimming event or a luncheon in her name a year or so from now."

The Olson brothers are snared by a couple of their female friends. Stella and I share greetings at the doorway. Aaron pokes his head around the girls.

"Hey, Doc," he extends his hand to greet me and pulls me in. "Glad you're here. We need to talk later if that's all right with you."

"Of course," I said. "I've decided to take a couple R & R days. These are specific orders from Tessa."

I look over the gathering.

"Come to think of it, I missed her at the ceremony."

Aaron chuckles softly.

"As luck would have it, she got a call on her cell just before services were to begin. I watched her take it and sulk back to the office. Your guess is as good as mine. She gets to handle daily hazard duty aside from a funeral. I bet she took some time off and got away. Think you might have an answer to that one?" cocking his eyebrows. "You can't keep your nose to the grindstone all the time. An exception is our old man, though. Now there's a prime example of how *not* to live."

He has a point, and I can't argue with that logic at all. Stress bombards us at all levels. Brother David is busying himself with the ladies and relishing the brought-on self-attention. Something he tells them has the girls giggling and covering their mouths. Standing deadpan like a comic, he taunts his brother by twirling his bolo tie.

Aaron's mind is elsewhere. "Bro, it's time to skedaddle. We got work to do."

"Yeah, I guess," David says flatly.

"Well, you take care, Doc, and if you see Tessa, tell her we need a couple of signatures on some documents of Dad's."

"Roger that," I reply. This leaves me wondering if it might be related to other things he mentioned. "When the party dies down, we'll get together."

Disappearing quietly was not in the cards. I am cornered by Gloria who gives me a full hug and slobbering lick on the cheek out of view from the others. Then there's Perky Paula who, I'm quite sure, had ulterior motives and coyly suggests meeting her for a swim later. This is soon followed by Vincent Bode, with the crushing grip and the full-on stare down.

"If you ever need a distraction, my souped-up tractor is the bomb. Give me a call and we'll go for a drive." His jaw is set tight, his legs wide apart like a football coach in a close game.

I hit him with my own come-back. "That sounds like fun. When's the next road trip?"

He cocks his head. A smile slides off his face, as if missing the punch line of an off-color joke. I continue.

"Let's just say my schedule is wide open for the next couple days, so I'll keep it in mind."

He rolls his eyes. "By the way, Tessa and you put on quite a dance show the other night. My guess is there was a little practice involved."

"It's merely pure talent," waving off the comment with a smirk.

After that, the exit was uneventful. I politely usher myself out the side door toward Tessa's office, knock and enter. Her chair is pushed in toward the desk. She's gone.

In my mind I'm trying to erase the deaths as coincidence: Ole in Africa, Darlene in the woods, Ray Perkins in the Nursing Home, the body in the cave, and the boy in the well from years ago, not to mention the destructive fire and my unconsciousness. Logically, there's absolutely no connection and I needn't dwell on it any longer. All were declared natural deaths to some degree, yet it's a fascinating thought. Erin is still missing, too, but that case is becoming colder day by day. Poor Tessa had so much on her plate even before I hopped aboard.

Back at the cabin I sit at the desk in my room checking e-mail, sifting through casework on my laptop, reviewing notes, and editing reports for clarity. The Texas family with the accidental overdosed son still bombards me with emails on a weekly basis, as is their right. Toxicology reports have yet to come back to me by Medfile on a latent case in Florida involving lethal levels of PCP prior to the suicide. No surprise there. Then from the west coast, someone's lost relative, a reclusive logger in Oregon, washed ashore a week back. Everyone is in shock and demands to have an answer. As usual, I'm informed that he had no health issues that they're aware of.

I sit back and close my eyes. None of this will be going away soon and the troubling apparition is adding to my ongoing stress. All in all, I am not accomplishing much sitting here, and my mind continues to drift toward Wasoon in a negative way. Why this big need to take extra days off or try to blend in with the townsfolk? The airport and rental cars are my home away from home, not this cabin-trap. Reunions like this complicate things. I begin to feel like a voyeur looking over the neighbor's fence.

Outside I hear trucks and cars starting. There is male laughter at the dock and a power boat revs up a couple times in between the idling motor. I can hear the first splash off the diving board and sixties music echoing near the registration driveway. Back to normal. As for me, CTRL-S and Shutdown are the right moves to make. I place the computer back in its briefcase with an emphatic zip.

The walk has no destiny and no direction. I learned the hard way how best to desert motel rooms when the rental car and Google map only mean another method to raise the angst level. Tessa and I are developing a relationship and that has me concerned. It's more than casual and more than necessary in our busy lives. A lump is forming in my throat. Emotional conflicts are coming at me from all directions and I don't want to lie to her about my feelings.

Soon I am beyond the boundaries of the resort, mentally lost in the magnitude of the live oak brambles and aged spruce trees with trunks the size of stadium poles. The single track slowly morphs into a deer trail with fresh scat near a clearing where they've been recently nibbling on juniper bushes. The treacherous pointed-leaf, tinted-red vines grow beyond ankle level and I carefully overstep the threat. I hear the pine tips creak in the breezes and somewhere nearby an angry ground squirrel is sounding off at my presence. Further ahead, the landscape becomes more familiar: sodden moss throughout the granite erosion and the crashing waterfall. To my amazement, this is where Tessa and I had swum. I pick up my pace like the fatalistic lemmings in stories of old.

The cooling updraft of the mist on my face laced with the roar from below can only mean one thing: I'm approaching the precipice where we both leaped. I'm spellbound. How in the hell did I survive that daring plunge? The rugged trail bends to the right along the cascade in a descent toward the river. With no hesitation, I continue this sojourn seeking some sort of semblance to the peacefulness the two of us shared on those rocks. Away from the falls, large loons swoop like F-20's toward the slowing banks, stopping occasionally to pluck something from the water line, then bee-line to the safety of the branches. The sunlight nudges around the vegetation until it gets to the water level and forms a brilliant reflection on the swirling dark stream.

Our private drying platform is again, inviting and comforting, a mental solace. At its narrowest, the cross-over is twenty yards of an ill at ease soaking, and yet the urge to recapture the journey's end is deeply set. The first footstep is more of a slip, bouncing butt-first into the icy depths and surfacing downstream beyond the exit point, the distance from roughly home plate to first. A couple of novice strokes later I grip the river rock eddy and slog ashore on the other side. No harm, no foul. Only a little soggy and relieved that the struggle is over.

The table rock surface is like a welcome stovetop warming tray. I draw my knees up and overlook the expanse of pristine emerald solitude. I drape my tee shirt alongside me and tap the gravel out of my sandals. How did Tessa know about the poison oak oils? With those chores accomplished, I lean back, close my eyes, and take in the quietude of the escape. Not a care in the world. Living the dream. Only a handful ever visit this rock, and I happen to be one of them. This moment is a bucket list check-off.

The stillness holds me in a cocoon-like slumber, and it takes the barrage of meddling jays and woodpeckers overhead for me to wake. Groggy and stiff, I sit up surveying the surroundings, identifying the interlopers darting tree to tree, branch to branch, until territorial rights are once again restored. My tee shirt is air-drying, and sand residue is caking between my toes. The smell of nearby wood smoke can be faintly detected, like campfires stoking, like the resort, like every night, like a comforting hug. Rotating left to right, stretching my back muscles, popping my spine, I notice a piece of soft fabric next to where I slept. It's a green headscarf, coiled in a small loop. Erin's headscarf. The internal roil begins again.

CHAPTER TWENTY-TWO

There remains a chronic mental burden that I carry of being careless or screwing up with the scalpel in my hand. Like accidentally slicing a vessel in a murder-stabbing case, or not identifying the bleed site, or missing an obvious thromboembolism cause of death, or the macerated stillborn with anomalies. They haunt me on a weekly basis, and the constant reminder is the annual professional liability insurance premium. In the fog of battle, the pressure is on HIGH and I've pretty much accepted the dull ache in the back of my neck just thinking about it. But this role as the 'answer' doesn't get any easier over time. How might others view me? Irresponsible? Untrusting? Not thorough? Indecisive? That's a guilt-filled sanitation truck under scrutiny, tumbling out of the gate and bouncing off my sorry ass.

Now the glove is on the other hand. The grip of reality is gone. In my haste, I've become lax, allowing emotions to ride the tombstone toward an unending resolve. There is no luster in my armor anymore. I have a dull pain forming in the back of my scalp. It's my inability to understand the cabin blaze and that haunting headscarf. I watch the sunset form against the dark tree line.

My chest heaves with a non-productive cough and I wheeze back to the resort. Each draw is painful. There are lukewarm stares on the faces of those seated at the picnic tables. They pause to look up, stop in the pathways, step aside with their food trays. Mouths open in surprise. I'm like an extraterrestrial to the group.

Anxiety is not the immediate problem, it's much more worrisome. Back in the cabin I close the door behind me, standing back against the framework. Evaluating. Contemplating.

Is it in the cards that I've been carrying around the headscarf in my pocket all this time not realizing it? Are there other answers to questions that I've yet to voice? I've associated it as belonging to Erin and that's my mistake. This piece of cloth is someone else's. Tessa or Paige's, or anyone who has ridden in this same vehicle. Jumping to conclusions without investigation is the dooming downfall and in relatively short order, I'm becoming prey to such an animal.

I step into the bathroom to check and re-check my throat in the mirror for redness, pull down my lower eyelids and look at my corneas.

A normal person passes it off as circumstantial, but I'm not the random thinker. There needs to be a logical answer that is yet unknown.

Timeliness. Punctual to a point. The resort has begun the sunset festivities: stoking the fire pits, hors d'oeuvres on the center table, and revving up the music from the decades of their youth. There is a fiery yellow glow coming from outside and shadows rise and fall on the wall. I change into jeans and sweatshirt, then scrunch up the headscarf into my back pocket. The air is a soft flume of haze and envelopes the tables like an opaque ceiling. Tonight's main course has the aroma of fresh bacon and grilled hamburgers.

"Well, it looks like you have risen from the dead, Doc."

Security Guard, Perry Brown, flings his hands in fake surprise and takes a wide stance.

"From how you appeared staggering down the driveway, I wondered if the bean salad was overripe at the memorial service today. Sometimes if you leave food out too long it has a penchant to be a little gamey. The Ladies Aid at the Lutheran Church mean well, but when they run low on mayonnaise, the next best thing is honey mustard." He taps his belly. "It's not a good combination."

"Thanks. I'll keep that in mind for the next time."

At least Perry still recognizes me as friendly. I keep my head down and meander through the early troops near the dining tables. My goal is Tessa's office in hopes she has come back. Moreover, I'm in need of some common ground. Considering the options, she's my best choice for now.

"She's not back yet. No one has heard from her all day."

Paige, the Intern, pokes her head from around the beer tap bar.

"I've been assigned extra duty pouring drinks and shooting the breeze. I could say that you're my first customer, but that would be lying. All in all, I estimate forty guzzlers were ahead of you."

Watching others with a satisfied smile she continues.

"So far so good. The old biddies are keeping it tame for now, but it's still early."

"Good luck on that one," I wrap my knuckles on the counter for emphasis. "Please tell Tessa I'm looking for her."

"She left nary a note or phone message," Paige adds. "It's not like her to off and disappear. Ooops." She covers her mouth.

"I understand," pausing. "By the way, have you been driving the company truck lately, picking up the mail or grocery errands to town for the staff?"

"Not likely, Doc," she shakes her head and points to her lips. "They keep me pretty busy in the front office. This is a 'vacation' for me. Why?"

"Oh, I'm missing my lightweight jacket and thought it might have been taken by mistake. I didn't pack extra outdoor wear and prefer to keep track of my lucky inventory for the next time it pours."

"Well, I'll ask around," she adds. "Dark navy or black?"

"It's navy, but with all the smoke and the fire, it's pretty grungy."

Then building up enough courage, I continue.

"How about Tessa's headscarf? She lost that too. It's forest green and was sitting on the seat the last time we rode together. She proclaims that's her good luck charm along with a favorite pair of earrings."

Paige ponders that thought.

"Can't say that I've ever seen her wearing one, Doc. She is quite picky with us dressing too casual in public. I'm her intern and still learning the finite points of maintaining the crew, so I really pay attention to those types of details. I have to."

"Don't ask around, Paige," I tell her, putting up my hand to stop.

"It will eventually show up. Forget that I even asked. No more extra duties for you tonight, but thanks."

Dusk has settled in the resort with a quiet hush instead of the usual music. There is a cool, after-rain freshness to the air. Crickets are in full staccato, and residual dampness to the asphalt streets and trees mute the sounds of slowing vehicles. Without any thought other than morbid curiosity, I drive into town and park across the street from the Kwik Stop.

Local adults zip in to buy gas and rush out on their way home to have dinner with their families. Some hurry into the store to buy a lotto scratcher or two. Teenagers in tanker tops and flip flops hustle in and out to purchase sodas and Polish dogs. The cockier ones tap the cigarette packs in their palms to act cool before placing them unlit between their lips. Liquor is the priority offense. Everyone puffs, legal or not. From where I'm parked, I see a handful of young males jostling in front of the store, lighting up, laughing loudly, and hounding customers while they fill their tanks.

Today's misadventure at the river has me rationalizing. If Erin was somehow snatched, then this might have been how it happened. Someone enticed her into a car to meet-up with friends and promised to bring her back. Of course, that was over forty years ago, and that filling station has been updated and remodeled at least a couple times over and now includes this convenience store.

I was trying to get a grip on the situation. Most people fill up at night and prefer to, without any delay. The main exception is the 'convenience' of other options grocery-wise. In those days, gas, soda, and candy were all that was available. Locals were fortunate that non-truck stops remained open for business beyond eight or nine o'clock. But perhaps it wasn't a station just for locals. Had she recognized the other driver, or was the conversation instigated by the stranger? It's impossible to say and I feel as if I'm making song selections on a broken juke box. Some habits are hard to break.

One thing for sure, rural lifestyle and youth are basically the same. High school graduation is still a big event. The community secures their futures. Everyone has a large pick-up truck -- and this includes some of the girls.

I recollect that Erin was one of the first to have a moss green VW bug with barely enough power in third gear to a wind-aided fifty miles per hour. It was never going to be a getaway car but was certainly unique and stylish for the era: very upscale and urban. She put-putted around town on errands for the church camp as I rode shotgun with the to-do list. I always managed to peek at her long, tanned legs, short-shorts, and Jesus sandals riding up her slender calves. It was distracting as hell and no amount of sermonizing was going to save this miserable sinner.

Two more guys with pickups are inserting their credit cards at the pumps, waiting, then leaning back on the fender as they gas-up. Some of them chat with fellow customers whereas others are checking their cell phones. The new norm. Over the past hour, only two females have stopped. There is a teenager-type who left her car idling and races into the store. The other is a young mother with two children in the back seat. She carries on a clamorous mommy conversation with them as she begins to fill.

Erin would do the exact same thing if push came to shove. Her beetle often refused to start and sometimes it took two or three attempts. On one instance, another male counselor and I had to jumpstart by pushing. I reminded her to have the spark plugs checked. She told me it's priority number one after counseling duties were over for the summer.

But I don't think this was the case for her disappearance. According to the scattered details, she was there to buy gas while a male driver in a dark-colored truck was using another pump. The clerk was reported to have recognized her. The puzzling piece is why she left her car and got in the other? It was so out of character for her to abandon the 'Pride of Wasoon', as far as I was concerned. If it were me, I'd stash the car keys in my pocket as it fills. In my younger days, by accident, I locked myself out of an idling car at the gas station. But teenagers take those dumb risks constantly. All the information

I can glean is that according to the store clerk witness, something was said by the driver which prompted her to get in the passenger side. The door was closed, and the truck drove off into the night. Her VW keys were still in the ignition.

What initiated that? Knowing her, I suspect she was merely going to sit in the vehicle to talk, not expecting to become a passenger. That meant she knew the person or, at least, trusted him. At any rate, that's all I had to go on for the past forty years. There was no visual contact or recognition, and the other driver wasn't ID'd. But that brings up another point. Was that person pursuing her to the gas station and if so, why? To talk? To argue?

Now I was speculating rather than sticking with the details. My jaw tightens as I grip the steering wheel, thinking how seated in the witness chair has a familiar tone. This Kwik Stop was once a locally owned business, but those people either retired, moved away decades ago, or died. Perhaps all the above. The garage portion was raised and expanded into rows of snacks, drinks, and a refrigerator wall. In addition, the new petroleum tanks and platform were replaced over ten years past, leaving me nothing but hypothetical thoughts.

There erupts a squeaky yelp as one of the young men races around to the passenger side of the car and extracts a soda can which he downs in two gulps. The female passenger is grabbing at his arm in vain squealing in delight and surprise. The taunting continues as she opens her door. The teaser backs away, arms in the air as if surprised to be blamed. He crunches the soda can and walks away before returning to his truck.

I speed-dial Tessa and it goes to automatic voice mail. A couple grain trucks rumble past, closely followed by an Air Stream fifth wheel. Approaching the city from the other direction is another SUV signaling into the Kwik Stop. This is life in the fast lane of Wasoon. A casual drive in the country.

Not yet ready to call it another night of isolation in the cabin, I pull onto the highway heading for downtown. Bee's Café is still open, its neon sign aglow, and I need a break. A cup of watered-down, late night coffee sounds like a good idea and how about a nostalgic piece of homemade pie.

Andrew Kvistad, the Coroner's Assistant, and Spencer Smith, the County Coroner, occupy a booth in the back. Andrew sits facing the door and acknowledges me. Spencer turns and signals for me to come over.

"It's a little late for breakfast, Doc. But how about if you join us for dessert?"

He's still in uniform and his face has a humidity-style sheen. Perspiration marks radiate from his arm pits. He slides over to allow me a space.

"Andy and I returned from a head-on near Cloquet. No one beats the dealer at the casino line on a tank full of booze."

He picks at his thumbnail, then bites the tip and spits quietly toward the window.

"We average four or five deaths like that a year. The state guarantees to put in a right of way, but we heard the same thing last year, and the last."

"Yeah," adds Andrew. "It's becoming a statistical news item, but domestic abuse still rules here in the sticks."

I settle in, noticing their empty dishes stained with red pie filling.

"Pass me the menu, please?"

"They call it strawberry rhubarb but it's not fresh harvest fruit," Spencer adds. "I suspect it's canned pie filling." He dips his head toward the dessert counter behind the bar. "Our season is short and to the point. April is best, June is worst. July fruit is unpalatable. It's stringy and sour."

The waitress pours more coffee into both their cups.

"Anything for you, Doc?" She steals a peek at Andy.

"It was recommended by these two gentlemen to try the pie. I'm game."

"Coming right back." She scribbles on the tablet and moves on to the next empty table, picking up the left-over tip.

"She's nice," says Andrew. "I know her older sister, Paige. You know, she works with Tessa at the resort."

"Paige has been very helpful," I add. "We sat together at the memorial service for Darlene Gabbert this morning. She is moved by the loss."

"We all are to some degree, Doc," interjects Spencer. He scoots his body into the corner of the booth and rests his leg on the cushion's ledge. "My appointed duties also cover sympathy calls to the next of kin. It's never a fun job."

"I hear you. That's the toughest function."

Our thoughts seem to be on a common wavelength. He sits forward, elbows on the table, a frown across his forehead.

"One of my first cases coming in was the Erin Garner missing persons. I was going to be *that* officer, who solved *that* mystery, and make a name for myself. With literally no follow-up information to use, and no witnesses, it was clearly becoming a lost cause, much to my dismay. I expect yours too, Doc," his head shaking slowly in defeat. "I piddled with that story, but there were no leads. I can't shake it, like in a movie, where somebody's bones show up in a wood pile or excavation site. She had family and friends. A good life, people say. Why, the other day, Tessa spoke her name like she's still with us."

He pauses as if waiting for my reaction.

"I bet you find analogous situations in your line of work. People struggle with the here-today, gone-tomorrow logic."

The waitress delivers the pie with a scoop of ice cream and I lean into it with gumption. Turns out, it's one of the best I've ever tasted. The fruit holds it shape on the inside, it's not overbaked, and the crust crumbles just touching it with my fork. The ice cream is like tasting gold.

"On the house, Doc, and thanks for taking care of my big sister today. She mentioned that you are the sweetest."

"I appreciate it, and I appreciate being able to help in any capacity." I sit up and lean forward over my dish in disbelief. "This sure is good."

"Enjoy," she says. "It looks like we might be closing soon. Will there be anything else?"

"We're good, Lacy," says Andrew, giving her strong eye contact. "Do you need a ride home?" Looking back at us, he pads his wallet pocket. "It's on me tonight, you guys. I insist."

"I've noticed that Tessa has been bothered recently," I continue, folding my arms in thought. "Is there anything we can do to help her?"

"It's a long road for her," says Spencer, stifling a burp. "Excuse me."

"We do what we can," adds Andrew. "She was AWOL today. At least a couple of times people asked me where she went. She's popular, I'll grant you that."

"None of our business, Andy," reminds Spencer, tapping his spoon on the rim of his mug. "She'll come around in a day or two. She always does."

"Are you saying this phase has a history?" I ask.

Another late-night hay truck slows as it travels through Main Street.

"A couple times a year she will get all fired up on mostly resort things. But Erin's name will surface like a curse word: 'Damn it, Sis' or 'Now what, Erin?' We allow her some space and the steam eventually dies down, so to speak. Soon, she's back to her own cantankerous self. Yelling at the staff. Trudging through the banquet room. Stomping into my office. Giving me the one-two."

"The one-two?" I ask, placing my fork alongside the plate, intently listening for clues.

"Yep. Like, 'what have you done for me lately?' stuff. For Erin. She's aggravated to the max, but I suspect her ex has something to do with the internal strife, too. He took her to the cleaners in more ways than one. The last time we saw him was when he drove through town in a twenty-foot U-Haul, towing a speed boat, packed with all the things she hated the most."

The food prep room goes dark and Lacy opens the register till. Andrew stands and begins to put on his coat.

"That's last call in Wasoon," sighing and tugging down his wrinkled trousers. "I'll catch up with you guys tomorrow. I'm going to bug

Lacy on that ride offer again, small town or not."

Spencer looks out the window, lost in thought, as the shadows coming through the blinds fall on his face. He scratches at his watch band and sighs. I know that feeling all too well. Some of my finest hours in hotel rooms begin like that.

Long-haul truckers travel best at night on highways connecting small towns. I notice up here it's the same situation, as another semi rolls by. This time, it's a petroleum tanker with whistling air brakes. The caution streetlight flashes but, unlike me, they have thrown caution to the wind.

"Let's get out of here," suggests Spencer.

He sighs in the direction of Lacy and Andrew who are talking at the counter. "I didn't know Erin Garner, but I sure as hell miss her."

"She's the one that got away," I add. "You probably aren't aware, but I knew her for two short months one summer. It seems like a lifetime ago."

"Somewhere, someday, she will show up. I'm still riding on hope for that," he says, pushing out of the booth. "Any change in plans, Doc?"

Despite my itinerary to connect with other potential cases, my intentions are to stay at the resort until there is some resolution. It's neither the pie nor the remorseful company tonight. It's Tessa.

"I'm going to give myself a couple more days at the resort. I deserve it, plus the weather is improving from tempest to temperate. Minnesota Indian Summer. It's my favorite time of year to be here."

No need for more reflection or wasted commentary. What Spencer revealed caught me completely off guard and I am still shaken by this twist of fate. How many other people have been involved in Erin's case over the last forty years? We enjoyed each other's company over a piece of pie and coffee, but internally, we were brainstorming scenarios as if the disappearance were yesterday. He expected to break Erin's case wide open. I wish he had. Disappointment is written all over his face. As for me, I leave the café without a clue where I'm going next.

By the time I look up, Spencer is two blocks away. I cross the street, open the door to the rental, settle in, seat belt secured, and watch the silhouettes of signals and taillights bounce off my hood until dawn.

CHAPTER TWENTY-THREE

The mysterious headscarf hangs over the rearview mirror like one of those aromatic tree car air fresheners. There are still no answers to grasp on my end. Emotion wise, it's either a mixed blessing or an anathema. But I prefer to think of it as the reminder, an accustomed memento, resolved or not. I make the drive to Ada, a working-class community that Erin once told me she frequented with classmates. All the northern cities have identical templates beginning with city limit welcome signs, populations hovering around fifteen hundred or less, GMC and Ford dealerships across the street from each other. Near the outskirts are the hamburger joints. Closer to downtown are situated old red brick churches. Main street is home to a fire department adjacent to the police station. There is the usual conglomerate of gray and white-colored cars, black monster trucks, and navy-blue SUV's meandering up and down the streets.

Winter is the worst time for vehicles and it's easy for me to understand car maintenance from the continuum of freezing and thawing. Grit and salt corrode the undercarriages like an ulcerating skin cancer and very few people use their garages for their commute vehicles. More importantly, things like jet skis, boats or trailers are housed like babies in a crib. August brings out the best of drivers. It's the last opportunity for vacations and visiting. There is pride of ownership in the means of transportation and the occasional restored Victorians. Of course, some are painted contrastingly like the homes in San Francisco along 19th Avenue, projecting a Norman Rockwell tableau.

I watch kids on bikes doing wheelies and a middle-aged woman, wearing fashionable jeans with tailored rips on the legs, text while walking her large dog. A mailman, wearing blue khaki shorts, hops out of his truck and scurries down cracked sidewalks lined with colorful flowers. Spunky mid-Americana on full display. The cost of living is significantly lower than in my hometown and I am convinced that purchasing a house can be done by using a credit card for the down payment and still stay under my card's max limit. That's crazy talk, but I'm beginning to grow some roots here -- if not physically, at least psychologically, like breaking free from a cocoon and rubbing the wax off my wings. More than ever, the lake life comfort zone has me hooked.

I recall that the original Garner family home was in Ada although its exact location is unknown to me. A visit to the local branch of the county's Public Records office might give me some help in that matter. Weak answers result from weaker questions and somewhere I long for a leap forward. I try calling Tessa and again it goes to voice mail. It's a better idea to let it go. If she sees how often I leave messages, it might suggest I miss her, and that's not entirely true. I need her.

At the Public Records office, I am greeted by a clerk. She's a cordial, elderly woman, her reading glasses rest precariously low on her nose. She ushers me from the modest entry-reception room with walnut colored captain chairs to a narrow hallway lined by other office furniture. Here, the smell of lemon polish is strong, and there are heeded warning signs at the doorway to *Watch Your Step*.

From another era, bound faded black ledgers are stacked on shelves beginning with the early nineteen-hundreds at the bottom. Most of the older books are flattened from the stacking weight, the covers are as thin and frayed as canvas tarps. The baby-boomer versions consist of two volumes: I & II. A closer inspection does not reveal any recent texts. Microfiche or ancient electronic data are probably stored elsewhere. Lucky for me, the clerk locates only one Garner family and the information is alphabetized. That makes it a lot easier. I jot down the address. There is a framed city map on the wall with both the street list and a close-up map of the city. We map-grid the Garner homestead on the east side, near the outskirts of a community park.

Driving from west to east through Ada gives me the impression that the newer developments faced the sunset. In most places, patios face south, out of the wind. It's a modest selling point but nonetheless, these structures are the first hit by atypical weather such as blizzards and tornadoes. Passing First Street East and Main, the over-crowded tract homes gradually give way to various average-sized lots with single-story modular homes dotting the streets like a Mayberry of the North. There is a brick middle school adjacent to the only high school, at least on this eastern side. Two hockey rinks overgrown with grass look askance. Homes on this side of town appear to be older, mostly of wood sidings, on narrow streets. The drive through the city is approximately two miles from end to end and the Garner place is on the last street to the north.

I pull up to a shuttered three-story Victorian with a front porch supported by large wood columns. Anything originally painted is either peeling or the paint is completely gone. The meager lawn is a patchwork of prickly, large-leafed weeds and crabgrass with numerous pinecones, giving the driveway a puckered look.

Sunlight pokes through birch and maple tree foliage leaving elongated dark lines on the roof top. Power lines strung from the street to the garage sag like thick old ropes. As a kid, my friends challenged each other for the record number of tennis shoes we wrapped by their laces on these lines. As we got older, our greatest fear was that one of them would eventually set off a house fire.

There is a hint of wood smoke in the air, not from this place, but nearby for sure. Jays, the theme bird of survival in this region, noisily dart from driveway to tree limb to rooftop, twitching, head jerking, keeping an eye on this new intruder.

Houses on each side and down the street look lived in. There are haphazard oil stains on the driveways and a couple of them have rusted auto heaps and old lawn mowers in plain sight. The irony of it all is that it's an upgrade from the staked lawn flamingos of the fifties. Those were the worst eyesores as front yards were trashy enough. Hand-driven snow removers are stashed alongside the garages, their shields rusting and laden with chalky bird droppings. Contrastingly, the closed community from where I live in California is made up of older homes, but those are mostly excluded from harsh weather.

Certainly not lived in for decades, the Garner house's exterior is in disrepair. I step out of my car to get a better view of a once original family homesite.

Close up, the weathered wood and hoary shabbiness give me the urge to roll up my sleeves and hop into a major restoration project. Pride of ownership has flown this coop. HGTV people: leap on board and announce your remodeling budget.

I slowly approach the front steps that are held in place by a rickety set of rails. Under the roofed portion, there is a leather sofa teetering on only three posts, its surface faded and pocked marked. Human depressions are long gone, and the matting and coils look like metallic centipedes. The screen door lists on its bottom hinge, ready to fall off with the slightest tug. On the side of the house is a cellar door nailed in aluminum siding, its flimsy deadbolt held on by only one screw. The backyard overcrowded vegetation encases the house and consists in large part of wild mulberry bushes and juniper saplings. A rusted screened rear entryway, half the size of the front porch, puts the finishing touches on my exploration.

At the end of the lot is a narrow building with a detached barn door. Old split logs, a couple of sixties-style gallon gas tin cans, and assorted pitch forks and shovels are piled on the side. Nothing here has seen better days, better months, or better decades.

There's a set of rusted clothesline poles leaning against the shed, the tangled cords and wooden pins litter the ground. The house well is covered with large boards, overgrown with thorny thistles. I walk over to the pump and take a couple attempts with the lever. The pipes gurgle and in due course, a slurry of foul-smelling black sludge spits from the spigot, leaving an oily stain that dribbles down the base and in between the wood pieces. I can hear the hollow splashes deep down. The back of the house has fewer windows. Vertical sliders are encased in cracked wooden frames and ripped screens. Desiccated animal scat is accumulating along the basement windowpane. It's no telling which varmint was using it as a condo, but my guess is either coons or skunks.

I make one last look and resign to the fact that this escapade into the past is both unsatisfying and disappointing. I'm stymied and press my lips together. This constant berating. Why do I obsess over why things happened as they did? Here is a place with much history and I am merely a recent observer. People once lived and loved here. Nothing more. Nothing less. Places like this need to be raised or gutted. It's way too much effort to restore it into anything suitable for a household, especially a financially struggling young couple wanting to buy. Erin couldn't wait to leave. I imagine for her it was a hop skip over adolescence, and the home life. That was until I passed her in the chapel hallway, and it all went to hell.

I hear a car start up and loudly pull away as I come around the corner to the front. Some smart-ass teenager spinning summer rubber, letting some steam off, or getting even with his parents. Other than that, the old hometown is picturesque and peaceful, as if I were never here. I take a moment to study the Garner house. The tattered upstairs linen curtain billows through the broken glass on the attic floor. In my mind I can see Erin waving good-bye through the broken dreams continuing to torment me.

My next stop is back to Wasoon and the Lutheran church that sponsored the camp all those years ago. I trust some specific records have been kept in the rectory library, and I'm eager to learn if the island pastor, Laverne Williams, is still alive. Photos of us camp-crazies in those records would be a big plus since my luck thus far has scored double goose eggs. I am feeling a little directionless and this recurring lack of emotional connection has me wielding up a little internal anger. I slam the car door behind me and trudge to the entrance.

My recollection of Pastor Williams is that this church was his 'calling' - - meaning first job. He was full of youthful exuberance, connecting and allowing us to carry the ball as overseers. He also directed the services and tried not to step on our toes, so to speak. His meet-you-in-the-middle attitude worked well because all of us counselors were doomed with overseeing adolescent hormones and the daily, never-ending taunts. We accepted our fate as babysitters and that became the focus over re-telling bible stories. In the cabins, it was never a message of love or understanding. That never worked out.

Tall, thin, and with porcelain skin, the Pastor became sunburnt with only a few minutes without some head covering. His sandy-colored hair and hazel eyes were no match for summer, but he was a trooper when it came to activities at dusk. With an old acoustic guitar, singing grade school style folk songs and urging us into two-part harmony were his element. My impression of his wife was that she was plump, plain, and perennially pregnant. Pastor Williams roared at the most unassuming jokes as if he were hearing them for the first time. Sequestered in religion and socially inept, he was never out of uniform. The starched-white collar and black short sleeve shirt and khakis was a reminder that he was always available when the need arose.

All in all, he was well-liked and respected. A vow of poverty is not a decision to be taken lightly. But I sometimes overheard the elders of the congregation complain he was overpaid and that he underserved the people in need. In my opinion, this was far from the main event. It was the pessimistic church leaders who tended to criticize and that took a toll on his persona. He tried to practice turn-the-other-cheek, but us counselors knew something was bothering him. Over time, his exuberance became lifeless. Sermons amounted to a few minutes. Benedictions even less. His shoulders sagged more each week as if carrying the weight of the camp's survival.

There was never enough the Pastor could do for the congregation. They constantly looked for excuses to let him go. Interest in church circles were diminishing. They believed he was instigating that the youth leave the church on a mission of mass migration once those high school diplomas were dispensed. It was a tough job, certainly not as bad as a used car salesman, but he continued to be positive and still pushed the product whether he believed it or not.

Back in the day, our local Lutheran ministers usually over-stayed their welcome and this Pastor was not out of the ordinary. He lasted four short winters in this Caucasian wilderness. Not long after, though, he took a parochial school principalship in Alexandria.

Unfortunately, I lost track of him although I meant to occasionally drop him a note after graduation. His smile and laugh weren't always sincere, and I sensed he was as lost as the rest of us, even more so. Perhaps he retired or even left the ministry for brighter pastures. This much I know: if he'd divorced that overbearing woman with bratty kids crawling all over her, Pastor would've been much happier. He was dying from the inside-out daily. I figured him now to be around eighty or eighty-five, playing golf or checkers, sitting in a church rectory somewhere flipping through pages of ancient sermon notes. Because of Erin, my curiosity of him is the key that might open another door.

The front entrance to the church is unlocked, and I descend from brilliant sunlight to an unlit, step-down corridor. I wait until my eyes adjust before moving along the hallway. There is a spartan rubber mat for overboots underneath a coat rack that's filled with flimsy wire hangars. The bulletin board meets me at eye level and a table of well-organized brochures is displayed next to the Guest Book. I read the open page and notice recent visitors from Oregon had signed in and left their email address dated from last week, no doubt they were attendants of the reunion at Ole's Resort. The room has the smell of day-old bouquets and pinecones. Signs point to the restrooms and office and I walk in that direction.

The mahogany front desk is manned by a late thirtyish, early forties gentleman busily scouring the pen drawer. He looks up, his fingers touching his parted lips.

"Oh my gosh. You caught me off guard," pushing away from the desk, his legs wide apart. "What can I do for you?"

He wears a plaid sweater vest over an ivory, short sleeve polo, with brown slacks and brown shoes. Very conservative. His dark eyes are narrow, rodent-like, with a well-defined pointed nose. His receding hairline is freckled with medium length streaks of unruly gray and brown tufts. The back of his scalp is spikey as if statically charged. His demeanor is spellbound, like being surprised, and simultaneously, he rolls his neck and gulps.

"I'm Dr. Kevin Michaels, a guest staying at the resort of the Olson boys. I apologize if I startled you." I place my hands on the counter in a relaxed manner.

"I used to be a member of the Summer Church Camp counseling crew back in the day and was wondering if there were any photos of the camp sessions that I might see. It's merely a trip down memory lane and I have a couple days without a case."

He drops his hands onto his thighs and rubs them together slowly.

"Well, we don't usually get visitors here in the church during the week." He looks past me. "Was the door unlocked?"

"As a matter of fact, yes," I answer, surprised of his concern. "I took a chance that someone was here to help."

"For sure," he begins. "I guess I was lost in thought. There's a funeral coming up and I'm not quite yet prepared. Ole Olson, the boys' father, is to have a service tomorrow. There's much to do." He stands. "I'm Pastor Williams, but call me Arnie," extending his hand.

"Nice to meet you," I say, cocking my head. "Is that any relation to Laverne Williams?"

"My dad was Laverne," he responds, chin high. "Twenty-three years a pastor, ten years a missionary, five years a deacon, another five doing on-call and interim duty. He never was without somewhere to go."

A smile eclipses over his face.

"We lost him three years ago. It was in one of those darn boating accidents. A propeller from a speed boat hit him as he was water skiing down at Lake Minnewaska. The body was never found." His gaze fixes on the floor. "That's a good thing. Those drive shafts can tear you up. All that torque, you know."

"I'm sorry for your loss, Arnie," I empathize. "I only knew him for a summer. He was young, anxious to please, and the perfect match for the Wild Bunch of so-called Christian teens."

"I'll grant you that," he rejoinders, his limp arms at his sides. "There are six of us brothers and sisters, complete with two adopted brothers from Korea. Big family in a small town. After graduation, they wanted to go back home to find lost relatives, but the rest of us scattered in the wind. Mom retired to Willmar after the accident. She still resides there and has a group of close friends, mostly widows like herself, waiting for grandchildren to visit and bragging up their kids' lives. I'm quite sure those stories have been repeated a hundred times, to the point of glaze, like on a coffee cake icing."

I smile. "Parents have a unique way of adding flavor."

Getting to the point, I continue. "Might there be some binders or photos of the campers from the 1960's?"

"From the time I took over, it's doubtful that anyone has opened a single volume," he shrugs. "That was years ago, but let's go take a peek."

Doing the math, I estimate that Arnie might be one of the middle sons, but his mannerisms are an irreproachable match to his father's. He's the son who followed the footsteps and pursued his dad's religious path. I bet his father beamed when he took the vows.

We walk down a corridor where outdoor light comes through the stained-glass as soft as tumbled bath towels. The carpeted floors muffle our steps and piped-in organ music can be heard in the ceiling speakers.

"It's a little flair the congregation likes," pointing up. "I got the idea from Roland Purdy at the funeral home."

"Fits the theme well," I add as we pass rows of framed photos of confirmation classes lined-up in chronological order by year of completion. Innocent-looking thirteen-year-olds in choir gowns and banners, displaying hymnals in front of each of them.

"Hold on a second." I stop in front of one of the frames looking and hoping for a glimpse of Erin from junior high school. At last, I discover some black and white photos with familiar Scandinavian last names: Kvistad, Perkins, Lundgren and two Garners. I see Erin and Tessa standing shoulder to shoulder in a row of young girls. Tessa is taller, but they are certainly related through the smiles and eyes. A tad of melancholy cascades over me and I close my eyes to trap the memories that this faded photograph churns up. More guilt. The best thing to do is walk away.

"Do you recognize anyone in the photos?"

"Not especially, at least I don't think so," I lied. "The names are not quite the same although I may be wrong. How about those summer camp records?"

"Let's see." He leads me to the end of the hall and the last door on the right. "If you have an allergy to dust, then this is the wrong place to be." He smiles and pushes the door open.

The mustiness of old paper materials is overpowering. The ceiling incandescent lamp hums like a dormant beehive. It gives off a faint umber glow. A scattering of dead flies is seen on the inside. It's more of a storage room than a library and there is total clutter. Boxes of church bulletins are spread on the floor. There are old blue hymnals and faded banners of Advent and Pentecost, a broken statue of Jesus without arms, and label-less stacks of black three-ringed binders launched into the darkness from the doorway. It looks like a religious exorcism of office supplies. Arnie enters first, looks at the mess, and sighs. I hide my reaction.

"This is a duty of the Assistant Pastor, but the new one doesn't arrive until next month. It's a make-or-break task. Some get a kick out of it, like the assistant we had a few years back. She stayed in here for hours each time, looking through these old photos, sorting them, categorizing, creating a reference list."

He chuckles and taps the first stack.

"A little older than most. I suspect she needed an excuse to get out of the house. That's not to say anything negative, but if you ever watch the TV show Jeopardy, then you certainly can understand. It's usually the 'librarian-types' who seem to know the questions to those crazy answers. They can recall the finer points. You know? The small potatoes. I never paid any attention like that in school. For me, everything was trivial, not trivia."

From the clutter, it's a foregone conclusion that this duty hasn't been done for some time. Little tidying up has been completed except for some binders. I walk over to the bookshelves, pull a few black binders from a stack, and find photos and programs from an assortment of years' confirmation classes. Some of the members are holding hymnals while others are clutching a bible. Most years they're wearing white robes, while other years they're decked in their Sunday best attire. Standing next to another stack is a solitary binder and I open it. The first sheets are in dingy transparent protectors chronically listing the years 1961-69. Each page itemizes the residing chaplain, dates of the camp, and the planned activities. The year 1966 is not there. Going back to the same stack of binders I skim the associated years, and find that same year is missing here, too.

Feeling a need to be left alone to further my search at a slower pace, I ask, "Pastor, do you mind fetching a flashlight? I might need it."

Tapping his forehead as if bringing up a lost answer in the back of his mind, he says, "I think there might be one in the kitchen underneath the sink. The plumber was always complaining about water spots down there when he tried to fix it last summer. He regularly checks it now. I'll be right back."

Where to begin? It looks as if all I've been doing for the past few days is pointless and now, I'm here, rummaging through another under-used room, enduring the same fruitless endeavor. My venture with fate might take longer than anticipated. I walk over to the corner where a folding chair leans against the wall and drag it to the shelves. Standing behind the chair on its side is a dark binder. I bring it up to my face in the dimness. Scribbled in red wax pencil: 1966 Summer Church Camp.

Bingo! My luck could be on the upswing, but I wonder why this is sitting separate from the others.

I look at the first three pages. Typical summer camp information. There is an illustration of the chapel, a folded brochure issued to each camper, and a list of the planned activities. Page four is missing. The following pages are group photos in front of the chapel, except the faces of several of the people are cut out leaving a circular defect in its place -- including Erin's and mine. I flip a few more pages to view some of the action shots taken from the picnic such as relay races, and lake swimming. Again, some are missing. Erin is easy to identify, lithe and tanned, but without the face I can't be certain.

Back in the day, the unruly kids constructed caricatures of the group leaders but none of these are here either. History of the 1966 Summer Camp is empty, negated, the end. I locate a rusted office scissors in the back pocket of the binder and hold it up to the light.

"Here you go, Doc. Let's hope it still works."

He extends the shiny chrome cylinder to me and I test it. The beam is not strong but it's enough to reveal the stirred-up dust that dispenses in a slow-motion haze throughout the room. I pan the other shelves looking for anything in this cave of gloom. Like in the storage facility downtown, where to begin?

"Pastor, I have to get back to the resort for an appointment with the Olsons. My search is finished here. There isn't much to see for the period I worked at the camp. The binders are in shambles, but I managed a few tidbits. I deeply appreciate that you were here to let me in."

"No worries," he says with a soft smile. "If there's anything else, come on by. The doors are always, err, unlocked."

He stands by the door waiting for me. I take one last look and head out, the mysterious scissors cupped in my hand.

I'm back at Wasoon by around four o'clock and decide to pay a visit to Nick Lundgren at the sheriff's office. A couple of late model trucks are in front of the office building. Two elderly men in coveralls and trucker's caps are jawing with each other in the doorway. Their resulting chuckles are bubbly and raspy. A middle-school-aged boy in a baggy tank top and cargo jeans whizzes by on his skateboard, gripping a dog leash attached to a bounding chocolate lab. A throne of pink cotton candy counterbalances his ride in the left hand, the lingering sweet smell still reminds me of county fairs. In relatively short order, a UPS truck pulls up. In a sweeping moment, the uniformed driver hops out, greets the men, and hustles through the entrance carrying a shoe-size box.

Other street activities consist of a rattling work truck that slows to the city speed limit as it drives by. A white church van coasts by, the stencil of hands folded in prayer are visible on the side door panel. Orthopedic devices and motorized wheelchairs are crammed and strapped on the attached trailer. I park in the shade off the street and pull in next to two vacant spaces reserved for the sheriff and clergy. Deputy Lundgren steps out of the front door of the building, with cell phone up to his ear. He stops, listens, takes a few steps, and responds, and stops again and listens. An odd, but well-rehearsed exercise in concentration. I've seen law enforcement multitask like this for decades. We all do the same. He pauses in front of my car, looks up, recognizes me, and holds up his hand for me to wait.

"Let's get a hold of both the Ada and Crookston police and see if they know anything. Chances are slim, but we have to catch a break somewhere," he pinches his lower lip between his fingers. "If all else fails, we can get a chopper from Moorhead." There's a muffled response from the phone, and he says, "Roger that. Good."

Disconnecting, Lundgren signals me over and I meet him on the sidewalk as he fumbles to put his phone in his side pocket.

"Doc, what brings you here?"

He pokes his tongue inside his cheek, looking for answers, for some sort of solution.

"You're obviously too busy, but I want to check on a couple things."

Surprisingly, he hasn't resorted to his impatient huff, so I go on.

"First of all, is there anything else on the skeleton that Tessa and I uncovered in the cave? I know it's been only a couple days. Secondly, Tessa once mentioned the accidental death of the boy in the well up by the old cabins that burned down. Do you happen to remember his name or the circumstances to his vanishing?"

He squeezes his eyes shut and spreads his hands, fanlike, on his breastbone.

"Never mind, Deputy. I'm being unpretentious and you've more important tasks."

"Sorry, Doc. We have a 'buzz saw' going on. Of all the luck, the

Wasoon bank was robbed during lunchbreak, so no one was held hostage or injured. Paula Johnson, the teller, was all alone. There are two suspects. One watched the door while the other leaped over the counter. Either that one knew about the security switch or caught her off-guard. She thinks it was only a couple hundred dollars in small bills, but she's a nervous wreck. I'm pretty sure her witness identification will be all over the charts. She has an annoying habit of overreacting."

He stiffens and draws in a huge breath through his nostrils.

"Where will it all end? We have an autopsy, a death, a fire, a skeleton, and now this." He exhales loudly. "Of all the luck, one of our cruisers is in the shop and here I stand waiting for Minot's Automotive to bring me a loaner."

"Let me help," I interject. "I'll drive, and you can check-in with the crew. Come on, let's go." I click and unlock the passenger door and wait for him to slide in.

"What the hell," he mumbles, grabs for his pocketed phone and punches in a number. "That's the best thing I've had happen all day. Hang on a second, Doc."

Holding the receiver up to his cheek, he speaks.

"Andy. It's Deputy Lundgren. Listen. I've got a ride to the bank. Doc Michaels is standing here. Cancel Minot's. Tell them thanks anyway." He waits for the response. "That's right. Go ahead and cancel the request. Doc Michaels has offered to drive. When I get back to the station, remind me to deputize him." He looks at me and grins. "Contact the highway patrol from Detroit Lakes, too. Yep. Bye."

"Let's go on silent approach," Lundgren smirks as he straps into the driver's seat.

"Most of my work is done on 'silent approach,' Deputy," I said, backing out.

He chuckles and rests his hat on his lap. There's an uneasiness, like a player sitting on the bench, waiting for the coach to put him in the game. He soon leans forward.

"To answer your questions, Doc, the remains results have come back only to confirm the bones were female, based on the pelvis and jaw. The age can't be positively determined yet. That will take a couple more weeks. Identification might take two months or more if we're lucky. There was serious carnivore damage and gnaw marks."

That comment relaxes him, and he sags on the back rest.

"Now having said that, I'm certainly not hoping that it's Erin Garner," he adds.

I attempt to pass a slow-moving Prius on the right but decide to wait and nose up on its bumper. Lundgren isn't paying attention and continues to watch the road. My impatience takes over and I edge past on the right narrowly missing a pickup truck. The Prius' passenger window rolls down and Alice, the beautician, flips us off until she recognizes my passenger. Thereupon, she hastily brings her hand up to her hair and straightens some loose locks from the side of her ear.

"Sorry about that," I say as I give a little flip of my wrist in her direction. We pull alongside each other at the streetlight.

"That was close," he sighs. "Leave it for Alice, the town spitfire, to write another editorial in the local gossip rag criticizing the drivers in this city. You might have taken over my role as Public Enemy Number One with that move. I held that glorious title for six weeks running last summer when the Sturgis Nomads, female Hell's Angels wannabees, gathered here, speeding, drinking, tattooing, and what not." He harrumphs. "Alice suddenly became the most conservative citizen ever, parading down Main Street, carrying a sign of Wasoon Lake with stupid gulls flying overhead, as if we live near the ocean. All I wanted was for them to eat at Bee's, spend a little money, buy gas, and move on down the highway. But here was this self-righteous Alice-clan of women claiming equal rights protection and having their lifestyle interfered with. That's a big crock of bull."

He shuffles his bottom on the seat, powers down the window, clears his throat and spits.

"This was a group who gave women a bad name. They painted the town red with anger. I'm certain that no husbands survived that physical torment, and I wouldn't be surprised if some are mentally scarred for life. Right now, it's legendary."

The poolside women came to mind and that stormy, near-disaster night of skinny-dipping.

"Do you think any of them masquerade as doting housewives at high school reunions?"

Lundgren tilts his head and furrows his brow.

"It's possible," he ponders and slowly rubs his elbow. "I'm not sure where you're going with this, though."

We move toward the downtown section. Bee's Café is on the right, a half block down. I see the flashing police cruiser car on the left and slow.

"My guess is the liquor was talking, Deputy," I begin. "Some of the women were acting out their inhibitions the other night in front of my cabin and caught me off guard, being a newcomer to modern-day hooligans in Wasoon and all. Everything was cool the next day at the memorial service. Sobering up does take some time."

"That's always the excuse," he adds pointing for me to pull up to the curb. "I'll take it from here, Doc. Thanks for the ride. Andy said he'll be over in about fifteen minutes, so you are free to leave. I appreciate your help."

He collects his hat and cinches his gun belt.

"I have to play the role of county official, even though they're all clueless. Political correctness rules the land." He feels for his cell phone. "There's been a slew of small-town robberies lately. Wasoon was immune for a long time, but now it's here. M.O. is always the same: local bank, mid-day attempt, and two suspects. A robber and a driver. They choose only small bills. We'll catch them someday soon. All the little towns in this lake region are ripe for picking and I'm guessing it's a group of goons from the Twin Cities looking for drug money."

"Good luck," I tell him as I signal to merge onto the street heading back toward the resort. "Keep me posted, please. Thanks."

He offers me a casual salute and looks toward the hurried deputy who I recognize but had never been introduced. Notepad in hand, the deputy recites his findings to Lundgren who sternly stands and listens. It reminds me of family members reciting their version of their lost one's maladies to me, and now I'm expected to side with them following someone else's actions, regardless of the circumstances.

As I pull away, the two are walking toward the bank door where a crime scene investigator is dusting the handle and frame for prints. The futile search for clues commences.

CHAPTER TWENTY-FOUR

People all around me have indiscriminate things to do, places to go, crimes to solve, funerals to consider, and reunions to enjoy. At the same time, I feel as bogged down as a large turd swirling in a clogged toilet. There is nowhere for me to go in a hurry or get anything done. My frustration level is at a breaking point and I'm convinced that the time has come to go back home to California.

I head back to my cabin. The regular pool demographic is present and accounted for. There are the glib loungers with drinks, aromatic sunscreens, noisy cannon-ballers ready for another jump, and the swimwear immodesty that vacationers love to share. Is it the time of day, or is it viable that the timely lawn mower always does laps around my building when I only want to be left alone? I yank open the screen door, the inside door is ajar.

My room is in shambles as if last night's storm tore through the door. The place has been ransacked. Clothes are tossed, mattress inverted, toiletries are strewn, and drawers emptied in heaps on the box spring. A knot grows in my stomach and I can feel the pulse through my temple. It's a high blood pressure showdown. Copies of autopsy files that were once in my briefcase are spread on the desktop in a haphazard manner. A large schematic "X" is scrolled on the front sheets in red pencil. My desk chair has been flipped and now stands against the back wall. I begin sorting through the damage. At first sight, I'm devastated, but as destructive as it seems, it's only cosmetic. I sigh deeply and sink onto the chair. Stapled pages are intact but now wadded into paper balls. Thankfully, there are no punctures or rips in the mattress. Toiletries were dumped in the sink basin but the basics: toothpaste, aspirin, mouthwash, and lotions are unopened.

I carefully side-step continuing to look for an entry site. The sill is deeply etched by something sharp, like a screwdriver or pocketknife.

There's a circular, palm-sized, smudge in the lower portion of the half open window adjacent to the latch. Clumps of mud and dark smudges lace the edges as if the person lifted, then grasped the sill to gain leverage. No blood. This was a planned hit, planned to occur when I was gone, planned to sustain maximum damage and fear. I have been targeted.

I think about yelling to the visitors meandering around the grounds but that's pointless. No one will be the least bit interested in anything outside a twenty-yard diameter. People come and go, and doors are usually left unlocked. Privacy is expected, but not required. It's a resort, for god's sake. This means the break-in happened this morning. Someone was watching my place and watching me. There are other options, but my trust level has plummeted like tumbling off that waterfall. It's becoming them-versus-me.

I close the door and think about moving my vehicle into the far lot, away from the cabin and underneath a canopy of elm trees. My suspicion is on overdrive. Groundskeepers. Security. Housekeeping. Someone who I had met. How about a memorial service attendee or reunion classmate, or even someone who had seen Tessa come and go from here? I park in the lot outside the diamonds, kill the engine and lock the door. If someone is watching from a distance, I need him to think that I'm gone. As luck would have it, I had discovered a deer trail leading around the campus from the registration building and outdoor picnic sites. I decide it's a good idea to take that trail back to the cabin and slip through my door.

In the room, I avoid the light coming from the inverted the blinds. Even vacationers on the loungers are under suspicion but they are way too casual, way too relaxed and no one is stealing glances this way. Where to begin? The room is a disaster. There's the aroma of spilt cologne near the dresser. Other than the reports, I carry nothing of any value. Copies of medical records are fanned on the floor like a deck of cards. My business camera is a provincial digital and at least five years old. Data on my work laptop is backed-up on thumb drives. Fortunately, these were stashed in my shaving kit side pocket in a disposable razor container. After a few depositions went south, I decided to keep the important stuff out of prying hands. I walk into the bathroom, expecting the worst, but other than my toiletries being scattered, nothing is out of sort.

My logic is that the forced entry is a cover-up. Everything on the floor, tip over furniture, flip the mattress, scatter work folders, and leave the place ajar. Rather than paranoia I feel a weird form of calming acceptance. I'm right. Someone doesn't want me here for intentions unknown. Unfortunately for whoever it is, I intend to wait. The next mistake is on you. I prepare for interaction, but foreboding is the constant reminder that I've screwed up other things too.

Putting things back in order takes a matter of minutes. In haste, I re-arrange everything on the dresser next to my bed, stack my notes in the briefcase, fix the bed, align pillows, and perform a snap-wipe of the windowsill. This time, I lock the door, but the damage is done. Any intruder won't know the difference except for the medical text on top of the nightstand. As a practice, my work phone number is written on the cover in case I forget to take the book with me from place to place. If that number is used, I can trace it immediately with a call-back.

I decide not to notify the police of the incident, but to maintain status quo, keeping my appointments, and watching for clues along the way. Consequently, a visit with the brothers is agenda item number one. Aaron had cornered me at the memorial service. I take out my phone and press his cell phone number. Five rings later, he picks up.

"Aaron Olson." Serious sounding. Not the Aaron I expected.

"Aaron, this is Kevin Michaels. How are you?"

"Doc, sorry for the harsh tone in my voice. I've been waiting for a call from the loan officer. We're doing some re-financing for our resort and I won't give him the wrong impression." Chuckling, he adds, "That jerk was at the memorial service and I think he caught me putting my arm around his daughter's waist and giving her a squeeze. We've been seeing each other on the side for some time, but he doesn't know that. What can I do for you?"

First impressions aside, his phone demeanor is upbeat.

"Good luck with that one," I tell him. "In case you didn't hear, Wasoon Bank was robbed today. I don't know the exact amount they got away with, but I bet the bank is shut down until an investigation is done."

"No way," yells Aaron. "You're kidding me, right?"

"Sorry, no. I drove Deputy Lundgren over to the bank a short time after he was notified."

"Man, we need that loan to go through," he exasperates, as if all hope is lost.

"Lundgren was telling me that other small institutions have been hit recently, and Wasoon was long overdue."

"The cards fell, I guess," Aaron surmises. "Anyway, getting back to this call..."

"You had mentioned at the memorial service that we needed to talk. I have some free time if that will work. My work schedule is beginning to gather speed and it looks like I'll have to shorten my stay."

"Oh, yeah, that's right. It's another witness signature on a form for my Dad's belongings. He was wearing a honkin'-sized ring made of South African silver. I don't recall ever seeing it, but both David and Aunt Gail claim he had one. I know you're not finished with the report and it will take several weeks, but was there any jewelry that you noticed during the examination?"

Frozen bodies, swollen, thawing tissues, decomposition, bloody icicles, and now this. When will it all go away?

With reassurance, I respond.

"My external examination was negative. I always check for jewelry, first thing. That's most important. I photograph the body and don't remove personal items unless they interfere with the examination." There is a pause on the other end, and I add, "Aaron, tell them that I carefully checked the wrappings and searched the pockets for belongings. There was nothing else."

"Good to know, Doc. I really appreciate it. You know, we're going to have Dad's service tomorrow, then cremation the next day. It might seem odd, but funerals have been the new norm up here lately. There's been a weird string of happenings I can't get a handle on. It's like a recurring bad dream."

The same thing is happening to me, too.

"If you'll be back later, I'll swing by to sign the form."

"Sounds good," he answers. "I'll give you a call when I get back to the resort."

We disconnect and I cautiously lift the blinds and peer out at the boisterous activities. It's only the clattering of the springboard launching another crispy visitor into the deep end and the maddening, piped-in country music from the speakers. This whole matter can be summed up as bandits waiting until people leave their rooms, then grab cash, credit cards, or a laptop in the process. These old-style skeleton keys and locks are easy pickings. Perhaps a little small talk at the coffee urn with the workers will give me a greatly needed boost to my mindset because right now, this emotional slope is waiting for the fuse to be lit and the avalanche to begin.

I slip around the cabin, quietly taking the deer trail back to the lodge. Near the fire pit, the young staff is busying themselves and not surprisingly, my abrupt appearance doesn't seem to affect their duties. I receive a few head bob greetings. One of the young female staff even asks if I need a beverage.

"No thanks," I reply, forcing a smile, and trying to move on. I realize then that some consider me to be one of the crew when I am called upon to help move a couple picnic tables to free up some room for a little summer music jam tonight. All in all, the workers are my witnesses, making pleasantries, and conversation. I grab a bottle of water and head for the registration building.

"She's not here," says Paige looking up from the monitor. "We're still waiting for her to call back," closing her eyes and rubbing the middle of her forehead. "I can't get this new program to work and she is the only one who can fix it."

Knowing my role in computer troubleshooting is closer to the late nineties, I can offer no consolation.

"Have you considered Aaron or David? They seem to know their way around all the new technology."

She shakes her head in agreement. "I have a call into Aaron's cell, but he has yet to respond. Thanks for the tip, though. We're on the same wavelength." Looking up from her monitor, in a half-pleading, half-frustrated voice, she adds, "Doc? Where is Tessa?"

Paige doesn't give me time to respond, and after a deep sigh, looks back at me and grins. "You know, I think a gremlin must have broken my computer."

Her grin turns into a smile.

"The service was nice this morning, wasn't it? I have a feeling things will turn around for Mr. Gabbert in a week or so back home." She softly exhales and holds her gaze upward in hope.

Death and travel have been the main ingredients for me the past couple decades and now it's replaced with dread and standing around waiting.

"His family will get him through the worst of it, Paige," I reassure her. "From the looks of it, his sister-in-law has a good grip of the situation. She gave a nice memorial. In my opinion, better than the minister's lengthy soliloquy."

"I guess my mind was elsewhere," she says. "David kept playing with his brochure, making a paper airplane out of it. It was so annoying."

Getting back to the present, I add, "Please call me when Tessa's back. I have some business with David and Aaron, and she needs to be involved."

"Will do, Dr. Kevin, and thanks for stopping by. It's always a good talk."

"You're only saying that because it's true," I say, buttering her up. "The next time we see her, we'll brow-beat Tessa to death for leaving us in a lurch like this."

With suspicions on red alert, I decide to forego a direct path to my cabin and instead take the long hike back by circling the softball fields and ducking into the woods beyond the outfield. No one is playing catch or prepping the diamond where my lack of athletic prowess was magnified a couple nights ago. I wrestle with the situation and a Field of Dreams image comes to mind, like when the baseball ghosts materialized in the corn field. There is another deer trail beyond the right field fence, and I take it around the property, parallel to the entrance gate where Perry Brown mounts his high-chair with his back against the door jam. His day shift must be over soon. From this vantage point, I have a clear view. He doesn't notice me slip by and I can sit and watch my cabin for unexpected visitors.

The unflappable breeze is doing a good job of keeping the mosquitoes at bay and my blood is Ground Zero for the few lingering in the bushes. I try not to swipe at my face or neck or make motion of any kind. This will be a safe viewpoint for roughly an hour until the forest sounds like a muffled buzz saw. Imagined or not, I sense pinpoint pricking on my arms and the back of my neck, and the urge to scratch is orchestrating.

The first vehicle to enter is a rumbling white Shelby Mustang convertible driven by David. He idles down and stops next to Perry Brown's booth. Perry stiffly stands from his chair and leans on the driver's side door, tilting his hat back, and smiling. I notice that both brothers are in the car. My stealth action might be delayed. They seem to be making small talk. Perry reaches in the car for a cigarette, grabs the lighter, sucks in the smoke, laughs, exhales, coughs, and repeats. Not your average cigarette, I'm sure. A comment from one of them creates a cackle. David hands Perry a bottle of beer through the window and he salutes them both before tucking it inside his long sleeve. Perry straightens and steps back as the boys drive off toward the registration office, probably to help Paige with the computer.

I settle back against the tree, rubbing my eyes then clasping my hands around my waist. Fatigue is catching up on me and I'm fixated on how close I was to burning alive. For the first time in a while, I can comfortably slouch, feeling all the vertebrae from neck to lower back begin to mold onto the stiff old bark. In the background is the clanging sound of a horseshoe game. A couple of acoustic guitars are being tuned. Loud voices can be heard, yelling instructions near the serving tables. The silence is broken by the appearance of a squeaky golf cart.

"Whoa, Nellie."

The driver nearly runs over Perry who's putting up the 'Closed' sign outside his booth. He grabs the gifted bottle from Aaron and toasts the golf cart driver with the opened beer. They follow suit with their own plastic glasses of iced amber before heading toward the clubhouse. Perry's outline is making its way toward the registration circle, but I lose sight of him.

The horizon is dramatic, indigo against the eastern tree line and the faint constellations are like a premier seat in one of those observatories at a university. The Big Dipper is directly above me and a breeze drifts through my vantage point stirring up aromas of barbeque pork ribs and something sweet, like buttery corn on the cob. Do I smell marinated chicken over a fire? Someone is either tapping a beer barrel or has dropped a malted pitcher. The bitter ferment is undeniable, and I yearn for an ice-cold bottle like Perry's. I'm becoming accustomed to the festive mood, good people, good friends, and good times. I find myself with an acknowledging smirk. It's becoming easier to be lulled away from my current prime objective and I quickly sit up, looking into the duskiness, still searching for answers. How long was I dozing?

Eventually, I fixate on Perry's unoccupied booth. The blinking welcome lights are off and a shadow of the structure extending across the lane is the shape of a rectangular black hole. That was a surefire exit. The campground is strung with night lights. These are similar duties we used to have as camp counselors. Very nostalgic, very peaceful, like slowly flipping through old albums.

I am distracted by the popping sound of an approaching car on the pea gravel driveway. There's a speeding vehicle flying past the guest entry then moving in the direction of my cabin. The parking lights are on as it loops the drive before eventually coming to a stop in front of my sidewalk. How late is it anyway?

It's a dark sedan, looks like a rental, like any of the other fifty cars. Gradually idling down and braking, the vehicle stops and kills the engine underneath a large spruce tree. The driver takes a foot off the brake and the red glow disappears. My cabin entrance is a mere fifty feet away.

The pool is closed for the day but that didn't stop the ladies from storming the water last night and yet, I wonder if that set of circumstances is about to take place again. For that simple reason, I decide to stay put. The driver's door opens, the interior light goes on, and a dark-jacketed figure slides out quietly. The person stands next to the car. I can't be certain if the image is motionless or not. If I sneak in that direction, perhaps the image will become more distinct. But is that something I'm willing to do right now?

"Who's there?"

Dried leaves shuffle and crackle, a flashlight beam bounces off my face.

"Doc, is that you?"

"Perry?"

"Yeah, it's me. What's going on?"

Caught red-handed. I can feel the guilty-as-charged look forming on my face.

"I, ah, took a stroll after supper, came across this deer trail." More lies. "Actually, I don't have an explanation. I sat down, lost my bearings, got too relaxed, and ended up nodding off. It's pretty lame and I apologize for catching you off-guard."

He sighs.

"Hell, I'm glad it was you and not some maniac from the loony bin." He moves in my direction, checking the ground, kicking branches, using his boots to clear the path. "If you're wondering as to *why* I'm here, it's because this is now the latest segment of my newly assigned daily duties. Jokers have been scoping this place recently to sit and drink beers and light up doobies." He chortles. "As if that's never happened."

He rubs the back of his neck. "It's getting harder to find summer help like they used to."

He clicks off the light and we stand face to face, but I'm still feeling a little uncomfortable at being caught red-handed.

"Well, I guess it's an honor to belong to such a famous club," I joke. "I thought the aroma was a little too sweet for wood smoke."

"Right on, dude," he adds jubilantly and snorts. "It's summer. Folks think up all kinds of excuses like high schoolers."

"It's a reunion, Perry," I said.

"You got me there," he says. "By the way, what's with all the secrecy, Doc? You are the most famous Californian in Wasoon these days. Everyone talks you up. How special it is to have you helping us, not to mention whacking the shit out of the softball."

Catching me off guard, I explain.

"Oh, it's not anything private. I prefer to be alone, do a little biking, or hiking, and such. My wife died a few years back and I never got back into the groove of life, I guess. I'm not that adept when it comes to socializing. This resort has seen more of me than I usually see of myself."

His eyes narrow and he remains motionless. I continue.

"As you can tell, I'm close to an 'outside looking in' type," I add. "By the way, how was that beer from the brothers?"

"Don't tell Tessa, please, Doc," he says, rocking on the balls of his feet. "I could get canned."

"Hey, not to worry," giving him a friendly tap on the bicep and thinking who else could they find to fill this dead-end job? I only wish there were another brew for me.

Standing erect, tugging at my coat lapel, I tell him, "Well, I better get going, now that's not a secret anymore. Have a good night, Perry. See you tomorrow sometime."

"Any word from your boss lately?" I add. "From all appearances, more folks need her besides me."

"Not a peep. It's a strange one. She usually is the first to call in with her whereabouts. We're all puzzled but, yeah, see you tomorrow. Let me light up those first couple steps to the road for you. Those dips are killers on the ankles."

I evade a few thorny weeds until finally safe on the dark pavement.

"Thanks, I needed that," I tell him, feeling a twinge of pain in my left forefoot.

"Good night then, Doc."

He proceeds along the deer trail and I watch as his flashlight bounces and streaks the tree limbs and footpath in sweeping fashion until he rounds a bend. By then, only the illuminated ghostly shadows remain. Looking back toward my cabin and re-focusing in the darkness, I'm suddenly aware of the empty space beneath the spruce tree. Whoever parked there is now gone.

"Well..." I murmur, unable to move for fear of returning to my place. I hunker behind the greeting booth for the next hour, cowering like a teenager with a smoldering joint as a handful of cars are coming and going, entering and leaving, opening and closing, nearly living and almost dying, belonging and losing.

CHAPTER TWENTY-FIVE

In due course, my ultimate decision to linger like a curious mole produces zilch and I decide to walk back to my cabin. Once inside, overly suspicious feelings come crashing back to earth. Although my earlier clean-up was still intact, the thoughts of who and why had me pacing through the two rooms, checking the closet twice, and securing the locks again. In my developing suspicious neuroses, I flip on the bathroom light and leave the door ajar.

I grab a pillow and the thick blanket and splay it along the wall beneath the window. If anyone wants to look in, let them think I'm gone. But in the short term, I need to form a plan of attack. Will I burst from behind the door and surprise him or will I get into an altercation, knocking the gate crasher down, pinning him on the ground until security arrives? These are crazy thoughts. CSI dramas gone wrong. I'm not that type of hero.

Not much to accomplish at this point, I decide it's a good idea to get some needed rest until morning, or at least until dawn. Fatigue tails me like a pet needing to be fed as I crawl down on the blanket and back up against the wall. The room settles from its slow spin and the moonlight casts an inviting gray-white glow on the bed and chair. My eyes wander over the wood frame, the headboard, the footboard, the illuminating nightstand clock, reviewing, and remembering, fading out like the credits in a movie.

There's a jarring CRACK beyond my door, the nearby sound of stepping on a large dry twig. I remain still. Options of all sorts flash in my mind. Someone is tiptoeing around within inches from me. A person's head forms an obtuse oval shadow on the floor beside the bed. The silence migrates to the backside of the cabin and there's an attempt to open the door -- once, twice, three times. I feel my heartbeat thrashing in my ears as I roll in that direction, into a crouch, reach up, unlock the door, poised and ready to pounce.

At that moment, I hear faint footsteps at the front of the cabin that morphs into a fast gait. They're coming from both sides. The person out back begins a trot, a car door slams and there's the sound of gravel shooting from under the tires. This is my chance, my opportunity to at least catch sight of the intruders. I fling open the front door and suddenly there's a loud shrill as someone flails at my head. By instinct, I react putting my hands up, grabbing the arms and flinging the figure into my cabin. We stumble, then collide with the bedframe and flop headfirst onto the mattress. Both of us are motionless, lying flat, looking back at each other.

"Thank God you're here."

Desperation in the voice. Palms pressed to the eyes. Sobbing. Sniffling.

I rear back, my thoughts scramble to understand.

"Tessa?"

"Kevin!"

I stand then bend down to bring her to a sitting position next to me. Her clothes are damp and gritty with a lingering smell of wood smoke. Her jacket holds the overpowering stench of something dank like an old room or a cement basement. She sobs into her hands and I clasp the sides of her head in disbelief. In the twilight we sit, hugging, wondering, waiting.

When she calms down, I stand to close the cabin door and flip on the light to the room. She looks like a homeless transient. Hands smudged with dark soot. Her hair is shaved to the scalp along the left temple. There is a linear crusting abrasion the length of a carpenter nail above the ear.

"What the hell happened to you?"

She takes a moment to compose herself.

"I, I don't know. It's like a nightmare and I can't wake up."

She grabs me by the wrists, squeezing, shaking.

"Where am I? Who...? Where...?"

I gently rub her forehead. "It's not the time to worry about that. You are safe here."

I grapple with the situation as I glance around the room. My brain whirls with the weight of being temporarily safe versus in eminent, potential danger. She struggles to stand, but I sit her back down on the bed.

"You need to contact Lundgren, the sooner the better. People have been looking for you. Everyone has questions. Make that call."

"No calls," she blurts out. "They might be watching."

"They? Who's they?" I ask, scanning the door for movement or the sound of a car.

Shaking her head back and forth she continues.

"It can be anybody, everybody." Her cracked lips are pressed and flat. "I either sneaked or was released. I don't know where or how but I got to the resort by using back roads."

She briskly rubs her arms.

"I was lucky once it got dark and dared to take off the blindfold. Kevin, there was suppressed anger, *real* anger. So much, it was palpable. I can't be sure of anything right now. It's all so confusing. Everything was dark and now it's all blank. I think I might have been drugged. The inside of my mouth feels like I swallowed sandpaper."

She faces me and gingerly touches her throat.

"It's not a good idea to sneak out. Whoever was in that car, whose car I don't know, has been looking for me at least for two or three hours. I can't be sure, but I've been running and running. Hiding and ducking behind anything possible."

Pulling up the hood on her jacket to cover her head, she adds, "Now I've put you in danger by coming here. See how they search, looking for any connections, driving by your place? They know something about me, and I have no clue."

We embrace as she continues to tug at my arm. Over time, Tessa calms down and lets her head to fall back on my chest. Suddenly, she raises her head from my clutch and scans the room. Shadows alternate with the slivers of outdoor lamps. A chimera of illusion pours onto the floor and bed. It is as if at any time the door will be kicked inward by who knows who?

"Tell me what you remember," I ask and cup her trembling hands in mine.

Her eyes close tightly, trapping images. There is a facial tick as she begins to relive the painful events.

"I was about to attend the memorial service for Mrs. Gabbert when I received this message from an unknown number. Actually, I was expecting a handyman to show up and thought it might be him."

There is a pause in her explanation as she continues to rub her outstretched arms.

"I was expecting a detailed conversation, so I went back to the office to ask him to call later when there was more free time to discuss."

She clutches her throat. A wild, harried expression falls over her face. I wait as she tries to sift the details from the tormented circumstances.

"Was that the call?"

"No, Kevin," rubbing her hands and slapping her thigh in frustration. "I can't remember. I must have blacked out. There was an old carpet. Smelled like grease or oil. My head bounced on it for some time." She rubs her eyes.

I recall seeing cars lined up at the entrance, dropping off guests for the service as valets were hustling to park cars and hanging keys onto the storage board. Was Tessa stuffed into a car trunk as the rest of us attended the service inside? Was that possible? Without anyone noticing?

"It sounds as if you were kidnapped. That must have been some powerful drug to take effect like that."

I begin to list the possible sedative pharmacological options in my head. Propofol comes to mind. Michael Jackson called it Mother's Milk. Tessa was probably unconscious in a matter of seconds.

"Tell me what else you can remember."

She shifts her weight and cringes.

"Ow, what's that?" She hikes up her open shirt at the waist. There is a red bruise imprint on her hip, crisscross, the size of a large locket. She gently rubs the indentation.

I lean over to get a closer view.

"This has some blistering, like a burn."

Branding iron-style is my fear. Nothing else quite looks like it, but I keep that forensic opinion to myself.

"It must have happened in this room-cave where I was kept." She pulls up her blouse and gently touches underneath her rib cage. "I'm sore all over, but that one is especially tender."

Curious, I ask, "How do you know that it was a cave? Was it damp or musty?"

"It stank like wet concrete or rocks. My face was covered with something thick like a wet beach towel." She cups her ears and trembles. "I had these earrings that were yanked off my ears. That's another fading memory, but I remember how painful it was. The next thing, I was back in a closed box, bouncing and jerking."

I begin to speculate. She was jammed in the back of a car and moved to another location.

"How did you get here?"

"I'm still not ready to piece that in place," she answers with resignation leaning forward, elbows on her knees. "I remember that the bouncing stopped. There was the smell of gas and a dinging bell, metallic, tapping."

"Perhaps you were at a filling station, gassing up. Was the car's motor running?"

"I think so," she sighs. "My face and hands tingled but it gave me hope, being able to flex them."

She squeezes her fists open and closed, testing her strength, her knuckles becoming white. She then reels, raising her hands, eyes widening, recalling.

"That's it! That's when I sneaked out."

She mimics pushing up a lid.

"There was an inside release latch and I pulled on it. I remember crawling out and trying to stand." She clutches at her throat. "I fell over and vomited, but somehow managed to take some steps. It was a filling station, and the hose was in the tank with the pump running. I was alone and, in that moment, the driveway led to a dumpster, the dumpster opened up to a field, a field became the highway."

I watch as she attempts to mentally sort it all out. Her eyebrows narrow, she purses her lips, and her frown deepens.

"After that, all is a blur. Where I was, how far I ran, or even how I knew directions to go. Kevin, I just don't know. I can't remember. I need help."

Tessa recoils.

"Who would want to do this? Look at me. Look at my hair."

"You are coming off some harsh sedatives, Tessa. Let's not rush into anything until your head clears a bit. I think it's still best if we contact Lundgren. This is a kidnapping and assault crime."

I reach in my pocket for my cell phone and begin dialing.

"No calls, Kevin, please," grabbing my arm, sobbing, begging. "Let's drive away from here. I don't want for that door to open again," her eyes widening.

"Wait," I hold her back from bolting. "I'll get the car."

She grimaces as if a mysterious pain is cascading across her wan complexion.

"Sit down, Tessa. I won't be long. It's safer inside. Safer than it's been in days. We will get to the bottom of this. I guarantee it."

I grab my coat, feeling for the keys.

"Oh no. I must have left my keys in the car."

She clutches her arms tightly around her body as her eyes dash from the door to the window, and back.

"Please hurry. I don't want to be here alone. Anything might happen." Her voice is brittle.

Another car drives by and pulls up to the fence gate. There are the sounds of all four doors opening and closing and women whooping with laughter. Last night's group of gals are back for another monumental moonlight swim.

"We'll be safe," I reassure her. "The ruckus that these ladies generate will scare off any intruders looking for you."

I squeeze her hands.

"I'll be only five to ten minutes. Maintenance was doing some drive work and asked that I move my car. It's in the north lot."

Lies are becoming easier than voicing my real concern. I force a downward glare, hoping she doesn't pick up the signals.

"Lock the door behind me. You did a good thing coming here," I add, kissing her on the forehead.

The departure through the back door, sneaking onto the walking path, and racing to the other side of the resort is an obscure mental stain in my mind. I tear through images of her helplessness and surprise capture, like a military strike in the middle of the day at that. Is it at all plausible? Is that feasible? Tessa is frenzied. She might even be delusional, her fears orchestrated to frightening levels. Distressed people can exaggerate scenarios that accent their behaviors or actions. I know for sure she is terrified and was tortured. Her lasting moments must have been horrible.

In the darkness I pause to get my bearings, careful to not trip or make unnecessary noises. The haunting stillness is both terrifying and tranquil at the same time. I cast a glance both ways for exits or wide driveways in case there is a need to escape. The other surprising sensation is extreme calm and confidence as if lighting a campfire. My phobias have been answered. Something is going on in the resort.

Without a lighted path the distance seems endless and inexact, like a coroner viewing the destruction and dismemberment of an airliner crash for the first time. Up ahead the pathway infringes onto the barbeque pit and I dart past the stacked glowing wood embers. There are skewers lined up along the concrete block border and an occasional empty beer bottle litters the ground. The stench of bleach and strong soap on the dance platform is the result of someone either hurling or spilling their cocktail. Patented moves on a past high school crush. I've been there, done that.

Once back into the safety of the pine grove, I begin to sprint. Another fifty yards and I'll be there. I weave through the dark. Where's my car? Odd. When I rolled in yesterday, there were four large spotlights, one in each corner. But now, I'm ducking, feeling, and darting between obscured vehicles, row by row, looking for anything familiar.

There they are. The landmark birch trees, next to the forest pines. I whirl and race toward them, my heart pounds.

There is a dark-colored car near the reserved spaces for campers and RV's. Idling. Lights off. I vault back into the protection of a large off-road truck and tuck down behind the tail bed, using the rearview mirror to look for the invader. The daytime staff are for sure gone and there is no need to be wasting gas at this hour -- unless, unless someone is waiting, waiting for me. Seconds slowly become minutes. I strain to make out anything that looks like my car in the shadows. Maybe I'm wrong. It could be on the side with the maple trees.

Sorting through my options, I mutter, "Damn it," and pound the truck tire with my fist. I'm being stalked, just like Tessa. But why?

I rush back to the cabin, sneaking through the back entrance. Someone is in the shower. The nightstand lamp shade flickers with a moth circling the bulb.

"Tessa? Tessa?"

The shower stops and there's the sound of the curtain sliding open. She's sobbing.

I knock on the bathroom door.

"Tessa. Are you alright? Can I come in?"

Her clothes are heaped on the floor next to the toilet. I need to keep them intact, in an evidence bag. Lundgren must see them.

"Kevin? Where were you?"

I falter.

"It won't start, dead battery," I lie. "Let's wait till morning and I'll call the tow company. With all the outside noise, we'll be safe staying here."

She emerges from the steam-filled shower.

"I was filthy," she explains. "I needed to be clean again."

She looks to the closed closet. "Do you have anything that might fit me: tee shirt, sweatshirt, warmups?" Her towel is wrapped securely under each arm, and there is a redness on her neck. Thankfully, the abrasion on her scalp had rinsed away clean, no bleeding, no weeping. I step aside to allow her to pass.

"I brought along some extra scrubs and a tee shirt. There is a light jacket hanging in the closet."

In the last hours until dawn, we snuggle under the bed covers. After an eternity of restless shifting back and forth, Tessa falls asleep in my arms. I can't blame her. What have we buzzed into? What is 'What'? The last time I checked the clock it was three-thirty. That's when the ladies outside stopped arguing about who stole a pair of slippers, then left giggling. First a liar, and now thief. What's next on my agenda for tomorrow?

CHAPTER TWENTY-SIX

My cell phone buzzes. It's 7:15.

"Hello?" My mind is foggy as I sit up in bed. Tessa is still curled in the blanket facing the other direction.

"Doc, it's Deputy Nick Lundgren," pausing. "I'm afraid there's some bad news. Your rental car was tracked down on the outskirts of Wasoon this morning, meaning that it was registered to you. So, I put one and one together."

He waits for a response. The ceiling fan rotates at low speed above my bed and I hear golfers carting up, laughing, and teasing each other about today's tournament. My room still smells of scented shampoo. Tessa stirs and sits up.

"My car?" I grab her arm. "Are you sure?"

"Pretty certain," he adds. "Your rental agreement was still in the glove compartment. Of course, I might be wrong, but I doubt it." He clears his throat. "The point is that it's been vandalized: windshield shattered, driver's door kicked in, and all four tires are slashed."

"Are you sure, Deputy?" A flush of adrenalin tingles through me body. I reach over and lock Tessa's arm in mine. The lost car keys.

"I got back to the resort pretty late last night and went to my cabin. I didn't hear any noise outside. I certainly hope I haven't created enemies over my stay."

I try to sort out potential suspects from my memory banks, but there's at least one still unidentified. Dawn pokes through the blinds in horizontal bands like a strobe.

"Well, how about if I come over to pick you up and we'll take a drive?" he summarizes. "See for yourself. By the way, did you purchase insurance for that rental?"

"Yes," I reply, "but the information would be in the glove compartment with the other paperwork."

Tessa sits up with a quizzical look.

"Let's begin at square one, then," interjects Lundgren. "I can be there in roughly fifteen minutes. Is that good?"

"I'll be ready. Thanks, Deputy."

I hang up. Tessa's face is puffy, eyes blood shot and the scalp wound opened over the night. A thin streak of fresh blood now tracks the side of her temple. The towel she placed under her head on the pillow is blotchy-red.

"Who was that?" Her brow wrinkles as she props herself up with a pillow against the headboard.

"Deputy Lundgren," I begin. "My vehicle was vandalized last night, sometime between midnight and this morning."

I begin to scroll my phone for other messages.

"Actually, he said there's big time damage to it -- from tires to windshield to door. Someone stole it and drove away from the resort."

Tessa sits forward and says, "This is crazy, Kevin. We've never had these issues until this spring and now there's a whole rash of them. We always blame it on bored high schooler's but none of the usual suspects fess up."

She brings her feet first over to my side and sits beside me. After she's slid her arm into mine, she continues, "Have you told him about me, Kevin?"

"Not yet. I'm struggling with who to trust; plus, I'm not sure on who to tell. If they know about my car, then they certainly know where to find me. Someone is trying to scare me off the resort and get me to leave. If Lundgren can help, that's great. But is there a connection to him? He has the ability to gather information and has the know-all."

We exchange concerned looks.

"And Tessa, I need to tell you that my cabin was tossed yesterday. I'm still not sure if anything is missing -- medical or personal."

"This can't be happening, Kevin." She looks to her palms, then rubs a hand through her scalp stubble. "I'm involved too, otherwise why all this?"

The option is to sit there all morning and quiz each other, but we would still come up empty.

"Here's my plan," I tell her. "We wait for Lundgren to drive over and knock. I let him in, stand back, and see if there's any reaction to my cleaned-up room. In the meantime, you stay in the bathroom with the door ajar. If he looks somewhat suspicious, then I'll take it that he knows. If he doesn't, then I want you to come out and we'll explain all that has happened. You and I might have to trust him to keep a secret. We have no one else. There's been no missing person's report for you. Everyone thinks you're on a business trip maybe to the Twin Cities or meeting with another caterer. The cooking staff thinks you're shopping for supplies. It's all speculation at this point. Paige is at a loss behind the Front Desk. She even has the Olson boys helping her with computer issues."

Tessa has a determined look, a blank canvass, collecting her thoughts.

"I don't like hiding, Kevin. Everyone counts on me, but I trust your logic. The less people see of me for now, the better are our chances that someone will crack. Act as if nothing has happened." She touches the lump on her head. "For the time being, if worse comes to worse, I'll do the same."

"In a matter of a few minutes, I'll have a new do, choppy and punkish, like Alice's, but explainable, given the situation."

"It's awful," I tell her. "It's uneven and certainly done with malice. This look is specifically designed to shame you. Thankfully, and miraculously, you escaped, and now there's a loose end. This wrongdoing will unravel soon, no doubt about it."

She goes on, "What if he wants to arrest us to cover his tracks?"

"Well, we can't attack and tie him up," I respond guardedly. "The game plan is to play it by ear. If he comes in with guns drawn, then we're in big trouble. He pretty much owns the town, and the news will spread in every direction. No one will believe us over his authority. For now, this happens to be our only alternative."

"Are you sure?" she asks, softly touching her temple wound.

"No, I'm not," I said. "It's all I can think of at this point. I've been lied to, made a patsy for malpractice, and had false accusations hold up in court. But this is an entirely new ball game, so we need to build our own defense."

"Then let's stick it to them," she says with anticipation and stands to peek through the corner of the blinds. "Nothing ever changes, Kevin. Up until your arrival, I longed for something to stimulate me. Something exciting." I join her at the window. Her frame is rigid, pale, and statuesque. "This is more like an electric shock. Like being struck by lightning."

I try to console her, but her mind has drifted elsewhere.

For the next ten minutes we straighten up the room and I fill her in on my venture yesterday to the Public Records office, and eventually to the Ada home site. She sits attentively and shakes her head in disbelief.

"I never knew that place too well. We were only there for a short time. It was more about Erin finishing high school. I was into skipping classes and flirting with the older boys more than she was. Little did I know that crazy behavior was ruining my young life for good."

"We can talk about that later. Let's get you out of those clothes. After being clean, it will clear your thoughts."

Tessa had arrived with only the clothes on her back which I bagged and jammed under the sink in the bathroom. Even as she showers and re-applies some aloe ointment, I reexamine door and window locks for obvious scratch marks. We share one bath towel to avoid suspicion of two being used. But the fear in us drips like a leaky faucet and neither of us have yet to show the will to conceal this deception with any measure of success.

We didn't notice Lundgren's arrival until his car door closes. I walk over to the now open blinds.

"He's here, Tessa. Let's hope this goes smoothly and we can get some help."

Pointing to the bathroom I tell her, "Remember to leave it cracked open with the vent fan running. When he comes in, I will excuse myself to turn it off, like I was in there moments ago."

Her eyes ping-pong from the door to me.

"I'm with you all the way, Dr. Kevin Michaels. You're my only help."

Lundgren puts on his hat and slowly pans the parking lot, acknowledging one of the attendants spraying down the deck. They do quick waves to each other. He turns and makes his way in my direction. He knows where I'm staying. I never told anyone about my cabin. Aside from the swimming vixens, Tessa is the only one who knows.

"Here he comes," I inform Tessa, lowering my voice. "Better stay out of sight for now. If he takes me with him, follow at a distance. Is there another vehicle available or can you slip into one of the worker's trucks?"

There's a tap on the screen door, then two successive louder knocks.

Tessa is in a fright zone, biting the inside of her cheek, her lips tremble. I am certain this is way too much to ask of her. "I don't know if I can do this, Kevin. I'm scared."

"Be right there," I shout.

She sneaks into the bathroom and behind the door.

I greet Lundgren as he stands there, serious, with hat in hand.

"Doc, I'm glad to see you, although not under these circumstances." He offers a condescending smile and shrugs. "Can I come in?"

"Of course," I say and step aside. "Excuse me a second. This old bathroom fan is noisy. The shower stall stays humid and this cabin is not that well ventilated."

He waits for me to finish this chore, then sighs. "Four months of damp, eight months of frost, or worse. Welcome to my world."

He looks around.

"When I stopped at Registration, I expected they reserved some sort of hospitality suite for you," he snickers. "This is too rustic, and noisy at that. The brothers have been talking you up ever since your arrival, so I thought for sure there was first-class resort treatment for you for the services rendered to Ole."

He grabs the chair by the dresser and gingerly sits, legs splayed and straight.

"My hip is killing me, lately. I think I twisted it last weekend wrestling a drunk driver. That was stupid of me."

He motions for me to sit and I occupy the foot of the bed.

Leaning forward, I ask, "Any word on the bank hold-up? Do you have any suspects?"

"Nada. We're a one-horse posse tracking down Poncho Villa and his gang of desperados. I have the neighboring police departments and the local dispatcher on the watch, though. According to forensics, the suspects wore gloves and that's unexpected up here. It appears more sophisticated than any locals if you ask me. According to the local paper, it's an organized syndicate from of the Twin Cities. These little banks are so susceptible. They're built along the main street, have minimal security, which makes for an easy get-away. The triggered alarms are minutes off target."

"Were there any weapons?"

He shakes his head and delivers an unconvincing smile.

"Just a note to the teller while the other hand is inside a pocket. According to her, it looked like a gun. Perky Paula won't sleep for a week. There won't be enough sedatives at the town's pharmacy to calm her."

Leaning forward and tapping me on the knee, he adds, "That's a joke between just you and me, of course."

"Understood," I tell him.

"So, about my car?" I ask, rubbing my eyebrows, then resting my hands back on my legs like that wary third baseman three nights ago. I try to not sound too eager and tip him off.

"It's pretty bad," he begins and shifts his butt cheeks forward on the small chair, using his hands to lift his leg over to the other side.

"Damn, this hurts."

"I can write you up a prescription if it goes too far," I offer with an internal reluctance.

"Thanks, Doc, but I prefer to tough it out for the time being." He glances at the bed momentarily, then the dresser top. He taps the brim on his cap.

"I have no back-up in the Department until next month, so I have to stay sober. Anything extra in my blood stream outside of the occasional beer will raise more concerns."

He settles back into the chair and it groans with his bulk. He presses his lips tight and narrows his eyes in thought.

"I'm giving up a little too much information to you, but even if those people claim Workers' Comp on any kind of silly ass excuse, be it lifting a box or grunting in the bathroom stall, I'm always under scrutiny as if the Superman tee shirt under this uniform will save them all."

He rubs his pant leg then fiddles with his shirt cuffs. His ears turn red.

"Mostly, I'm embarrassed. Wasoon has this reputation of being heaven on earth. Dorothy and Toto never had it this good."

"We all need some time off, Deputy," I console him. "But crimes usually don't solve themselves without dedicated people like you in the background. Stealing others' property is centuries old. Only the faces are different. I'm glad there was nothing of value in my car. That's the good thing." I stand. "I'm ready if you are."

He gathers himself and rocks forward.

"Good idea. Thanks for the pep talk. I need to step outside and check in with the Dispatcher."

"Let me get my wallet in the bathroom and we can go."

"Roger that."

Lundgren ambles toward the screen door and stops.

"We still haven't heard from Tessa and it's coming on a couple days. How about yourself, have you heard anything?" He frowns and taps his collar intercom.

The moment of decision has arrived, and I'm torn between honesty and an evolving courtroom drama. Shaking my head, I answer.

"I'd be the last one to be told. People call her the glue for this resort but from what I've seen, they've been well-trained and doing quite well in her absence."

Lundgren meditates on this, his brow furrows, then relaxes as if the comment is genuine.

"I'm with you one hundred percent, Doc. I'll be right outside."

The screen door closes with a loud slap and I watch him gingerly step down to the ground level and walk toward the tree shade. He stops and puts in his earpiece. All clear. I walk into the bathroom to tell Tessa to wait. The back door is ajar. She is gone.

CHAPTER TWENTY-SEVEN

We enter Wasoon from the south loop, which adds another five miles. I'm uncertain as to why Lundgren chose this course unless it's to travel the crime route. Nary a cloud is in sight on this unspoiled lake drive. There is the occasional pickup camper towing an aluminum fishing boat toward the city launch. Huge elms along the bike path house heavy wooden picnic tables strewn with Styrofoam beer coolers, paper goods, and smoking barbeque grills. Scruffy fishermen in dark tee shirts and blue jeans wearing trucker caps are trying their luck from the shoreline as spouses and girlfriends busy themselves around camp sites. Some soggy striped jean shorts and flimsy halter tops dangle lifelessly on cords between large tree limbs. Noisy blue jays balance on the cords, screeching for their territorial rights. The weathered wooden pins align like tired soldiers. There is a half-full, plastic grocery bag clipped to the edge of the biggest table. I gaze out the passenger window. The air conditioning on low and a comfortable ride thus far.

Lundgren points across my line of sight and says, "About fifty yards off this shore is where I put my fish house. Last year, an eleven-pound walleye paid a visit to my ice hole and I had supper for a week. It was on the local news," he chuckles. "I'm frickin' famous."

A jet ski skims directly offshore and sends a picturesque spray in the direction of the fishermen. The older man with the cigar flips him off, while the younger is busy tugging his arcing pole toward the water's surface.

"Lucky bastard," comments Lundgren in surprising language to me. "That's a chance catch this early in the day. I bet it's about a twelve-pounder."

My dad hated the sport, but out of obligation he took my brother and me bullhead fishing which consisted of baiting the hook with anything mushy-soft and setting the red and white bobber at a three feet depth. The catch was often so plentiful in that murky green water that the eagles and hawks patiently waited in the dead cottonwood branches for the discarded smaller catches such as carp or perch, the ones with a million tiny bones. The fish were delicious in butter with some seasoning, but the effort to clean them was not five-star restaurant-style. Our prep room was next to the stand of birch trees accompanied by hundreds of curious wasps and hornets. At supper time we continuously pulled toothpick-sized ribs from our mouths. It might have been easier to eat a hot dog on a bun with a side of potato chips, but we never told Dad. The grape soda was our mandatory cocktail.

We slow as we enter the city limits and allow a church van to pass ahead of us. A thin smile forms over his face.

"That's Pastor Arnie dropping off someone for dental work from the retirement center. He also serves as a caretaker and offers to drive them to and from. Nice guy."

"Yes, I met him yesterday when I drove over to the parsonage to satisfy my nostalgic obsession. He was immensely helpful, although the trip wasn't."

"That's a surprise," interjects Lundgren. "With the reunion and all, he volunteered to be the main lead at chasing down ex-classmates. If you want to know the classic definition of the term 'anal retentive', look up the word in the dictionary and there will be a picture of him."

Lundgren enters the local implement dealership lot. Shiny red tractors aim nose-first toward the highway, accompanied by ten or so semi cabs on both sides in a V-shape, like a flock of geese. Patriotic-colored company flags dance in the breeze on tall white poles. There is a balding salesman standing on the sidewalk wearing a button-down short sleeve dress shirt and dark slacks. He chats with an elderly woman who stands next to an orthopedic walker, shading her eyes to the sun's glare.

"That's Simon, Bill Simon, AKA the Simonizer. Fairly good guy but a lousy card player. He has a magical way to keep the truckers and farmers from going elsewhere to buy machinery. The way I see it, he steals a high portion of sales from other regional markets."

Lundgren lifts his sunglasses from his face to rub his eyes.

"I don't know how he does it on truck sales alone. Guess that's why he sells snow removal and blower equipment. He's also the city's main towing force on the side."

"Is he a member of the reunion crowd too?"

Lundgren rubs his eyes and scratches the top of his head.

"Everyone is either a classmate or related to one by marriage or death, graduate or not. We're trapped in an eternity of fight songs and the school mascot. I wouldn't be surprised if the women are shopping for matching tops and dresses with the school colors no matter where they graduated. Hell, it might be matching underwear for all I know."

He promptly head-signals to the left.

"Anyway, I like to sneak attack around the back, especially where all the junk vehicles line up like old toys. You know how it is. Kids think they can pull something over on us if they can hide between old semi's and combines, drinking in the back seats and such."

He looks across my chest and points to a side driveway.

"Here's where Simon drops off the wrecks and that's where I spotted something out of the ordinary. This wasn't the usual crash damage like ripped-off door frames, or asphalt scars on the under-carriage, or pieces of weeds stuck in the wheel rims. This looked way too intentional. I saw tons of these when I worked in Duluth along the docks. They all had that trademark kicked-in-the-door look. I stopped to get the license plate number and called it in. That's when I thought *holy shit*. Doc Michaels has been in an accident or something worse."

Little did he know that's not even close.

"What's the damage?" trying to rationalize anyone's intentions and connecting the exact chronology. Which came first: meeting me, knowing of me, talking to me, trashing my room, or vandalizing my car?

Lundgren drives around the building until we're circling the back lot. Fender benders, four-by-fours, and old sedans wearing a patina of road dust and bird splatter abound.

"See for yourself," pointing to my rental that had been backed into the narrow space next to the recycle bin.

I would've never recognized it as mine. Wedge-like indentations on the driver's door, forceful cobwebbing of the front windshield as if using a sledgehammer or heavy piece of pipe, and drip-dried spray paint over the hood. We pull to a stop and both of us get out. Am I the reason for this sudden explosion of hate?

"Easy now, Doc," he warns me, "because this is still a crime scene. I have forensics from Parkers Pointe coming around lunch time, but I still think you can call the rental agency, if you so desire."

For emphasis, he taps on the dashboard.

"There was no boot print if that's what you are thinking," directing my attention toward the dented door frame. "But I don't know of anything else that does that type of damage."

In forensic training, we are introduced to psychological profiles of a serial killer's evolution. It usually begins with adolescent bed-wetting and torturing small animals, followed by vindictive personal property destruction, like setting small fires. The suspect gains confidence and progresses to stalking human victims. They graduate into murder because of the psychological rush. For all intents and purposes this fits a similar M.O.

I pull out my cell phone and hold it up to him like displaying my credentials card.

"You mind if I take a photo or two for the rental people?" choosing my words carefully.

His gaze is probing. A wry smile overshadows his face.

We are no longer alone as Bill Simon briskly hustles around the corner to greet us. His tie flaps in the breeze and his white shirt is bunched at the waistline. Loose strands of thinning brown hair on his damp scalp give him the appearance of a short, wet ostrich plume. He palm-covers his eyes exactly like the woman he was greeting in the front of the building.

"Be my guest, Doc, but hurry up. Simon is picky about damaged cars going online with his name as the location. Bad for business, I guess."

"Good morning, Deputy," he greets us, nervously looking around behind him. "Do you think next time the city's police officer signals into my drive, he could give me a heads-up call? I have customers arriving in ten minutes."

"Didn't I tell you?" Lundgren elbows me and tilts his head at Simon.

"Bill, this is Doctor Michaels. The car *not* for sale is his rental. On a routine drive-by, I noticed it last night crammed next to *your* dumpster. To be more specific, aren't those mixed recyclables, oils, grease, paper goods, and paint cans?"

Lundgren looks around and continues.

"I thought you had installed a lock to your chain link fence to prevent nighttime loiters from getting back here. That's what tipped me off last night around two o'clock when I drove by."

"It must have been unhooked, or I forgot," Simon surmises. "I got a little busy with a couple who wanted to trade-in a fifth-wheel. They wasted my time and never were interested. Sorry."

"It's okay," Lundgren adds. "I'm messing with you."

He looks toward the flagpole in the front of the building.

"Are those security cameras set up like I suggested a few months back?"

"It's on my list. I've had to post an ad for a new tire mechanic and the applicant pool has been quite slim."

He produces a stained handkerchief from his back pocket and dabs his forehead.

"This time of the year is slow in the sales division. Sometimes I allow Amanda to handle the phones. I was doing a little landscaping of the dead flowers and got hooked by Sally Brunstad, our 'Make Wasoon Beautiful Again' spokeswoman."

He slowly steps back into the strip of shade alongside the building.

"She gave me her patented lecture about the danger of chemical herbicides. Believe me, I got an earful of how pricey new cars don't fit into the aging economy. But I had her interested in a test drive, that is, until your silent approach scared her off."

"So, you have no idea when Doc's car arrived?" says the Deputy. He cocks his head and pulls out a notepad and pencil from his chest pocket.

Simon thinks for a moment and then says, "No, not really. I closed at six o'clock and went home for supper. We had an early meeting at the Lodge."

He straightens up, chest out. "I'm the current Chapter President and we've been discussing a little get together for our past and present members attending the big reunion at the resort."

"Well, that's all good and fine, Bill. I understand the community bonding thing, but Doc's time here has led us to this scrapheap, and I need to right the ship somehow."

He looks to me as he clears his throat and swipes at an annoying fly.

"Crime isn't supposed to happen in the middle of God's providence, and this isn't a petty visit."

Tempers are rising, so I interrupt. "Do you mind if I check the console? Then we can get going. Will that be all right if I put on gloves and do that?"

Lundgren breaks his concentration on Simon.

"That's a good idea, Doc. Let's give him a little time, Bill. I sure need a cold bottle of water, though."

Simon huffs and says, "I'll be right back. Take all the time you need."

He unlocks the metallic back door with one of the keys on his large key ring and disappears inside.

"Let's get the hell out of here," mutters Lundgren. "Once a salesman, always a salesman."

Back in the car, he signals toward the resort.

"Is there anywhere I can drop you off? I automatically went toward the resort."

"Can I buy you coffee and a sandwich, Deputy?" I tilt forward in the sticky seat and tug my saturated tee shirt away from my chest. "I owe you that much. It's been an event I don't want to re-visit."

"I can use a little cooling off myself and the Bee sounds like a good idea. Let's do it."

He huffs and whips the car into a fishtail. The car's powerful engine hums along like a jet's take-off.

I glance into the side mirror, watching as he nearly clips the curb. A white pick-up truck is behind us, maintaining a fifty-yard gap, keeping up with our city speed limit.

It's Tessa.

CHAPTER TWENTY-EIGHT

I go back to the cabin and change into a pair of swim trunks. My status quo composure needs to be maintained even though whoever is responsible knows this innocent-looking maneuver is a false front. The crowd has dwindled down to only me. It must be geriatric nap time and I have this giant sloshing tub to myself. It must be a resort record of some sort. Solitary water confinement. The opportunity to swim unimpeded is a welcome relief. I step out of the pool and settle in on the chaise lounge. The dramatic ordeal has become taxing, including the privacy issues and possible tampering with client's information on my laptop. I squeeze my eyes shut. Where to go from here? I have yet to receive a call-back from the car rental agency and it's been over three hours. I suspect Tessa is lying low and I hope she has a safe hideaway place that no one else knows.

The sun's shadows slowly claim territory on the west side of the fence. So much has happened and most of it is against the grain. It's becoming time for my daily addiction of checking for emails and messages and I begin to scroll. Other than the usual advertisements, it's as if my connection to the outside world has taken a vacation too. Either I'm getting poor reception in this remote region or the company has discontinued my services, a reminder to check my accounts when back in the security of home. Anyway, it doesn't matter that much, and I retrieve from my cell the photos taken at the dealership.

Shots of the crime scene gallery: front, both sides to compare doors, the smashed windshield, all four tires, and the hood. All are over-exposed. Nonetheless, I'm sure the rental agency concurs with my assessment that this was malicious.

The hood tagging is a puzzle. It's white paint, for sure, but I can't discard something worse -- like construction glue or spackle of some sort. Not being able to feel it only leaves me to speculate. The random streaks and splatter, the thick and thin straps of the material, as if it were art-museum worthy. To be certain, I photographed both the front bumper and over the hood, much like documenting details in an accident. I double tap to enlarge the picture and see the hood work has some sort of design. I shield my face from the glaring sun and hold the phone closer. The tag doesn't reflect well on the dark surface. It consists of irregular lines, bold strokes, like when a highlighter is used. I can't figure out the exact images, but it's graphic for sure. Perhaps it's script? Moving it back and forth with my finger, then up and down, I wonder if it's a version of a doctor's poor penmanship? According to medical transcriptionists I've worked with throughout my career, mine falls into that same category. I bet it's wording. Some sort of warning. Some sort of message directed at me.

"Come on, dumb ass," I mumble, putting down the phone on my lap and briskly rubbing my face. "One more time."

Profanity works wonders. It comes in handy during autopsies in morgues where furnace-type heat, the encompassing odor of days-old decomposition, and lack of ventilation are my brethren in crime. With a heavy sigh I pick up the phone again and slide the images back and forth, from left to right. The caricatures are Greek-like, angulated, and with divots. The only letter for sure is the first, carved like a P. This next one is a W. No, it's two original letters that merged into one. My guess is this one is V or a U, and next to it is the number 1 or a capital L, followed by an attempt at a W. The squiggles are throwing me off. Could it be an excessive drip or is it un-capitalized, like an E? Then it hit me.

Pitiful?

Pitiful. No doubt. Aimed at my failed attempt to fit in.

Is Tessa sending me a message? Or worse, is Erin still alive? All these years. She's still here. When Tessa burst into my cabin yesterday, this never came up. I hope that she trusts me enough. I've been looking over my shoulder way too long. I need to know. I need to understand. I lean in and study the lettering, trying to decipher another word. Maybe it's a phrase or wording related to something else, like a secret code.

Pitiful.

I'm not going to be swayed again. This time, I'm convinced. No doubt, it's Erin signaling me to find her. This immediacy has been my downfall and now is not the time to put the cart before the horse. Stick to facts over assumptions. But my mind is on overdrive, shifting into a higher gear. Nonetheless, this mental con job loiters, even though my gut churns along with the white-knuckle gripping of the arm rest.

I set my phone down next to my thigh and pretend to nap, acutely aware of the surroundings. Lord knows I've been here a few times, so it's not that unusual. I think back on the unabashed vixens, dragging their chairs noisily along the concrete and prancing around the circular drinking table. It's obvious that Gloria, the leader of that pack, has had work done. Her front points out like nose cones on a rocket and they hardly jiggled as she gymnastically leapfrogged a stark-naked Abigale who straddled on the diving board. Then there was the surprise of Tessa knocking on my door. I'm still not fully prepared for the way she's entered my life.

I awake with a start as the book fumbles off my lap. My thoughts are fuzzy. The sun has set behind the tree cover and dusk is a delicate palate of purples and pinks. The wind has died down and the smell of freshly added chlorine and murky lake algae battle the air currents in equal strength. I fixate on the lakeshore for the next hour, pretending to be in deep thought, realizing that fear no longer holds my attention. My phobia is the next phase in this whodunit. It's as unpredictable as slipping on a wet boulder and bombing butt-first into an icy pond. I'm at a loss. My next step is uncertain, but it better be well-calculated. I decide my best course of action is with the Wasoon law enforcement pecking order. Someone's rage is baiting me, waiting for my reaction. I pray Lundgren is trustworthy.

I scroll to Aaron Olson's phone number and press the 'call' option. He answers on the fifth ring.

"This is Aaron."

"Aaron, this is Doc Michaels. I apologize for not getting back to you sooner, but when is a good time for us to meet? You mentioned that I need to go over some documents for body release."

The attendant saunters past in front of me, lugging two plastic gallons of liquid chlorine. A friendly hello, earphones, sunglasses, unshaven, iridescent visor, Bermuda shorts, tank top, and flip flops: the quintessential teenage summer uniform. In contrast, I look like a typical businessman closing a deal, dressed down after a day of golf, or a conventioneer needing a private moment to check-in at home with the wife before having supper with cohorts. Either way, I fit the appearance and he doesn't look twice. Summer help is still faceless and replaceable, much like I was years ago.

"Oh, hey Doc," Aaron says. "Thanks anyway, but we figured your signature wasn't needed. David spoke with Aunt Gail yesterday and she told him that the paperwork was in order and we can go ahead with the funeral arrangements for Dad."

There's a brief pause, then he continues. "I hope this doesn't screw-up your travel plans too much. If so, send us the revised statement and we'll take care of it. For the record, you helped us get closure. I want to thank you sincerely."

"It wasn't a problem on my part, Aaron," I tell him. "You know that I used to work as a counselor at the church camp a hundred years ago and have been enjoying the time travel, so to speak. My compliments go out to both David and you for keeping this place running."

Hoping the flattery is working, I continue.

"I want to close my stay pretty soon and meet with Tessa one more time to thank her. Has she returned from playing hooky?" I busy myself by adjusting the back of my chaise lounge. It feels like I'm under scrutiny at every opportunity.

"Paige talked to her briefly this morning by phone. She said that she was checking in. David and I were helping Paige at the front desk yesterday which took most of the afternoon. We're going to change service providers. For all the money we're paying those people, their service sucks."

Tessa reconnected with the resort, but from where?

I continue.

"Has she left a contact number or indicated when she might be back?"

"Not as far as I know, Doc, but I'll surely let you know. Dad's funeral is currently scheduled a couple days from now, but that's not set in stone. Roland says the plumber discovered additional repairs needed in the back room of the chapel, so he might need the water off and order new parts. Up here, life is too slow and way too remote. A funeral home is usually the last place a repairman wants to spend working, especially if he has to drive three hours one-way and receive payment a whole three weeks later. I guess that's understandable. We have a hard time with that too. Once we even called in a paver crew from Fargo because the local company dropped the ball."

Getting back to Tessa's whereabouts, I probe.

"You've been very accommodating and because of that, I want to donate toward the weekend reunion. Perhaps some sort of monetary gift or a case of champagne for the celebration?"

"There's no need to do that, and I appreciate the offer. People up here are mostly beer drinkers, but I'll be sure to pass that along to her the next time we chat."

"Please do," I request. "I'll be here for a couple days at most, doing some hiking or biking and will have to have another burger and milkshake at Bee's for sure. It's like a home away from home for me."

"Well, let's do supper there tomorrow, if that's all right with you. By that time, Tessa should hopefully show up."

"Sounds good, Aaron. Thanks." We disconnect. I gather my towel and toss it into the USED bin and leave with more concerns than when I sat down.

Back at the cabin paranoia sets in big time. I'm a combination of hypersensitive and dead tired. Besides, the feeling of being watched or followed is like a chain around my neck. I scour the living quarters and bathroom. The gilded luminescence creates faint and ill-defined shadows on the walls. There is the mustiness in the damp towels from the previous night. A lone cricket scampers for safety behind the dresser. Like that insect, I want to disappear, but if I'm here, I'd better be ready.

My intentions are deliberate. Pass by the half-opened windows and appear to be doing nothing. No hurried motions. Nothing unusual, except for the packing in full view. No doubt someone is watching. I spend a moment to fluff-up the pillow, pausing to adjust the blanket, walking into the bathroom, and flapping the towel in front of the open door. Next, I fumble in the medicine cabinet, then back into the main room, and sit on the chair.

I imagine the door flying open and this stranger bursting in. With that concept etched deeply in mind, I fumble in my pocket for the cell phone. Time to re-check emails and messages, all the time scouting for quick exits either front or back, depending on which one is broken into first. Paranoia 101. My phone vibrates.

"Dr. Michaels."

Click.

I rush to the door and hear the screeching of tires. A car engine revs near the resort's entrance. In moments, a dark sedan races past the registration building and nearly hits Perry Brown who leaps off the driveway in the nick of time.

He mouths a profanity as he gathers his spilt coffee mug and lunch bag from the pavement.

I hold up the phone and dial 911.

Three rings.

"Wasoon Police Department. Is this an emergency? How can I help you?"

"This is Doctor Michaels. I'm staying at Ole's Resort and want to report a reckless driving incident. This car almost ran over the Security Guard. Is Deputy Lundgren available? I need to speak with him."

"Hold please."

A minute or two passes.

"Dr. Michaels? Deputy Lundgren is off-site. There's been an

accident on Highway 22. Roland Purdy, the funeral director, had a roll-over in the van. The ambulance has taken him to Detroit Lakes. It's not looking good." She stops with further information and waits for my response.

"I'm deeply sorry to hear that. Is there anything I can do?"

She begins, "Deputy Lundgren has requested you at the accident site. It seems that the Coroner is busy as well as the Deputy Coroner. Deputy Lundgren has consulted with the Coroner, and he feels comfortable with your offering organizational assistance. Is this doable?"

Into the swarm I go again. I rub my eyebrows and tightly close my eyes. This is how the attorneys yanked my chain last year. This is how I almost lost my medical license. Luckily, I can still practice in Minnesota. Now this. How am I going to explain the lost keys? All this constant planning and obsessing. At this point, I'm ready to do anything.

"Absolutely, but I need a car. Mine was vandalized last night. How can you get me there?"

"We're sending an officer to pick you up. She'll be there in ten minutes." There's another static pause. "Thank you for offering. By the way, I remember meeting you at the Welcome reception three days ago. You crushed Tessa's toes dancing in the disco line. No fault of your own and I'm not pointing a finger, but she favored that foot around the office the next day. I knew, though."

"What happens in Wasoon stays in Wasoon," I joke back. A choking thickness forms in the back of my throat recalling how that straightforward line has gone wrong.

"Thank you and please tell the driver I'll be outside."

"Finally," I let out a huge sigh. The weight on my chest is lifting ever so slightly.

The crash site is cordoned off with two squad cars, one facing in either direction, flashing in unison to the slowing rubber-neckers. A foggy mist emanates in the headlights like cold steam. The moon is banked behind a wall of ominous clouds, only its faint outline is visible. Scorched tire marks at least a hundred feet long, lead from the centerline to where they disappear beyond the graveled edging. Two uniformed patrolmen lift their booted feet through the matted vegetation toward the tilted funeral van, its engine drips dark fluids from the chassis. There's a fire truck parked diagonal to the road with two firemen in yellow coveralls aiming a collapsed hose at the vehicle. Suppressant foam drips from the nozzle. One of the men amidst the group raises a flashlight overhead in broad sweeps as if to signal us to walk in that direction. It's Lundgren and he wants me to follow. We walk past the van debris and broken glass. He places the lantern at his side and lights up the intended pathway.

"Thanks, Doc," he says aiming his flashlight at the van. "This is hard to take in. It looks like it flipped only once, then landed on its side. But to get a bottom-heavy load like this upright requires big-time momentum."

He pauses to surmise.

"I presume Roland was going beyond the speed limit at the time and therein lies the puzzle: clunky funeral van with no hurry to ever go anywhere fast. He's the slowest, most careful driver in Wasoon. The guy even stops at unused railroad tracks."

His voice trails off.

"There were no passengers, either living or the other, as far as we know. I got the boys carefully searching the perimeter, though."

"How did it happen?" I ask, forming my own suspicions.

"It's dark, but the skid marks are straight, long and wide, meaning that he had to brake hard to stay on the highway. My guess is that he had to swerve, a judgement call, and that was that."

He shouts to the patrolmen in the matted grass. "Anything?"

The closer one swings his flashlight back and forth, "So far, no, but it's getting darker. I found the gurney and cover about fifty yards beyond the van's location. It wasn't fastened down in back and hurtled through the open door."

He aims his light toward the other patrolman who is searching the site too, step by step.

"Wally is carefully covering every foot. I hope to hell that only the driver was involved. By morning there could be an infestation of insects."

Lundgren tilts his head upward and folds his arms tight against his chest.

"Roger that. Take all night if you have to."

He taps me on the shoulder.

"I know you don't have any jurisdiction, but I want to show you something. Follow me."

He leads me to the crushed van on its side and aims the light toward the driver's door.

"I want your professional opinion on this here," pointing to the frame. "Tell me that it's not what I think it is."

I lean in and gently sweep my fingers over the blood-speckled indentations. Jagged residue pokes through the door insulation. Gravel and asphalt slide freely into my other palm, along with multiple, dark BB's. Lead pellets. Shotgun pellets. I bring up the mysterious foreign bodies for a closer look and rub the fragments together as Lundgren steadily holds the flashlight. I sniff and close my eyes, concentrating.

"It smells like sulfur. Gun powder is my guess. You need to send some of this to the lab first thing tomorrow to be sure. Have the patrol check for wadding in the weeds."

"Already in the works." Lundgren deeply sighs. "When I arrived, the paramedics were extracting Roland from the seat. His left cheek had these pock marks that I originally thought was glass or dirt abrasions, but it was only on his face. I know he always ran the air conditioning day or night. With the van's tinted windows always closed, we never knew if he was the driver. That's a no-no in this county, but it became an exception for our funeral director."

We step back as the van is hooked up by Bill Simon, the tow truck operator, whose stature is solemn. He wears coveralls over his white shirt and tie and slips on a pair of leather gloves. The cable becomes taut as he controls the hand lever.

"Deputy. I'm going to upright the van and get it out of the ditch."

Fifteen minutes later, we stand alongside the trailer where the funeral van lists on bent axels and tire rims. Only the W is visible on the side panel and the remaining lettering is covered with mud. Simon latches it with thick tie-downs at each precarious corner. My impression is that the vehicle's damage has the look of texting while driving. To save himself, that driver's survival story might be an amended version.

"I got off the phone with the Medical Emergency unit. Roland's status is dire. He's bad off. The next two hours are critical."

A shock to the system, my jaw drops open. I feel like the rug has been yanked out from under me.

"Deputy," I continue to analyze the wreckage. "I need to tell you something because I believe somehow this is related to my presence here at the resort."

Lundgren holds up his hand, pausing as if to carefully choose his words.

"Stop right there, Doc. You don't have to go any further."

He steps back into an unlit area next to his cruiser, pondering, deliberating, hands hooked on each side of his utility belt. He continues.

"I used to be a big believer in coincidences, that things inexplicably happen. You know, like three famous celebrities dying within a couple days of each other. But this is unlike that. When I told you 'Welcome to my world,' I wasn't kidding. You work under the microscope for tiny clues, and I work under a big fat target for answers. Sure as us standing here, it's the same entity. Don't take this the wrong way but we're being watched. I know that for a fact."

Lundgren's shoulders sag as he kicks at some loose gravel. We listen to the tow truck's back-up *beep-beep-beep* signal.

"I paid a visit to your cabin yesterday looking for you and saw the nasty whirlwind in there. For sure, you weren't there, but my initial concern was that you were dead in the bathroom. I checked, you weren't, so I closed-up and left ASAP. You're a secretive guy and like me, protective to a point of distrust. It's been like that lately, if only to survive. So, I thought the best offense is some sort of defense. Let you tell me instead of me telling you which is the last thing you want to hear from a local cop. But I trust you, Doc. Until then, until there's a clue of some sort, it's a waiting game for us. Both of us are going into reverse-stalking mode. The prey is becoming the predator."

Glancing around, no exit, no help, I reply.

"I apologize for not trusting you, Deputy. It's self-preservation on my part, plus I'm a little concerned that people are dying because of me."

"I'm with you on that. For the time being, let's stay on the same page. If you come across anything, anything at all, I need to know." He taps his intercom receiver, "Marsha, you there?"

There is a scratchy, electronic reply.

"Go ahead, Deputy."

Cupping the speaker, Lundgren looks intently at the wreckage and tilts his head. He lowers his voice for only me to hear.

"The next time you hear from Tessa, like last night, tell her from me that now is not the time to make a surprise guest appearance. Maintain status quo. Keep calling in. Tell them she has personal issues to take care of. We have a killer amongst the clan who is slowly widening the spider web around Wasoon."

CHAPTER TWENTY-NINE

By the time the transport deputy and I conclude our work at the accident scene, the sun is arcing over the ridgetop, as if being coerced by an invisible grip. I am official support for Lundgren's crew, directing them over the importance of sampling and photographing from a medical standpoint. Other than that, they are well-versed in handling these middle-of-the-night accidents of which, I suspect, aren't all that unusual with weekenders and their hundred thousand-dollar watercrafts. I settle in the passenger seat and check my phone for messages. It shows the rental company called sometime during the night, so I press the 'call' option. There is a lengthy explanation of the insurance coverage by a benign voice of someone in the claims department. But eventually, I hear that I'm not responsible for any of it, and I'm placed on hold. The deputy tilts her head toward me. Her eyes never leave the road.

"Not to worry, Doctor," she glances into the rearview mirror. "Deputy Lundgren informed me under no circumstances that I share this information with anyone. He and I have been discussing our plans without setting off the alarm to anyone, especially the Resort. This is where, we believe, most of the problems are originating."

She slowly drives past the resort entrance a half-mile, pulls onto a widened section of the road in the opposite direction and leaves the engine running.

"Deputy Lundgren?" she taps on her intercom.

Lundgren immediately responds.

"Go ahead, Officer."

"Duty completed. I am returning to the Department."

She looks first down the road ahead and then checks her side mirrors. The first tint of dawn slits the skyline. A doe and her two fawns suddenly bound in front of us, disappearing into the pine grove. It's unusual to see such young animals this late in the season. Perhaps she lost her other offspring to coyotes or wolves. Hopefully, the mother and her twins will survive doe season this November. No doubt, life in the wild is not as forgiving.

"All clear, Doctor," she exhales loudly and tilts her head on the rest. "Deputy Lundgren wants us to be 'stealth,' as he put it. Act normal and pull over to the typical speed trap spots and wait."

She checks the ditch, then the grove of pine trees beyond. "If you don't already know, there are single-track bike trails twenty yards deep to the road right there," pointing to a gap in the bushes. "It will wind you all the way back to the resort on the back side. No one will know if you've left. The trail leads to the adjoining cabins."

She smirks and cocks her eyebrows. "We were all teenagers at one time or another and not just a bunch of silly class reunion folk. You can sneak into your cabin from the back entrance."

I study the direction that she's pointing.

"Right through there?"

"Roger that, but don't let your legs drag onto the scratchy vines. That's poison ivy, our beloved state flower." She softly chuckles.

My phone wait was over.

"Hello, Doctor Michaels? I apologize for the delay. We have a driver delivering a second rental to your address as we speak. He'll arrive around eight o'clock. Once again, we're sorry for the inconvenience. If there's anything we can do to further help, please feel free to contact us at our 1-800 number."

"Thank you, and yes I will. I sincerely appreciate your help. Good-bye."

"That's done," I exhale with relief. "Tell Deputy Lundgren he's a good man. I sure hope Roland is going to be okay."

She gives me a concerned look, her eyes narrow as she glances at her watch.

"I better get on the road. Now's a good time to sneak out because no one's coming from either direction. Good luck and happy sleuthing."

I unlock my door, duck down and head for the tall ditch grass, listening and waiting for traffic, behaving like that protective doe. At the same instant, the deputy merges her cruiser onto the road. The conversation with her borders more on the secretive. I'm wondering if she and Lundgren are closer than merely a professional relationship.

I tilt my head back, look up, and shudder. I'm either coming or going to this damn wooded resort. It's either the front door, back door, opening, closing and all this time, questioning my purpose. I'm not any further along in this investigation, although I suspect that not coming forward with the truth to Lundgren has not made matters worse. I'm grateful for that. I presume he also knows about the scribbled word on my car hood.

Pitiful.

Yes. It is pitiful.

Not in the usual sense, either. It's more individual, like someone who I wasn't polite with, or someone who doesn't see eye to eye with my socializing at the resort, or someone who hates tourists? Put up a good front, but back-talk when out of earshot. I recline in the bucolic rocking chair on the porch with my empty coffee mug, watching the habitual jays darting between pine branches to my railing, scavenging for breadcrumbs that I had begun to pile on the ledge from Day One here at Ole's Resort.

I doubt anyone is spying on me at this hour, but someone is calculating the next move after peppering the funeral van and almost killing Roland last night. That news will spread in relatively short order as an accident, but his role in this whodunnit is obscure. Our hope is that he regains consciousness and can give the Deputy a solid lead.

Last night's attendant is up early, rearranging the furniture into neat four-chairs-to-a-table. He's disheveled and his baggy cargo shorts looked slept-in. There are endless wrinkles on the front of his polo shirt and his sunglasses slide down his nose like a watchmaker's. Again, the distinct smell of liquid chlorine permeates the air as he reaches for the pool brush. The pool pump motor hums softly like a baby's humidifier after a bath. The sunlight pokes through the fenced grove of poplars. In another hour, the complex will be in full bloom.

But how am I going to get past all this weed infestation of secrets when there is so much good with this place? Checking my messages has been futile. Tessa is in hiding, my work schedule is nil and per Lundgren's request, I am refrained from making calls to him unless I use the cabin phone.

Comparing myself to others and obsessing with my flaws has me acutely apprehensive. I take to the sight of a shiny, navy-blue SUV as it slows, passes the booth, then parks in front of the registration office. No doubt, Security Guard, Perry Brown, is still fast asleep in his Wasoon apartment. Besides, things don't get hopping until later in the morning when the first tourist bus and limos begin lining up. That's when he will once again shine for the company -- all salutes and smiles.

It dawns on me that this is my rental replacement: a mid-size SUV, the undercarriage muddy from the roads, and an unusual blue, out-of-state license plate.

I casually stand, stretch, and pretend to take a sip of coffee from my empty cup as the driver pulls into the resort entrance. Minutes later he returns to the car and slowly passes each cabin.

I signal him to my walkway. A young man, he has the ruddy, athletic look of a serious wakeboarder only taller than most of the others I've recognized. There is scruff on his lower lip, his wavy hair is thick and blond, pulled tightly into a man's bun, the company shirt collar disguises bold tattoo lettering of some sort. I sign revised rental papers, we do fist bumps, and he informs me he is to be picked up within the hour. Works for me, even though I offer to drive him where he wants. I plan to head next to stop at the Sheriff's department and follow-up on Roland's accident.

I avoided a meeting with Lundgren, feeling that a little distance between us might be useful for the time being. Upon my arrival, I'm relieved to see his patrol car isn't in his reserved space. I check-in at the reception desk and introduce myself as an assistant for Lundgren at the accident site last night. I inquire as to the status of Roland, thank the staff, and walk back to my car -- a smooth operation for the med-ops specialist.

Feeling a little strapped sitting here, I begin to list the available options in my head. A transient-type walks by and tosses his cigarette butt toward the gutter drain and misses the mark, much like Alice, the beautician, a few days back when Tessa and I went to the storage building. He steps off the curb and drags his weathered shoe over the grate cover until the mission is accomplished. He juts his chin and cocks his head. The acid in my stomach churns.

I might tool around town in my new wheels along Main Street. I'll back under an ancient elm at the city park and watch for any suspected dark-looking cars. That's not going to satisfy me because my impatience doesn't have that sort of life span, plus even criminals have non-working hours. I decide to re-acquaint myself with Bode Trucking and talk to my pal, Vincent.

Like the old Burma Shave domino signs of the fifties, his advertising is on four-by-fours as drivers enter the city limits. Vincent once offered to take me for a ride on his souped-up tractor, and this seemed to be a good time as any to see if it still holds true. My impression of him is that he's not only the most eligible stud bachelor to the dwindling stable, but also has a social eye for the local folks. A sort of who's who privateer with fewer pretensions.

A full-size, souped-up, semi-style, hot rod, black, with red rims, and a double stack behind the cab fills the showroom facing the street. The stenciled racing number '43' is boldface on the driver's door. It's the pride of Bode Semi Racing. I open the door and look up toward the ceiling with admiration.

The room brings back fond memories of my dad's garage back in the late sixties. First on the list was Dad's annual racing calendar on the back of the bathroom door with fabulous bikini-clad models. There was the smell of engine fluids and hand degreasers, the citrus air fresheners, and permanent oil stains on the carpets, along with a squeaking overhead ceiling fan. All of these were coming of age landmarks for me. Vincent's office is remarkably similar.

Behind the Parts Department counter, a pudgy, dark-skinned man in jeans and tee shirt, sporting a bushy moustache and wearing a 'Bode Trucks' baseball cap gives me a bullseye look as if I'm a target. Papers are splayed over the counter under his meaty forearm, as a customer dribbles his fingers and clears his throat. There's a sheen on his forehead as he rubs the back of his hand and holds his cell phone at the ready. Beyond the counter I notice Vincent at his Ikea-style desk, phone at one ear, writing something down on a yellow tablet.

He doesn't bother to look up, which is acceptable because I usually don't either, unless it's to check the wall clock. His door is ajar, but I surmise by his posture that the caller's berating him. Vincent leans back on his chair and massages his temples, then he sees me in the doorway and stands, signaling me inside.

"Charlie, I'll get back to you on that bid. Can I call you in, say, half an hour? Great. Thanks."

He hangs up the phone and softly F-bombs under his breath.

"Doc Michaels, what brings you here? Have I done something wrong or offended someone?" rolling his eyes, his chin drips downward as he plays with his shirt pocket. There's a guilty blush in his deeply pigmented trucker's scalp.

I slide up the massive captain's chair opposite of him and plop down.

"This is an awesome cushion. Now I know how you corner the trucking market. You lull them to sleep, then sign the deal."

Shaking his head and closing his eyes, he answers.

"My secret's out."

Pointing to the office window facing the counter, he continues. "For what it's worth, the backrest is so high that I can sit in it and face my desk, and it looks as if no one is here. I dim the lights and nap time never feels so good, come around three o'clock."

He tosses his head back and grins. "Do you think anyone has figured it out yet?"

He points to the tablet in front of him.

"Scheduling deliveries has become an art form as opposed to a political science subject in college. When I took over this business from the previous loser, I was certain to make it work with only a couple part-time employees. But those days are long gone."

He tips back and cups his soiled hands behind his head causing his baseball cap to list on the top of his scull.

"Believe it or not, most of my calls are after closing."

He looks past me toward the counter.

"Was he actually doing something when you arrived, or blowing smoke out of his ass? I've had a few complaints about his lack of urgency when it comes to getting things done."

I give him an affirming blink.

"The customer is growing impatient. At least, it looks that way to me."

"He's slow as molasses, that's for sure, but being an Einstein is not a job requirement. Actually, it's the opposite." Bode taps his chin with a pencil. "I guess I can fire him, but let's give him another week and see if he turns it around. I'll get him in here tonight for a little heart-to-heart."

"Good call, Vincent," I respond, as if I have any power in the decision-making process. "Sometimes border-line employees need a little kick in the pants to shape up. Medical staff included. But their ineptitude is usually unforgiving to the patient."

We spend an uncomfortable minute under self-evaluation. Bode fiddles the page corners on his scheduling book with his thumb as I glance at the certificates on the wall behind him. He has his hands in a spate of local organizations and holds offices from President to Treasurer to Good Will Ambassador. On his desktop, facing the customer's direction, is a framed picture of him proudly standing beside his dragster, with one leg resting on the running board. Muscle cars and trucks have always been the norm up here. Chest out. Chin up. If there ever was an opportunity to show off, this is it.

"That's a beauty, Vincent," pointing to the photo. "Is that the ride you offered me at the Meet and Greet a couple nights ago?"

"The same, Doc," he exhales and coughs. "I figured we'd tool Main

Street and blast 'em until everyone is deaf. Even put you behind the wheel."

He brandishes a wide grin then fends off a bubbly, smoker's style hack.

"What gives?" His eyes narrow. Small talk is over.

I feel reluctant to answer, but I need to ask. I need to trust my judgement. I need to believe that he will not surprise me.

Clearing my throat, I begin.

"It's nothing, but I'm getting an impression that my presence in Wasoon is not welcomed by everyone."

I slowly adjust in my chair, back and forth for a comfortable spot to sit.

"There have been some strange happenings. Perhaps you over-heard some talk or complaints?"

He sits forward as in confidence and lowers his voice.

"So, you pissed off Tessa? Is that it?" exhaling through his nostrils, jerking his head back as if astounded. "If that's the case, then it's the ideal recipe for me because I'm on her good side again."

The Cock of the Rock slaps his thigh.

"To be honest, when you arrived, it was as if she had met her match. Someone exactly like her. Put up or shut up. No more false prophets. You lit a fire under her seat. She had a sharp tongue before, but after your arrival, it was lights out."

He flops back in his chair and moans.

"Mind you, there was never anything between us except the bantering, but she loves the attention and the challenge. It stirs up that fire in her behind. Lately, like the past month or so, I overheard folks at the resort talking about dating websites, like FindAMatch. com. You know, one of many promising the 'ultimate consummate' relationship."

He slaps his knee then reaches for his coffee mug and takes a sip. "If it worked, then I'd been a happy camper years ago. Unfortunately, it's not in the cards for the Gambler of Love."

Softly pounding his fist on the desktop, he goes on.

"All joking aside, she looks stressed to the bones so maybe a little sex, or something like it would help. The horizontal hula. The Big Nasty. You know what I'm talking about, Doc."

My hope that he knew something valuable is dead in the water. It's becoming a safe guess that my private Deep Throat isn't sitting across the desk from me although, nonetheless, he's relishing in another fantasy.

Feigning surprise, I tell him.

"This is news to me, Vincent. We're getting along like friends. It's nothing more than that."

"Yeah, bullshit," he interjects, frowning with a hard smile. "You are not talking to a mannequin, Boss. Word is, you are the anointed one. If ever there was someone to tame this she-devil, it's you. The other day at Bee's, Paige was grumbling over some computer issue at the resort and there was no Tessa in sight for at least couple days." His eyebrows bounce a couple times. "Any idea where she might have gone?"

"She is not with me," I retort, reflecting blame, raising my voice in defense. "Have you seen her in town lately?"

"No. And that was news to me, Doc. I figure she's meeting with contractors or caterers off-site. The boys are lax in that respect. Responsibility was never instilled when Ole left the dock, so to speak. They prefer to spend first, repair later."

Sweeping his hands as if to offer good riddance to the topic, he adds.

"Other than that, it's business as usual. Farmers never have enough rain, folks kvetch about the Twins and Vikings losing seasons, and the number one gander is when your neighbor buys a new pickup every other year. You think the Olsons would have developed a thicker hide by now, too." He chuckles. "I guess you know, everyone has their own sad sack story. You can't please them all."

Vincent scratches his head. "Gutting a deer is normal for these folks, and actually carving up a human is totally beyond reason. That action only takes place on cable television. It goes to show how they think."

I check my watch and instantly slide into another fib.

"Which reminds me, I'm to meet with them later this morning to iron out some residual paperwork." I push back in my chair to stand. "I'd appreciate if we keep this conversation in confidence, Vincent. More than likely, it's over-reaction, but I thought if anyone has a pulse on the Wasoon Nation, it would be you."

Pointing back to the racing machine in the front window, I continue.

"I'll be leaving in a couple days but will take you up on that ride sometime soon."

He doesn't bother to stand. A relaxed smile forms over him like a lion waiting to pounce on a guaranteed kill.

"If you're around tomorrow night, say, six o'clock, and if the weather holds, I'll haul ass in that MF'er to the resort. It'll be a show that those cronies will never forget."

There's a rap on the door and the employee from the counter pokes his head inside.

"Excuse me, Vince. Two things. First, we have a grain haul to Fargo scheduled in the morning." He allows that to settle in, then goes on. "The second item is that the sheriff has arrested David and Aaron Olson for armed robbery and attempted murder."

"The hell you say!" Vincent pushes away from the desk and begins to rub his throat.

A sudden coldness hits me at the core as I fixate on the room's ceiling fan, its broad blades slicing the desk lamp's soft light into reflected shards.

CHAPTER THIRTY

The trip over to the sheriff's office is snail-speed sluggish. There is continuous stop and go traffic. Countless television news vans are competing for parking spaces nearest the courthouse. Cable hook-ups and people from as far as Minneapolis television stations jostle and shout instructions. Microphones and cameras in hand, the women newscasters primp as their male counterparts knot their ties and tug on the front of their sport coats. The major news anchors are seated on stools as their assistants' bustle around them with a makeup brush. I roll down my driver's side window and overhear a soundman with boom and headset, giving orders to a couple of vans.

"Get the hell out of the way, butt face. We were here first."

It's like a news vulture feeding frenzy. The hell with leftovers. This 'just-in breaking-news' is the mainstay.

To my surprise, Bee's has a lunch table set up in front where a mix of newscasters and lighting crews hover near the freshly barbequed meat table. They hold their plates in front as the juicy beef is sliced into thick portions. I recognize one of the national nightly news celebrity anchormen: a slightly built, short, fifty-something, in a tailored blue stripe suit and a quaffed haircut. His receding hairline is dyed the same color of the cut surface of a timber log and there's a contrasting streak of gray along his temples. He's rehearsing some lines on the teleprompter as his assistant stands motionless, one arm in the air, waiting for the signal to go live from a director on headphones seated nearby. If they corner me, do I have a story to tell.

Fortunately, humidity is not a competing element. Late summer breezes linger like company not wanting to leave. There is a hint of wood smoke in the immediate air. A remote forest fire has been spotted, but that's yesterday's news compared to this. My deputy escort from a few hours ago is now providing traffic control. This time, no one is diving or ducking in between cars or under four-by-fours. Her tone is sharp as if plucked from a night's sleep as she chastises another rubbernecker. She aims her chin at a news van driver who was bartering for a prime spot to unload equipment. A yellow and blue helicopter with a large "TV 20" on the side hovers above the scene. The cameraman pokes a large zoom lens through the chopper's door.

As difficult as it is to conceive, this crime was not only local, but that two favorite sons are arrested for it. My lack of plausibility hovers like an ominous dark cloud. I feel gut-punched, blown away. How is it possible those signs haven't smacked me in the face? My weakness is that I have an inherent tendency to take people at their face value and had to learn the hard way it's a trait brought on by over-friendly plaintiff attorneys. Friendly, that is, until the courtroom doors close behind any semblance of medical truth. But thinking these two young men have the capacity to steal or murder is beyond me. I ease up alongside as she directs another news van.

"How's it going?" I dare to ask her.

She stops the waving and ducks down to eye level. Beneath her cap's stained brim, beads of perspiration collect. She groans. Her breath is warm with the odor of caffeine.

"It's the job of a lifetime. Living the dream. How about yourself, Doc? Are you still free of poison oak?"

I feign scratching my elbow and rub my neck as if being unconsciously reminded of the close call days ago.

"This is too unreal, Officer. Any news on the arrest?"

"Lundgren received an anonymous tip." Suddenly, her shoulder intercom beeps, she listens, then continues.

"Someone called it in late yesterday with a vehicle description matching the Olson's truck, but with its plates removed. It was seen idling along the side street of the bank for a long time and the caller said a couple men were sitting inside. It seemed suspicious, especially with the recent string of bank robberies."

She scans the cars lining up behind me.

"We searched the Olson's home site and the Resort, and finally found the pickup parked behind a storage building at the Resort. It was a little dusty, but smudged handprints were found on the door handles and fenders. There was also a loaded twenty-gauge behind the seat."

She steps back and points.

"Listen. You'll have to stay behind these idiots, or better yet, circle back along Oak Street to the east. There's a residential alley that few people know. One block from Headquarters. If you want to meet with the Sheriff, it's the best way to circumvent this melee."

Tapping on my door, she adds.

"Tell them Officer Melissa gave you permission. My reputation precedes most of them. Also, please convey to Nick that he owes me big time. Tell him a supper or two is on the bargaining table."

"Nick?" I inquire.

"Lundgren, to you, Doc," she smirks and pinches the brim of her cap. "Now, you better get going."

The back entrance is a side door adjacent to a benign-appearing garbage bin. No one would think twice that it leads to anywhere important because the alleyway is barely wide enough for a pickup truck. I'm allowed in after a couple knocks and a brief introduction to a young deputy guarding the exit. It is my opinion, most of the department either knows Melissa or doesn't give a second thought as to why I might be sneaking past the front security. Lundgren stands at his desk, gathering his hat from the hook and a notebook from the drawer, looking as if he is leaving. I tap on his window, he looks up, and signals me inside.

"Officer, I came by to see if you need any help. I'm in total shock."

His smile is rehearsed, nodding, noncommittal.

"Me too," he motions me to close the door. "But I've seen crazier things. As for me, it's all a little too schematic and under-planned for a couple of young men. Neither of them has an ounce of gangster in them. Don't lead on, but I think this is a set-up, like it is with the two of us and yet, here we are: evidence in hand."

He looks past me through the glass, tilting his head from side to side.

"This isn't my first rodeo. Six of one, a half dozen of the other. That's the way I see it, but the press doesn't care as long as the story has legs and sells to the public."

I follow his gaze. A tall, grey-haired officer wearing dark blues and carrying his hat in front of his service belt moves in our direction. The Chief of Police from Ada momentarily waits at the door, then loudly knocks twice, and opens.

"Hey, Lundgren."

A friendly greeting and yet there's a terse tone of authority. Straight as an arrow as he struts inside.

Lundgren acknowledges him.

"Dave, glad you could come."

He directs his attention to me.

"This is Doctor Michaels. He stepped in to help me last night at the accident outside of town, where our funeral director was shot."

We shake hands.

"Hello," I begin. "Actually, I offered my services until the Coroner arrives. I'm the pathologist who was hired by the Olson boys to autopsy their father, Ole."

"We are all aware of Ole's misgivings," the veteran officer concedes, "especially how he unloaded the business into their laps." He chortles. "It looks like that escapade hasn't worked out too well for them either. Too much free time and in no measured terms, too much play."

"They are quite popular with the locals, despite their genetics," I mention. "Is there any indication of the resort faltering or being delinquent on payments?"

The Ada officer moves his hand to and fro.

"All I know is that same vehicle was seen on camera in front of our local bank the other day. My guess, they were scouting the scene looking for the best getaway option."

He looks back to the office, lowering his voice.

"If you're asking my opinion, I stayed a couple times at Ole's Resort and thought the whole shebang was overrated. It's metro-expensive to dine and the golf course is only average. Just saying. The greens need manicuring and fallen branches were everywhere. Now there's an opportune catalyst for the bank heist: steal cash and help pay for repairs. Historically speaking, no one takes on a bank teller for the fun of it, armed or not. As for the night shooting, maybe poor old Mr. Purdy was just in the wrong place at the wrong time?"

Lundgren interjects, "Well, we're still looking at all the facts, Chief. I need to take a step back and view the big picture again. News people dive headfirst into every lead as if it's the solution, but I won't go there."

The desk phone rings and Lundgren answers.

"Lundgren."

He glowers and looks at the main office.

"Okay, I see you. Be right there," and disconnects. "That's my signal for a press conference. The party is on."

He pauses and sucks in his chest. "Gentlemen?"

We stand aside as the deputy slowly tromps toward the reception of news people and lights, leaving the two of us in his office.

"Nice to meet you, Doctor Michaels." He makes for a friendly fist bump but holds back. "Come visit us in Ada and with any luck, on a more cheerful occasion. You will appreciate the fishing, the food's cheaper, and the stay is way less hectic."

"It sounds like a plan," my concealed fist is clenched behind my back and I masquerade a smile. "Unofficially, of course."

"Of course," he smirks and slips through the same side door I used to enter.

It looks as if my services to the staff are redundant and the brothers lawyered-up, meaning that this is going to be a wait-and-see case for at least another couple of days. The concocted stories will become kindle that burns the midnight oil in all the local lakeside communities. Even though the Chief of Police from Ada drove down with corroborating information, I still question whether I've missed something in the town where Erin and Tessa were raised.

My crazy thoughts need to become grounded. Am I assuming that Erin is sending me coded messages from beyond? It's more practical that someone is stretching my emotional wit. The word *pitiful* is still a word, no matter the hieroglyphic style. I head to my car and sit there, weighing the options: my cabin, be a target driving through downtown Wasoon, or elsewhere. Has this mystery come to an unsuspected conclusion? Medically speaking, fellow doctors always refer to work as practice, but this resort game is an unresolving batter ram without rehearsal. I decide on that little farm town with the broken-down Victorian.

CHAPTER THIRTY-ONE

This old house doesn't leave me any compulsion to crawl through the bushes or break into the back door. For that matter, I need to use common sense and remind myself not to become irrational considering everything else that has happened. I drive past the front of the Victorian, lean over my steering wheel, and peer at the entry steps. Neither Erin nor Tessa ever mentioned growing up in this shuttered eyesore. The house has seen better days and the upper level has caught the worst of it. It looks harmless enough, but I recall from my first visit just the other day the animal scat along the basement windowpane, and I fear those critters scurrying beneath my shoes, looking for pant legs to crawl up. I look up and see pigeons perched on the attic sill, and those frayed linen curtains still waving at me through the windows with the broken glass.

I move along the exterior, taking it all in, cautiously walking along the side to avoid the thorny vines, testing the cellar hatch cover, surveying the backyard and shed from a safe distance. Nothing much has changed since my previous visit. I step onto the back porch where the screen door is unlocked and ajar. My jaw tightens, and I carefully check my tracks. Things seem to be moving beyond my control. There is a heaviness in my gut, as I enter with uncertainty, feeling trapped, taking the plunge, the last man standing.

The musty, bitter odor of rat urine is overwhelming and even the wallboard has memory-jogging hints of crumbling-wet secrets. The old porcelain sink has become the final resting place of dead moths and remnant hulls of beetles. Instinctively, I peer upward, shading my eyes for fear of dangling bats awakened from the extra noise. The kitchen sink window is half-cranked open and has a limited view into the back yard, reminding me of how my mother kept an eye on my brother and me as we wrestled until one of us told on the other for playing too rough. I averaged two warning shouts from her each day, telling me not to hurt my little brother. But that was his problem, not mine.

An old wooden table with heavy, block-style legs had been pushed against the wall leading to the sink. There are no chairs, but I recall from the last time that the backyard firepit ash held skeletal remains of furniture seats and castings. The sunlight pokes through the room like a skewer onto the cupboards. I shuffle through the dining room, trying to stay within the most obstacle-free path, second-guessing my decision thus far. My thoughts race for a better alternative to this mistake and I tentatively stop to listen. Outside, a truck's brakes squeal as the air locks release with a *Whoosh*. There are a couple toots on the horn and the machine ambles down the street.

At the base of the stairwell is a framed and faded painting with the image of a shoeless little boy in a straw hat and bib overalls sitting next to a well. Over the years, I've seen variations of this serene theme. Cassie and I would browse antique shops often and this had been a popular sixties print: the cherubic farm life from a different era, the yapping cocker spaniel, the sloshing water bucket, and the speckling of clouds. I never had the talent. I trace my fingers over the canvas. Original. Some of the paint flakes off in chunks. Who has the patience to do this? Odd. The boy's face has been deliberately carved out leaving a vacant oval in its place. My pulse thumps in my ears.

Save yourself. Leave now.

Suddenly, there's an explosion of pigeons from somewhere upstairs. Wings violently flap to escape the room and their shadows zip across the front yard. That's how they come and go: through the attic window with the broken glass and shredded curtain. That's their nesting cover, their safe home. There is a flustering, a prickling in my scalp, as I grip the railing to ascend.

Remember. I have come this far. No backing out now.

Upstairs, the Victorian hallway is quite typical. There are three doors on each side. All are closed and the wood frames are splintered from the outside. At the far end, filtered daylight displays swirling dust and debris too fine to grasp. I am distracted by inkling sounds. The frantic bird activity in the attic has hurtled me on edge. I scan the area for the quickest exit knowing this is plain stupid. Attempts to open each door results in increasing levels of retreat mode. Dracula comes to mind. The irrational fear from the psychological scars of my youth still flowing through the veins in my neck.

The old-style oval knobs wobble and each door opens with a mild protest, the hinge plates and screws loosening with each attempt. I tally five of six empty rooms, and there's that strong smell of mice activity in each. But the stark metallic blinds in the sixth room at the end of the hallway are bent downward as if someone spent time peering through them. Stashed in this room is a dirty, military-issued style cot with a dull green woolen blanket and small pillow covered in dust and mildew. There are indentations of a body shape. As with the other rooms, the faded, floral-printed wallpaper is curling with age and brown water stains in the ceiling indicate decades of a leaking roof. The floors are darkly stained planks that bow and creak with each stride. Next, the attic.

I find a latch on the heavy attic door, open it, and secure it to the hook. Once inside, my attention shifts to an eerie wavy glow and the frayed linen curtain rising in the breeze. I survey the vaulted ceiling, checking for any provoked movement. This is a definite multi-generation bird haven. Dried mounds of crumbly feces mask the floor beneath the overhead beam. White down feathers are trapped like giant moths in elaborate corner cobwebs. Looking out the window, eaves are pocked with bullet holes. Someone has been using the feathered fowl for target practice.

On the floor are seat cushions that have been picked apart by attic mice. Stacked in the corner are two pairs of ancient work boots sitting atop discolored magazines. There are dismantled cardboard boxes and a stack of unused mailing labels. On the opposite wall is an old denim field coat on a nail hook. Leather work gloves stiffly protrude from the pockets.

Pigeons have been living in the vast attic space, secure from predators. But more animal activity is evident, including fragmenting bat guano, the usual choking odor of rodents, and a cat-like carcass of black fur. I hunch over, careful not to step on broken glass or rusted shingle nails. From this vantage point I can see my rental car parked underneath the elm trees on the other side of the street. A younger Erin or Tessa sneaked up here on cool summer nights. Watching. Dreaming. Hoping. I know this to be true because I used to do the same thing at my home.

I notice some of the old lawn chairs are collapsed and lined-up against the wall. All have seen better days decades ago. Backrests are missing, legs are dismantled and lay on the floor, but those broken pieces of chairs are indeed puzzling. According to the woman at the county office, the next owners, after Tessa's family left, assured her that not everything was salvageable and was going to sell only the intact pieces as antiques. Whoever that was had good intentions to fix it up. To-do items were stashed in the attic. But from its appearance, this house hasn't been lived in for decades. I rest my hand on the sill, and then I see it: a green headscarf on a stool. A shiver crawls up my back.

I feel trapped and flustered and hold up my hand in front of me as if warding off oncoming dread. It's Erin's, no doubt. Like a beacon, her infamous head badge has been relegated to the attic. This must be a signal. This time there will be no more springing to conclusions. I tentatively scan the room, looking for other unidentified items, anything that she might have worn that I can remember, like a hair clip, a pair of jeans, or a sweatshirt. Decades-old dust billows as I throw boxes, move broken chairs, toss the overcoats into never-to-be-moved-again piles. I sneeze, then continue to wildly search for any clues of her whereabouts.

WHOOMP!

I recoil at the impact from behind me and I release an old bundle of textbooks from my grasp. The attic door is dropped from its hook with a resounding "BOOM" followed by the locking sound of the latch. Someone is here. Moments later there are loud, hollow footsteps on a wooden floor, bounding downward, heavy tromping in the far reaches of the hallway. Then there is silence as I wait for more audible signals.

My chest tightens and I rush back to the attic window, hoping to see someone racing away. No such luck. Moments pass, and then, there are more echoing steps to the main floor. The screen door creaks and slams shut. There are still no signs of anyone escaping. I crush the headscarf into my fist and pound on the wall in frustration.

CHAPTER THIRTY-TWO

Lundgren braces against his squad car and chomps on his gum. I overhear him offering up a few choice words under his breath. He shakes his head and folds his arms. It's time for me to face the music. The dull turquoise color of sunset reflects on his complexion beneath the brim of his patrolman's cap. There are sweat stains under each arm and his temple has bulging vessels with the earmarks of tortuous blue worms.

The smell of fresh cut lawns is all around. Someone, probably a neighbor sprucing up the houses, is weed whacking around the dilapidated Garner mailbox. A couple of teenage boys wearing football-logo tee shirts cut off at the waist cruise by on Fat Tire bikes, doing wheelies, hopping curbs, and offering up habitual spitting contests at the passing mailboxes. I drape my arms over the hood of the car and take another chug from the plastic water bottle.

"That was a hot mother up there, Doc," he repeats a second time in the past five minutes as if for emphasis. "You're a better man than me."

I cap the bottle and let out a deep sigh. "It's pure luck that my cell phone was still in my pants pocket. I thought I had left it in the car to recharge."

"Don't ever do that, even for a minute," he scowls and looks back at the house. "Please don't pound on the walls or yell again for attention. This might look like small town USA, but idiots come in all sizes and from all directions."

His mouth becomes tight as if biting down on overripened fruit.

"I suspect the same happened up there," pointing to the attic. "You caught someone red-handed rifling through the Garner household. Hell, they could've been living there, but according to the mortgage records, this damn building has been vacant for at least twenty years."

He straightens and simulates an enforcement-like stance.

"People are survivors up here. There is no new economical vir-tue. Transients and vagrants multiply like rabbits. As for the cot you mentioned, all I saw were empty rooms: six of them upstairs and four down below. I'm not dragging my fat body into that basement without some canine service support. Every time I see an opossum's yellow eye reflection it freaks me to the max."

Replaying the events in my mind are acutely fresh.

"I'll grant you that, Deputy, but you know both of us are being watched and it stands to reason that we're on the losing end, one and the same."

Lundgren's patrol car is parked behind mine. Passerby's would consider us as two old friends visiting, chatting, comparing notes with fishing tales. Hopefully, no one suspects anything else.

Streetlights are gradually illuminating, the bulbs clicking like moths in an electrical zapper. I hear the faint sound of televisions and radios in nearby houses. We watch an elderly man at first, peer through his front door, then mosey out and struggle down the porch steps. He grimaces a little too much as he picks up the garden hose. He busies himself, pretending to examine the shrubbery, but all the while, standing within nosey earshot of us. I wished like anything to be him right now. Crickets hum in anticipation of calling mates and in the distance, a train engine hoots as it enters the city limits.

"Why the cot?" Lundgren questions. "What's the point of that? This isn't CSI Ada, and we're a long way from the Wasoon resort, Ole's Resort." He squeezes me by the arm like a coach consoling a player. "Please stay within the city limits from now on, Doc. We need to be careful. Maybe it's another homeless person sheltering up, waiting to pull the police brutality card. Maybe not. But regardless, a criminal is innocent until proven guilty."

I stand up straight, shrugging.

"That's the easy solution, but we need to connect all the dots, Sheriff. I'm trying to protect Tessa as much as you. I bet in the realm of recent events that this house has been used illegally. More than likely it's all connected somehow."

"I read you, Doc," he blurts. "My skeptical brain neurons are working overtime and the realistic ones are on vacation, but I need viable proof."

He faces me straight on. "Remember what I said. Don't go 'unofficial' on me. If there's something, anything, you're doing *within* the law, I want to know about it."

Thanks to the villain, this is how it plays out. Lundgren still has his doubts.

"Are you absolutely sure about this?"

He nods and continues.

"Yes. My quandary is that I initially trust people at face value. No matter your thoughts, we're still working the same side of the street. I strongly believe this all ties in somehow with the deaths, the accident, and you getting trapped up there." He lets that sink in.

"Roland Purdy has been taken off life support." His arms droop down to his sides and he looks at his open palms. "Poor bastard. Now it's Murder One."

We arrive at the resort by sunset. Lundgren has taken the lead, but I know firsthand that he wants to narrow my search boundaries and chastise my efforts. Perhaps he associates our budding alliance to Roland Purdy: common ground, common enemies. It is now painfully clear to me this chain of events, my presence and becoming trapped in the Garner attic, are the next phase of the mystery.

Lundgren leaves me to ponder my mistakes and quickly pulls onto the highway, heading toward Wasoon. I give him a dismissive wave which he doesn't return. Like a rebellious teenager being punished I decide to park near the boat launch instead of the cabin driveway. My blood is boiling, and I let out an ugly laugh. A solitary twelve-foot aluminum fishing craft putters toward the dock. A man's silhouette wearing a broad-brimmed hat and lit cigar in his mouth slows the craft, levering and steering up to the pier. He gathers his rod and tackle box and begins to stiffly stand and walk away before stretching back beneath the seat to gather two good-sized walleyes. With all equipment in hand, he throws the anchor rope on the landing and steps up to the dock. I bet nothing *pitiful* has ever happened to him.

There's a wooden bench and I decide to spend some time sitting there. Lake water laps on the smooth rocks like the sound of a wet bed sheet being softly snapped dry. The algae-filled, foamy scum accumulates onshore with each sloshing surge. I inhale deeply, bow my head, and close my eyes. This inability to associate with others clings to me like static electricity and discharges a dreaded fear. There is no one that I can trust, and I have no other options.

I stare out at the lake. How many missing bodies can end up in cold deep water such as this before floating to the top? How many winters can pass before people forget about it? I feel a bottomless migraine coming on, slowly thickening, like early ice, the oxygen trapped in small pockets under the surface. On the contrary, a starry night such as this can lull even the most mistrustful asleep.

My cell phone vibrates me awake. Unknown Caller. Another text from an irate client or a message to contact the business phone. It'll have to wait. I'm not in any hurry and click it OFF. Setting the phone aside on the bench seat, stretching, clasping my hands behind my head, I close my eyes. Right now, it's the perfect combination.

This ordeal is unending. The week has morphed into a maniacal monster from what began as a straightforward postmortem, to an accidental death, to an explosive cabin fire, to a missing Tessa, to vandalizing my cabin, to a murder, to being trapped in an ancient attic. I can't accept that, to say the least. My stamina is wilting. In this powerless pace, it's as if nothing will ever be the same. The signals are too strong. I need to pack up and leave and avoid Harm's way.

Pitiful.

What does it mean? Pathetic? Despicable? Worthless? How does that all apply?

I bring the phone out and scroll through the photos of the malicious hieroglyphics on my car hood. The first shot is underexposed because of night and is useless. But subsequent overhead ones are conspicuous. I often examine body photos during a positional death scene investigation in a like-minded fashion. Cross-hatchings, X's, and lines scored with something sharp and with force. Could it be a screwdriver or nail? I enlarge the lettering with my index finger and thumb to broaden the less defined markings. Looks like letters. P's or D's or F's. Straight-lined I's or T's but maybe something else altogether. No doubt, this is a crapshoot.

The first three scores are symbolic but dissimilar from the others in a roundabout way. I first think P-I-T, but the last, an *L*, appears to be deeper and bolder. What about *L*'s doubled-up? It's the middle four markings that's puzzling. Don't overlook the obvious. Stick with what I know for sure.

Oftentimes, those who are considering suicide, compose frantic notes of desperation. There's a fear of not being able to follow through. This is similar, nearly illegible, done in haste. The first letters are decipherable, as are the last. Control, then chaos is followed by a sense of peace and acceptance. People in need can often mask the inevitable to the rest of us. It appears that the middle letters are smaller words. How about a number 1 or a lower case *i*? What if the middle word is '*is*', then it becomes a phrase? 'Pit is full.'

Pit is full.

Pit *is* full. *The* pit is full. It makes no sense.

He's the Joker to my Batman. At any rate, that maligned soul is enjoying these clues of confusion. He wants to be found out. It's a given. Considering the consequences, I need to play the role of prey with these tidbits. It's a Who-Done-It game, a campfire game, the kind we played as teenagers, and hated as counselors. When this resort was a church camp, we had firepits and toilet pits. Ash and ass collectors as they were called by us 'fine young Lutherans.' The physical structures are gone, and the last cabin Tessa and I inspected was engulfed by fire. Another sign. Another piece to the puzzle. It's unfair to assume I've arrived at a meaningless conclusion. This unprovoked solitude alongside the lake and the harmonious loons calling in the marsh are clouding my judgement.

"The hell with this," I yell, frustrated, running my hands through my hair.

"Have a nice night, Doc?"

The fisherman ambles by, arms down by his sides, lugging a tackle box, pole, and the two caught fish.

"It's Simon. Bill Simon. You know, the implement dealer."

I look up from my phone.

"Hi, Bill."

I take a moment to admire his catch. He stops to stand and display them trophy-style.

"Those are nice-sized. I watched you take them from the boat. At first, it looked like you forgot them."

He softly laughs then becomes serious.

"I guess my mind is elsewhere. You heard about Roland Purdy's accident. He's in ICU right now. Folks say it might take months to recover from those flips." Shifting his stance, he continues. "As it was told to me, he was on a delivery call to Thief River Falls when it happened."

He fixes his eyes on the lake. There is a fat pause between us. I don't know how to respond. The whole story is still being withheld, and Deputy Lundgren is playing it close to the vest.

"It's a tragedy, Bill. You know that I was there with the deputy at the accident scene," I tell him. "As often as I see these cases, it never gets any easier. I decided to sit and relax here because I need some quiet time, especially today."

Acting like a local, I lift my cap and scratch my scalp. "Let's hope for the best. Humans have this amazing will to survive. I see it all the time: heart attacks, cancer, and even through addictions."

"Agreed," he says. "I'm with you on that one. I pray he's going to be all right, though."

"Have a good night, Bill," trying to deflect the moroseness. "Try to take care and don't forget the fish next time."

He studies the two fish dangling from the cord. "This is two hours each of work and roughly two minutes of pure pleasure. That totals at least four hours of R & R. Fishing and math were my favorite classes. And in that order, too."

He pulls the brim of his cap over his forehead.

"Get it while you can, Doc. Of all people, I'm sure you know the days are numbered for most us."

"Roger that."

Ten minutes later he motors off with the boat loaded on his trailer leaving only the soft sounds of road gravel and a shift into higher gear. Everyday should end like this. Suddenly, I have an epiphany and pull out my phone.

"Hello, Deputy. I bet you didn't want to hear from me so soon." A pause. "Yes, I know it's late, but you gave me this number in case of emergencies. Listen, I have an idea and I need your assistance. Swing by and pick me up. I'll explain?"

The deputy answers back.

"Great. See you in a half hour."

We drive the narrowed logging trail overlooking the scorched cabin site from a few days back. His patrol headlamps are on dim. At the rise, Lundgren kills the engine and leans forward over the steering wheel.

"You are certain we can't do this in the morning?"

In the dim console reflection, I can see his mind churning as he exhales through his nostrils and rubs his hands together.

From a short distance, we contemplate the unlit survey of trees and remnants of cinder and door frames. Insomnia is taking its toll on me. My eyes have a continuous dull throb as if the back of both sockets is filling with coarse sand and there's a gnawing neck ache that I've carried for hours.

"More and more, there's a direct connection with me coming to the resort."

I bring my cell phone out to show him photos of my car hood.

"I've studied these photos and originally thought that it's the word *pitiful*; but now, it appears closer to *pit is full.*"

I hand him the phone.

"Here. It's weird but rotate it and magnify the image."

He takes it and begins rotating and spreading the screen to

enlarge the image. I watch his interest rise as he pulls his glasses down over his nose for a closer look, then his jaw drops.

"Son of a gun. I think you're right. I can see the phrase *Pit is full.* But how does that pertain to you?"

Taking back the phone, I point it toward him for emphasis.

"It's all some sort of game, Deputy. Whoever it is, wants to toy with us, fool us. He thinks we're being outsmarted. The etching is a greater game. He's a seasoned veteran. That time was a dress rehearsal. But here's where we begin to draw a line in the sand. There's a definite lack of maturity in this folly. The teasing clues have suddenly become deadly. The accidents have morphed into killing and that will go on to bigger catastrophes. He likes the feeling of power. He's mysterious to a fault. I'm certain we're dealing with a sociopath, emotionally a teenager, and most likely younger than us."

He cocks his head to the side and raises his chin.

"I've read about this in training manuals, but sure as hell never thought Wasoon was ever going to be the center of a sociopath universe. Do you think there's a history of abuse or hurting other people?"

I hesitate. Carefully considering the answer. Calculating in my head the correct response. Internalizing the options. Hoping to convince him.

"No doubt there's a trigger for these events, whether it's parental torment or an inability to connect with people the same age. This memory bank is on full tilt, initiated by all these people from around the country showing up for a reunion. Reminiscing. Laughing. Doing goofy pranks to each other. Adolescent behavior."

I tap the dashboard with my fist.

"He might have self-diagnosed as a loner. I've witnessed aberrant activities in criminals who have blamed their transgressions on others. Arson is a test to see if it can be done without drawing attention. It's not that uncommon, but the evolution to something serious is hiding off-stage and now 'Look at Me' is front and center."

Lundgren sits motionless, his eyes narrowed and focused on the screen. I go on with my explanation.

"To this person, we are in the way of progress. He's the diamond in the rough. I might not be the exact reason but my arrival here at this time stokes the fires. The brothers were blind-sided because they are gullible, and the bank robbery is an easy set-up based on their past relationship with their father. Roland might have discovered something. He became a target, so he had to be eliminated."

I let that sink in. Lundgren blinks as if having a revelation. Moonlight casts a half-shadow across his face. He smirks.

"I knew the boys were innocent all along, but the indications point to them."

"Blindsided, boss man," I add. "We're following rules being dictated to us. It's a setup and the pieces are falling into place for both the hunter and the prey."

I steer his attention to the seared ground down the hill below us.

"This is where it all began, and I surprised him. This is where he hit me from behind. This is where the EMT's noticed my vehicle. But who called? Who knew I was coming up here?"

"You think that the scratching on the hood means something?" Lundgren rubs his jaw and focuses on the tinder's destruction. "I don't get it."

"It hasn't sat well for me either. But when you consider Erin missing and then Tessa's recent disappearance, I'm thinking he's been around the area from the beginning. At first, everything was in place: an unknown amongst the knowns. But I believe he's a known among the knowns. This is no stranger to Wasoon. It's someone seen daily: a resort worker, a guest, or a local, hiding behind a cloak, using his dark personality as a veil. That's the ploy. That's the phantom's style. There is someone or something under his skin that created another itch on the trigger finger. Hence, the gouged carving on the hood. That announcement is some sort of challenge, an invitation, like a maniac in wait. In addition, this look-at-me individual wants us to know that we're being watched."

"Let's go down and take a closer look, Doc," Lundgren responds, eagerly reaching for his flashlight and cap.

"Remember. We are not alone, ever," I warn him. "That's why stealth is best. I think the answer is down there, buried in the embers. The fire was fabricated. All the lightning storms and humidity, it's quite easy to cover up a crime without accelerant. It's a matter of holding a flame to the ceiling near the highest point."

Lundgren grovels.

"It's dark as ink down there. Scrounging around is pointless."

"We're taking a chance for sure. But the fewer people who know, the better."

I agree. "Neither of us are experts in fire forensics and yet, between the two of us, law enforcement and medical, we could get lucky. The signals are strong. I can feel it."

The next fifteen minutes we head in opposite directions and do a large circle sweep making broad arcs with our flashlights. I'm more cautious. Thinking of my smoke-damaged lungs, I cover my mouth with my hand for fear of inhaling particulate matter kicked up by my shoes. Sweeping gently to-and-fro with a charred rake handle, stopping to pick up carbonized pieces of wood and metal, holding them up to the light, then discarding, our teamwork is on full tilt. With the lantern held high in front of my face, I explore the collapsed fireplace brick remnants. The soot I scoop up disappears in the breeze. Lundgren loudly huffs in frustration a couple times. I hope my enthusiasm doesn't collapse into futility or frustration. There are tons of unidentifiable burnt materials, melted utensils, and shattered glass, but nothing specific is spurring my interest.

The smoky stench permeates my sensitive nose as mucous drips down my mouth and chin. It's all too familiar, bringing back memories of identifying bodies burned beyond recognition, their pugilistic, blackened forms of contracting, hyper-heated muscles and thickened skin bark.

"Anything?" I shout from across the destruction.

He emerges from behind the half-standing chimney and plays the flashlight back and forth, shaking his head.

"No, but there are bed springs and mattress bits everywhere. Did you say how many kids were in each cabin?"

I must think back. Some of the campers were day-to-day. Others stayed the duration of a week.

"I think the most we had were ten or twelve at a time," I yell back. "Seriously, it was no vacation for any of us counselors. Most every night was a campfire bitch fest."

I aim my lantern in the direction of the still erect well house.

"Let's check that old structure. I remember when Tessa and I came here the first time, there were some old paint cans lined up against the studs. Our luck might change."

Lundgren leads, carefully stepping over tree corpses and branches that crumble into soft ashen powder. "Keep your distance. I noticed some eroded tree roots behind the cabin. More than likely, it's from badgers or fox. Once they dig a safe tunnel, it can go for tens of yards deep into the subsurface. In the dark and with all this muck... ahh hell. I just went boot-deep. These critters are territorial and will attack. Remember, unofficially, you are my guest."

"Roger that," I answer, hoping he will catch my coy response to something he had told me a couple days ago. "One thing I know, Deputy, is oftentimes the perpetrators like to re-visit the original crime. They admire their creativity and tap the self-ego a little bit."

A faint needle-like green light sweeps across my line of vision.

Pffft.

The sound whistles past my ear like a large wasp. There is an explosion of bark in the tree by my head, disseminating splinters onto my cheek. The lantern glass shatters in my hand and I drop it like a hot iron.

Pffft.

Lundgren suddenly hunches forward, losing grip of his flashlight and falls face-first onto the ground.

Pffft.

Hard clumps of caked dirt burst like sharp powder between us. I jerk my head back in that direction and lose my balance in the darkness, flailing into the brush tangles. Lundgren is moaning like a wounded bear twenty feet to my right. We are pinned down, ambushed with a laser scope and a suppressor.

"Fuck me," he whines over and over, each time a little weaker and more distant. "We need to call for backup. I think I'm hit in the chest."

He groans and musters a cough. I manage to crawl and roll toward his stilled body. The shooting has ceased and there is no additional laser illumination. Lundgren's flashlight has fallen in front of him and ends up pointing toward the cabin, glowing in the mist of fine ash.

"Don't reach for it," I yell. "How bad are you?"

I begin to clamber to his dark form, all the time conjuring up images of where he might have been shot. If the bullet hit him near a vital spot and he collapses like a boxer walking into a knockout punch, it could be much worse.

"I'm closing in, Lundgren, don't move and don't talk."

"Fucker," he wheezes, "got me below the vest protector and it's hard to catch my breath. There's blood oozing on my beltline and coming out of my shirt."

He coughs and tries to spit.

"I'll be damned. Tastes like blood."

I kneel next to him. Lundgren is on his back with both arms clutched in toward his body. His shirt is saturated with dark fluid. Chest wound. No doubt. This is critical. If I can't plug the hole and stop the bleeding, he'll be a goner.

I sit up and tear off my jacket.

"Hold on and press hard against the pain. Keep the vest snug and pull on the strap if you can. The Kevlar will help tighten the seal."

"Easy for you to say, Doc," he mumbles through the pain. "Rule Number One: never assume. Rule Number Two: never sneak into a snake pit without a spear. I failed on both."

I grab hold of the caked soles of his boots.

"Push on my hands, slowly, then harder."

He struggles but wiggles them back and forth which is an incredibly good sign. At least he's not paralyzed.

"If you're anything like me, I want to be up and running right now, too. But we need to be cautious and wait. It's unfinished as far as he's concerned."

The back of my mind is on overload and not a good time for irrational thinking or sacrificing something important for the unknown. If we can't get immediate help, Lundgren dies right here in a matter of minutes.

There is a *click* as he hoists the Glock 9mm up to his vest and aims in the direction of the assault.

"Send him my way, Doc. I'll be waiting."

I feel him rocking back and forth, then onto his side as he forces himself up, propping against the tree and speaking in between gasps.

"This is Deputy Lundgren. I'm on Fire Trail Road Number Eight, near the mountain cabins. We have an Officer Down. Repeat: Officer Down. Request assistance ASAP. You got that?"

"Good call, Deputy," I whisper, but my concentration is fixed on the faint bouncing flashlight flicker of yellow in the ridge beyond the cabin site fifty yards ahead of us.

Lundgren squeezes my arm.

"Don't do anything Dirty-Harry-stupid, Doc. Find him and I'll do the rest."

"Copy that." I blink a couple times, harried, powerless, the taste of bile surging in the back of my throat.

A few days back, Tessa had shown me the treacherous cycling trails that I now duck and dart along. In a matter of a few yards, I stumble over a large trunk and do a face-plant and the taste of blood and dirt in my mouth is immediate. Burn marks over my kneecaps cry out with each stride. For certain, the wounds have re-opened. Eventually, I become accustomed to the darkness, and soon begin to vault over flat, luminescent limestone rocks as if in a higher gear, an exhausted marathoner in the nineteenth mile. No need to quit. The urgency keeps me pressing on.

I reach the bifurcated trail and stop. Which direction? The chilled air slithers down the back of my shirt like a snake. Tessa's whereabouts and Lundgren's life cling to the right decision. Focus. No more negative thoughts.

Go right? No. Left. That's the way.

I set my jaw and pick up the pace like the nocturnal predator ahead of me, but it's as dark as a raven. Like a hunter in the woods, I stop to listen. Then there's a faint, familiar sound.

CRACK.

The silence is smashed, and the hunter now becomes the hunted. One hundred yards further, I propel toward fallen tree limbs, dodging, and torqueing my ankles on softball-sized pinecones. The chase catches up with me and I slow to a brisk walk, still panting, assessing in my purpose to this idiocy. I raise my flaccid arms above my head. This is pointless. Lundgren warned me to not be heroic, but this is no time for contemplation of moral decisions. I can feel my temple pulsate and I'm drenched with sweat, but ready to begin another round. A fight. A knockdown brawl. I'm closing in for the final round.

There's CRACK nearby and instantly another CLICK. A green laser beam points a button-sized dot at my heaving chest. Squeezing my eyes shut, I launch into the prickly brush.

Pffft.

Above me, dried evergreen branches rattle, then cascade like a wood shower on my neck and back. By the time I dare look up, the lit figure is once again bouncing away, this time faster, more pronounced, as if sprinting. There must be a clearing ahead. For the next few minutes, I tip toe along a less-trampled pathway. The silence of the forest envelopes me. Sweat pours from my face and neck and I weakly hold back the need to vomit. My eyes water from the irritating wood debris and I rub the sides of my brows and cheeks to keep any foreign material away from my face. There has not been a sound in any direction for quite a few moments. My heart sinks. If he's gone...

Suddenly, there is another CRACK, and I slink into the underbrush. Yards to my right is a deer bed and I begin crawling through the matted grass. The green beam scans the woods nearby, double-checking, triple-checking, forward and back, up and down, like a medical conference pointer. But my podium is vacated although the killer is still here, waiting for the next presentation in this poorly attended lecture. Out of the darkness, I can barely make out a slight motion fifty feet ahead of me. A standing-upright-human formation taking shape in the darkness, between two large evergreens. That's all the excuse I need. Busted, you motherfucker.

This valiant charge through the brush generates an adrenalin-filled, Cowardly Lion roar in me and he reels as if electrocuted. He trips on an upturned root and clumsily bounds through and over this poorly lit obstacle course. I am the risk-taker again, closing the gap, tightening my fists for the first strike. His silhouette is upright, legs driving, arms flailing, toting a rifle, darting through low-lying branches, wedging his arms in front like a road grader. I hurdle toward the form on my own trail, feeling the thorny scratches clip at my unprotected arms and legs. There is no stopping me this time.

The ground gradually becomes mossy as the two trails merge into one. I see him struggling with the traction, splashing, and kicking up pungent dark spray from the soggy conditions. He is a mere ten yards ahead, but I can hear him wheeze. From the rumble, I can tell we are nearing the river rapids and recognize the falls constant rumble. I can sense the cooling mist and the fear in both of us. At the trail's end, the waterfall berates its warning. He skids forward, losing balance, slipping backward on the trail with a thud, smacking his head on a stump. I have him trapped. He struggles to stand, wobbly, exhausted, his right leg taking all the weight.

"Don't do it," I yell. "It's at least a hundred-foot drop."

He slowly faces me, zombie-like then plods toward the edge, dragging his left foot and gripping the inverted rifle by the stalk. It's too dark to get a good look. I'm uncertain, but...

"No!"

The figure fades into the dark mist. Never yelling. Never looking back. Never trying to let me save the both of us.

I crawl to the precipice and peer over the rim, listening to the engulfing currents bubble and churn, swallowing anything foolish enough. The water spirals down a vortex as I look through the mist and release a primal shout.

"Damn it."

Above me, the bold moon begins to flank a large grey cloud, leaving its reflection on a relic by the slippery ledge. Something of substance. Something I can pick up. Something to hold in the palm of my hand. Something that dangles on a saturated cord. Sadly, through all that has happened, I am, once again, left alone to wonder who the winner is.

CHAPTER THIRTY-THREE

The next morning is an eyesore to this remote area. I'm living on adrenalin and stale coffee, coping with a crime scene search party downstream along the river. So far, the first two miles of rapids, rocks, and driftwood yield zilch. No life jackets. No rifle. No body. I've read reports of violent undercurrents spinning remains for days, spitting the corpse to the surface, bloated, the shredded layers of soft tissues, chew marks from carnivorous fish, eyeballs missing, scraps of fabric still attached to disarticulated limbs.

Local authorities have taped off both the cabin site and where my confrontation with the shooter had ended. A dig team with backhoe is setting up a crime scene zone next to the old well. Divers in thick wet suits are checking their masks and goggles on the cemented lip in advance of being hoisted downward into the darkness. The imprisoned smell of diesel combustion and exhaust is overwhelming. There is a gray haze trapped in the treetops like a vaporous umbrella.

Word of the shooting is materializing and yet, tidbits of untruth, or rather, half-truths, perform verbal loops like paper airplanes. The babbling 'on location' news reporters are easy to pick out, wearing rustic windbreakers with strategic station monograms on the chest pocket right next to their microphone. I stand in the background behind the booms and listen as each rehearses their news clips. Lines of electrical cable snake through the trampled landscape where it connects to various news vans.

I check my watch. It's been daylight for roughly an hour and the treetops are slowly bowing from the breezes.

The sheriff's department and I are on the same page with an explanation: An anonymous source contacted the sheriff's department advising there was suspicious activity at a previous cabin fire. Because of the potential for additional incidents like this, the county arson crew was notified. Deputy Lundgren was summoned to assist in the investigation, where he encountered an armed suspect hiding in the forest nearby. Gun shots were exchanged. Deputy Lundgren was struck once on his left chest, immobilizing him from further pursuit. The gunman escaped. Speculation is that this person of interest either leaped or fell off the cliff near the Ottertail waterfalls and yet, no body has been found. No weapons or vehicle, either. Deputy Lundgren's condition has been upgraded from 'guarded' to 'serious.' He was transported to Regional Hospital in Moorhead. The investigation is ongoing.

My presence was missing from the equation.

An anchor woman corrals a fireman by the arm as he scurries behind the set.

"What can you tell our viewers of the impending situation?" she dramatically pleads and holds the microphone up to his mouth. "Is it true that there is evidence of money taken?"

Some of the fire crew are acquainted with me through the Olson brothers, but their attention on Lundgren is foremost. As far as they've been told, I was out for a run, showed up shortly after the incident, and upon request of the Department, stayed to help coordinate the team until the ambulance's arrival.

Like the funeral van accident, another life has been claimed. We step back as the EMT's barrel down the broken pathway with equipment in hand. Lundgren is hooked up with IV's and loaded onto a gurney. Two of the more burley firemen hike him up the hill to the ambulance. I come up from behind them on the gravel road through the trail, acting like an early morning jogger. No one knows different. My shoes squish with water. I'm filthy and sweating profusely. In anyone's opinion, I'm as bewildered as they are.

Lundgren's expression is as flat as a corpse, his eyes dull. There's this distant dreadful vacuous stare that I've seen a million times and his flak jacket is blood-soaked. I continue to monitor his pulse until he is carted into the EMT transport van. The last thing I tell him is that I'll wait along his patrol car until the others arrive.

I receive a ride back to the resort where I quickly shower and hop in my car, racing from the lake country and onto the fertile, flat agricultural lands toward Moorhead. By the time I arrive at the hospital, Lundgren is out of surgery and in ICU. The nursing staff allows me to poke my head into his private room. I feel light-headed and unzip my windbreaker and undo the top button of my shirt. There are enough electrical lines on his chest and catheter tubing to cover at least two worthy candidates. I've had comparable clients wheeled and slapped onto the morgue examination table, mostly because of cardiac failure. I pray that this won't be a similar situation. On the left side of his chest, there's a flexible drain tube taped to a sutured wound pocked with lead shot. A gradient collection bag is filled with blood-tinged fluid and taped to his side railing. His face is enveloped by a ventilation mask. Monitor indicators record his pulse at eighty-five BPM and blood pressure at one hundred-fifty over ninety. To me, these are good signs following all he's been through.

My mood plummets as I walk over to the side of his railed bed. Consumed on his sordid state, hoping he will survive, my chest feels weighted as if piled with sandbags. There is an ache in the back of my throat. In that moment of anguish, his eyelids flicker and half-open.

"Deputy Lundgren," I begin, but struggle to continue. Emotion wells in my eyes. "You might have to write me up for excessive speeding."

Tilting his head toward my direction, his left eye slowly blinks twice, the eyebrow half-raises as if the physical effort is painful. His left index finger slowly straightens and points toward my chest.

"He missed me, but he got away." I bring him up to date. "My guess is he accidentally fell over the falls, but the sharp boulders did the rest all the way down. Between the darkness and the undercurrent, there's no way he'd survive, plus he was favoring his hip after he slipped and hit his head on the tree roots. I was about twenty yards back when it happened."

I wrap his hand in mine and squeeze.

"It's still our secret, Deputy. The story is that you were by your-self. I wasn't in the patrol car. More importantly, you need to get better, so I can be the first to see you discharged."

His other hand slowly uncurls and gives me the thumbs up.

Outside, I pause at the hospital's entrance and look upward. Benign puffy cotton ball clouds splatter the sky, forming small shadows that slide over the hoods of cars, like schools of fish. The warming breeze has kicked in and there's the aroma of late summer field harvest. It's still a resort's paradise despite the chain of events. The two-hour drive back to the resort is painstakingly slow. The road morphs from two open lanes, to a single. There are 'No Passing' signs every half mile until I eventually make it to the paved county road. Pretty much how my life has been going recently.

I sit in the car and grip the steering wheel. Hopelessness. Total loss. A dull knot grows in my gut. From all appearances, Lundgren's chances of surviving are slim to none. Have I done more damage and less damage-control? To go along with that, I am so exhausted the back of my throat is scratchy again. Is the virus claiming its next victim or is it simply the smoke? My departure from the resort is long overdue. An over-analyzing, pencil-pushing Quality Assurance Manager is in his glory watching me squirm. I'm on an invisible leash of doom.

My suitcase and carry-on lay open on my bed as I stuff underwear into the zippered pouch. Enough of this rouse. I've been replaying the events over and over. My jaw tightens and a knot forms in the back of my neck. The recurrence is that I usually open my vulnerable self when my best defense should be to stay out of it. By keeping my shrinking circle of trusted friends to a minimum, no one gets hurt. Lying has been a good ally, if not caught. It's always been my go-to defense against the odds. Trying to fool everyone in this charade, especially Tessa, isn't working. From the deadly beginning, I trusted her more than anyone else here.

Over the past two days my email and phone messages are pinging like the birth to new music. I need to respond ASAP, lest I get trapped in this mini-Lake of the Woods. The gestational period of my stay here has gratefully come to an end and it's time to cut the cord. My phone buzzes and shows 'Unidentified' caller and I eagerly answer.

"Hello, Tessa?"

Click.

CHAPTER THIRTY-FOUR

The lot is otherwise empty as I park next to an old Silverado step-side with a 'Jesus Saves' license frame. I admire the steeple and the weathered image of a Christ-like four-pointed star. The light is on that leads to the office and I make my way across broad red steppingstones to the door and knock.

"Yes?" inquisitive, unsure.

"Pastor, it's Doctor Michaels. Can I come in? Are you still open?"

"Yes, of course. The door is *always* open."

He sits at his desk immersed in the laptop monitor, the glow on his half-silhouetted face highlights his brow and nose like any number of paintings by nineteenth century artists. He looks up from deep concentration and sighs. The neckline of his clerical collar is yellowing and his black coverup is ruffled.

"I was reading about the deputy and the shooting. It says he was transported to Regional in Moorhead, but nothing else. I'm wondering whether to wait or drive to Moorhead and pay a visit."

He pushes back from his chair, folds his hands in front, twirls his thumbs, and continues.

"Anyway, what brings you here at this hour?"

I lean against the door frame, feeling as marooned as one of those fishermen in Lake Wasoon caught offshore in a storm. It's all slow motion. There is tightness in my ears, and I grit my teeth. The feeling of being watched is incessantly acute as I scan the hallway.

"I looked everywhere at the resort, but I might have left my favorite watch in the storage room along the wall when I was here a couple days back."

Shifting my weight from side to side, I continue.

"I'm scheduled to leave tomorrow for Boston to meet with some defense attorneys on an expert witness case. The watch was a gift from my late wife when I graduated from medical school, so you can imagine what it means to me."

He nervously smiles, his chuckle lingers.

"That I do, Doc. Trust me. My dad handed mementos to each of us kids. Funny. I don't, for the life of me, remember mine anymore." He closes the laptop and begins to stand. "I'll follow and turn on the light for you. As usual, it's unlocked."

He leads me down the hall and stops at the library door.

"If you want me to come in, I can. Otherwise, take your time. I'll be in the office when you're done."

I hold up my hand and grimace. "As is happens, I might need some help sliding a large stack of boxes out of the way. My back is killing me lately and moving those boxes is the last thing I remember doing before taking off my band. Do you mind?"

He checks his wristwatch then rubs his hands together eagerly.

"Let's get to it, but I have devotions at the convalescent home in a half hour. No one waits for the Lord, especially those without many days, so to speak." His words are rushed as he leans forward and stands.

"Unfortunately, their care is so impeccable that possibly they'll outlive the two of us. Don't you agree? I mean, in your field, I'll bet there's little that surprises you anymore."

"It's not the same office every day for me, travelling from town to town. I learn something new all the time."

In the back of my mind, nothing will ever be the same.

The two of us slide a teetering column of office boxes filled with old hymnals and bibles to the other wall and carefully lean it against the wall to prevent collapsing.

"I guess in retrospect, we had better take them down one by one. It will be easier on the back."

He stands upright and rocks his neck side to side.

"Being a Pastor is not that demanding, you know. But I need to play the part of infallible once I enter the pulpit. You are cordially invited to attend Sunday's worship service, but I guess that will screw up your travel plans."

I kneel and extend my arm deep into the dark recesses of the now open space in a sweeping movement. "You know, I think I might have something where that broken statue of Jesus had fallen." Fishing in the dark, stretching. "I bet this is it. Hold on. Here it is."

I get back up on my knees and examine the object in my hands: a gold metallic cross, moss-stained and muddy.

"Does this look familiar, Pastor?"

"It most certainly does, Doc."

He raises the broken statue of the Savior over my head, cocking his eyebrows, holding his head at an angle.

"The Lord doth work in mysterious ways."

Thwack!

Stunned. Groggy. Ears ringing. Straining to focus. Strapped to a folding chair. Christmas tree lights gouge my wrists and feet. A dismantled wire wreath is coiled loosely on my head like a Steampunk crown of thorns. Warm blood trickles down my tingling brow and over the bridge of my nose.

"I had to do some sprucing up," he says with a smugness, plucking at his shirt, unblinking, a smile flashes across his face. He lifts the last box on the floor and places it against the wall.

"So much to do. So little time. So many to save. So few believers."

He taps me on the top of my throbbing skull.

"The beast given authority over every tribe, people, tongue and nation. I had this gut feeling you were getting too close, even though the clues were lining up. It's too bad I couldn't finish the deputy with that one shot."

He exhales through his nostrils and puckers his lips. His body language hardens.

"The plan was for them to find you unconscious with the rifle by your side. Poor Lundgren was to have joined the others at the bottom of the well."

"Pit is full," I said, spitting saliva and blood.

"Exactly," he responds, still smiling, and searing beneath the surface. "Now that was a good clue, if I say so myself."

He walks over to the bookend-style piece of old mahogany furniture and rearranges a display of plastic flowers, the kind you see in large glass vases at cemeteries.

"You don't recognize me, do you? Does this give you any clue?"

Holding up the faded petal collection to his cheek, he gazes upward as if looking for divine acceptance. He waits, then cackles.

"Lavender. I'm *the* Lavender, the one from your church camp days who was to be protected from the others by *you*. But you told me I needed to fend for myself."

He rises, arches his back, and points.

"Do you even know my name? From the beginning, I was Lavender to the bunk bullies. To them, I was Lavender, the Flower Power. Lavender, the Golden Shower. Lavender, the Girly Cower. The name is Arnold or Laverne Junior, but Arnie is preferred."

I recite his name with a sneer.

"Arnold Lavender Williams."

"Close, but no cigar, Doctor Michaels."

His closed fist comes out of nowhere, snapping my head back. White flashing spots appear.

"Now you will remember."

Bunching the artificial stalks into his hands, he shuffles toward me, now favoring his left leg. Tapping the bunch on the top of my head, smirking, sneering, he explains.

"It's not all about you, though. My indentured servitude originated at home with dear old Dad, Pastor Laverne Williams, the Great Evangelist. But you know that, I'm sure, based on your *vast* forensic knowledge."

"I never profiled you, Arnie," I utter, closing my eyes to the constant throb evolving in my head and neck. "We were all kids at the time and only a few years separated us. What did I know about counseling? No one else is to blame how two elemental months of camp changed our lives."

"Oh, but it is for all of us, including you."

Stiffening his stance over me, balling his fist.

"Your groin was set on warp speed for a particular counselor. Erin Garner, I believe. I watched the two of you canoodle beside the campfire. I saw you sneaking to rendezvous at the lake. Miss Bare Breasts. All nippily in the cold. Speaking of that, how about you, Mr. Hands Everywhere? Now that was one hell of an education for us sinners. Why you had to ruin all my fantasies is a question for the ages. Out of unadulterated luck, you consented to do Ole's autopsy. Keep in mind that it was me who recommended it to them."

Artie relaxes his fist and brushes his finger at my chin. "With Ole's body coming back, it was going to be so simple. One plus one makes two. My old man would shout to the heavens with pride."

I'm speechless. The skin on my back tingles as if covered in ice. My hands are numb. But by stretching and clinching my fists over and over behind my back, the knots begin to loosen. I need a little more time to keep him distracted and for him to believe I'm in excruciating pain.

"This isn't meant to be a recipe book of *Find Lavender Waldo*, chapter by chapter, so here goes and not in any specific order."

He braces against the doorway and folds his arms as if beginning a recitation in high school English class.

"Number One: Years of Daddy yelling, correcting, and chiding led him to a watery grave. He loved to water ski despite a total lack of any athletic skill. I added a few punctures into the life jacket. He was such a terrible swimmer, flopping in the water like the world was ending. He couldn't float to save his own soul, let alone, anyone else. In a matter of seconds, he was under. The beginning of the end. I was free of his incessant matchmaking me to the hometown cheerleader. Either Dad was blind as a bat to my impulses or his strict regimen rejected that possibility. Mother must have known that I wasn't interested. Right in front of her eyes, for God's sake."

He sneers.

"Dad had this painting of himself that he framed, kneeling, and facing the church. To top things off, he hung it in the living room above the television. Can you believe it? Bible in hand. Looking toward the heavens. It was our constant reminder of a richer life. A better lifestyle. Saturday morning cartoons were our only escape."

He suppresses a shudder.

"If you look closely at the canvass beneath the paint, it looks like little crosses, millions of them."

He fumbles in his pocket and comes up with a switchblade. Holding it up to the light, he studies it, then flips it hand to hand.

SNAP!

He slashes back and forth at the invisible intruder. Seconds later, he becomes disenchanted and shivers as if shockwaves pour over his body. The muscles in his neck are like stretched, giant rubber bands. He taps the top of my head with the knife handle.

"Used to drive me nuts looking at those tiny crucifixes. Sometimes, he scowled at me the same way. He called me *pitiful.*"

He takes a step back. Spittle builds in the corners of his mouth.

"He quoted to me time and time again: show them no mercy, judgement without mercy will be shown to him who is not merciful. Enough said on that tiring topic."

The car hood scratches. Now it's becoming clear. My head flips with fear.

"Number Two: Arson 101. Now that was even easier and deliciously delightful."

He primps his receding hairline, then inspects his nails.

"No one ever suspected the Soul Savior's son."

All at once he flings the bouquet aside, smashing it into the stack of boxes. Manic destruction and then frivolous joy emanate on his face. The psychosis is becoming paramount.

"Number Three: Stalking 101. Everyone is on Facebook these days. It's a no-brainer."

He touches the tip of his tongue with his bloodied finger.

"Back then, it was actual face time."

"Number Four: Animals are so vulnerable. Let's leave it at that."

"Number Five: Girl in cave? Come on! That's a failed Lazarus experiment. My Dad preached it, but only Jesus can raise the dead. This was *my* first-love thing and way beyond crushable if you get my drift. Everyone had their sights on *your* missing girlfriend and that deception became so much easier to kill *mine*. Once again, timing is everything. As far as I was concerned, any 'body' would do. No one will identify the cave girl."

He scoffs.

"Hippies. Runaways. A dime a dozen back then."

"What happened to Ray Perkins, the old man in the retirement home?" I ask, stalling, still working the wrists.

"Dear old Ray. Now *that* was a mercy killing," he sneers. "Actually, that was respect for Dear Old Dad. Ray was the last one alive from the committee to fire Dad. That was on the account of putting up with everyone's demands. According to the synod higher-ups, ordained pastors are not allowed to give communion to non-Lutherans, even if they ask. Ray had to eventually learn that his beliefs were a mortal sin."

Arnie puffs up his chest.

"I had to be patient on that one," he snorts and displays a wide grin. He then slaps his thigh and continues.

"I had to wait until he was feeble enough. Fortunately, county authorities came into the room and declared him dead. He was my first 'vespers' subject."

I rock back and forth in my chair, still working the wrists, snorting, tugging.

"Take it easy, Doctor. Relax. I'm not done. I thought about retiring from the business, so to speak. The joy I experienced was rapturous, but it was sadly becoming too dangerous. Then, I got an idea, a revelation."

"Darlene Gabbert," I said solemnly.

"I've lost track of the Number's game, but it's not her. I consider that collateral damage."

He folds his hands as if in prayer.

"She was hiking and got lost, of course. Old people can lose their way so quickly. Darlene came upon me as I was in the middle of a feral tomcat burial. I named it Willie after my most despised teacher from grade school back in Iowa. It spun in that wire loop like a top, until I got my leather gloves around its scrawny neck. What a scratcher. I have wounds to prove it. Made me angry, too. But lucky for me, no one was interested in the critter that washed up two days later. I was going to dispose of it anyway. It was time. Is it any wonder what God can do?"

"Bank hold up and Roland Purdy." I've resigned myself to ask about the ultimate nightmare.

"Bingo." He exhales loudly, hangs his head, and closes his eyes. Then, he slowly looks up. In an instant, the smile becomes a snarl.

"The brothers have a reputation for mismanagement. Even their Aunt Gail confirms it."

He snickers and leans in.

"By the way, she is an excellent driver. As for Roland, he was way too nosey, always asking around town for information that should've been recorded on their death certificates. It was Roland who tuned you in to the spongy neck on that Gabbert pig. He couldn't leave anything alone, insinuating that between the two of you she might've been strangled. Where there was once no interest, now all Wasoon needed to know. That was not the fork in the road he should've taken."

He hesitates, then adds, "That was a messy one."

Just then, the portable air conditioning unit automatically engages and hums from the corner. Arnie smiles and fans himself.

"Good timing, Doctor. I was getting a little toasty."

"Tessa."

I squeeze my eyes shut, hoping to erase the image of her brutalized soul. Selfless and unassuming. We'd driven to the outskirts of Wasoon on a whim, dined and flirted, slept together, woke up together. Now, I regret every moment.

"Your Tessa, Doctor Michaels," he taunts. "Well, let me tell you. It was not my idea to bring her any harm, but she needed somehow to be taught a lesson and keep her nose out of others' business. I think it worked well. Call it a mini torture. She bolted like a surprised fox in a hen house. I knew her stress level was near the top, but then you came along: Mr. Avalanche of Love."

His eyes dart around the room and he lowers his voice. "It was my intention to release her eventually. The mouse urine stench was nauseating even to me, plus she was always dry heaving through the hood. I was worried that she'd aspirate and die. I like her new hairdo, don't you? Much better than Alice the Malice with a comb and scissors could ever accomplish."

He rubs his scalp back and forth. A mirthless laugh boils out.

"Every time I go in for a trim, that fat pig's spunkiness melts my ears off. She is the self-proclaimed Queen of Blabbing. Birthdays, engagement parties, marriages, baptisms, vacations. It's all fair game to her."

I have one last query, the ultimate question. An upsurge of ice forms on the back of my neck. I'm dizzy, my mouth is dry. One last time, I gather enough courage to ask.

"Where's Erin?"

He remains motionless as if pondering the question, then moves forward and squats down. His breath is sour and warm, white spittle is caked in the corners of his mouth, his voice becomes raspy and faint.

"That's for me to know and you to never know."

A car horn alarm blares in the driveway and he jerks his head in that direction.

"Have you brought company, Doctor Michaels?"

WHAM!

My hands become untangled, and I bash him hard in the chest. He yelps like a wounded coyote, stumbles, and falls backward, crashing into the wall headfirst. I'm on him with all my reserves, pummeling his chest, pounding his head, yanking him by the hair, slapping his face back and forth. My still-bound legs clatter and scuffle in the chair's legs, but I'm able to pin him down with my weight as he struggles to roll over. He fights to free his arms from my grip on his neck, clawing like a captured wild animal unable to move. There is a gurgling cry emanating from deep inside his throat. With one last effort, he yanks my arms off his neck, and smacks me in the jaw with his fist, stunning me. He lunges for the knife on the floor behind him. I fall back and onto the edge of the chair seat.

"AAHHHH!"

In that moment, he manages to get his arms underneath his body and struggles to crawl away. Suddenly, he stops, his mouth agape, his eyes locked in horror.

"Oh, my God."

CLICK.

"Is it really you?"

A pencil-thin green laser lights up on his forehead.

Pffft.

CHAPTER THIRTY-FIVE

Duluth Harbor is a mind-boggling monstrosity to a land-lover like me. There is a flurry of functional bustle. Blocks of colorful containers are stacked by the dozens, row upon countless row like a Legoland for adults. In plain sight, cargo ships of all sizes are either docking or offshore. A beehive of commotion begins with the deafening cranes that are taller than the downtown skyscrapers: lifting, transporting, or loading freight. Semis line up for at least a half mile in wait. The eastern horizon is the color of a school of rainbow trout in a clear stream. From shore, the rippling water is crystal clear. Waiting for Spring, like the rest of us.

From the shoreline, I arrive at the main entrance exhausted from having to crawl up on all fours over granite boulders. Besides, I can't shake the biting throngs of a so-called February warming trend. I left the house miserably unprepared, wearing only a long sleeve tee shirt and a baggy pair of gym shorts. What the hell was I thinking? I'm dressed like a thirty-year old fitness instructor and acting like a three-year old, steadfast and adamant.

The solitude is broken from a blaring tugboat horn. From my observation deck in front of the food truck, the goings-on look as if it is quite efficient. There are occasional shouts of instruction, but otherwise, the only maritime cacophony is the sound of mechanical hoists or forklifts. I huddle against the wind-protected wall, shivering, clutching my espresso with both hands close to my lips, watching the activity in the fisherman's wharf portion. All the dock workers are wearing insulated coveralls and stocking caps. By the time I arrive in shorts and tee shirt, all they do is shake their heads and gawk. Their silence speaks volumes and to them, I am another rich idiot weekend tourist from the Cities.

Above me is a noisy avian contrast, a counterculture of low-flying sea gulls and mid-level Canadian geese. Shearwater gulls dive-bomb the wooden platforms, shitting, and irritating the humans enough for them to either relinquish food scraps or mutter and dart indoors at the Quik Stop for shelter. A drenching cold shower of sleet passed through the region last night, leaving in its wake the freshest air this side of Alaska. There's a northeasterly breeze and the onshore glints with froth. All told, the tapestry of the Lake's immensity with the gigantic swells crashing onto the rocky shore... if I closed my eyes, it's Big Sur, California.

Walking south along the bike path, away from the progressive work, I am captivated at how serenity over-claims the supertankers. The graying, murky dock water from a couple miles back is nearly transparent here. In the rocky shore below, I pause to watch schools of sardines moving through the safety of warm shallows like veils of dark soaked linen scarves. To my right, the sharp cliffs of gran-ite rise two hundred feet where the morning mist evaporates into energizing sunlight. Unquestionably, this is a jogger's paradise and way too narrow for the novice mountain bikers. No unnerving clicks of downshifting gears coming from behind, no shredders on full tilt, nothing but rhythmical pants coming fast and steady.

Those few souls I encounter going the other direction, are low on caffeine, too. That Espresso truck back at the harbor is the only link to a civilization and the chain restaurants downtown street are a mile back. On weekends, I witness drivers looking for that imme-diate jolt, waiting sometimes a half-hour before ultimately giving up. The blocked traffic honks for minutes as irate drivers maneuver in the middle of the road. Like me, their reward with a double-shot, non-fat, no-whip, will be well worth it.

Three months into this new job at the County Coroner's Department and I am still learning the ropes. I had basically fibbed my way through the job interview, citing medical conferences that I attended (not), listing pathologists under which I interned (week-ends only), and questions regarding my opinions on various tech-niques and divisions of responsibility at crime scenes (yawn). In between, we chatted about Duluth tourism and new fishing holes for trout. I'd name-drop favorite mountain lodges or skiing getaways to Colorado. That's how serious they were about getting me on board. Not to brag, but I can impress most of them because I was a traveler. It's like telling scary night-time stories to children then tucking them in for the night. They soak it all in and I'm the center of attention.

Their biggest concern is why leave California for six months of winter? The truth is that I'm tired of living alone. Not that I miss the cold, but in the end, I traded isolation for some sort of consolation. They need to replace a vacancy and I'm available. I require medical liability insurance coverage to practice. Lucky for me, they either know little about the Wasoon resort or it isn't an issue for employment. My medical license was up for review because of the legal discharge I encountered when Cassie died. I wasn't about to divulge any of that, and they didn't ask.

Up here in the land of hockey sticks and flannel plaid, the cases I confront are mostly natural-related. There's alcoholism, some pulmonary fibrosis and mesotheliomas from mining and shipyard workers, not to mention the over-the-top obese diabetics. Three hundred fifty pounders who were supposedly 'healthy' living on biscuits and gravy are commonplace. Sometimes morgue workers can be quite crass and label this condition as a 'table goiter.' It's an inside joke and I've come to appreciate it. There is also the occasional murder-suicide. Blue collar and chronic unemployment. Interesting bed partners. After all, depression can wear many hats. I should know.

The incident at the parsonage left me with a mild concussion syndrome, which the emergency doctor assured me will subside over time. Migraines have dwindled down to a whirring in my ears but I'm still sensitive to loud noises. Looking back, this trip to the docks is a bad idea and the stiffness in my knees exaggerates the decision.

My working territory is extensive: roughly twelve hundred square miles. Oftentimes, I have become that same traveler who entered Wasoon a couple months ago. The other day, I was, once again, in Lake of the Woods for a convalescent home issue. Believe it or not,

Canada was across the river. Pretty cool. Today is Saturday. I don't have to fly, drive, or work weekends. I am like the rest of the Duluth diehards, except for the dock workers.

Northern Minnesota is breathtaking, and I make a vow to explore the coastal highway next summer. But learning to stay at home when the weather turns sour has its rewards too. Because of the demand in the market, I easily sold my Central Valley home and was soon motoring a rental-sized truck nineteen hundred miles through two continental mountain ranges and endless farm country. It's amazing how the time passed in what seemed an instant. By coincidence, on the drive crossing over the southeastern Iowa border, I happened upon Vincent Bode at a truck stop. He's alone in a booth in the back, chowing down on a pile of steaming pancakes. I join him and the tales begin. He boasts some, listens less, and eventually offers me his leftovers of extra bacon and home fries. That was unexpected, but I wolfed them down back in my truck. Vincent and I formed a mini convoy all the way to Saint Paul where he had to meet a grain shipment deadline. He's my new BFF and checks in on me from time-to-time. If he's coming to Duluth, he calls to see if we can "hook up for lunch." Nice guy once you get to know him. He's a major memory that I don't ever want to lose.

A surprise to me, my savings account held enough to afford a remodeled A-frame that faces the sunrise at the end of a bluff. No neighbor is within fifty yards in either direction which allows me to keep my curtains always half-open. This house has that rustic log cabin guise, but the property is immodest, at least for me. One cleared acre, two bedrooms, two baths, a finished deck with hot tub, full kitchen with functional island, and a living room that surrounds the central fireplace, and not vice versa. The realtor sold me on the 'entertainment' value, but she knew that I preferred to keep my trusted circle of immediate friends as tight as a rusty faucet.

Trust is not something that came with the new job even though it looked good going in. I was reminded that the probation period will be a year. Come to think of it, as I researched the website, there had been two other short-term forensic pathologists prior to me, who had moved on to higher ground within the past four years. In that regard, I was not alone. That's not a good track record for pathologists, but I was through bustling away from the problems and planned to stay at least through April. What are they going to do? Fire me?

I decided my new purchase needed another addition and thus, I invested in, of all the things that were much less demanding, a dog. By 'invested' I mean a companion who will have my back without question, although there is a 'food-available contingency.' She is a rescue, like me, but not quite as terminal. An Italian Greyhound mix, sleek like her larger racing cousins, brown with grey highlights around the ears, weighing only twenty-three pounds. She's as skittish as hell and her survival skills are still on the back burner, which puts her in the same category as me. I suspect her international toy-dog value appealed to the previous owner who lost interest over time and investment. But this hound can track a jackrabbit which is her favorite passion. I don't walk her with a leash because she prefers to trail or stay alongside me, stride for stride. Separation anxiety is not just for humans anymore.

The two of us mount the wooden stairwell as I begin to clomp the slush and grit out of my shoes. Dark smoke quietly paints a flat line from the chimney as if there is a silent exhaust fan directly sucking the house's entrails into the trees. I had intentionally left the kitchen light on. The early morning sun is a timid visitor on the front porch leaving only a seasonal hue on the door frame and curtained glass. My off-season purchase is a road bike that is banked against the side wall. I hardly ride it. The tires need air, and the derailleur needs a tune-up. I am quite aware it demands a more attentive owner but I'm working on it. First things first. The last time I rode was two weeks ago, after I spent another unsettling day in court as an expert witness. Weekend weather has not been accommodating as of late and without daylight savings time in the rear view mirror, I've compiled excellent excuses to refrain in spite of the fact that the recently converted rail-to-bike-trail is packed with a variety of bikers every day, come rain, snow, or shine.

I've incorporated on my bucket list a new pair of cross-country skis and re-learning to fall like a one-year-old. By a strike of fortune, those end-of-season sales haven't pressured me much yet.

I make it to the porch, stomp the grit from of my soles, and unlock the door. My canine pal anxiously waits to be allowed inside, at least that's my interpretation. In this frigid country, I can leave the furnace on at a comfortable temperature without guilt of dimming the power grid. The fireplace glows with the two logs of fresh cut pine I had tossed in prior to the espresso jog. Every time I come inside, I get this euphoric, giddy, sensation of guilt. It's amazingly quiet, like lying on the summer grass and soaking up the sun.

The bedroom door opens and Tessa peers out from behind and rubs her eyes. She shivers, then scampers to the sofa, rifling for a blanket which she throws around her birthday suit nakedness. All the while, I stand at the kitchen sink in a puddle of melting snow. I never grow tired of seeing her like this. Uninhibited. Her small breasts jiggle some. Her hips are rounding with age, but her toned thighs and behind still turn me on. Although her late summer tan lines are fading, it bears to mind nearly every day how it felt to caress her inside that green-colored cabin. That will never dim. It keeps me from dwelling on the neurosis that encloses me, coffin-like, on a regular basis when I'm by myself.

I tried once to emulate this playful freedom of hers, prancing in my birthday suit, but that was short-lived. As the years passed, I felt very insecure of my lean look in the mirror. There's this boney butt, not to mention the pitted acne scars of adolescence on my back. But the internal scars of Wasoon resort will always be there.

Despite the abuse of travelling for a living, sitting in cramped airplanes and compact cars, or dining on cheap foods, I give myself a fifty-fifty chance of seeing eighty years old. Tessa and I still shower together on occasion, but I prefer the lights be off when hopping into bed with her and let the fingers do the walking, so to speak.

She tightens the woolen blanket around her in a snug wrap, looks to me, smirking.

"Morning."

Tessa often complains of having cold feet and thus, if she wears anything at all, it's socks. She offers up her best skating moves over the tiled floor and presses me into the kitchen counter. I open my arms wide and she burrows in.

"You're shuddering."

"Morning."

"How was the jog?"

"Freezing, but ok." Holding back the enthusiasm, I pretend by tucking my hands in my shorts. "Taking up jogging again was nuts. They're loading tons of freight this morning and the gulls are complementing them with equal amounts of poop. I'm like an icicle. Even my shorts are brittle. Here. Check it out."

"Now that's too much information." She elbows me and looks at the steaming kettle, then shakes her head and groans. "Do you have to keep it so damn hot in here? Try living with menopause."

She rests her head on my chest. Her hair is damp and smells citrusy. She wears it long and straight to cover the raised scar over the left temple, a dark reminder, a palpable knot embedded under her scalp. Strands of white are beginning to show in her roots, but I don't think that's the most important item on her table. It's taken some time, but since we've been together Tessa has learned to live through the sleepless fidgeting and nightmarish talking in her sleep. Usually around eleven o'clock or so, the battle with fatigue and anguish is over and she snuggles on my side of the bed. That's when I turn off the light and cover us both. Come to think of it, by morning, it's as if we sleep in a twin bed. I can't complain, though, considering the alternative.

She cried in her sleep again last night and mumbled a few words. The Sandman caught up with her around three o'clock. I'm totally baffled to see her up.

I have decided to go spiky-short, crazy-little-boy-colic and all, along with a low-profile manicured beard. My closet holds trendy leather goods from moccasins to cowboy boots to a plush bomber jacket. I like the new me, but Tessa thinks I'm going through another mid-life crisis like the other half dozen men in her life. The promise to prove her wrong is challenging sometimes.

We embrace and watch the embers glow. The dog is curled up off to the edge of her flannel bed. Tessa stiffens.

"Lundgren called and woke me up. He was chuckling over the phone, like it's a big joke. The Jerk. He still likes to tease me for over-sleeping and never ends the conversation without insisting that I call you Loverboy."

I scoff. "You're not the only one. I'm trying to live up to that anointed title. He constantly emails or texts me photos of tiny homes with a loft and deck."

She arches her back.

"What's in his krall this time? Another idea for the ultimate fish house with solar panels?"

She draws up the corners of her blanket shawl to her neck and offers up a labored huff.

I mock her frustration with a noisy exhale.

"I've explained this to you twice. Lundgren has an ulterior motive. He wants me to be available when the Wasoon murders go to trial and I'm called upon as a witness. As padding for my threadbare resume, I'll be able to explain I'm locally employed, in an official capacity for the county."

Tessa relaxes. "Sorry. I'm using Lundgren as my vent."

I place my arm around her and hug.

I was relieved to learn the brothers were released from jail and all charges dropped. But during the extensive financial investigation, it was discovered the Resort was thousands of dollars in the hole. Examiners found Aunt Gail had embezzled over four hundred fifty thousand dollars at last count, and they are now looking for forensic accountants to serve as expert witnesses at her trial.

"Actually, I think that he'd be the ideal host for a new HGTV program: Fish House Hunters."

She burrows her head into my neck. "He has way too much time on his hands with this disability case. Any specific plans for today?"

A couple of noisy joggers go by on the street in front of the mailman as he trudges toward my driveway.

"Sorry, man," one of them shouts in passing.

He throws up his hands, flips them off, and mumbles something caustic. Vaporous condensation clouds his face, but he still barks back at them like my loyal hound does with a treed squirrel. His moustache is as iced as his glower. His steps to the doorway are deliberate and loud. Today's weather outlook is on the decline as far as I can tell in his expression. Any dreadful attempt of mustering up a happy greeting will be futile.

In my hapless defense, I'm also beginning to increase my endurance distances now that the four-footed Italian joins me on a regular basis. I can't tell if she enjoys my unwieldy pace or is putting up with the exercise until the event is rewarded with a smoked ham hock back in the house. She spins at my feet, Pavlov-style, with anticipation each time I open the refrigerator. But I avoid running anywhere close to lumbering mailmen.

Two days ago, I completed a five-mile loop and was totally wasted for the remainder of the evening. Later, Tessa and I shared a bottle of Central Valley zinfandel in front of the fireplace and the turkey chile and garlic bread were awesome. I felt as drained as if finishing a marathon. She sternly warned me yesterday morning that better not happen again tonight.

"There's a Brat and Cider tasting festival up in Two Harbors. I thought we'd drive a few miles further west and see the million-dollar log cabins. You know. The second homes for the Cities rich-and-famous. Sound like a plan?"

She sighs and shrugs.

"I don't know. I'm a little low on antacids. Let's stay here and do a bike ride later, that is, if your roommate approves."

We both check the dog cushion where the Italian is as motionless as I get after a spaghetti dinner and a bottle of red wine. Come to think of it, I have yet to name her. I'll let Tessa have the honors on that.

I give Tessa a gentle squeeze and kiss her on the nape of her neck. "How about your ideas? Care to share?"

She moves toward the couch and plops down on the corner cushion. Slowly, her blanket slips open. There is plenty cleavage showing and I'm quite sure that act is for my indulgence.

"It's that time of year for the annual review of the resort's summer events before we hand the books off to our CPA. I've been arguing with the brothers. Actually, it's a working monologue."

A red flush covers her face. There's a fat pause as she pokes her tongue inside her cheek.

"They have this hair-brained idea to generate a Daytona Winter Wonderland of ice fishing contests and NASCAR-style snowmobile races with big time sponsors. That's meant to raise eyebrows of the Wasoon environmentalists, at least until the ice melts. And I can only imagine the cost for liability insurance."

I picture a snowmobile ramping snowdrift over Ole's Resort as the Ladies of the Coven are soaking in the hot tub, drinking their hot toddies. A combination Dukes of Hazzard County versus Cannonball Run riders yelling and saluting as they go airborne over the fence line. With all this hoopla and infectious enthusiasm, I envision Gloria stoking her pack mates to drop their tops. Now *that's* a story for the Wasooninans.

All in all, it's the other-side-of-the-galaxy image that lingers. The limp body of Arnie Williams draped over me like a large horse blanket, his head at an obtuse angle to his neck, a golf ball-sized defect in his hollow left eye socket, the right eye bulging as if popped from the pressure exploding inside his head. Large fragments of his skull bone and brain matter had splattered the front of my jacket and forehead as we struggled for the knife. One of his arms still gripped my shirt and the other arm was fulcrum-style beneath him.

The final report of the investigation is still pending, and no arrests have been made. By the time I righted myself, his arm collapsed, and the shooter was gone. The hallway was dark, and I was helplessly strapped to the chair. The only witness was Pastor Arnie and sadly, he'll never tell.

Maybe it's selective memory. Maybe I don't want to remember. Maybe I don't want to know. At any rate, Wasoon is pretty much back to normal. The fifteen minutes of fame brought the worst, and recovery can be a living hell. The class reunion group 'regrouped', and the extended weekend plan went on without other dramatic hiccups. The Gabbert's were nominated as Honorary King and Queen of the reunion and the class erected a memorial banner for Mrs. Gabbert in the high school gymnasium rafters.

Accidents, funerals, and burglaries aside, murders can certainly take the wind out of the sails. The sheriff's department only releases specific information in tidbits, piecemeal enough to be inaccurate, but not a total wash of the events. The killer of Roland Purdy is dead, but the execution of Lavender Williams is open to speculation. I overheard rumors of Hollywood types showing up in large black SUV's wanting to get background material for a movie. Believe me, three hours in this backwoods country and they'd be gone. Fact into fiction is still fiction. Anything screenwriters conjure up, won't hold a candle to the actual events.

"Hey, come back to earth, Dr. Michaels. Antisocial hour is over. I missed you enough for two people."

I sometimes catch myself, stuck in place, waiting for the turbines to stop. Both of us still have gaps to fill in our relationship and she is my closest friend ever. It's my hope there will come a time soon that guilt calls a truce and something more lasting can germinate.

"Sorry," I tell her, my arms fall at my side. "I'm still learning to survive. I missed you, too. That was a long week for me."

She motions to join her on the sofa. I move a cushion aside as she scoots over to plop on my lap.

"Hey, I was kidding." She collapses in my arms. "No more hiding, as you can plainly see. I'm all for a drive, but breakfast is required. Let me shower and we'll have some fun. What do you say?"

"Did I actually hear you wanted to put some clothes ON?" I cock my eyebrows.

She stands and races for the bathroom, giggling and taunting me all the way as her blanket drops off her back and falls in a heap on the floor. The Italian raises its head from the cushion, then drops back into her winter nap with a big exhale and twitching eyelids. My four-legged roommate has seen this exercise a dozen times.

In a couple minutes, the shower turns off and the exhaust fan clicks on. It's going to be a stellar day, I convince myself. Above me, the ceiling fan whirs in a calming motion. Outside, there's the metallic scraping sound of a snowplow on frozen asphalt surfaces. Thank you for modern equipment. Welcome back to civilization. We can make that date after all. No more passive voice, no more frustration or dwelling on how unfair life has become. The sun's rays poke over the hearth and the lit logs crackle. I gradually unclench my fists and unlock my jaw.

As I wait for her, I stand next to the fireplace and sort today's letters. Like a dealer playing twenty-one at the local Indian casino, I flip and toss unopened junk mail into the flames. For the moment, a water bill, a garbage bill, and a bank statement are stuffed under my arm pit. But then there is this manila envelope, taped-sealed over the tab and forwarded with no return address. Odd. Am I still getting mail from California? It's a Wasoon postmark. I glance toward the bathroom door and hold the envelope up to the light. Interesting. I surrender to impulse and tear it open. There's a single sheet of paper stapled to a familiar faded green headscarf.

I found you, now you find me.

Tessa announces a countdown through the open bedroom door.

"Ready in ten minutes. You're next."

Stay cool. Relax. I hear a blue jay pecking at millet on the sill corner. Tap. Tap. Tap.

"Spinach and mushroom omelet with bacon," Tessa sings. "Espresso. Double shot."

She pokes her head through the doorway, a bath towel wrapped around her hair.

"Anything good in the mail?"

I shake my head and watch the fire. With one flip of my wrist, the tossed envelope contents are aflame. Tears well-up behind my eyelids as I walk over to the opened doorway and contemplate the thin grey trails of smoke leaving my chimney. At last.

"Just more junk mail. Okay. My turn, then let's go."

ABOUT THE AUTHOR

Brace Ruben (a pen name) is a retired pathology professional who specialized in anatomy and postmortem examination. During his career, he instructed at the college level, presented seminars, and published several articles on pathology. Finally, he's devoting more time to creating fiction that flows with visual metaphors and unforgettable characters based on personal experiences. As a dyed-in-the-wool husband to his devoted wife of over forty-six years, they have raised two adult sons, been honored with a precious daughter-in-law and two grandsons that are so much like their parents. Raised in the farm country of Minnesota, he resides in Northern California. *Pitfall* is his second novel.

Made in the USA
Las Vegas, NV
10 February 2021